RENEWAL AFTER DARK

GANSETT ISLAND SERIES, BOOK 27

MARIE FORCE

Renewal After Dark
Gansett Island Series, Book 27
By: Marie Force

Published by HTJB, Inc.
Copyright 2024. HTJB, Inc.
Cover Design by Diane Luger
Print Layout: E-book Formatting Fairies
ISBN: 978-1958035672

View the McCarthy Family Tree
marieforce.com/gansett/familytree/

View the list of Who's Who on Gansett Island here
marieforce.com/whoswhogansett/

View a map of Gansett Island
marieforce.com/mapofgansett/

CHAPTER 1

*D*uke Sullivan waited more than a week to move the lovely McKenzie and her son, Jax, to the apartment at his place after the hurricane flattened her cabin next door. With Blaine working around the clock and Tiffany feeling poorly, McKenzie had offered to stay with the family that'd rescued them during the storm to help with their girls. Tiffany had gratefully accepted the offer, and Duke had his plans on hold until he got the text that McKenzie was ready to move to his place.

He couldn't recall the last time he'd been so excited about anything as he was at having McKenzie and her adorable son come to stay at his garage apartment, which had been empty for years. After his last tenant moved out, he'd decided not to bother renting again because he usually preferred the solitude of having the property to himself.

It was just as well that their plans had been delayed, because his tattoo studio had been nonstop since the power came back last weekend, thankfully just in time for his friends Shannon and Victoria's wedding to go off without a hitch. The tourists had returned for late-season fun in the sun and were keeping the tattoo studio booming, which was good news after six days with no power and no business.

The island had breathed a collective sigh of relief at the return to mostly normal after a tumultuous week. As far as he knew, only one island resident had been presumed lost in the storm—Billy Weyland, who owned the gym. He was a good guy, and Duke had considered him a friend. But no one could believe he'd decided to ride out the storm on board his sailboat in the Salt Pond.

After the storm, the boat had been found partially sunk with no sign of Billy.

The Coast Guard and local public safety were still looking for him, but no one expected to find him alive at this point, which was freaking sad. And so unnecessary. But what could you do? People made their own choices and had to live with the consequences.

Showered, beard groomed and as cleaned up as he ever got, Duke was about to leave on the most important errand of his life.

The dramatic thought had him laughing at his own foolishness as he stepped out of the shower and reached for one of the towels he'd washed after the power returned. Everything he owned had been washed, polished or swept for the first time in longer than he cared to acknowledge in preparation for his important guests. He was glad he'd gotten to vacuum when the power came back on.

Duke usually looked forward to the post-Labor Day time of year when things slowed down from the madness of the season. But after being shut down for a big chunk of September before and after the storm, everyone was hoping for one last burst of business before the island buttoned up for the winter.

Despite all the other things he needed think about, getting his guests settled had become a priority. He was probably a little too excited about them coming to stay.

Before the storm hit, he'd noticed someone staying at his late friend Rosemary's cottage next door. He'd also noticed that the woman was young, stunning and caring for a baby. He'd meant to get over there to say hello but had been so busy preparing for the storm that he hadn't gotten around to it.

Then Ethel flattened Rosemary's cottage, which sent Duke into the storm to look for them. When there'd been no sign of them in the wrecked cottage, he'd gone to see Blaine Taylor at the police station.

The chief told him he'd found them and taken them to his house to ride out the storm.

Duke had been unreasonably relieved to hear they were safe.

So much so, he'd gone next door to the cottage to retrieve what possessions he could find and had delivered clothes, a backpack with a laptop that hadn't been damaged and other personal items to the Taylors. He'd learned McKenzie—her name was McKenzie—was one of Rosemary's granddaughters, and the little guy was her son, Jax.

Then he'd spotted a teddy bear in the rubble, brought it home to clean it up and delivered that to her, too. That's when he'd asked her if she might be interested in his garage apartment until she figured out what to do about the cottage.

Now, finally, the day that McKenzie and Jax would move into the apartment was upon him.

As he stared at his reflection, he tried to see himself the way McKenzie would. He was disappointed to realize that a gorgeous woman like her would probably have no use for a guy like him if he hadn't been offering her a free place to stay after the storm rendered her homeless.

His face was pleasant enough, and he'd gotten enough compliments on his blue eyes to decide they were his best feature. They sure beat his beak of a nose, that was for sure. He'd taken the time to clean up his unruly beard, and as he ran a comb through long, dark blond hair, he wondered if it wasn't time for a haircut.

Colorful ink decorated every inch of his torso, stopping just below his jawline.

He smiled when he thought about how Rosemary used to tell him to stop using himself like a coloring book and get a hobby. She'd been a delightful friend and neighbor, regularly baking her famous banana bread for him and the guys at the studio. Much of what he knew about life and adulthood had been learned one lesson at a time as she showed him what he needed to know. He'd looked forward to her arrival every spring and had missed her when she went home to the mainland for the winter.

She'd become "family" to him, not that she'd known that. When

3

she died, he'd mourned her loss more than he ever had for a single other soul. His mother was still alive and living up by Boston, but she'd been in and out of his life so many times, he hardly thought of her as a parent. He'd spent most of his childhood in foster care while she was either in rehab or prison.

Rosemary had been the mother of his heart. He'd missed her tremendously in the two years since she'd passed and would be eternally thankful for her friendship, especially since that friendship had helped him convince her granddaughter to accept his offer of a place to stay. Without Rosemary's stamp of approval, McKenzie probably would've been afraid to be the guest of a strange, long-haired, bearded, tattooed dude.

It'd taken hours of elbow grease to make the garage apartment livable. While he'd scrubbed the place, he'd aired out clean sheets, towels and blankets that had been in the closet for years. After the power returned, he'd washed anything that smelled funky and made her bed with clean, fresh-smelling sheets.

The power had continued to be spotty at times. He'd heard in town that one of the main conduits had been severely damaged and needed to be replaced. Apparently, the electric company was waiting on parts that had to be ordered and were hard to find, since the island's grid was so outdated. In the meantime, island residents made do with what they had while hoping it wouldn't go out again. Thankfully, the ferries were back to regular runs, bringing food and gas for generators that'd worked overtime all over the island. Everyone he knew had refilled their gas cans in case they lost power again.

As he'd finished up at the apartment, it occurred to him that she might want to borrow some sugar or something. That'd sent him into a cleaning frenzy in his own home. He sure as hell didn't want her to think he was a slovenly bachelor who couldn't take care of himself, even if he might seem that way at first glance.

And honestly, why did he care what she thought of him? She'd come to stay briefly, until her cottage was rebuilt, or she decided island life wasn't for her. No sense making her arrival out to be the most important or exciting thing that'd happened in years, even if it was.

In a life marked by chaos, moving to Gansett Island had been the best thing he'd ever done for himself. He'd come for the first time with a friend from school, whose family had invited him for a weekend. He'd loved the place from the first second he stepped foot on the rugged, remote island as a sixteen-year-old.

After he'd aged out of the foster system, he'd come back to Gansett, willing to do whatever it took to make a home for himself there. In the ensuing eighteen years, he'd been a dockhand on the ferries and a bartender at the Rusty Scupper, among many other odd jobs. He was eventually hired at the tattoo studio in town, due to his ability to draw anything and everything.

They'd trained him in the trade, and when the owner retired, he'd turned over the shop to Duke, which was how he'd become a business owner at twenty-nine. Seven years later, the shop had grown beyond his wildest dreams and was providing him with a very decent living in-season. The off-season was much quieter, but he'd come to welcome the slower pace and had learned to save up for the slowdown.

On the island, he'd found the peace and quiet that'd eluded him for the first half of his life. Here, he'd found the home of his heart, a family of friends who loved and supported him like no one else ever had, especially Rosemary Enders, who'd shown him more about how to live than anyone else ever had.

His phone rang with a call from one of his close friends, Mick Jacobs from the gym.

"Hey, what's shakin'?"

"Have you talked to Sturgil since the storm?"

"No, but that's not unusual. I only say hi to him at the gym, and even that's a stretch after the way he treated his ex-wife. Why?"

"No one's heard from him since the storm, and his folks are pushing the panic button. They thought he was on the mainland, but no one has seen him over there either."

"Is there any chance he was with Billy on the boat?"

"I suppose it's not impossible. The two of them were friends back in high school. Billy was one of the few people who didn't turn his back when Sturgil made a mess of things."

"I was afraid you might say that. Don't think much of the guy, but I don't wish him dead."

He glanced at the clock on the wall in the kitchen and saw it was inching closer to five. "I gotta run. Let me know if you hear anything."

"You do the same."

Damn, Duke thought. Sturgil might be missing. He wondered if his ex-wife, Tiffany Taylor, knew that and whether he ought to ask her about it when he picked up McKenzie.

Nah, he decided. Wasn't his place to tell her, and besides, it wouldn't take long for word to get out on Gansett that Sturgil might be missing.

"I DIDN'T THINK anything of it, you know?" Tiffany sat at the kitchen table with a cup of tea McKenzie had made for her. "He missed his visit with Ashleigh last night, but that's happened before. I've gotten to the point where I don't even tell her he's coming because I don't want her to be disappointed when he doesn't show."

McKenzie wished she knew what to say to Tiffany, who was trying to hold it together since the phone call she'd received from her former mother-in-law, asking if she'd heard from her ex-husband, Jim, since the storm. McKenzie had pieced together enough to realize the breakup had been ugly, and Tiffany didn't know how she should feel about him possibly being missing.

"I mean, I'm sure he's fine. He's probably off somewhere, oblivious that anyone might be looking for him. Maybe he's somewhere with no power."

"I'm sure that's all it is."

"It's such a weird feeling. I've secretly wished he'd go away and never come back so many times in the last few years, but hearing he might be missing was so…"

"It's very upsetting."

"It is, and I wouldn't have thought I'd care, to be honest. He put me through hell."

"I assume you spent a lot of years with him."

Tiffany nodded. "From high school through to a couple of years ago."

"At times like this, we tend to focus on the good times and not the bad."

"That's true. And here I thought my biggest issue this week was going to be figuring out what to do about my poor squished Bug." A tree had fallen on her red Volkswagen Beetle during the storm.

"I'm so sorry about that. It was such a cute car."

"Blaine says we'll get another one, but that seems so trivial now that I've heard Jim is missing."

She'd no sooner mentioned her husband than Blaine came bursting through the kitchen door, taking them by surprise. "I came as soon as I heard."

Tiffany perked up considerably at the sight of her ridiculously handsome husband. She wiped a tear from her cheek. "I'm fine. Don't worry."

"Don't do that."

"What am I doing?"

"Thinking you can't be sad about Jim in front of me."

As if a dam had broken, Tiffany dissolved into sobs.

Blaine wrapped his arms around her and lifted her right out of the chair to carry her from the room.

Whoa.

McKenzie fanned her face, feeling as if she'd witnessed a scene straight out of a romance novel. It was a revelation to her that men like Blaine actually existed. She'd certainly never met one like him. The ones she knew were all frogs, with nary a prince among them.

A soft knock sounded at the door.

She got up to greet Duke.

As she opened the door, she realized he'd seemed more... polished than he had during his earlier visits. Had he done that for her? She couldn't help but notice that he was handsome in his own unique sort of way or that his blue eyes twinkled when he smiled.

"I didn't want to wake the little guy if he's napping."

She couldn't believe he'd thought of that. Most people didn't. "That's very kind of you. Come in. He should be awake any second."

"Take your time. I'm in no rush." He lowered his voice even further. "Does Tiffany know about the ex?"

McKenzie nodded. "Her former mother-in-law called."

"Ah, okay. I know him from the gym. Got a call from a friend asking if I'd heard from him. Was sorta hoping I'd get here and find out he'd been in touch with his daughter."

"They've had no word, and he missed a planned visit with her last night."

"Crap."

"I guess that's happened before, so Tiffany didn't think anything of it."

Ashleigh came into the kitchen. "Miss McKenzie, Jax is awake."

"Thank you so much for letting me know, honey."

"You're welcome."

After Ashleigh had skipped out of the room, Duke said, "She's her mother all over again."

"I know. She's adorable."

"I really hope for her sake that they find her father soon."

"I hope so, too. Let me grab Jax and tell Tiffany we're leaving. I'll be right back."

"I'll be here."

She stopped and turned back to him. "I just want you to know... I appreciate your generosity so much. I'll never be able to repay you."

"You don't have to. It's my pleasure to help you out. It's what Rosemary would've wanted me to do."

He was so very sweet and adorable in a slightly awkward and endearing kind of way.

She'd no sooner had that thought than she stopped herself. *You have no business finding any man adorable or endearing when you're basically a homeless single mom to an infant with almost everything you own lost to the storm. You've got much more important things to think about than whether your new friend is adorable, so knock that off.*

Upstairs, McKenzie retrieved Jax from the portable crib Tiffany had set up for him in the guest room and then broke down the crib to take it with her. Tiffany had told her to use it for as long as she needed. The Taylors wouldn't be traveling for a while with a third baby due soon. Thankfully, Tiffany was feeling better after a week of intense nausea and heartburn that'd made her miserable.

McKenzie swallowed the huge lump of fear that landed in her throat as she collected the last of their meager belongings into the grocery bags Duke had used to deliver them. Thinking of him picking through the remains of the cottage to find their things made her heart do that wobbly thing again. It'd been a long time since anyone had been as kind to her as Duke, Tiffany and Blaine had been.

Jax let out a whine and reached for his bear, which had also been rescued by Duke.

"Oh, we can't forget Mr. Bear."

Jax gurgled with delight.

That sound filled her with unreasonable joy, which drowned out the fear. As long as she had him and he had her, they could get through whatever was ahead for them. Or so she hoped. The task of rebuilding her grandmother's cabin was daunting. How did one even undertake such a thing on a remote island?

She'd managed to avoid having to deal with that over the last week while she helped Tiffany with the kids. Once she was at Duke's, she'd have no choice but to finally confront the wreckage of the cabin where many happy memories had been made with her grandmother.

"One step at a time, MK. One step at a time."

CHAPTER 2

"*E*verything okay?" Tiffany asked when she appeared in the doorway.

"Oh wow, you caught me talking to myself."

Tiffany offered a small smile. "I do it all the time."

McKenzie noticed that Tiffany's face was red and puffy from crying. "Are you okay?"

She shrugged. "I don't know how I'm supposed to feel about this."

"I'm sure it's so confusing."

"It really is." Tiffany took one of the lighter bags to carry it for McKenzie. "You're still planning to stick around, right?"

"Absolutely! I'm looking forward to getting started at the shop if you still need me."

"I do need you. I'm in denial that my faithful Patty is leaving me right before this little one arrives." Tiffany patted her pregnant belly. "I just need a minute to catch my breath after this news about Jim, and then we'll get you started."

"Take whatever time you need. I'll check in tomorrow."

"Sounds good."

"Duke is here, so we'll be getting out of your hair. You have my number if there's anything I can do to help you."

"Thank you. I appreciate that and everything you did to help me this week. You ended up saving me."

"No way. I'll never be able to thank you enough for taking us in during the storm and letting us stay this week." McKenzie gave Tiffany a one-armed hug that put Jax between them. "Thank you again for your kindness, Tiffany."

"Thank you for yours. I'm so glad we got to meet you and Jax. We love making new friends. I'm going to text my lawyer friend Dan Torrington about your situation with Jax's father and see what he has to say about it. He and his wife had to go to Maine for something with her family, but he'll know what you should do."

"I'd appreciate it. Part of me wants to leave well enough alone, but the other part of me wants Jax to have everything he needs."

"It's the right thing to get a lawyer involved. You won't be sorry. Sometimes all it takes is the threat of legal action to get someone to do the right thing." Tiffany led the way downstairs. "Hey, Duke."

"Hi, Tiffany. Not sure if I should say I was sorry to hear about Jim..."

"I was, too. I hope they find him."

"If there's anything I can do..."

"You're sweet. Thank you."

Duke shifted his attention to McKenzie and Jax. "Are you guys ready?"

"I think so."

He took the portable crib from her and carried it out to his truck.

McKenzie followed him out and thanked him for holding the door for her so she could get Jax settled in the car seat Tiffany had loaned her.

His truck smelled like it had been freshly cleaned. Had he done that for her, too? So what if he had? It's just that it had been such a long time since anyone had done anything nice for her, other than the Taylors, of course, that the smallest act of kindness felt huge to her.

Tiffany waved them off from the back porch.

Jax gurgled and played with his toes as Duke navigated winding island roads.

"He's awfully cute," Duke said with a chuckle.

"He's obsessed with his toes."

"I suppose babies like to chew on them while they can still reach them."

"True."

"Rosemary would've been crazy about him."

"I know. I so wish she could've met him."

"I'm sure she's still around here somewhere, keeping an eye on things."

"I'd like to think so."

"Were you always close to her?"

"Very. She lived next door to us when I was growing up. I spent more time at her house than at mine. She taught me to cook and sew. She bought me my first glue gun and taught me how to make every kind of craft. We were best friends."

"I can picture all that. She tried to teach me how to cook, but I never made it much past the basics."

"Was she exasperated with you?"

"Highly."

McKenzie laughed at the way he said that. "She wasn't known for her patience. She'd often say, 'MK, I taught you better than that!'"

"MK?"

"Yes, she gave me that nickname when I was a baby and never called me anything else."

"I remember you as a teenager."

Surprised, she looked over at him. "You do? We met before last week?"

He looked as stunned as she felt. "Once. She invited me to come to her house on the mainland for Christmas one year, and I remember meeting a granddaughter named MK."

"I'm trying to remember meeting you. She was always inviting people to holidays and stuff."

"I have a photo from that Christmas. I'll show you."

McKenzie wondered how old he was but didn't want to ask. If she had to guess, she'd say late-thirties, which would make him at least ten years older than her twenty-six. Not that it mattered... She was just curious.

He took a left turn into a dirt driveway that led to a shingled two-story saltbox-style house with a two-story garage to the left side. The driveway circled around a firepit with lights strung above it.

"Home sweet home."

"It's lovely."

"It's not much, but it's mine."

"You own property on Gansett Island. That's quite something. Gran always talked about how crazy the prices are out here."

"She helped me buy this place by making the down payment, and I paid her back every month for ten years."

"Oh, I love hearing that! She was so generous."

"She changed my life by showing me what it was like to have someone in my corner."

McKenzie looked over at him. "You'd never had that?"

"Not until I met her."

Duke was reeling from the realization that he'd met McKenzie years earlier, when she was still a teenager. He remembered her. She'd been a beautiful kid who'd grown into a stunning woman. She was probably far too young for him to be dazzled by her. Out of respect for his dear friend Rosemary, he would keep his distance from her lovely granddaughter while helping her the way Rosemary had once helped him.

"Can I carry that for you?" he asked of the baby seat, which looked heavy.

She handed it over to him. "That'd be great. Thanks. He's a load all of a sudden."

Duke made a goofy face at the baby, which made the little guy giggle. Having never heard a baby giggle before, he was briefly stunned by the flutter in his chest at having been the cause of such a joyful sound.

So naturally, he did it again and again.

"He likes you," McKenzie said as she followed him up the stairs to the apartment over the garage.

"He's a cutie."

"I'm so lucky that he's such a good baby. He slept through most of the storm."

Duke had so many questions. Where was the baby's father? How had she not heard about the hurricane before it was too late? What was she going to do about the cottage next door that'd been flattened by the storm?

Now was not the time to ask any of that, however. He wanted to get them settled and comfortable. "So this is it. You've got a living room-kitchen combo, a bathroom and a bedroom."

"It's all we need. And it smells so clean. Thank you again so much, Duke."

"I'd like to lie and say it always smells clean, but I spiffed it up a bit for you."

"That's very nice of you."

"Least I could do. Is there anything else you need to get settled in?"

"I'll take a walk into town to get some groceries and diapers."

"Let me know when you want to go, and I'll drive you. No need to walk."

"I'm sure you have other things to do."

"I've got time. Just let me know when you want to go."

"Thank you again for everything. I feel like I'll never be able to thank you enough."

"You don't need to thank me. I owe your grandmother so, so much. This is how I can repay her. You know?"

"She'd never want you to feel like you had to repay her kindness."

"Believe me, I know. I had to force her to accept my monthly reimbursements. She said she didn't want it, but I told her I needed to believe I'd bought this place myself."

"That also sounds like her."

"You were lucky to have her in your life, as was I."

"I guess we may as well go to the store now, before Jax's bedtime."

"Let's do it." He carried the baby carrier back to the truck, realizing he should've offered a trip to the store when they were still in town. But he'd been so flummoxed by having her in his truck that he hadn't been thinking clearly.

Duke drove them back to town and went with her into the grocery store in case she needed help with the little guy. He was amazed by how she propped the seat on the shopping cart like an old pro and wheeled him into the store.

"Nice to have the power back," he said as they entered the brightly lit space. It'd been like a cave in there while they relied on generators.

"Sure is. I'd never given the first thought to how this place would function without power."

"We had a days-long blackout last summer. A lot of people bought generators after that, myself included. I had one running on my fridge all last week."

"Blaine and Tiffany had one going, too."

"We'll get you some ice just in case the power goes out again. The grid is old, and the storm identified new vulnerabilities."

"Is that why it keeps going on and off?"

"Yep. I heard they're looking for parts that are hard to find because the system is so outdated."

"Is it weird to be more anxious *after* the storm than I was during the storm?"

"Yes, that's very weird."

She laughed, as he hoped she would.

"You were in much greater danger then than you are now."

"I know, but it's just so sobering to realize how isolated we are here."

"You want to know a secret?"

"Sure."

"I love when things go askew out here. It's fun figuring out how to cope without the basics."

McKenzie rolled her eyes. "I prefer a more sedate kind of fun than living without the basics."

"You need to tap into your sense of adventure."

"I don't have much of a sense of adventure. Never really have."

"Well, this is a good time to get one because you never know what's going to happen out here from one day to the next."

McKenzie put a bunch of bananas in the cart. "You don't see mention of that in the tourist brochures."

Duke laughed. "Nah, it's our little secret. The year-rounders take care of the tourists when need be." He put two jugs of water into the cart. "They're recommending bottled water for a while longer."

"Right, Tiffany mentioned that."

"It's fun the way the community comes together to take care of each other at times like this. It reminds me of why I love it here so much. People are always willing to help."

"That's a nice way to live."

"I'd never experienced true community until I came here," he said.

"How long ago was that?"

"Eighteen years ago. Been here half my life now."

"So that makes you…"

"Thirty-six last week," he said with a grin.

"I never have been able to do math in my head."

"Me either. I also can't spell out loud. I'm always sure it's wrong."

McKenzie laughed. "Me, too! Spelling bees were a nightmare for me."

"Same. I refused to do them after sixth grade because I was sick of coming in last place."

"I came in last place in sixth, seventh and eighth grades. Thank God they didn't do them in high school."

"What were you good at in school?"

"You're going to laugh."

"Hit me," he said.

"Math—as long as I didn't have to add in my head—and wood shop. I loved it."

"That's cool. Have you done anything with it since then?"

"A little. Some home improvement stuff. That sort of thing, but I want to get more into it again someday."

"It's good to have a dream."

"That's all it is at this point. Right now, I need to focus on supporting myself and Jax. Tiffany offered me a job at her store, which was a huge relief."

"That place stays busy all year."

"That's what she said. I'm excited about it, and she said I can bring Jax to work, which is huge."

"So you're planning to hang here for a bit?" he asked, hoping he didn't sound like he was fishing for info.

"I think so. I was really liking it here until the storm hit."

"I kept meaning to get over to say hello, but work was insane on top of storm prep, and when I got home, it was usually dark over there. Didn't want to freak you out."

"You would have."

Grinning, he said, "It's the tatts, right?"

"Nah, they don't bother me. Just any guy showing up out of the dark would've given me pause."

The more she told him, the more he wanted to know about her. Woodworking, of all things. He never would've guessed that. He would've said art or music or something much more cerebral. Although learning she couldn't do math in her head or spell out loud made him feel like less of a dummy next to her.

"I was good at the art stuff." He held out both arms to show off the sleeve tattoos. "My own original design."

"It's incredible. I thought so when you first came by Tiffany's."

"It's the one thing I've ever been good at. Used to drive my teachers crazy that all my papers were covered in drawings. They told me I needed to focus on more serious things, but to me, that was as serious as it got."

"And now you own your own art-based business. I'd say you showed them."

"I doubt they'd be impressed."

"I think anyone who finds a way to support themselves through their own business and talents is hella impressive. That's the dream come true, in my opinion."

"It's pretty cool."

"Sure is."

She added a box of diapers, pouches of baby food, some powdered formula and other items for the baby—things he'd never noticed on the shelves before now.

"Babies need a lot of stuff."

"*So* much stuff."

He was further surprised by how much it all cost. A hundred and twenty bucks, and she'd barely gotten any food. Should he offer her some money? Before he could decide about that, she'd whipped out a card and was collecting her receipt.

On the ride home, she gazed out the window at the sun setting over the beach. "I'd forgotten how beautiful it is here."

"Did you get out here much as a kid?"

"Not as much as I wanted to. My mom sort of resented how much time I spent with my grandmother, and the minute Gran left for the summer, Mom thought I should spend all my time with her. Except that wasn't what I wanted."

"What did you want?"

"To come to Gansett with Gran for the summer, but my mother wouldn't have it."

"Why not?"

"I don't know. I never have been able to explain her to people. Gran used to say she's a narcissist. Everything was about her, all the time."

"Your mom is Cecelia?"

"Yeah. I guess she probably told you about her."

"She mentioned that she was difficult."

"That's putting it mildly."

He wanted to ask her to elaborate, but it seemed like a sore subject, so he left it alone. But even though he'd decided he was way too old for her, and she was way out of his league, he wanted to hear more of her stories.

Much, much more.

CHAPTER 3

Tiffany didn't know what to do with herself since hearing the news that Jim might be missing. Thank goodness her mom and Ned had come to take the girls to their house for a few hours so she could get herself together.

Her emotions were all over the place, from sadness to fear to anguish for Ashleigh to relief, which made her sick with guilt. How could she be *relieved* at the possibility of Jim being gone forever?

She couldn't let her mind go there, or she'd be unable to live with herself.

Blaine's strong arms came around her from behind, and she melted into his embrace. "I can tell you're spinning."

"I don't know what I am."

"It's okay to be upset, Tiff. Anyone would be."

"It doesn't feel right to be upset about him. I don't have any right to be."

"Of course you do. You were with him for years and had a child together. I'd be worried if you weren't upset."

"The last time I saw him... when he brought Ashleigh home before the storm... All I could think about was how I wished he'd go away and never come back. And now..."

"It's not your fault that something might've happened to him. He was probably taking risks he shouldn't have been taking during the storm. People do that stuff. Deacon and his team rescued thirty people off the rocks on the north end before the storm hit. They'd gone out there to watch the surf. People are so stupid, and my guys had to risk their lives to rescue them. So many think they're invincible. Jim was probably one of them."

Tiffany turned and looked up at him. "What'll I tell Ash?"

"Nothing until we know for sure what happened."

"What if we never know?"

"Let's take it one minute at a time and see what happens. I've got my whole crew looking for him, the Coast Guard is assisting, and Jack has brought in additional state police help to look for him and Billy. We'll find them."

Tiffany rested her head on his broad chest. "You should be out there with them."

"I'm right where I need to be, babe. With you."

Her phone rang, and she pulled back from Blaine to grab it off a table. "It's Maddie."

"I'm sure she's worried about you."

Tiffany took the call from her older sister as she leaned on her husband's unwavering support. "Hey."

"I just heard the news, sweetie. I don't know what to say."

"Me either. I'm all over the place."

"I'm sure. Anyone would be. Has there been any word?"

"Nothing yet. Blaine said everyone is out looking for him and Billy. They might've been together."

"What can I do for you?"

"I have no idea. It's a wait-and-see thing at this point." Her voice broke on that last word. "I've had very bad thoughts about him, so many times, but I never wanted anything like this to happen."

"I know that, Tiff. We all know that. Do you want me to come over?"

"That's okay. Blaine is here with me, and Mom has the girls."

"Call me later?"

"For sure. Thanks for checking on me."

"Love you. No matter what happens, we've got you."

"That makes everything better," she said as tears rolled down her face. "Love you, too."

How in the world was she crying over a man who'd broken her heart in every way it was possible to break a heart? He'd been a monster to her, and still... She wept. In front of her new husband, who was the undisputed love of her life.

That wouldn't do.

She wiped away her tears and made a valiant attempt to rally. "Are you hungry? You must be. I'll see what we have."

He took her hand to keep her from walking away. "Stop, Tiff. Just stop."

"I need to be busy, or I'll go crazy."

"You don't need to worry about feeding me or what I might think about you crying over Jim or anything else."

"I want to feed you. It'll help."

"Okay then, but only if you let me be your sous-chef."

She forced a smile for his benefit. "You're my sous-chef for life."

He gave her a soft, sweet kiss. "No matter what happens, we'll be okay. I promise."

As long as she had him and their blissful life, she would get through this.

But she sure as hell hoped her pain-in-the-ass ex-husband wasn't dead.

AT RHODE ISLAND HOSPITAL in Providence, Kelsey Gordon adjusted the sling that supported her surgically repaired broken right forearm, which was now encased in plaster. The meds she'd been prescribed kept the pain manageable, which was a relief after a rough couple of days following surgery to pin the broken bone. She waited by the nurses' station, hoping for an update on the condition of her fiancé, Jeff Lawry.

Her fiancé.

She still couldn't believe they'd gotten engaged during the storm, before the roof over her apartment collapsed on them, leaving Jeff seriously injured. Other than the broken arm, she had bruises and lacerations all over her body, but she was in good shape compared to him.

He'd suffered a broken pelvis and fractured hip, injuries that had also required surgery. For a time, they'd feared he wouldn't survive long enough to be airlifted off the island to get the urgent care he needed. Thanks to Dr. David Lawrence and the team at the island's clinic, he'd been stabilized to travel by helicopter to the mainland.

Her parents had spent a week in Providence with her and Jeff and had left this morning to return home to Illinois. Jeff's brother John had also been with them until yesterday when he went home to Gansett. Kelsey had been staying with Jeff's mother, Sarah, stepfather, Charlie, and grandparents, Russ and Adele, at Frank McCarthy's home, which had been made available to them for as long as they needed it.

Debbie, the nurse who'd cared for Jeff overnight, approached the desk and smiled when she saw Kelsey waiting for her. They'd gotten to know most of the nurses who worked on the floor. "He had a restful night, and the doctor upgraded him to good condition when he came through on morning rounds. They're working on a plan to discharge him to a rehab facility in the next week to ten days." She squeezed Kelsey's shoulder, reassuringly. "It's all good news."

"Oh, yes, I know. It's still a lot to process."

"He's young and strong, and he'll bounce right back. Try not to worry."

"Thank you. It's been..." The dreadful twenty-four hours she'd spent fearing the man she loved wouldn't survive had taken a huge toll on her. The fear had been far more painful than the broken arm. She'd never forget the way he'd lunged to cover her in the one second they'd had to prepare as the roof came down on them. A beam had landed on him, resulting in the most serious of his injuries. "It's been hard. He got hurt saving me."

"He's on the road to recovery, honey, and everything will be all right in a month or two."

"I appreciate your kindness."

"Go see your love. He was asking for you. I'll be back tonight."

"We'll see you then." Feeling better after her talk with Debbie, Kelsey walked down the hallway to Jeff's room.

Sarah, Russ and Adele were outside the room with Jeff's eldest brother, Owen, who'd come over yesterday, hoping to convince the others to go home to the island so they wouldn't wear themselves out. Jeff's recovery would be a long one, and they'd been encouraged to pace themselves. Sarah wasn't having it, though, and as long as she was staying, so were Charlie and her parents.

"The morning nurse is in with him," Owen said. "He asked for a few minutes."

Kelsey nodded. "I just saw Debbie. She said he had a restful night."

"That's good news." Sarah wore a pinched, stressed look about her since her youngest child nearly died in the storm. The four of them had been in Italy on vacation but had flown home when Sarah sensed something was amiss. She'd been right about that, and Owen had filled her in on Jeff's condition after they landed in the US.

Charlie approached, carrying trays of coffees that he distributed to each of them.

Kelsey smiled at him as he handed one to her. "Thank you." Charlie was such a love. He'd asked how she took her coffee a week ago and had kept her supplied ever since.

"How're you feeling, honey?" Charlie asked.

"Sore, but better knowing Jeff is improving."

She would never forget the ordeal of being pinned under him and a ton of debris for hours while firefighters and townspeople worked frantically to get them out.

Tears flooded her eyes as she relived the horror.

Sarah's arm gently encircled her shoulders, giving silent support that Kelsey needed badly. The four of them had been so good to Kelsey. She'd be forever thankful to them and her own parents, who'd come running when they heard she and Jeff were badly injured after the storm.

Kelsey was also thankful for her bosses, Mac and Maddie McCarthy, who'd been a huge source of support from the island. Mac was one of the people who'd worked so frantically to get them out of the rubble, and she'd never forget the comforting sound of his voice reassuring her as she awaited rescue.

Both Mac and Maddie had checked in regularly, had offered anything either she or Jeff needed and had told her not to worry about her job. It would be waiting for her whenever she was ready to come back. In the meantime, the grandmothers were pitching in to help with their five young kids.

A male nurse she hadn't met before emerged from Jeff's room. "He's all cleaned up and ready for guests. Is one of you Kelsey?"

"That'd be me."

"He's asking for you."

Kelsey ran the fingers of her left hand through her hair, pinched some color into her cheeks and took a couple of deep breaths, preparing herself to give him whatever he needed while bracing herself once again to see him badly injured. She smiled brightly as she entered the room, wanting to project only positivity and optimism.

Every day, it was all she could do not to crumble when she took in his bruised face, the tubes, machines, monitors, IVs. It was a lot.

"Hey," he said gruffly. "There you are."

She went to his bedside and took his hand, noticing the bruises on his face had begun to go yellow, which one of the nurses had told her was a sign of healing. "Here I am. You look so much better today." That wasn't true, but she'd never tell him otherwise. He'd been lightly sedated for much of the past week, so she hadn't had much of a chance to talk to him.

His cracked lips curved into a small smile. "Is that the kind of wife you're going to be? The kind that lies?"

"I'm not lying! You do look better, and you're awake, which is a huge improvement."

"I asked for a mirror earlier. I look like shit."

"No, you don't."

"It's okay. I had a barn cave in on me and lived to tell. That's what matters, right?"

"Yes, definitely." Kelsey's emotions were like a kettle set to boil. "I can't stop thinking about what you did, Jeff... You got hurt so badly saving me."

"It's worth every ache and pain to know you're okay."

She shook her head. "I can't bear to see you hurt like this."

"I'll be okay. Eventually."

"I'll be right here for all of it."

"I want to send you home because a hospital isn't a fun place to hang out when you're recovering from your own injuries, but I'd miss you too much."

"I'm not going anywhere."

"How's your arm feeling?"

"A little better. The meds are helping."

"I hate that you got hurt, too."

"It's nothing compared to what happened to you."

He gazed at her with love and affection. "I can't stop thinking about what went on before the roof fell in."

At times like this, Kelsey wished she didn't blush so easily.

"Do your rosy cheeks mean you've been thinking about it, too?"

"I've given it a little thought."

"Only a little?"

"I was too busy worrying I might lose you."

"Well, you didn't, so don't go thinking I've forgotten that you agreed to marry me."

"Did that really happen?"

"You bet it did, and as soon as I'm standing on two feet again, we're going for it."

"I'll look forward to that."

"So will I. It'll give me a goal to work toward in rehab."

For a few minutes, they gazed at each other like the fools in love they were.

"You were okay after the other thing, right?"

"I was okay."

"Sore?"

"A little, but it passed." That'd been the least of her concerns after the roof fell on them.

"I'm glad."

"Is it okay if I let your family in? Your mom needs to dote on you."

"Sure but give me a kiss first."

Kelsey leaned over the bed rail to kiss his rough lips. She needed to get him some more lip balm from the hospital store.

"One more and make it a good one."

She smiled as she complied with his directive. Then she went to let in his eager family members.

Sarah went right to Jeff's bedside to hover over him the way she had from the minute she'd arrived in Providence.

Of course, Kelsey was focused on Jeff and what he needed, but lurking in the back of her mind was panic over being out of work for an extended period. Thankfully, they both had health insurance through Mac's construction company, but with a broken arm, she wouldn't be able to care for Mac and Maddie's children—including twin infants—for six to eight weeks.

She had a car payment, car insurance, cell phone bill and other regular expenses she wouldn't be able to cover.

Not to mention most of her clothing and personal belongings were under a mountain of rubble back on Gansett. Sarah and Charlie had gone to the store to buy her some basics, and she'd need to reimburse them.

Eventually.

Worries about finances had kept her awake last night, long after the pain pills had finally kicked in and taken the edge off the sharp ache in her broken arm.

She could borrow money from her parents, but that was a last resort. They'd helped her and her siblings through college and were now excited to travel. She'd hate to do anything to hamper their plans.

Kelsey wished she could calm down and not worry so much. They were both alive. That was the only thing that mattered, but as someone who'd been born practical, according to her mother, she couldn't help but fret about the details.

Mac stood before the wreckage of the barn he'd managed to avoid for most of a week, staring at it while trying to get his head around what'd happened there during the storm. Kelsey and Jeff had come close to being killed. He'd never forget the frantic race to get them out from under the rubble before it was too late.

He shuddered as the horror resurfaced in vivid, graphic images that would haunt him forever. He'd refused to go near the site until now because he'd been too raw over what'd happened there and how lucky they were that Kelsey and Jeff had survived.

The former barn-shaped structure had been reduced to rubble by Hurricane Ethel. Mangled boards had formed a pile ten feet high in places, relieved only by the area where they'd worked in the wind and rain to free Kelsey and Jeff.

Big Mac joined him, striking a similar pose as he, too, stared at the ruins, probably reliving some of the same memories that'd tormented Mac for days now. "Thank God they're on the mend," Big Mac finally said after a long moment of silence.

"Indeed."

"Have you heard how they're doing today?"

"Kelsey texted earlier to say that they're arranging for Jeff to be discharged to a rehab facility. Probably in the next week to ten days."

"That's good news." He glanced at Mac. "Did you hear Sturgil's missing?"

"What? No. Does Tiffany know?"

"Ned told me her ex-mother-in-law called to ask if Tiff had heard from him. That's how she found out."

Shocked to hear the news about his former brother-in-law, Mac pulled out his phone to see he'd missed two calls from Maddie. Turning the phone on its side, he saw that the ringer was off and turned it back on.

Son of a bitch.

He called her back.

"Hey, have you heard about Jim?" she asked.

"Just now. Sorry I missed your calls. The freaking ringer was off, probably thanks to Thomas playing games on my phone last night."

"I figured something like that, or you were busy."

He was never too busy to take a call from her, which she certainly knew by now. "How's Tiffany?"

"She's not sure how she's supposed to feel. I think she's far more upset than she would've expected to be."

"I get it. He put her through hell, but she doesn't want him dead."

"Yes, that exactly."

"And poor Ashleigh."

"I know. She and Addie are with Mom and Ned for now. I offered to go to Tiff's, but she said Blaine's with her, and she's doing okay."

"That's good."

"Where are you?"

"Dad and I are at the barn to figure out what to do about it. I was also going to see if I can salvage some of Kelsey's stuff."

"Don't endanger yourself by going in there. Do you hear me?"

"I won't. My mom is still there with you, right?"

"She is, and she said she'll stay until you get home."

"Tell her thanks, and I'll be home by three. Four at the latest." He'd been working nonstop since the storm hit, damaging thirty homes on the island at last count. As one of four local construction firms, two of them one-person operations, Mac and his team would be straight out for months, which was not how he'd planned to spend the off-season. They'd get it all done. Somehow.

"We're fine. Do what you need to."

"Love you."

"You, too. Be careful."

"I will."

"How's she doing?" Big Mac asked.

"Shocked about Jim but hanging in there thanks to Mom."

"She's happy to help for as long as Kelsey is laid up. We all are."

"Thank you. It's very comforting to be surrounded by family at a time like this."

"I want to get some money to Kelsey and Jeff," Big Mac said. "I'm sure there'll be expenses and other needs with both of them out of work for the time being. Can you help me make that happen?"

"Sure, Dad. That's very nice of you."

"It's the least I can do after my building collapsed on those poor kids."

"They don't blame you for that."

"Maybe they should. Hell, I wouldn't be surprised if they sued me for damages."

"They won't do that."

"But they could, and they'd have a case, so let's give them enough that they don't want for anything while they're getting back on their feet."

"I have their bank info for payroll and could get it to them. How much do you want it to be?"

"Maybe a hundred each?"

Mac turned to his father, eyes gone wide. "*Grand?*"

"Yes. I talked to your mom, and she agrees we need to do everything we can to make this right."

"That's incredibly generous of you both, but surely you had an act of God clause in the lease."

Big Mac's gaze shifted ever so slightly toward Mac. "What lease?"

"You gotta be kidding me."

His father shrugged. "That's not how I do business. Those kids got hurt in my building, and I want to do something for them. If I write you a check, will you take care of getting it to them?"

Mac wasn't as surprised as he should be that there was no lease with Kelsey. His dad operated on faith and gut checks that'd served him well over forty years in business. He was as old-school as it got, and generous as hell.

Mac wouldn't change a thing about him. "Yeah, Dad. I'll take care of it."

"Thank you."

"You're a kind and generous man."

"Least I can do for those kids."

Mac patted his dad on the back. "It'll mean so much to them."

"Tell them there's more where that came from if they need it."

"I will not do that. That's more than enough, and I'm sure they'll tell you it's far too much."

"I'm just so damned thankful they weren't killed."

"We all are." Mac handed his dad one of the two pairs of work gloves he'd brought. "How about we see what we can do about finding some of Kelsey's things?"

"Let's do it."

CHAPTER 4

*D*uke insisted on carrying the baby and most of the groceries upstairs to her new apartment. As McKenzie followed with two of the bags, she was filled with a warm feeling of homecoming, which was odd since she'd never stepped foot in this place until an hour ago.

But he'd made her feel so welcome and had gone above and beyond to make sure she and Jax would be comfortable. While he made a second trip to the truck, she asked herself when was the last time someone had considered her needs and tended to them the way he had?

Never.

One of her earliest memories was standing on a kitchen chair making scrambled eggs for herself and her mother while her mom was in one of her low periods. She didn't recall learning how to scramble eggs. Maybe she'd been born knowing how. That wouldn't surprise her. She couldn't remember a time when her mother had taken care of her. It had always been the other way around.

That could be why she often put up with crap she never should've tolerated in her relationships with men, always hoping to find someone who'd put her first. Thankfully, she was mostly prepared to stand on her own two feet, except for when a hurricane came and knocked down the beloved cabin in which she'd planned to make a home for herself and her son.

The part of her starved for someone who gave a shit about her wanted to wallow in Duke's TLC, but she knew better than to go there. If she'd learned anything, it was that there was no point in investing that kind of hope in other people. They always disappointed her.

Jax's father was the latest in a long line of people who'd let her down.

"Thank you again for everything, Duke. I don't know what we would've done without your help."

"Happy to do it. I'm right across the yard if you need anything."

"That's good to know."

He gave the baby's foot a little tweak that made Jax giggle. "Sleep tight and don't let the bed bugs bite." He quickly added, "Not that there are any of those in here."

McKenzie laughed. "I'm not worried about that."

"Okay, then. Sleep tight, both of you."

"We will, thanks to your kindness."

"No problem."

McKenzie walked him to the door and watched him go down the stairs, whistling a chirpy tune as he went.

Though she knew she had nothing to fear from him, she still flipped the lock on the screen door before she went to feed and bathe Jax and get him down for the night in the portable crib. Thank goodness for the new friends who'd made sure they had everything they needed, including the car seat.

She and Jax went through their usual ritual of a final feeding, story and snuggle before she tucked him in with Mr. Bear. He was rubbing his eyes, which was always a good sign that he was ready to sleep.

With the baby down for the count, McKenzie made herself a salad and sat on the sofa to eat. This was the time of day when loneliness set in, making her aware of how alone she was in the world, other than Jax, of course. He was the purest joy in her life and had been from the second he was born, even if single motherhood had been the most daunting thing she'd ever faced.

She'd made it through the first nine months, a day at a time, most of it living with her mother until that'd become untenable. Desperately needing a change, she'd decided to come to the island to check out the cottage her grandmother had left to her, even if the idea of living on a remote island with an infant had been almost as daunting as single motherhood.

She'd loved the time they'd spent there before the storm hit. Now that Duke had taken care of her most pressing need for a roof over their heads, she had to figure out what to do about the cottage. The insurance company had told her an agent would be coming to the island this week to survey her damage and that of a few other residents. Once she knew what the payout would be, she could determine the next steps. In the meantime, she'd been putting off viewing the damage personally because she'd been afraid to see the cabin destroyed.

Tomorrow, she'd go over there to sift through the rubble and hopefully find some more of her things. Thankfully, her grandmother had paid the insurance for three years, which would end next year, so the repairs should be covered. Or so she hoped, but she had no clue how to go about rebuilding a house on Gansett Island.

One thing at a time, MK. The words came to her in her grandmother's voice, which made her smile because that's exactly what Rosemary would've said if she'd been there. And she was right. Today had been a good day, thanks to Duke, Tiffany and Blaine, new friends who'd stepped up for her when she needed them most.

In the morning, she'd begin the process of figuring out her next steps. Duke had been on the island for years and knew everyone. He'd mentioned Mac McCarthy, who ran a construction business. Maybe Duke could put her in touch with Mac.

McKenzie went to close the inside door and spotted Duke sitting next to a fire under lights that'd been strung through the trees, giving his firepit area a magical vibe. He was working on something, but she couldn't see what.

She checked on Jax, who was sound asleep. After cracking the window in his room so she'd hear him if he awakened, she went down the stairs, crossing the yard to the firepit and stopping short when she saw what Duke was doing. "Are you... *cross-stitching?*" Nothing in her life had ever surprised her more.

He gave a sheepish grin and a shrug. "Rosemary taught me how years ago. It's oddly relaxing. Don't tell the guys at the shop, okay?"

McKenzie smiled, ridiculously charmed by his confession. "Your secret is safe with me." And then she had another thought. "The pillows in the apartment... Did you make them?"

"Maybe?"

They'd been the first thing she noticed. "They're incredible! You're very talented."

"I don't know about that, but it's something to do at night rather than rot my brain in front of the TV. Not that there's anything wrong with that."

McKenzie sat in the Adirondack chair next to him. "She taught me how, too, but it never took with me. My attention to detail isn't what it needed to be, or so she said."

"That sounds like her. 'Duke,' she'd say, 'if you don't apply yourself, you'll never learn anything new.'"

McKenzie laughed. "I've heard that one a time or two myself. I used to say, 'I *am* applying myself. *This* is what I'm capable of.' She didn't like that answer."

"No, she wouldn't have cared for that."

"I still can't believe you're a cross-stitcher."

"Messes with my image as a tough guy, huh?"

"Kinda?" She tried to suppress the giggle that gurgled from deep inside but failed miserably.

His eyes danced with amusement, which was when she realized that not only was he handsome, but he was also kind of sexy. "Are you laughing at me by any chance?"

"I'd never do that."

"And yet..."

"Sorry."

"Don't be. It's funny. A long-haired, tattooed dude like me isn't exactly the target audience for cross-stitch. I was next door one day and saw her doing it, asked what it was, and she showed me. I thought it looked fun and a bit challenging, so she set me up with a simple sampler, and that was that. I've been at it ever since."

"I'm seriously impressed."

"I see it as a way to be creative without having to expend as much mental energy as I do at the shop when I'm permanently marking someone's skin with art."

"I get that. What're you making?"

He turned the sampler, which was held tight by a wooden loop around it, so she could see it. "I'm making this one up as I go."

McKenzie was stunned by the gorgeous field of wildflowers in an array of dazzling colors, shapes and sizes. "You're making it up? Not following a pattern?"

"Nope." He handed her a drawing done in colored pencil. "I'm following that—loosely."

"Now, that is seriously impressive."

"I've been freelancing for years, so it's not that hard anymore. Takes forever to get stuff shipped out here. I started making up my own designs so I wouldn't get bored waiting for new ones to arrive."

"You're very talented."

"Art is the one thing I got."

"You're lucky to have that one thing. I'm still looking for mine."

"I thought you were a woodworker?"

"I'm a wannabe woodworker. I have the interest but not the skills. Not yet, anyway."

"What do you do for work?"

"I've kind of bounced around from one career to another—my degree is in fashion, but I've never really used it. In hindsight, I probably should've majored in something that lent itself to a real salary. I was working in retail when Jax happened."

"So he was a surprise, was he?"

"You could say that. I'd been seeing his dad for a year when I got pregnant. I was on birth control that didn't work, which was a shock, to say the least. When I told him I was pregnant, that's when I found out he's married with a wife and two kids and wasn't interested in another. He told me he'd had a vasectomy, so the baby couldn't be his. That was almost worse than the wife and kids, since he knew I'd been faithful to him, which was more than he could say."

"I'm so sorry. That's awful. What a *loser*."

McKenzie smiled at the emphatic way he said that last word. "Yeah, he was. He lied to me about everything, and I found out the hard way. But it's okay. I'd rather raise Jax on my own than have him around a man who lies and cheats and runs from his obligations."

"That's the way to be."

"I really loved him, though, so it was a rough time. It got better after Jax arrived. It's hard to be sad when he's the most cheerful, happy little guy."

"He's a cutie."

"He really is. The way I see it, I've got a built-in best friend, at least until he becomes a cranky teenager."

"I bet he'll always be your best friend."

"That'd be nice." She glanced up at the lights. "I like the lights."

"I do, too. They're solar. I have them on a timer to come on every night."

"That's cool. They look great strung through the trees."

"I love them."

"Well, I'd better get back upstairs in case Jax wakes up." He never did, but she didn't want to outstay her welcome when Duke was trying to relax.

"Don't rush off on my account. It's cool to have someone to chat with."

"You're a very nice man, Duke. Why aren't you married with a bunch of kids?"

He grunted out a laugh. "Came close once, but that was ages ago."

"What happened?" She asked the question before she took the time to think about it. "I'm sorry. You don't have to tell me. I shouldn't have asked that."

"It's fine. She didn't like it here, and this is my home. In a choice between her and Gansett, I chose Gansett."

"What did she say?"

"At first, she couldn't believe it, but when I refused to change my mind, she finally got the message. If she wanted me, she was going to have to live here. I guess she didn't want me that much, which is fine. I'd rather find that out than have her suck it up and make me hate it here, too, you know?"

"Definitely."

"Took me a long time to find a place that felt like home. I wasn't willing to give it up."

"I'm glad you stuck to your guns."

"Rosemary was very good to me after that happened. I was a little heartbroken at first, but she told me I'd done the right thing not to give up something that meant so much to me."

"She would know. After my grandfather died, her children pressured her to sell her place out here. They didn't want her coming out alone for the summers. She flatly refused and told them all to mind their own business and quit telling her how to live her life."

"She told me about that. She said we have to fight for the things that're important to us. Gansett was more important to me than the girlfriend was, she said, so I made the right choice for myself. She knew I wouldn't have been happy somewhere else. As always, she was right."

"I love that you two were such buddies."

"We really were. She was very important to me."

"For what it's worth, I agree with her. I think you did the right thing. No one is worth giving up the things that mean the most to you."

"That's true, but it was still a rather bitter pill when you think you've found 'the one.'"

"I'm sure."

"What about you? Never been married?"

"Nah, I'm not a big fan of marriage," she said. "I don't get why people are still bothering to get married. Why not live together and have a family and be together every day by choice rather than because you're legally bound to someone?"

"That's a good point. I think people like the tradition of it."

"Which is fine, but when it's so damned complicated and costly to get out of a marriage, and half of them end in divorce anyway, why does anyone take a risk like that?"

Duke thought about that for a second. "Hard telling. I guess in most cases, it's a leap of faith."

"Definitely. A scary leap of faith that I'd prefer not to take. I love the idea of two people choosing to be together because they want to be, not because the law says they have to be."

"Playing devil's advocate… People who get married seem to like the comfort of knowing that one person is theirs for a lifetime."

"I don't like the thought of someone *belonging* to someone. We all belong to ourselves, not anyone else."

"Also a good point. I should've said the comfort of commitment, not belonging."

"That's fair. Sorry if I got a little heated."

"You didn't. It's an interesting point of view."

"Especially from a woman my age who's supposed to be enthusiastically in the market for a husband."

He cracked up. "You said that, not me."

McKenzie laughed with him. "Yes, I did because it's true. After you hit twenty-five, everyone thinks something's wrong with you if you're not married or heading that way. I hate that kind of societal pressure."

"Have you felt that pressure?"

"God, yes. My mother wants me married yesterday, especially since both my sisters got married in the last few years."

"Why is she pushing it so hard?"

"Who knows? It makes no sense. Marriage ended badly for her twice. I'm not sure why she's still such a fervent believer."

"Rosemary told me when she got divorced the first time, from your father, I guess."

"Yes, he was first. The second one was worse than the first, which I wouldn't have thought possible."

"Ouch. No wonder you're not exactly jumping for joy at the idea of getting married someday."

"Exactly. I've witnessed two ugly divorces up close and personal. No, thanks."

"Understandable."

"What about your parents? Are they still together?"

"I was raised mostly in the system. My mom resurfaced when I was an adult, and I talk to her occasionally, but we're not close. Never knew my dad."

"Oh." McKenzie was momentarily stunned. "That must've been tough."

"It was. At times. Other times, it was fine." He shrugged. "I survived it."

McKenzie had so many questions she had no right to ask him. As messed up as her family had been, she couldn't imagine growing up with no family at all.

"Hey, don't be sad for me. I'm okay. I swear. I've created a family of my own that makes me very happy, which is why I wouldn't leave the island even to save the relationship with my girlfriend. All the other people I love are here."

"That makes perfect sense."

"It didn't to her," he said with a smile.

McKenzie loved the way that smile softened his hard edges. "No, I'm sure it didn't, but sometimes we have to do what's best for us, even if it's not best for others."

"That's so very true. Is that what you did when you came here?"

"Absolutely. I had to get away from well-meaning people who wanted to tell me how to live my life and raise my son. My mother and sisters were a huge help to me when he was first born, but after a while, I felt like I wasn't making any of my own decisions. And listening to my mother tell me every day that I'd made a mess of my life wasn't helping anything."

"Yeah, that's not something anyone needs to hear on the daily."

"It chips away at you and makes you question everything, especially coming from someone whose whole life had been a mess of her own making. At least out here, for better or worse, whatever happens, it's my choice. Well, except for the part about the house falling down."

Duke's laugh was a rich, joyful sound. "Sorry. It's not funny."

"It kind of is. I run away from my entire support system to end up homeless in a matter of days."

"You're not homeless."

"Thanks to you!"

"If not me, someone else around here would've stepped up for you and Jax. That's how it works on Gansett Island."

"I like it here."

"So do I."

"The insurance adjuster is supposedly coming out this week, but what do I do about fixing the cabin?" she asked.

"Tomorrow, we'll talk to Mac McCarthy about rebuilding. He's got a construction company and a bunch of guys working for him, most of them his cousins, and they get shit done around here."

"I hope he can fit me in."

"He'll do what he can for you. He's a good dude. I'll give him a call in the morning."

"Oh wow. Thank you."

"No problem. One of the things I love best about island life is how we all step up for each other. If someone needs something, people find a way to make it happen. When my friend Lisa was dying from cancer, her neighbors Seamus and Carolina O'Grady helped take care of her young sons and then took them in after she died."

"That's lovely and so sad."

"It was all the things, but she got to die knowing her precious babies would be well loved and well cared for by good people who'd keep them here in the place that was their home. They wouldn't have to change schools or leave their friends in addition to losing her."

"How're they doing now?"

"After a rough few months, they're thriving. And, in an interesting development, their biological father showed up out here a while back, after having done time in prison, and is now part of their lives as well. He didn't know Lisa had died, and by the time he found out, they'd already found a whole new life. We were thankful that Jace didn't upset their new lives. Rather, he's become a friend to all of them, and as Seamus and Caro say, it's one more person who loves the boys."

"What a story. It's funny that I think of this place as vacations and sunsets and beach days and sailing and all the fun things. But real life happens here, too."

"Lots of it. Especially when a hurricane comes along to remind us how vulnerable we are."

"Yes, for sure." McKenzie glanced at her phone and was shocked to realize an entire hour had passed while they chatted like old friends. "I, uh, should go check on Jax. It was nice to talk to you."

"You, too."

"Sleep well," she added.

"I always do. Hope you will as well."

"I'll sleep well tonight in your comfortable apartment."

"I'll make that call for you in the morning."

"Thanks again for everything. You've been an amazing new friend."

"Pleasure's all mine."

As she went up the stairs to the apartment, she said a silent thank-you to her grandmother for making a friend of Duke. Rosemary always had great taste in people—she hadn't liked either of her daughter's husbands—and because of that, it was easier for McKenzie to immediately put her trust in him. There's no way she would've invested her time and energy into Duke if she hadn't seen true potential in him.

The Rosemary seal of approval meant the world to her.

She checked on Jax, who was sleeping soundly, and closed the window she'd opened so she'd hear him from downstairs.

As she got ready for bed, she thought about the things she'd learned about Duke over the last hour, from the cross-stitching—she'd never get over that discovery—to being raised in the foster care system to giving up a woman he'd loved for Gansett, which he loved more. He'd led an interesting life, to be certain, and talking to him had been easy, as if they'd known each other much longer than the ten days since he'd come looking for them after the storm and found them at Tiffany's.

The sheets and pillows smelled of fresh air, which meant he'd gone to some trouble to make sure she was cozy and comfortable.

He was sweet, thoughtful, handsome in his own special way and had already stepped up for her more than some people she'd known all her life ever had.

For the first time in a while, she was looking forward to what tomorrow might bring.

CHAPTER 5

*L*ong after McKenzie went upstairs and the lights went off in the apartment, Duke sat watching the fire and thinking about the things she'd told him about herself. The baby's father had deceived her terribly before bolting. That made him a loser of the highest order. She and the baby were better off without him.

Her mother was complicated and difficult, which he'd heard before from Rosemary. She'd often lamented about her daughter Cecelia's challenges in getting along in the world. He remembered her saying how she and her husband used to call Cecelia their little porcupine, which was cute until Cecelia grew up and became even more contrary and difficult to deal with as an adult.

Cecelia's many struggles had caused heartache for her mother. "All a mother wants for her kids is an easier life than she had," Rosemary had said. "That was never going to happen for that girl because all she did was make things harder for herself than they needed to be."

He'd never thought about what that sort of behavior might be like for Cecelia's kids.

That McKenzie would rather be alone with a baby on Gansett than at home with her mother said a lot about their relationship.

Duke was glad she'd come to their island and looked forward to getting to know her better. The more time he spent with her, the more intrigued he became, even as he tried to slow his roll. He had nothing but respect for her as his dear friend's granddaughter, who was coming back from a tough couple of years.

The last thing she needed was an older man following her around like a dog in heat.

He grunted out a laugh at the way he'd described himself. He wasn't quite that far gone, but he needed to mind his manners around her. Right now, she needed a friend much more than she needed another complication with a man.

While she figured out a plan for herself and her son, he would be her friend and would help her navigate the maze of insurance and reconstruction of the cabin.

Maybe something more would come of it. Maybe it wouldn't. Either way, he was content with his life and would continue to be no matter what happened next.

Even as he told himself that, he couldn't wait to see her and Jax tomorrow.

BLAINE TAYLOR WOKE from the deepest sleep he'd had in days. Ahead of the storm and after, he'd worked around the clock to ensure the safety of the island and its residents. As the chief of police, he felt a deep responsibility for every one of his seven hundred year-round residents, as well as the thousands who came each summer to enjoy the island's beaches and other attractions.

It weighed on him that two men were missing after the storm. That one of the missing men was his wife's ex-husband and the father of his beloved stepdaughter made things even more complicated.

Blaine turned toward his wife's side of the bed and realized it was empty. The clock read 4:06. Where the heck was she? He rolled out of bed and went to find her, checking first in the girls' rooms. Both their little ladies were sound asleep. Hopefully, they'd stay that way for a few more hours.

Downstairs, he followed the glow of light to the half-bath off the kitchen, where his pregnant wife was on her knees scrubbing the tile floor.

"What're you doing, babe?"

She turned to him, startled by his sudden appearance.

That's when he saw the yellow rubber gloves that covered her hands and forearms. Something about those damned gloves struck him as ridiculously adorable.

"You scared me."

"Sorry. Didn't mean to. I woke up and couldn't find you, so I came looking. Why are you cleaning the bathroom floor in the middle of the night?"

"It needed to be done."

"Tiff, honey, come on. Let me help you up."

"I want to finish this."

"Let me do it if it needs to be done right now."

"I need to do it. It helps me to stay busy."

"Why don't we sit together for a few minutes and see if that helps?" He could tell she didn't want to take the hand he offered but did it for his sake.

He helped her up and waited for her to get her bearings before leading her to the living room. After they'd sat next to each other, he tugged the gloves off her hands and put them on the coffee table. Then he reached for a throw blanket and arranged it over her to keep her warm.

"I'm sorry if I disturbed you when you needed sleep so badly."

Blaine put his arm around her, encouraging her to rest her head on his chest. "You didn't disturb me. When I woke up and you were gone, I had to come find you." He wished he could take away her pain and sorrow.

"I couldn't sleep, so I figured I should get something done while I could."

"You want to talk about it?"

"What's there to say? My ex-husband, who I despised, is missing and presumed dead, and all I can think about is how will I ever explain this to Ashleigh."

"We'll tell her together. We'll tell her how her daddy loved her more than anything, that she was the brightest light in his life and how he never would've wanted to leave her. We'll make sure she knows she's loved by us and everyone else in her life and always will be."

A sob shook Tiffany's body.

He held her close as he ran a soothing hand over her back. "Let it out, honey."

"I can't cry about my ex-husband all over my new husband."

"Sure, you can. The new guy isn't at all threatened by the ex."

She laughed even as she continued to sob. "It's so bizarre for me to be sad about him."

"I know, honey, but I'd be surprised if you weren't. You have the biggest heart of anyone I've ever met. Of course you're sad over this."

"That biggest heart has contained a whole lot of ill will toward him in recent years."

"For very good reason. You're only human for feeling the way you did about him. He put you and Ashleigh through hell. But the Tiffany I know and love will grieve for the man she loved once upon a time, for the man who gave her our precious Ashleigh, for all the things that could've been."

"Yeah, that's it exactly. I've been thinking a lot about when we were first together. I never expected us to end up the way we did."

"Why would you? You were a devoted, loyal, loving wife to him."

"How do you know I wasn't a hag?"

"You wouldn't know how to be. You gave him everything you had, which, in my experience, is a hell of a lot, and he was too stupid to know how good he had it. That, and everything else he did before and after your split, is on him. And he knew it. More than once, I caught him looking at you with yearning. He understood what he'd let get away."

"He did not look at me that way. He couldn't stand me."

"That's not true, Tiff. He frequently looked at you with longing and regret. I saw that as recently as two weeks ago when he brought Ash home from dinner and you went out to meet them. I was watching from the kitchen window. I saw how he looked at you and the house where he used to live with you. He knew what he'd lost. I'd bet my life on that."

Tiffany had gotten the house in their divorce agreement, and they had decided to stay put after they got married since Ashleigh had already been through enough upheaval.

"You really think so?" she asked.

"I'm one hundred percent positive that any man who was lucky enough to be loved by you would regret losing you for the rest of his life. I sure as hell would."

"That'll never happen."

"No, it won't, because I'm smart enough to know I hit the jackpot the day you decided to love me, and I'll never take that for granted."

She laughed. "Decided to love you. As if it was a decision."

"However it came about, it's the best thing to ever happen to me. The difference between me and him is I'm able to see that and he never was until it was too late. I've always been thankful for that if I'm being honest. I mean, if he hadn't fucked it up, I never would've had my chance to love you."

"And what a tragedy that would've been."

"Definitely. I understand the heartache you're feeling, even if I don't feel it the same way you do. I feel it for you and for Ash and Jim's parents. Despite what I thought of him, I didn't want this for him or any of you."

"You were right. It does help to talk about it. Thanks for coming to find me."

"I'll always come to find you, babe. Always."

"I've had faith in that from the beginning. Knowing you were out there waiting for me to be free of him was what got me through a very rough time."

"I thought I'd go mad waiting for you."

"And then you still had to come after me."

"You didn't make it easy for me, but every second since then has been worth the wait and the chase."

"Thanks for this, for being here for me."

"I'm here, sweetheart, for you and Ash, and I'm not going anywhere." Blaine nuzzled her hair and breathed in the strawberry scent of his love. "Do you think you could go back to sleep for a while?"

"I can try."

He helped her up, followed her upstairs, waited while she looked in on each of the girls and then sat on her side of the bed to tuck her in. "Close your eyes and put it all aside for a little while."

She reached for him and brought him close enough for a kiss. "Love you."

"Love you more."

"No way."

"Yes way."

Smiling, she shook her head.

He kissed her again. "Sleep, love."

She closed her eyes but kept smiling while he stood watch over her. As soon as he was confident she was asleep, he got up to check in at work, hoping for an update on the search for Jim and Billy.

He needed to get some resolution for his beloved wife and daughter.

HIS RINGING PHONE pulled Fire Chief Mason Johns out of a deep sleep. Hoping that Jordan would stay asleep for a while yet, he grabbed the phone and took it into the bathroom, closing the door.

"Johns."

"Hey, it's me," Blaine Taylor said. "Did I wake you?"

"Uh, well, it is five o'clock in the morning, so kinda. What's up?"

"Sorry, I was awake and hoping for an update on the search. Having Jim missing is taking a huge toll on Tiffany and the family. I'm sure it's the same for Billy's family."

"Linc and the Coast Guard searched until around ten last night. They were planning to resume the search in the Salt Pond at first light. We believe they were probably on Billy's boat, so they might've tried to swim to shore when the boat sank. Might've been drinking…"

Blaine's deep sigh was loud and clear.

"I can't imagine how tough this is on his family and yours. We're doing everything we can to find them."

"I know. Thank you, and I'm sorry I woke you. I wasn't even thinking about what time it was."

"No worries. I need to get going anyway. Not sure which is worse, the storm prep or the cleanup."

"Definitely the cleanup. What're you hearing about Jeff and Kelsey?"

"Both are on the mend. He's got a stint in rehab ahead of him before they can return to the island, but he should make a full recovery."

"Thank goodness for that."

"Indeed. I'll never forget the sight of that barn collapsed on them."

"Me either."

"All right, I'll let you get to work. I'm sticking close to home for now but call if you need me. My team is available for anything you need."

"Will do. Please tell Tiffany that Jordan and I are thinking of her and Ashleigh."

"That'll mean a lot to her. Thanks."

Mason ended the call, thinking about how weird it must be for Tiffany to be upset about Sturgil being missing when he'd been such a dick to her. He headed for the shower, still pondering the mysteries of love and grief and hoping for Tiffany and Ashleigh's sake that Sturgil was found alive. But the longer he was missing, the less likely that became.

Even if he was a dick, he wouldn't make his loved ones suffer this way.

He turned on the shower and was grateful for hot water. Power had been spotty since it returned over the weekend, so he never knew what to expect.

Mason turned his face up to the hot water and tried to relax muscles gone rigid with stress over the last few tumultuous weeks.

Having their island under assault by Mother Nature had taken it out of him and everyone else who worked in public safety.

Because his eyes were closed, he had no warning before Jordan's warm, sexy body was pressed against his back. Just that quickly, he wanted her. "What're you doing up so early?"

"I wanted to see you before you leave."

"I'm glad you did." He moved carefully to turn to face her, wrapping his arms around her and holding her close. "Best way to start the day."

"Mmm, for sure."

"How're you feeling?"

"Not nauseated for once."

"I'm glad." He hated how difficult her pregnancy had been so far and wished he could do something to ease her burden. "I hate when you feel shitty."

"I do, too." She looked up at him with the eyes that had captivated him from the first time he ever saw her—after saving her life. Then she'd turned right around and saved his. "But I'm not feeling shitty now." She slid her hand down his chest and curled it around his straining erection.

His legs went weak under him as she stroked him and kissed his chest. "Jord... Uh..."

Her giggle echoed off the shower walls.

"Are you laughing at me?"

"Maybe a little."

He put his arm around her and lifted her, pressing her back against the wall.

She batted her eyelashes at him. "Whatever is happening, Chief?" she asked in the coy tone that drove him wild.

Hell, she drove him wild simply by breathing.

He pressed his cock against her heat. "*This* is happening."

"Yes, please."

Everything about her did it for him, from the way she looked at him with pure adoration to her silky soft skin to the lips that skimmed over his neck, setting him on fire, to the tight fit that required him to go slowly so he wouldn't hurt her.

He loved her madly, passionately, eternally.

She curled her arms around his neck and her legs around his waist as they moved together in the sort of perfect harmony that had eluded him before he found her. Now, his whole life was perfect, and it was because of her.

"Jord…"

She gasped. "Right there with you."

He pushed into her and held on tightly as they hit the peak together, which was another thing that'd never happened to him before her.

For a long time afterward, they stayed where they were, joined and breathing the same air before he carefully withdrew and put her down.

"Nice way to start the day," she said as she snuggled up to him under the warm spray.

"Best way ever."

They took turns washing each other, which had him hard and ready for round two in a matter of minutes.

"You're insatiable," she said, laughing.

"Only with you."

"Better be only with me."

"Who else could I possibly want if I have a goddess like you at home?"

"That's a good point."

He adored the curvier body and fuller cheeks that had come with pregnancy, but he didn't dare say so because he knew she was sensitive about her changing shape.

As they left the shower and wrapped up in towels, she looked back over her shoulder and caught him staring at her. "What?"

"You."

"What about me?"

To hell with it. "You're always sexy, but pregnant sexy is a whole other level."

"No way."

"Way."

"How can that be? I'm huge."

"No, you're beautiful."

"You have to say that. You did this to me."

"I did, and I can't wait to do it again."

"Easy, stud. Let's see how this one goes."

"So far, it's going great from my perspective. My baby mama is the sexiest baby mama on the planet."

"We need to get your eyes examined."

He gave her a playful pat on the rear. "My vision is perfect, and I like what I see."

"Well, thank goodness for that, because anyone else would've sold me back to the aquarium by now. Whales are a big draw, you know."

"Stop that."

She turned to him, brow raised, unaccustomed to such a sharp tone from him.

"I don't like to hear you saying stuff like that about yourself. If you could see you the way I do, you wouldn't be thinking about aquariums."

She came to him and flattened her hands on his bare chest. "Thanks for the ego boost."

"I didn't mean to snap at you."

"You didn't. You snapped me out of my prego pity party."

"Please don't be down on yourself. You're growing a baby human in there. When I tell you you're a goddess, I'm not just saying that."

"I know and thank you for the kind words. I'm used to looking a certain way. Pregnancy has been a bit jarring."

"As far as I'm concerned, you're even more beautiful pregnant, and I wouldn't have thought it was possible for you to be more beautiful than you already were."

"You're very good for the baby mama's self-esteem."

"Any time you need a reminder, let me know." He kissed her and went to get ready for another long day of searching for the missing men and other hurricane cleanup. "Will you be okay by yourself today?"

"I'm going to Eastward Look to hang out with Nikki since the Wayfarer is still closed." Her identical twin sister was the general manager of the beachfront venue the McCarthys had restored and reopened last year. They'd continued to have power issues that kept them closed after the rest of the island had reopened.

"Be careful on the roads. Still lots of downed trees and other junk."

"I'm always careful."

"How about I give you a ride there when you're ready?"

"You don't need to do that."

"What if it would make me feel less anxious all day?"

She tipped her head, calling him out on the manipulative phrasing. "I can't have you wound up in knots all day, so I'll allow you to get away with being pushy just this once."

"Thank you."

"You're welcome."

Smiling, he came over to kiss her before he left. "Text me when you're ready."

"Love you, even when you're overbearing and manipulative."

"Love you all the time, every second of every minute of every day."

"Nice recovery, Chief."

"See you soon."

"I'll be here."

Mason drove away in his department SUV, smiling the way he did most of the time since Jordan had come into his life in the most dramatic way possible. She'd turned his life completely upside down, which was fine with him. He'd never been happier than he was with her, and he knew she felt the same way about him.

They needed to get serious about planning their wedding as soon as they got past Nikki's big day in November.

On the way into town, he drove around massive puddles and crews working to remove the debris that continued to come ashore since the storm.

As soon as things calmed down a bit with storm cleanup and the search for the missing men, they would start making plans for their own big day.

CHAPTER 6

*C*oast Guard Commander Linc Mercer filled a travel mug with coffee and headed to the dock for another day of searching for the missing men. They'd focused their efforts on the Salt Pond since Billy Weyland's boat had been found partially sunk there. Linc, his officers, Harbor Master Deacon Taylor and others had warned Billy against riding out the storm on his boat.

But Billy hadn't listened.

A week later, Linc was fielding almost hourly calls from Billy's frantic friends and dealing with his brother, Morgan, who'd come to the island to assist in the search and keep the gym open. Linc wished he had something he could tell them other than that they were continuing to search for Billy and his friend Jim Sturgil, who was also missing.

Morgan Weyland had been helping by walking the perimeter of the pond at least twice a day, looking for any sign of either man. Linc appreciated that the man was helping where he could while allowing them to do their jobs. He was also relieved that Morgan wasn't doing anything risky that would only make their efforts more complicated. He'd also seen Sturgil's father out every day in his boat for hours, navigating the pond as he looked for his missing son. The whole thing was heartbreaking, and the worst part was that it never should've happened.

Dealing with the family members of missing boaters was part of Linc's job, but one of the more difficult aspects. As was managing the media that had gathered on the island seeking updates on the missing men.

Linc wished he had something to tell them all. He took a call from the admiral in charge of the Southern New England region.

"Good morning, sir."

"Morning, Commander. I wanted to let you know we're giving the search until sunset tonight before we call it."

Linc had been waiting for that directive and had been surprised it hadn't come sooner. "Yes, sir. I'll notify the families."

"Please tell them we'll continue to search during routine patrols, but we can't devote the full resources any longer, unfortunately. You know I hate this as much as you do."

"Yes, sir. I understand. Thank you for the update."

"Keep me posted on how today unfolds."

"Will do."

They said their goodbyes, and Linc continued toward the dock to break the news to the crews that'd spent a full week searching during every minute of daylight—and often well into the evenings on their own time, in their own boats.

"Just heard from the admiral that today is it for the official Coast Guard search."

"I wondered how much longer we were going to look," Harbor Master Deacon Taylor said.

He, too, had been missing for a time during the storm before being rescued at sea by Joe Cantrell and his crew on one of the ferries.

"I'll continue to send out a boat every day for as long as it takes," Fire Chief Mason Johns said.

"Of course we'll continue to search during routine patrols," Linc said.

"Understood," Mason said. "Let's get to it."

Linc captained one of the Coast Guard boats with a crew of three on board to assist. Another boat transported the divers who'd work underwater for a seventh straight day. They were focused on the eastern half of the pond, near where Billy's boat had been moored.

In truth, he'd expected to find them days ago since the pond was large but somewhat contained, making for a much easier search than would've transpired in open ocean. But after more than a week of twelve-hour days, they hadn't found a trace of either man. They hadn't even known they were looking for Sturgil until his parents made them aware he was missing.

They'd had the help of numerous agencies and departments, including those who mapped currents and tides to direct them on where to look. He wished that no news was good news, but at this point, he had no hope of finding either man alive.

At lunchtime, they returned to the station to eat and take a short break before resuming the search.

Linc checked his phone for the first time in hours and found a text from his new friend Monique. She was Dara Watson's sister, and he'd met her when Monique recently came to the island for a visit. They'd kept in touch since she returned home to Boston. Linc had started to look forward to hearing from her because her commentary was always entertaining.

She was newly divorced and figuring out her next chapter.

They'd fallen into a fun, flirty friendship that he greatly enjoyed. Because they were keeping things light, he hadn't mentioned that he'd spent much of the last week searching for two men who were probably dead.

When are we going to see you back on Gansett? he asked by text while he ate one of the delicious Italian sandwiches Mario's had sent over to feed the people searching for Billy and Jim.

Not sure yet. Got some things to figure out, but I hope to get back there in the next few weeks.

Keep me posted.

Will do.

Back to work I go.

All work and no play makes Linc a boring guy.

Haha. Right you are.

If you're up for some time off, come see me. I could show you around Boston.

I might take you up on that.

Offer stands.

Talk soon.

The more he talked to her, the more he wanted to talk to her. He wanted to know what things she needed to figure out and what her life was like. He'd met her when she was on vacation and looking for a good time. What was she like in her real world? And why was it that he'd started to look so forward to their text exchanges?

He took those questions with him as he returned to the boat to continue the search.

As MCKENZIE WENT through her morning routine with Jax, she thought about Duke and their conversation from the night before. He was such a nice guy, which was incredibly hard to find these days. She and her friends had withstood every possible dating and relationship disaster, from infidelity and lies, in her case, to the physical and emotional abuse of her friend Talia.

Many of her friends, herself included, had sworn off men forever —with good reason.

"They're simply not worth the bother," Rochelle had recently declared after the demise of her second marriage. Two husbands by twenty-six. Rochelle, who'd been McKenzie's friend since high school, wondered if that was a world record.

McKenzie had to agree with Rochelle's take. Every woman in her life had a story to tell about being ghosted, deceived, led on, lied to and, in Talia's case, injured enough to file a police report and go through the motions of having her ex charged with assault. McKenzie's own father had washed his hands of his three daughters after his wife divorced him. She'd seen him twice in twelve years, and neither time was memorable for the right reasons.

It was exhausting.

It was demoralizing.

It was often devastating.

Hearing that her boyfriend, Eric, had a wife and children had shattered her, especially since she'd discovered a year's worth of lies three days after finding out she was pregnant. That'd been one hell of a week.

They'd been fighting a lot leading up to that momentous week, so she'd debated whether to even tell him about the baby.

When she'd finally decided to share the news with him, he'd told her he already had a wife and kids, as if that wouldn't be the most shocking thing he could say after a year together. But then he went and topped himself.

"The baby can't be mine," he said. "I had a vasectomy years ago."

She'd stared at him in disbelief. He knew full well that she hadn't been with anyone but him. He also knew she was in love with him and hadn't so much as looked at another man since the day she met him.

"There's no one else, and you know it," she'd said, her chin quivering.

"Well, there must be, because I can't have kids."

She'd wrapped her arms tight around herself, trying to hold it together until she was alone. "You should go."

He'd tipped his head and given her the charming smile that had made her knees weak before she found out he was just another scumbag. "Why do we have to ruin a good thing?"

"The good thing was ruined the minute I found out you've lied to me about everything."

"I didn't lie. I never said I wasn't married."

"Please go and don't come back."

Stepping toward her, he'd put his hands on her hips and kissed her neck. "Come on, baby. You know I care about you."

It'd taken every ounce of fortitude she could muster to push him away. "Get. Out. *Now.*"

"You need to grow up and get with how the real world works, little girl." He'd put his coat on. "See ya around."

McKenzie had stood perfectly still as the door slammed shut, as he went down the stairs and as the door to his truck had closed. When the engine had started, she'd dropped to her knees and sobbed.

Many difficult days followed that confrontation, leading up to their son's birth seven months later. Heartbreak and fear had been her constant companions. Her mother had urged her to end the pregnancy or to give the baby up for adoption.

But a funny thing had happened on the way to the maternity ward... She'd fallen madly in love with the little being moving around inside her. From the first second she'd heard his strong heartbeat, she'd vowed to do whatever it took to make them a family. They didn't need anyone else.

But then he'd arrived along with a healthy dose of reality. She couldn't do it alone, after all. She couldn't work and take care of a baby and pay for daycare and diapers and the endless supplies newborns needed. She couldn't work if she didn't sleep, and she'd hardly slept for the first two months.

Her life had quickly become unmanageable, especially after she'd been forced to move back in with her mother because she couldn't swing rent on top of all the other new expenses.

Once again, her grandmother had thrown her a lifeline.

Two years after her passing, Rosemary's estate had finally cleared escrow, along with the cabin she'd left to McKenzie, the only family member who'd loved the island and the cabin as much as Rosemary did. Her mother had come home one day with keys that she'd dropped into McKenzie's lap while she breastfed the baby.

"Taxes and insurance are paid for three years," her mother had said. "The rest is your problem."

From that second on, McKenzie's only goal had been getting the two of them to that cabin. She'd planned to figure out the details after she arrived.

The entire ride from Coventry to Point Judith, she'd listened to her mother tell her she was a fool to take a baby to a remote island with God-knows-what for medical care or jobs or basic supplies.

McKenzie had tuned her out. This was the right move for her and Jax. She'd known it in her heart, until Hurricane Ethel had hit, and she'd been convinced for hours that they were going to die.

After she'd fled the cabin, she'd tried going next door to the home she now knew belonged to Duke, but he hadn't been home. Thank God Chief Taylor had found her hunkered down by the side of the road, because who knew what would've become of them if he hadn't come along when he did?

So far, her independent adventure to Gansett had been anything but. Two men had come to her rescue, and without them, she would've been dead and/or homeless. They both seemed like nice guys, but who ever knew that for certain? They were all nice at first.

She couldn't stop picturing Duke sitting by the fire *cross-stitching* for relaxation like an old grandma. She laughed to herself every time she thought of him in all his long-haired, tatted glory pushing a needle through the sampler like it was the most normal thing he could be doing.

Despite his appearance, which gave off a tough, untouchable vibe, there was something so sweet and almost pure about him. It was an odd contrast, and she wasn't sure which version was the real him. One thing she knew for certain, however, was that he hadn't had to offer her a free place to live while she figured out her next move with the cabin. He hadn't had to drive her around or offer to help her navigate insurance claims and reconstruction.

She refused to stick him with the sins other men had committed. So far, he'd been nothing but a good friend to her, and she looked forward to getting to know him better, comforted to know her grandmother had obviously adored him.

DUKE TOOK his morning coffee outside to call Mac McCarthy. "Hey, Mac, it's Duke Sullivan."

"Hi, Duke. How's it going?"

"Hanging in there. Getting back to normal. How about you?"

"Same. Still on cleanup and eyeing some rebuilds."

"That's why I'm calling. Remember Rosemary Enders, my next-door neighbor who passed a few years back?"

"Of course. She was a good friend of my parents'."

"Ah, that's right. She thought the world of them."

"And vice versa. We all loved her."

"I did, too. She was a good friend to me. Her granddaughter had come out to stay at Rosemary's cabin before the storm and is staying in my garage apartment since the place collapsed."

"Is she the one Blaine rescued?"

"That's her."

"Heard she had a baby with her, too."

"Yes, little Jax. Thankfully, Blaine came upon them before they got hurt, but she's in a bind with the cabin being destroyed. I know you're probably slammed after the storm, but if you guys could fit her in over the next little while, I'd sure appreciate it."

"I'll see what we can do to get out there as soon as possible."

"She's fine at my place for as long as she needs a roof over her head, but I'm sure she'd like to get back to her own space before too long."

"Of course. I've put her on the list and will prioritize it since she's Rosemary's granddaughter and a single mom."

"That's very good of you."

"I married a single mom. I know how challenging it is, even when her home isn't knocked down by a storm."

"I remember when you and Maddie crashed into each other on Ocean Road."

"And the rest was history," Mac said with a chuckle. "I'll be back in touch soon."

"You're the best. Thank you."

As he ended the call, he saw McKenzie come down the stairs to the yard, carrying Jax and a full backpack.

He jumped up to relieve her of the bag. "Where you headed?"

"Into town. Tiffany hired me to work at her store. I figured she might need some extra help right away, with her ex-husband missing and all of that."

"I'm sure she'd appreciate the offer. How are you getting to town?"

"I was going to walk."

"That's a long walk carrying a baby."

"I can do it."

"Or I could give you a ride."

"You've already done so much for us. I don't want to be a pain."

"You're not a pain. I need to run by the studio anyway. We're closed today, but it's the dreaded paperwork day."

"As long as you'd be going in, I'd appreciate the ride. Let me just go get his car seat."

"Want me to hold him for you while you do that?"

She gave him an uncertain look that passed as quickly as it'd come. "Sure. Thanks."

He took the sturdy little guy from her and held him carefully while she dashed for the stairs to fetch the seat.

"Hey there. I'm Duke. What's your story?"

The baby studied him intently. "Gagagaga."

"You don't say? What do you think of the island so far?" Duke walked over to give the baby a closer look at his rosebushes, which had exploded with late-summer color. "That one's red, and then there's pink, peach, yellow and white. And they smell good, too, don't they?"

"Yayayaya."

"You like the roses, huh? The ladies love them—most of the time. I've met a few who don't like them, but that's rare. You're usually safe with roses."

"Are you giving him life advice?"

Duke turned to her, smiling. "It's never too soon for such things."

"I suppose that's true."

When she reached for the baby, he handed him over, sorry that he hadn't gotten to tell him about the puffy, blue hydrangeas. Maybe another time.

"Your garden is gorgeous."

"Also thanks to Rosemary. She helped me plant it all and taught me how to care for it."

"I used to help her in her garden at home. I knew the names of all the plants and bushes by the time I was ten."

"Took me a while longer, but I eventually got the hang of it."

"It looks amazing. She'd be proud."

"I hope so."

She bit her lip and glanced in the direction of her demolished cabin. "I should go over there and deal with that, but it's been more than a week, and I still can't bear to look."

"It's not going anywhere. It'll be there when you're ready to deal with it. I called Mac McCarthy this morning."

"Oh wow. Thank you so much."

"He said he'd come by to take a look."

"I really appreciate your help with that. I've never had to deal with contractors before."

"Mac is awesome. He reminded me that your grandmother was close to his folks and that he married a single mom, so he's partial to them."

"That's nice of him."

"You'll be in good hands with him working on the cabin. Try not to worry."

She already felt better about the daunting task, and again, it was all thanks to Duke. He seemed to step in and help with whatever she needed. How easy would it be to come to rely on someone like him? Too easy.

"Ready to go?"

"Whenever you are."

"Let me just run inside to grab my wallet and keys. The truck is unlocked if you want to get him settled."

"Thanks."

He moved quickly, eager to get back to them and to talk to her some more. Last night's conversation had been... unexpected, to say the least. He'd been surprised by how much she'd told him about her baby's father and her life before she came to the island.

"Knock it off," he said. "She's Rosemary's granddaughter, and she's way too young for you. She's got enough going on without you bugging her."

Her situation had made her vulnerable, and there was no way he would take advantage of that. If he found her fucking gorgeous and interesting as all hell, well, that didn't mean he had to do anything about it.

CHAPTER 7

*D*uke was pissed off with himself by the time he slid into the driver's side of his truck.

"Are you okay?"

He looked at her over the baby seat between them. "Yeah. Why do you ask?"

"You looked upset when you came out of the house."

And she was observant, too. "Oh. No. I'm fine."

"I really can walk into town. It's no problem."

"You shouldn't walk with the baby on the roads out here." He started the truck and threw it into Reverse. "People drive like lunatics on the curves. Someone takes out one of the stone walls at least once a year."

"Well, I'll have to walk since I don't have a car."

"I'll take you anywhere you need to go."

"You sound pissed."

"I'm not. I swear. It's not safe to walk out here."

"You've already given me a place to live. Now you want to be my chauffeur, too?"

"Whatever you need. I'm happy to help you."

"Why?"

He looked over at her, seeming stunned by the question. "Because that's what people do for each other. They help when help is needed."

"That hasn't been my experience."

"Maybe you've been hanging out with the wrong people."

Her snort of laughter eased some of the tension that'd built up inside him as he tried to talk himself out of being attracted to her. "Ain't that the truth?" She quickly added, "I have the best girlfriends, but we all have stories about other people, mostly men, that would make your hair curl."

"My hair doesn't curl easily."

"We could make it happen."

"It's tough to be optimistic about the future when the past has been messy."

"Yes, it is."

"Took me a long time, a lot of years, to put the past where it belonged so it didn't screw with my present every day anymore."

She looked over at him. "How'd you do it?"

"I decided to focus only on what was right in front of me at that moment rather than putting it in the context of what'd happened before. Not sure that makes sense…"

"No, it does, but I still don't see *how* you can just do that."

"You make up your mind to look ahead, not back. There's not one damned thing you can change about the past, but the future is yours to map out as you see fit."

"That sounds great, but *how?*"

"You wake up every day with a choice about how you want to live. Do you want to be mired in a past you can't change or focused on a future that you direct?"

"You make it sound so simple."

"It is once you get the hang of it. You ever heard the saying that it takes three weeks to create a habit, whether it's a good habit or a bad one?"

"Yes, I've read about that."

"Usually, they're talking about going to the gym or starting to walk or dieting or whatever. In this case, you wake up and decide to focus on all the positive things you can think of. You give them your full attention for all your waking hours. Whether it's your work or your child or your garden or whatever brings you peace, pleasure and prosperity. I love my job. I love my studio and the people who work with me there. I love doing things to grow the business, such as partnering with the McCarthys to offer weekend getaways that include a tattoo. That was my idea, by the way. Brings in some business in the off-season. It gives me a kick to think of stuff like that. I love my art and my cross-stitching, my garden and puttering around my house. Those things bring me joy."

He worried he was talking too much, but when he looked over, she was watching him thoughtfully. "You think I'm nuts, right?"

"Not at all. What you say makes so much sense, but—"

"No buts. It works. I swear it does. For the first year I was doing this, any time something from the past wanted to sneak in to ruin my day, I did something to manifest the future I wanted for myself. One day, I went into the shop and spent the whole day building a website for the business. Let me tell you... That took all my mental energy for that day and a couple of others. There was no space for anything else."

"So, you're saying that by keeping exceptionally busy, you can start to replace the bad stuff with good."

"For the most part. You don't want to work yourself into an early grave, though. I mean, what good would it be to overcome a difficult past by creating a positive future if you're too dead to enjoy it?"

McKenzie laughed. "Good point."

"Like today, for example. What positive things can you start your day thinking about?"

"Jax, of course. He's the most positive thing."

"He sure is."

"The apartment you loaned us is definitely a positive. Also, a new job, some new friends, more time in my favorite place."

"All good things. Stay focused on them, and you'll have a great day."

"I'm adding your kindness in calling Mac for me to the good things to focus on today."

"That's the way to play the game. Doing that for you got my day off to a good start. You see how it works?"

"I'm beginning to. What do you do when your mind wanders to the bad stuff?"

"You pull it back on course by thinking about the good stuff. You don't give the bad stuff any oxygen before you come swooping in to change the conversation you're having with yourself."

"The conversation I'm having with myself..."

"That's what our thoughts are, right?"

"How did you get so wise?"

Duke huffed out a laugh. "I wouldn't describe myself as wise at all."

"Well, I would. How did you learn this stuff?"

"I got tired of the darkness. I wanted to focus on the light, so I did. Took a while to make it happen, but one day, I realized it'd been like two weeks since I'd thought about the bad stuff. That's when I knew it worked. That I could truly decide where to put my focus and energy. Now, I'm not saying I never think about the past, because I do. Comes at me at the oddest of times, usually when I'm really happy. It'll show up as if to say, 'Hey, dumbass, don't get cocky. I'm still in here.'"

"That's funny."

"Sorry to swear in front of Jax."

"You didn't."

"I said a-s-s."

"Oh, whoops," she said with a laugh. "I think he'll be okay."

Duke pulled onto Ocean Avenue, which was largely deserted except for crews from the electric company, which were still working on the grid, and the town's public works department shoveling seaweed off the street and into trucks. The storm had produced higher-than-usual tides that continued to deposit sand, seaweed and other ocean junk on the streets.

He parked in front of Tiffany's store, Naughty & Nice, where mannequins in lingerie filled the windows. "Are you sure Tiff is planning to open today?"

"Nope, but I figured I'd come in and see if she needs help."

He reached for his phone and found her contact. "You want to give her a call?"

"Probably should've done that before I asked you to drive me into town."

"It's no problem. I needed to come in anyway."

McKenzie called Tiffany and put it on speaker. "Hi, it's McKenzie, calling on Duke's phone. I wanted to check on you and see if you need help at the store today."

"Thank you so much for calling, but I think we'll stay closed today, since I didn't sleep much last night."

"Is there any word?"

"Nothing yet."

"I'm so sorry. Is there anything I can do for you?"

"I think we're good. Blaine is working this morning, but he'll be home after lunch. We're going to my sister's house for a bit this afternoon so the kids can play."

"If there's anything you need, please call me. I'll text you my number."

"Please do, and I'll keep you posted on when we're reopening."

"Sounds good. I'll talk to you soon."

McKenzie finished the call and handed the phone back to Duke. "Welp, I guess I've got the day off."

"Want to see my studio?"

"I'd love to."

DUKE'S CALL about McKenzie's cabin was the fourth of the day that Mac received from island residents in need of construction help after the storm. Ethel had upended his plans for the off-season, which he'd planned to spend mostly at the family's alpaca farm, finishing the renovations so they could be ready for the first of the weddings booked there for late May.

Now he had a single mom with a wrecked cabin to consider, as well as his friends Slim and Erin Jackson, whose island home had also sustained serious damage.

Mac was exhausted, and the day hadn't even begun yet.

Maddie returned to their room after tending to the twins and got back into bed. Sometimes they went back to sleep after an early wakeup. He hoped today was one of those days, because he could use a few minutes with his love before another day of madness began for both of them.

She curled up to him and rested her head on his chest. "What's wrong?"

"Nothing, why?"

"You looked worried when I came in."

"Just thinking about all the new work that's coming from the storm and how I'll fit it in with the other stuff I've already committed to, especially now that Jeff is out for the foreseeable future. I've gotten four calls already today, including one about the cabin owned by the single mom Blaine rescued in the storm."

"Well, you have to take care of that one right away."

He smiled. "I told Duke when he called that she'd be a high priority. She's Rosemary Enders's granddaughter."

"Oh, I loved her. She worked at the summer camp I went to when I was in elementary school. Such a sweet lady."

"Are there pictures of you as a summer camper?"

"Somewhere."

"I think I'd like to see them."

"I'll ask my mom if she has them. Is there any word about Jim?"

"Not that I've heard."

Her deep sigh said it all. "I'm so worried about Tiffany. I can't imagine her having to tell Ashleigh this news."

"Hopefully, he's off being oblivious and will turn up like nothing ever happened."

She looked up at him. "Do you think that's possible?"

"Probably not. I think he and Billy were riding out the storm on Billy's boat, which was beyond stupid. They're putting divers into the pond again today to look for them."

"God, I can't imagine what they must've gone through."

"They shouldn't have been on a boat in a hurricane. Hopefully, they were both drunk and didn't know what hit them."

"It's horrible. I couldn't stand him, but I never wanted something like this to happen."

"Me either. I keep thinking about Ash and how she has no clue he's even missing. I don't envy Tiff and Blaine having to explain that to her."

"I know. My heart aches for her."

"She'll be okay. We'll all make sure of it." Mac knew he should get up and get going on what promised to be another very long day, but they so rarely got a minute of peace that he stayed put for as long as it lasted.

"What's on the docket for today?" she asked.

"I'll swing by Rosemary's place to look at the cabin and see what we're going to need there, and then to Slim and Erin's, then back to the marina. Dad decided to open back up for the rest of the season."

"You knew he would."

"Yeah, I figured he would despite what he said. He's not going to want to miss out on another month of doughnuts and BS with the boys."

"True." She reached up to stroke his face. "I'm sure you're stressing out about how much needs to be done, but you're one man and one company. You can only do what you can do. Take it a minute at a time and don't let it trigger the anxiety, you hear me?"

"Yes, dear." For the second time in his life, stress had led to a panic attack that'd scared the hell out of him and everyone who loved him. He was trying to do better about managing it, but at times like this, that was easier said than done.

"You do so much for the people on this island, but there's no point in you working yourself to death. It'll all get done. Somehow."

"You're right. Thanks for the reminder."

"It's available any time you need to hear it."

"Are the grannies coming to help today?" Having their nanny out of commission was another thing adding to his stress. All that mattered was that Kelsey was okay and would recover from the broken arm. But being without her for a few weeks would be tough on Maddie, who was still recovering from the twins' birth and adjusting to caring for two infants in addition to three older kids.

"They are, thank goodness."

"I'd better get to it. Gonna be another long one."

"Remember you're not God out there, okay? Don't take on more than you can handle. It's okay to say no."

"Really? It is?"

"Yes, Mac, it's okay. I promise."

"I hear you, honey. Now give me a kiss and make it a good one. It's got to last me all day."

Smiling, she reached for him and gave him a kiss that made him moan from wanting more.

"That wasn't fair with hours to go until you can finish what you started."

"Something to look forward to later."

"I'll think about it all day."

"When's your vasectomy follow-up appointment?"

"Next week and let me tell you how much I'm looking forward to that."

"Your sarcasm is duly noted."

"I'm looking forward to having fun with my sexy wife, no condoms required." He kissed her again and then gazed at her gorgeous face.

"What?"

"You're just so pretty. I never get tired of looking at you."

"You know just what to say to me."

"I only tell you the truth. Call me if you need me today. I can be home in a few minutes."

"I will. Love you. Be safe out there."

"Love you, too. Be safe in here."

"Haha, it's a jungle in here."

"And you're the queen of the jungle."

Their daughter Hailey came into the room, her hair tousled and her cheeks rosy with sleep. "Baby Mac is awake, Mama."

"Thank you, honey." Maddie got out of bed and bent to hug their tiny girl. "Did you sleep well?"

"Uh-huh. Can we watch Bluey today?"

"As long as we keep power." Maddie took their daughter by the hand and went to get Mac.

"That mean old storm took Bluey," Hailey said.

As he got up and got ready for work, Mac chuckled as he listened to his family through the monitor. Maddie was so great with them, and they were lucky to have her. She was right about him managing the stress and that he was only one man.

He would try to remember that as the post-storm demands stacked up.

CHAPTER 8

"*A*fter I show you the shop," Duke said, "we'll go home and see what we can salvage from your cabin."

"I'm sure you have better things to do today," McKenzie said.

"Not at all. It's our day off, and I'm happy to help you. Besides, you shouldn't be over there by yourself. It's not safe."

After a period of silence, she said, "I thought I was being so independent coming out here to start over and to figure out what's next for me and Jax." She sighed as she looked out the passenger-side window. "We all know how that's worked out so far."

"Blame it on Ethel. She's the one who messed things up."

"How could I have come here with a baby and not known there was a hurricane in the forecast?"

"You didn't have Wi-Fi, TV or a good phone connection. It's not your fault. I should've gone over there to make sure you were okay, but I didn't want to freak you out by just popping in."

"Freak me out?"

"The tats scare some people. They think I must be a menace or something."

"That's ridiculous."

"I agree, but I didn't want to scare you, so I stayed away. I regret that now."

"I went to your house first that night when I left the cabin, but you weren't there."

He winced. "Oh crap. I was at the Beachcomber with some friends. We closed the place ahead of the storm."

"That sounds like fun."

"It was, but I wish I'd been home when you came by."

"Thankfully, Blaine saved us."

"I'm so glad he did."

He took a right into the ferry landing parking lot and drove to the far end where his shop was located alongside the massage studio in a two-story building that had apartments on the second floor. The rent from those apartments helped to keep him afloat in the off-season when the studio was slow. Not that she needed to know that.

He waited until she'd removed Jax from the car seat before he got out of the truck and went around to open her door.

"Thank you."

Her smile was so dazzling, it made him go stupid in the head. "No problem." Duke hoped it was okay to take hold of her elbow to help her down from the truck.

He was so out of practice when it came to being around women, and he never wanted to be anything other than respectful. But he couldn't let her trip and fall, especially with the baby in her arms.

As he put the key into the metal door that bore the logo he'd designed himself with DUKE'S TATTOOS in the center, he felt the familiar pride that hit him any time he walked into the studio he'd made his own over the years.

A red-brick wall bearing the same logo was the first thing visitors saw when they entered the space. To the left was a reception desk he'd built and varnished himself following an online template that'd looked much simpler than it'd turned out to be.

He flipped on the lights, which flickered for a second but stayed on. "The power is still kinda sketchy."

"I hope it stays on."

"You and me both. I'm out of business without it."

"This is such an amazing space." She took in the exposed ductwork that lined the ceiling, which had been painted black, and the leather sofa in the reception area. "I'm not sure what I expected, but this is really nice."

"Thanks. Took me a few years to get it the way I wanted it, but it was worth the effort."

"Tell me everything. How does it work?"

"Never had a tat?"

"Nope. I'm untouched by ink."

"Well, that's a crying shame." The words were said before he took a second to decide whether they should be.

McKenzie laughed. "I'm *such* a baby when it comes to needles. I can't imagine willingly sitting still and letting someone poke me with them for hours."

"It's not that painful. Well, most of the time, it isn't. Depends on where you're getting the ink. Joints and bony areas tend to hurt the most."

She shuddered. "I couldn't do it."

"Sure, you could. You survived a hurricane—and childbirth. A tat would be nothing after that."

"Right." She rolled her eyes. "The only reason I survived the hurricane is because Blaine rescued me. Who knows what would've become of us if he hadn't come along when he did?"

"You would've figured out something. But anyway, enough about that. We're all about positive thinking, remember?"

"Right."

"Come in."

They walked into the main part of the big, open room where four stations were set up to the specifications of each artist. "This is my area." He gestured to the deluxe table he'd saved up for over two years to buy and then special ordered from the mainland. It had arm and leg rests that made his customers comfortable while he worked.

"Do people usually know what they want when they come in?"

"About half the time they do. For those who just want something, we have books over there full of designs to give them inspiration."

"So the person picks what they want and then what?"

"We discuss the design until I'm sure they're happy with it, reminding them several times that there's not really a do-over once it's done. For instance, I discourage people from tattoos with boyfriend or girlfriend names."

McKenzie laughed. "Probably a good call."

"They always think they've found 'the one.' I've had a few people come back to have them altered after the breakup. I always want to question spouse names, too. Like, are you sure this marriage is solid before you put it in permanent ink?"

"I never would've thought of any of that, but you make good points. I bet people don't love that question."

"They don't, but I ask it anyway."

"What happens once you're settled on the design?"

"I run the design through a thermal printer, which spits out a template that I apply to their skin after it's cleaned, shaved and prepped. The template peels off, leaving an outline of the design that I then fill in with the ink we've agreed to ahead of time. Sometimes people want all-black designs. Other times, they want color."

Was he talking too much and giving her more info than she wanted?

"That's when the needles come into it, right?"

"Yep. And we have a bunch of different sizes and types, depending on what the design calls for."

"It must've taken years to figure out how to do this."

"About a year before I was fully trained and comfortable with flying solo. I was lucky to have a great teacher who then helped me to buy him out when he retired. He set me up with a very nice life here."

"That's so great. I'm sure you worked your butt off to deserve that kind of help."

"I did, but I loved it from the start, so it was a good fit for me. I love the camaraderie with the other artists, and the customers are fun, too. We get a lot of vacationers and first-timers looking to do something a little crazy—by their standards, anyway. They're so excited, which makes it fun for us."

"I'm sure that is fun. Other than the breakups, do they ever regret it afterward?"

"Not that we see. They're usually still high on the adrenaline of it when they leave us. If they regret it, that probably happens after they get home. You want to see some of my stuff?"

"I'd love to."

He gestured for her to take a seat on the sofa. "That little guy must get heavy after a while."

"He does. He's not so little anymore."

"You need one of those stroller thingies."

"I had one at the cabin. Maybe it survived the collapse." She pulled a blanket and some toys from her backpack and put them on the carpet for Jax to play with.

Duke sat next to her, bringing his leather-bound portfolio. "If it did, we'll find it and clean it up for him."

"Thank you for being such a great friend to me when I really needed one."

Her kind words went straight to his already-overcommitted heart. "It's my pleasure to help you. Your grandmother did the same for me once upon a time. I'll never forget her kindness or how much it meant to me. I'm just paying it forward like she'd want me to."

"She was forever telling us that kindness matters and to take care of people who need it."

"That sounds like her."

"It drove her crazy that my mother was nothing like her. She takes care of herself before everyone else."

"I might've heard something about that a time or two."

"What did she say?"

He shook his head. "I'm not spilling any secrets. All I'll say is that she saw it and wished it wasn't like that."

"It wasn't easy to be her kid."

"Rosemary saw that, too."

"Yeah, she did. Thank goodness for her. Anyway, show me your work."

For the next thirty minutes, she flipped through each page of his portfolio, studying every design with interest and curiosity that amused and aroused him.

That last part was a bit unsettling. Despite his best intentions, he'd have to be dead and buried to not be attracted to her, especially as she exclaimed over his work.

"You're incredibly talented, Duke, but I'm sure you know that."

He shrugged, embarrassed and delighted by her praise. "It's the one thing I'm really good at, so don't be too impressed."

"Too late. I already am, and you're also very good at cross-stitching."

"That's easy, and it's similar to what I do here. Just another artistic expression."

"Cross-stitching is not easy, especially the way you do it without a template, and don't try to tell me otherwise. I made a mess of every sampler I ever started. Gran eventually gave up on me and patted me on the head as she told me I'd have other talents."

Duke laughed. "That also sounds like her."

"She certainly didn't suffer fools."

"No, she didn't, which was why I liked her so much. There was no BS with her, you know?"

"I sure do. She had no patience for my teenage nonsense. She'd tell me my bad attitude would get me nowhere in life and to come back when I could be pleasant. Since there was nowhere else I wanted to be but with her, I sweetened up quickly, so she'd let me come back to her house."

"I can't imagine you as a nasty teenager."

McKenzie snorted with laughter. "I was the worst, but thanks to Gran, it didn't last as long as it might've otherwise. She wasn't having it." She continued to turn the pages, giving each piece of art her full attention. "I can't get over how detailed your work is. How hard is it to get the fine details into the final product?"

"It's not that hard once you know what needles to use for what effect. The art is the easiest part of running this place. It's the business stuff that makes me crazy. I hear the words QuickBooks, and I nearly break out in hives."

"Oh, I *love* QuickBooks. I used it to keep the books of a couple of businesses at home when I was in high school and college."

Duke looked at her without blinking. "You know QuickBooks?"

She glanced over at him, smiling as she nodded. "Uh-huh."

"Will you help me with it?"

"I'd love to."

"I'll pay you anything you want to make it so I never have to open that hateful program again."

She lost it laughing. "You don't have to pay me. I'm living in your apartment and letting you drive me around. It'd be the least I could do to pay you back for all you've done for me."

"You don't have to pay me back for anything, but I'd love some help with my accounting. It's the bane of my existence."

"I've got you covered."

The door swung open to admit his next-door neighbor Sierra, who owned a massage business. She had spiky dark hair, sleeve tattoos he'd done for her and a body that made the guys who worked for Duke drool. "Saw your truck out there on your day off." She stopped when she saw McKenzie and the baby. "Oh, sorry. Didn't realize you had guests."

"Sierra, this is McKenzie and her son, Jax. She's Rosemary's granddaughter. Sierra owns the massage studio next door."

"Oh, hey," Sierra said. "Loved your grandma. She was dope."

"Yes, she was."

"She made the best banana bread. I miss that."

"I know the recipe."

"Don't tease me unless you plan to come through."

McKenzie smiled. "I'll come through."

"I'll hold you to it."

"Guess what else she knows how to do?" Duke asked with a big grin.

Sierra stole a mint from a bowl on the reception desk. "What's that?"

"QuickBooks."

"Stop it. Really?"

"Yep," McKenzie said. "And I'm good at it. I even took a class."

Duke stared at her. "You took a class."

"I did." McKenzie's smile was nothing short of dazzling. "I aced it."

"Name your price," Sierra said. "I'll give you everything I have."

"That's not necessary," McKenzie said with a laugh. "I'd be happy to do it for you."

"If you do it, you'll be paid," Sierra said. "Handsomely."

"We can fight about that another time."

"When can you start?"

"Maybe tomorrow?" She glanced at Duke, as if to ask if that worked for him. "I just have to see what Tiffany needs at the store."

"We'll take what we can get." He glanced at Sierra. "Meet here around this time tomorrow?"

"I'll be here," Sierra said. "My first client is due any minute. Very nice to meet you, McKenzie and Jax. Have a good day, you guys."

"Nice to meet you, too."

When Jax started to fuss, McKenzie put the portfolio on the glass coffee table and picked him up for a cuddle. That settled him right down.

"You're good with him."

"I'm lucky that he's an easy baby. Now, anyway. At first, he wasn't at all, but we figured it out, didn't we, buddy?"

"Yayayayaya."

"Ya is his first word."

"He's a cutie."

"So's Sierra. She's freaking gorgeous."

"Yes, she is. The guys that work for me follow her around like puppies."

"But you don't?"

The question surprised him. Was she asking if he and Sierra were a couple, or was he reading too much into an innocent question? "Nah, we're just friends. Have been for years."

"I see."

He had so many questions he didn't dare ask her, but all at once, he needed some air. "What do you say we head home and see what we can salvage from the cabin?"

"That'd be great. Thanks for showing me your studio. It's absolutely amazing."

He thought she was absolutely amazing. "My pleasure."

CHAPTER 9

cKenzie had experienced the oddest feeling of jealousy or something like that when Sierra had walked into Duke's studio as if she owned the place. She'd been friendly and said such nice things about McKenzie's grandmother, so why had her hackles gone up the second she came in?

For one thing, Sierra was the kind of fierce, confident woman McKenzie wished she could be. What would it be like to be that comfortable in your own skin? McKenzie wouldn't know because she'd never been comfortable in hers. In addition, Sierra's easy camaraderie with Duke had made her wonder if the two of them were more than just friends and fellow business owners.

He said no, but she wasn't sure she believed him. Although why would he lie to her about that? The internal debate was stupid, especially since she had many more pressing things to think about besides wondering if Duke was romantically involved with the sexy woman who worked next door to him.

What did it matter to her if he was? It didn't. If only she could get the message to her raised hackles to simmer down and mind their own business.

She'd been blown away by his hip, stylish studio, as well as his incredible artwork. Since the natural-talent train had managed to ride past her, she was always amazed by people who could draw, paint, sing, write or create something from nothing. She'd gotten none of those things. Her one skill, if you could call it that, was an affinity for numbers that had served her well in a variety of jobs, even if she couldn't add or subtract in her head to save her life.

Once a boss found out she was good at math, she inevitably was asked to take on more of the admin tasks, which made her feel good about herself, even if it didn't come with more money. One of the store managers she'd worked for had sent her to the QuickBooks class, and she'd found she genuinely enjoyed bookkeeping—as long as a computer did the math for her.

"I bet there's plenty of businesses on this island, besides mine and Sierra's, who'd kill for a bookkeeper who knows QuickBooks."

"You think so?"

"I'm sure of it. You could have yourself a nice little business and work from home with Jax."

She glanced over at him in disbelief. "You really think so?"

"Absolutely. There's no one out here who does anything like that, but there're a ton of small businesses who need the help. We all muddle through, but I'm sure many of them make a mess of it the same way I do."

"How big of a mess are we talking?"

"It's pretty bad. You'll probably be appalled."

"I'm sure I can straighten it out for you in no time."

"That'd be such a relief. I stress out about it because I know I'm not doing it right, and I worry about the IRS knocking on my door."

"I'll take a look when Jax goes down for a nap, if you'd like."

"Sure, that'd work."

He pulled into the driveway at his place—or was it their place now? *Shut up, MK, and quit being weird.*

"Let me feed Jax some lunch and change his diaper. Then we can go next door."

"I'll be here whenever you're ready."

She went upstairs and fed Jax some of the baby cereal he'd recently begun eating, along with applesauce. While he was strapped into the baby seat, she went to use the bathroom and then made herself a peanut butter sandwich.

When she was ready to meet Duke, she decided to carry Jax in the baby seat so he could sit and play with his toys while they surveyed what was left of her cabin. She'd put this task off for days, dreading what she would find there.

When Duke saw her coming down the stairs, he got up from his chair by the firepit.

He took the heavy baby seat from her as if it was the most natural thing for him to do. For someone who'd mostly raised himself, he had lovely manners.

She walked next to him down a well-worn path that led next door. "Rosemary and I made this path over years of visiting back and forth."

"That's very sweet. I'm so glad she had such a good friend in you out here."

"She had a ton of friends out here. Everyone loved her."

McKenzie thought she was prepared to see the damage to the cabin, but nothing could've prepared her for the sight they encountered around the final bend in the path. The cabin she and her grandmother had loved so much had been reduced to splinters.

"Oh. Oh my God." Tears appeared out of nowhere and quickly spilled over. There was nothing left but rubble.

Duke put an arm around her shoulders. "I know it looks bad, but the good news is you guys got out of there before it collapsed."

She nodded, but the tears kept coming. How could there be anything worth saving in there?

While Duke held the baby carrier, she walked around the pile of wood and shingles and other building materials, looking for anything salvageable.

"Don't get too close," Duke said. "You don't want it to shift and come down on you."

"I can see the stroller!"

"Let me get it." He walked around to join her, handing the baby seat to her to hold while he got down on his knees to reach in to retrieve the folded stroller. "Here you go."

She pushed some buttons and had the stroller unfolded in a matter of seconds. "Well, that's a relief. One less thing I need to replace."

McKenzie's phone rang, and she took the call from her mother, who'd texted yesterday and asked her to call.

"Thank goodness you finally answered."

"I'm so sorry. I should've called, but I've been figuring out what to do about the cabin—"

"What's wrong with the cabin?"

"It's a pile of rubble."

"Oh no. Well, I guess you'll be coming home, then."

That's what she'd prefer, but McKenzie couldn't go back to living with her mother and her nonstop critiques of every decision she made. "We're talking to the insurance company and a guy out here who does construction."

"What do you do in the meantime?"

"A friend of Gran's has loaned me an apartment over his garage. He said I can stay there as long as I need to."

"In exchange for what?"

McKenzie had to bite her tongue to hold back the sharp retort that was dying to get out. But that never helped anything. "Nothing, Mom. He's a nice guy who was close to Gran. It's how people are out here. They help each other."

"No man helps a pretty young woman without an ulterior motive."

"I've got to go, but I'll text you soon."

"You should come home with that little one, McKenzie. It's probably not safe out there."

"We're perfectly safe. Talk soon." She ended the call before her mother could say something else that could never be unheard. That was her special gift—inserting the most negative, unhelpful comments into any situation.

McKenzie was outraged by the awful things she'd said about Duke, a man she didn't even know.

"What set you off?"

"Huh?"

"You look furious."

"My mother, as usual, with her commentary about what a man who helps a pretty young woman would want in return for his kindness."

His expression went flat with shock. "She said that?"

"She did."

"Well, it's not true."

"I know that. That's how she is. If she thinks it, she says it, with no filter or regard for the feelings of other people. She assumes I'll come home because the cabin is wrecked, but I can't go back there. I just can't."

"You don't have to. My place is all yours for as long as you need it, with no strings attached."

"I'm sorry she said that, and I'm sorry I told you what she said. I should've kept it to myself, but she makes me so damned mad."

"I can see why. It's funny how I always wanted parents, but the more I hear about other people's, the more I see I might've gotten lucky."

"They're not all like mine are."

"I know, but enough of my friends got the short end of the parent stick that I'm glad to not be dealing with that as an adult. It would drive me crazy to have someone judging everything I said and did."

"It's tiresome." She forced a smile. "I'm sorry to derail our day of positive thinking."

"Eh, life happens. You can't let it get to you."

"How do I do that again?"

"You look at this perfect little face." He gestured to Jax, taking in the world around him from the seat. "And you realize that no matter what's going sideways at the moment, you'll always have him to remind you of what's really important."

His words went straight to her heart and had her looking at him with even more admiration and, let's face it, *interest* than she'd had before. "What a sweet thing to say."

"Just telling it like I see it. What else matters besides him and whatever's best for him?"

"Nothing else matters."

"Well, it'd be nice if you could make yourself happy in the process of making him happy."

"That'd be good."

"You'll get there. Don't let her take up rent-free space in your thoughts."

"I still want to know how you got so wise."

"Life does that to ya."

"When is it gonna do it for me?"

"Seems like it's happening as we speak, if you ask me."

"It's happening since I got lucky to meet Yoda next door."

Duke threw his head back and laughed as hard as she'd seen him laugh yet, stirring the most intriguing feeling of desire and curiosity to know more about him. She wanted to know whatever he was willing to tell her, and that should've scared her senseless.

But because it was him, because he was so wonderful, the feelings she had for him didn't scare her at all. Rather, she was excited to find out what might happen next.

She no sooner had that feeling—and that thought—than a big black pickup truck pulled into the driveway. A handsome guy with dark hair and blue eyes emerged from the cab. He wore a faded T-shirt, cargo shorts and work boots.

"That's Mac." Duke went to shake the other man's hand. "Thanks so much for stopping by."

"No problem. Wow, when you said collapsed, you weren't kidding."

"Nope. Mac McCarthy, meet Rosemary's granddaughter, McKenzie, and her son, Jax."

Mac shook her hand. "Nice to meet you both. What a cute little guy. Reminds me of my Thomas when he was about the same age."

"How old is he now?"

"Six, which I can't believe. I've also got a three-year-old, an almost-two-year-old and new twins."

"Holy moly."

"My wife and I say that every day." Mac moved around to take a closer look at the damage. "Looks like a total loss. I assume it was insured?"

"Yes," McKenzie said. "My grandmother paid for three years in advance."

"Well, that's handy. You can rebuild to your specs, which is nice."

"How soon do you think that could happen?"

"I could do it in the next month or so. I'd just need to order materials, and that takes a minute with us being on an island."

"I thought I heard someone say you're booked out until the spring," McKenzie said.

"I am. I mean, I was, but I'm shifting some things around so I can fit in jobs like yours for people impacted by the storm. We'll get it done for you."

Once again, the kindness of a stranger overwhelmed her. "I don't know what to say."

"Not sure if Duke told you that I married a single mom. Thomas was nine months old when we met."

"That's how old Jax is now."

"I thought so. Thomas and his mom quickly became the best thing to ever happen to me. I'm happy to do whatever I can for you."

"Thank you so much. I wish there was something else I could say..."

"No need. Glad to help. I'll get some guys over here this week to get the site cleaned up so you can see what's salvageable underneath. Give me your phone number so I can get in touch when we're coming by."

McKenzie recited her number. "My service has been spotty here, so call Duke if it doesn't go through."

"Will do."

"I, um, I can't pay you until the insurance settlement comes in."

"No worries. I'll be ordering in bulk for several customers in the same situation as you are. I know you're good for it. I gotta keep moving. Got a lot of stops to make today. The storm did a number on this island."

"Is there any word on Billy or Jim?" Duke asked.

Mac shook his head, his expression grim. "Not looking good."

"No, it isn't. So sorry to hear."

"Yeah, it's very sad. Did you get the word about the get-together my folks are doing at the marina tonight?"

"Ned texted me. I'll definitely stop by."

"Feel free to join us, McKenzie. Everyone's welcome."

"That sounds fun."

"It always is when everyone gets together. Well, I'm off. I'll be in touch. So nice to meet you and Jax."

"You, too, Mac. Thanks again."

"You got it."

"Wow," she said to Duke after they'd waved him off, "what a nice guy."

"He's great. The whole family is. You should come to the hurricane survival party tonight."

"I won't know anyone."

"That's how you meet people. Everyone is welcome at everything on this island. That's how we roll here."

"I'm beginning to see that, and I love it."

CHAPTER 10

*J*ared James, his wife, Lizzie, and their baby daughter, Violet, arrived at the ferry landing a few minutes before the three-thirty boat from the mainland was due to arrive, bringing his older sister Kendall and her sons, Henry and Elias.

"So when did Katherine change her name to Kendall?" Lizzie, who was holding Violet, asked as they stood waiting for the boat that was visible in the distance.

Jared would've offered to take the baby, but Lizzie loved holding her so much that he didn't. He'd never seen his Lizzie happier than since Violet had come into their lives. "Kendall is her middle name, and she always wished it'd been her first name. When she filed for divorce from Phil, she decided to go back to James as her last name. Since she was changing her last name, she decided to finally use the first name she preferred."

"Good for her. I hope I don't slip up and call her by the wrong name."

"She won't care if you do."

"Who won't care about what?" Jared's brother Quinn asked when he and his wife, Mallory, joined them.

"I was telling Lizzie that Kendall won't care if she slips up and calls her Kath by accident."

"That's good," Quinn said, "because I'm worried about that, too. Who changes their name at our age?"

"Our sister did, so get on board."

"That's what I told him," Mallory said.

"You should listen to your wife and brother, Q," Jared said. "Clearly, we're smarter than you are."

Mallory coughed to cover a laugh while her husband frowned at her.

"Traitor."

"What? He's funny."

"No, he isn't."

"I really am," Jared said.

Quinn reached for baby Violet. "Come see Uncle Quinn, angel. Everyone's being mean to me."

Lizzie smiled as she handed over the baby to her uncle.

"My goodness, she's a beauty," Mallory said as she leaned in to kiss the baby's chubby cheek.

"We think so, too," Lizzie said, "but we're kind of biased."

"You're allowed to be. She's perfect. Is she sleeping any better?"

"Nope, and neither are we," Jared said, "but that's fine. We're told she'll sleep through the night before she's twenty, so we're looking forward to that."

Mallory laughed at the face he made.

"Here comes the big boat." Quinn turned so Violet could see the ferry coming. "You're going to meet your aunt and cousins."

"She's very excited," Lizzie said. "Insisted on wearing her best dress."

The others laughed.

"You're the cutest new mom ever," Mallory said.

"I'm a bit silly, but I blame the sleep deprivation."

"You're not silly. You're madly in love with your little girl. That's the way it should be."

Jared slipped an arm around Lizzie, wondering for the umpteenth time if a heart could burst from too much happiness. He'd thought he loved Lizzie as much as possible before, but watching her become a mother, after an awful battle with infertility, had been the most incredible experience of his life. Not to mention his own pure joy and bliss at becoming a father.

Before Violet had arrived in their lives through a series of still-unbelievable events, he'd thought he'd be okay if they couldn't have kids. After all, he got to love and be loved by the incredible Lizzie James and had a life anyone would envy. But after just a few weeks with Violet, he was glad to have been proven wrong. She was the sun, the moon, the stars and better than just about anything, even ice cream.

They'd breathe a little easier when her adoption was final in a few months, but they were trying not to worry too much about that. Violet's biological mother, Jessie, had left her with them because she knew they would care for the baby when she couldn't. She'd willingly signed the adoption papers after they'd finally found her. They didn't expect Jessie to have regrets, but until the ink was dry, that was always a possibility.

Jared couldn't allow himself to consider any scenario that disrupted their happy little family, so he refused to let his mind go there. He was pretty sure Lizzie was following the same plan. They never talked about any outcome other than her officially becoming their daughter.

Kendall and the boys waved to them from the bow of the big ferry as it came into port.

"I still can't believe Joe and Seamus took the ferries out to sea to ride out the storm," Jared said to his brother.

"I know. I can't even think about that without wanting to be sick. And that they rescued Deacon Taylor while they were out there." The island's harbor master had drifted out to sea on his overturned boat.

"That was a freaking miracle."

"Indeed."

After the ferry backed into port as smoothly as always, cars and trucks began disembarking before people followed. The group was smaller than usual, since the number of visitors tended to dwindle after Labor Day.

The boys bolted off the boat ahead of their mother. They were ten and twelve, with sandy blond hair and big smiles as they came running toward their uncles.

"Holy moly, have you guys been eating Miracle-Gro or something?" Jared asked as he hugged them.

"That's not for people, Uncle Jared," Henry said with preteen disdain for dumb adults.

He'd gotten tall since Jared had seen him six months ago. The sprinkling of freckles across his nose indicated a summer spent in the sun, as did the blond streaks in his light brown hair. His brother was about six inches shorter than him with braces on his teeth. Both boys had their dad's brown eyes and bright smiles that were like Kendall's had been before life had kicked her in the teeth. They were funny and inquisitive, and Jared loved being around them.

"So I shouldn't feed it to baby Violet?"

"No!"

They hugged Quinn and shook hands with Mallory and Lizzie, telling them it was nice to meet Mallory and to see Lizzie again.

"Meet your cousin, boys," Jared said. "Violet, this is Henry and Elias."

Quinn bent at the waist to give the boys a better view of the baby as Kendall caught up to them.

"She's wicked small," Elias declared, seeming disappointed that his new cousin wouldn't be able to play with him. Not yet, anyway.

"She won't be for long," Jared said.

"Thanks for the help with the suitcases, boys," Kendall said, sounding exasperated as she rolled two suitcases in each hand.

"Whoops," Henry said, grinning.

Kendall hugged her brothers and sisters-in-law. "It's so nice to finally meet you in person, Mallory."

"You, too."

"We were all relieved that someone finally took Quinn off our hands."

While Quinn sputtered with outrage, everyone else laughed. "You're not allowed to think any of my siblings are funny, Mallory."

"Whoops, sorry."

"No, you're not."

"I like her," Kendall said. "I think we'll be best friends."

"Oh God." Quinn moaned as he gathered Kendall's luggage to roll it toward Jared's SUV. "That's just what I need."

"My little brothers would try the patience of a saint, so you ladies must be saints."

"How long do we have the pleasure of your company?" Jared asked with a fake smile that made Kendall laugh.

"I'm not sure yet. Things are up in the air at the moment."

"You're welcome for as long as you want to stay," Jared said, all kidding aside. "David and Daisy moved out of the apartment over the garage, so that's all yours. We thought it would be better to put you there, so you don't have to listen to a screaming baby all night long."

Kendall reached out a hand to her baby niece. "I'm sure she doesn't scream all night, do you, princess?"

"Sometimes it's all night," Lizzie said, smiling.

Kendall and her kids had been through a lot with her husband and their father's addiction battle. If they needed a fresh start, Gansett Island was a great place to be.

"We can't wait to get to know Violet, right, boys?" Kendall said.

"Yes!" Henry gave a fist bump. "We love cousins."

Jared had a lot of questions, such as what her plan was for the boys and school, but he'd never seen Kendall look so fragile. Though she was her usual wisecracking self, she had deep dark circles under her hazel eyes and a pinched, stressed set to her mouth. If his sister and nephews needed a reset, that's exactly what they'd get on Gansett Island.

AFTER SEVEN STRAIGHT NIGHTS TOGETHER, Piper still couldn't believe she was waking up naked in bed with Jack Downing.

The brush of his hairy arm over her stomach gave her goose bumps.

He was the sexiest man she'd ever laid eyes on, and he seemed positively smitten with her—and she was smitten right back. Ever since the night she'd gone after him and realized he was upset because he'd forgotten his late wife's birthday, they'd been all in with each other. She'd never enjoyed anything more than being all in with him.

She smiled, recalling the nights of decadent pleasure in his arms. The memories came back to her in a rush of erotically charged moments that gave her more goose bumps and made her nipples tingle. They'd had sex *three times* the night before. She'd never done that with anyone else.

"What're you thinking about?"

His gruff morning voice had become her favorite thing to wake up to.

"You."

"What about me?"

From behind her, he cupped her breast and ran his thumb over her tight nipple.

That was all it took to get her thinking about round four. Who was this person she became when he was around?

He'd told her she was the first woman who'd interested him since he'd lost his beloved wife to breast cancer a few years ago, and she was honored that he'd chosen her. Even blissed out on happiness, however, she worried about what came next. She'd read that the first relationship after a great loss usually failed. The thought of that happening to them made her ridiculously emotional.

She coughed on the lump that suddenly appeared in her throat whenever she wondered what would happen now that they'd gone from months of low-key flirtation to a full-on relationship or whatever this was.

"Hello in there. Are you going to tell me any specifics?"

"Just that you're here, and how glad I am that you are."

"Even if I messed with your sleep once again?"

"It was worth it."

"I'm glad you think so."

"Do you? Think it's worth it?"

"Hell yes, I do. You can't tell?" He pressed his hard cock against her back as he continued to toy with her nipple.

She loved how affectionate he was. That'd been a problem in her relationship with Ben, not that she was comparing them, because that wouldn't be fair to Ben. She almost laughed out loud at the direction her thoughts had taken. She'd come to realize her ex-fiancé had done her a favor by calling off their wedding, as traumatic as that had been at the time.

After a week of intense passion with Jack, of counting the hours until they could be together again, she was at that weird point of wondering what it was, exactly, they were doing.

The night she'd gone after him, he'd told her he wanted everything with her, but was he ready for that?

Were they only about great sex? Or was it destined to be more? She hoped for the latter because she liked him a lot—even more so after becoming addicted to sleeping in his arms. She who hated being touched when she slept couldn't get over that particular development.

Piper turned onto her back, tucking the covers in under her arms. The sun streaming into her room at the Sand & Surf made her feel naked in more ways than one.

Jack smiled at her, and damn, was he gorgeous with scruff on his face and his dark hair standing on end, probably from her pulling it. The memory of why she'd had cause to pull his hair had her face heating.

He ran a finger over her cheek. "You're very cute in the morning when you're having all sorts of naughty thoughts."

"How do you know what I'm thinking?"

"Because I'm hoping you're thinking the same thing I am." He leaned in to kiss her. "And I'm thinking... Holy. Moly. What a night."

"Oh, well..." She cleared her throat. "Yes, it was." *You sound so stupid, Piper. Why are you acting like a blushing recent ex-virgin in front of this guy?*

He touched a finger to the furrow between her brows. "What's going on?"

"Nothing. Just, you know... Wondering what it all means, as I tend to overthink everything."

"Nothing wrong with that. If I could have anything I wanted, it'd be more time with you." He kissed her again. "Lots more time with you."

"Oh, okay. That sounds good."

"What did you think I would say to that?"

"I wasn't sure, and that had me spinning a bit, if I'm being honest."

"No need for spinning or uncertainty." He took her hand and linked their fingers. "I woke up this morning, like I did the last seven mornings, feeling better than I have in a very long time, and that's all thanks to you."

"I'm glad to hear that. You deserve to feel good."

"So do you. I don't like to hear you're spinning and uncertain."

"I'm sorry to be weird. I never used to be this way. I guess this is what happens when your fiancé calls off the wedding a month before."

"He's a fool."

"You think so?"

"I really do. Anyone lucky enough to have you in their life should be smart enough to know it."

She hadn't realized how much she needed to hear that.

"Remember when I said I wanted everything with you?"

"I do."

"I meant that, Piper. This is a very big deal for me, and I know it is for you, too. We've both been through a lot and have no patience for games or foolishness."

"What you've been through is much bigger than my thing."

He shook his head. "Heartache is heartache, sweetheart. Moving on from that takes courage, no matter how it happened."

"Yes, it really does, and if you'd asked me if I was ready for... well, this... I would've probably said not really. But now it's happening, and it's been so special."

"For me, too." He tucked a strand of hair behind her ear and ran his

99

fingertip over her cheek. "It occurs to me that I've missed a very important step in my quest to bring the glorious Piper into my life."

"What step is that?"

"The take-you-out-on-a-proper-date step so you won't think I'm just after more of this." He squeezed her breast to make his point. "Although more of this is never a bad thing."

He made her want to giggle like a girl who was in love for the first time.

Yikes. Take that back. No one was in love here.

"What do you say about a date tonight?" He kissed her shoulder. "Hmm?"

"Sure. That sounds good."

"Excellent. I saw a text about a hurricane survival party at the McCarthys' Marina if you're into that."

"That might be fun."

"Any time the McCarthys are involved, it's fun. But I'd still owe you a proper date with wine and candles and tablecloths."

"You don't owe me anything."

"Yes, I do."

She was about to ask him why he thought that when his phone rang. He took the call and did more listening than talking. "Thanks for letting me know. I'll be there in fifteen minutes." After another pause: "Yeah, I'll call it in. Okay. See you soon." He let out a deep breath as he ended the call. "They found a body in the Salt Pond. They think it's Jim Sturgil."

"Oh God. I was so hoping he'd be found alive." Jim's ex-wife Tiffany was her friend, and she ached for Tiff and her daughter.

"I know. I've got to call the coroner to come over from the mainland."

While he made that call, she thought of Tiffany getting that news and having to tell her sweet little girl that her daddy had died in the storm.

After he ended the call, Jack leaned over to kiss her. "One of these mornings, we're going to loll about in bed and have coffee and breakfast and more of the fun we had last night."

"That sounds like something to look forward to."

"Yes, it does."

"Don't you have to get going?"

"I do, but I don't want to." He kissed her again. "In case I forget to tell you, this last week has been a very big deal for me, as you know. Because it was you, it was perfect. You're perfect." He left her with one last kiss. "This time, I'm really going."

While he showered in her tiny bathroom, Piper got out of bed and put on her robe.

Ten minutes later, he emerged from the bathroom, wearing his sexy state police uniform, kissed her one last time and was gone, promising to text her later. The door had almost closed behind him when he turned around and came back into the room.

"Forget something?"

"Yeah." He kissed her again. "I mean it this time. I'm going."

She released the handful of uniform she'd grabbed while he kissed her. "Good luck with everything today."

He grimaced as he remembered the grim task that awaited his attention. "I'll be back as soon as I can."

"I'll be here."

"I can't wait."

CHAPTER 11

*I*t took Piper a full minute after he left to catch the breath he'd stolen from her lungs with his sweetness. She might want to tell herself this wasn't about love, but with every minute she spent with him, it was getting harder to deny that's where it was headed.

Half an hour later, showered and dressed for work, she went downstairs to check in with Laura at the hotel's reception desk.

"Funniest thing just happened," Laura said.

"What's that?"

"A sexy state trooper came down my stairs in full uniform. I said, 'Officer, is something amiss in my hotel?' He just grinned and said everything is just dandy. Do you know anything about what that hot cop was doing in my hotel first thing in the morning, young lady?"

Piper was trying her best not to bust up with laughter at Laura's teasing. "I've got to move out of here ASAP."

"Don't do that! How will I know that Hot Cop spent the night—again—if you leave?"

"I feel like my mom is catching me doing the walk of shame."

"So was it shameful, then?"

"Laura!"

She lost it laughing. "You're so cute when you're mortified."

"I must be flat-out adorable right now," she muttered.

"You are! You're glowing. So things are going well, I take it?"

"Duh."

Laura let out a yelp that would've been a scream if they weren't standing in a hotel lobby. "This makes me *so* happy!"

"Tell me how you really feel."

"I just did. I love when great people find each other in this world and do wicked, wicked things in one of my beds."

"I'm getting my own place."

"How come?" Owen asked as he came down the stairs, toting all three kids and making that look easy, as only he could do.

"Your wife is harassing me."

"Hot Cop just left," Laura told him. "Again."

"Ah," Owen said, grinning. "I see. She's obsessed with this new romance unfolding under our roof."

"Which is why I need to move out."

"Don't go," Laura said in a dramatic tone. "I *need* you here with me."

"Then you have to leave her alone about Hot Cop," Owen said as he put Jon down to run around.

Piper used her thumb to point at Owen. "What he said."

"You guys are no fun. I'm an old married lady. I'm living vicariously through you, Piper. How can you shut me off this way?"

Before Piper could answer her, the front door opened as Dara Watkins and Erin Jackson came into the lobby. Erin carried a massive bouquet of flowers.

"Ladies!" Laura said. "What's going on?"

"These are for you to thank you for your hospitality during the storm," Erin said. "We got the first batch off the boat this morning."

"They're gorgeous!" Laura juggled the flowers as she hugged both women. "But you didn't have to do that. We loved having you."

"We sure did." Piper had enjoyed getting to know both women during the storm.

"How's it going with Hot Cop?" Dara asked.

"Funny you should ask," Laura replied. "We were just talking about how there was a very handsome state cop in full uniform coming down my stairs this very morning."

"I'm going to muzzle you," Piper said, even though she was amused by Laura. She'd never had girlfriends quite like the ones she'd found on Gansett Island, and she adored them.

"Oh, do tell," Erin said.

With all three of them looking at her, Piper said, "I have no idea what she's talking about."

"Liar," Laura said.

"I'm getting my own place," Piper told Erin and Dara. "This is like living with my mom again."

"I'll behave if you promise to stay," Laura said, "and if you promise I get to see Hot Cop in that uniform at least once a week. That's better than coffee."

"I can hear you, dear," Owen said with a chuckle as he chased Jon, Jo and Holden, who ran toward their toys in the family room.

While the others laughed, Piper hoped that she wasn't getting her hopes—and Laura's—up about Jack prematurely.

"Are you okay, Piper?" Dara asked.

Dara's question made her feel madly vulnerable, but since she was among friends, she spoke the words weighing on her heart. "It's scary, you know?"

"What is?" Erin asked.

"All of it. I've been down this road before. Didn't work out so well for me." Her fiancé calling off their wedding had been among the more shocking things to ever happen, even if she'd since come to realize he'd done the right thing for both of them. If how she was feeling about Jack was any indication, Ben had definitely done them both a favor by ending their engagement.

"But this is kinda different, right?" Laura asked.

"Yeah, it is, and that's the scary part. It feels..."

"Bigger?"

Piper nodded as she bit her lower lip.

"I know it's super scary, but bigger is a good thing. I promise."

"Was it like this for you with Owen?" Laura had met Owen shortly after her first marriage had ended in dramatic fashion.

"God yes, it was so big from the get-go that it scared me to death. But he kept showing up and proving I wouldn't regret those big feelings. Not with him. I never have, in case you're wondering."

"Anyone who knows you two can see there're zero regrets."

"After what my ex-husband did, it was hard for me to even think about taking that kind of risk again, but with Owen... It wasn't a risk, you know? It was just right."

"It helps to hear that. Thank you."

"You're welcome. Just be happy for this moment, Piper. This isn't something that comes along every day."

"She's so right," Erin said. "The last thing I thought I wanted was what I have now with Slim, but it's the best thing ever. We all want that for you, too."

"Thank you guys for talking me off the cliff."

"Any time, pal," Dara said. "Speaking of romance... My sister Monique just texted that she wants to come back soon because she's still talking to Linc."

"Linc, as in Coast Guard Linc?" Laura asked.

"One and the same."

"Oh wow. I didn't realize they met while she was here."

"They did, and she was cagey about the details, which isn't like her. She's fresh off a messy divorce, so I'm not sure how serious she is about anything."

"Well, you'll have to keep us posted about that," Laura said.

"Of course I will."

"Did you guys hear that they think they found Jim Sturgil?" Piper asked.

"Oh God, no," Laura said. "Poor Tiffany—and Ashleigh."

"I know. It's terrible."

"I was thinking I'll make them dinner," Piper said.

"That'd be nice."

"What are you hearing about Jeff and Kelsey, Laura?" Dara asked.

"Both are doing better. They're working on getting him moved to rehab in the next couple of days."

"So glad to hear they're on the mend."

"I've got to run to meet Slim and Mac to talk about repairs to our house, but maybe we'll see you later at the McCarthys'?" Erin asked.

"We're hoping to go," Laura said.

"We are, too," Piper added, realizing she was speaking for Jack, which was still strange but oddly elating, too.

"See you there," Dara said as she followed Erin out the front door.

"Where do you need me today?" Piper asked Laura.

"Front desk for the morning, and then we'll see what the day brings. We're gearing up for a busy weekend, but today ought to be slow."

"That'd be nice."

"Because you didn't get much sleep, am I right?"

"I'm quitting you, Laura."

Laura walked away, laughing, as Piper settled in for a morning at the reception desk. She'd be needing some extra coffee that morning after having had very little sleep. But it'd been worth it. So very, very worth it.

CHAPTER 12

The pain had begun in the middle of the night and had intensified as daylight broke and flooded Abby McCarthy's bedroom with warmth. She'd tried turning over to ease the ache, which wasn't as simple a thing as you'd think with four babies competing for shrinking space inside her. The change in position hadn't helped. Nor had lying on her back or sitting up or anything else she'd tried to find relief.

Now it had reached the point where she was going to have to say something about it, but the words were trapped inside her, laced with terror at the possibility of losing the babies she wanted so badly. This didn't feel like the pain she'd had when she miscarried an earlier pregnancy, but something wasn't right.

She sat on the bed, listening to Adam talk to Liam as he got him up and changed.

The baby laughed at everything Adam said and did. He was his daddy's best pal, and nothing made Abby happier than to watch Adam in dad mode.

"Let's go see if Mommy is awake."

"Mamamamamama."

"That's right, buddy. Your mama can't wait to see you."

Adam carried Liam into the bedroom and stopped when he saw Abby sitting on the bed. "Everything okay, hon?"

"I'm not sure."

"What do you mean?"

"I've got a pain that won't quit."

"Where?"

She placed her hand on her swollen abdomen. "Right here."

"I'll call Vic."

He was gone before she could reply or say hello to her son or do anything other than try not to panic about worst-case scenarios.

For weeks, she'd been bemoaning her burgeoning belly, the lack of mobility, the constant need to pee, the fears of how much tighter the tight squeeze might get before the babies came. Now, none of that mattered. All she cared about was that all four of them were strong and healthy. Any inconvenience or discomfort was a small price to pay for four more sons to love.

Even the thought of five babies under the age of two was nothing stacked up against the fear of losing the quads who'd been such a shocking surprise to their parents. They'd been told their likelihood of conceiving was low, so no one had seen two sets of identical twin boys coming, least of all Adam or Abby.

Adam came back into the bedroom, still carrying Liam. "Vic is sending the rescue. I called my mom, and she's coming to get Liam to take him to Maddie's to play with the kids today."

"Is the rescue necessary?"

"She said she's not taking any chances, and she doesn't want you to do anything but sit tight and wait."

"Did she sound worried?"

"Not particularly."

Victoria might not have been particularly worried, but Adam was. His brows were furrowed, and his mouth set in an expression that told her he, too, was trying not to panic.

They heard the door downstairs open.

"There's my mom. She was already in town, so she said she'd be right over." He brought Liam to Abby. "Give Mommy a kiss before you go with Grammy to play with the kids."

"Kids."

Abby smiled as she kissed and hugged her little boy. "Have the best time and be good for Grammy."

"Good."

"He's becoming a regular parrot," Adam said.

"He sure is."

Adam lifted him into his arms. "Be right back."

"I'll be here."

She heard him go down the stairs. She heard him talking to his mother. And she heard the urgent tone of his voice as he asked his mom to be gone with Liam before the ambulance arrived to take Abby. "I think it might scare him."

"Of course, honey," Linda said. "Please give Abby all our love and let me know what's going on as soon as you can."

"I will. Thanks for coming running."

"Always happy to have some time with my pal."

"Pal," Liam said.

Abby smiled and then grimaced as the sharpest pain yet took her breath away. Suddenly, she was deeply grateful for Victoria's over-abundance of caution.

Adam came charging up the stairs. "How're you doing, hon?"

"About the same." He didn't need to know the pain had gotten worse.

"Ambulance should be here any second."

Just as he said that, they heard the siren in the distance.

"I'll go let them in."

Five minutes later, paramedics came storming up the stairs, following Adam's direction to their bedroom.

One of them was Adam's sister Mallory.

"Hey, honey, what's going on?" Mallory asked as she hooked Abby to a blood pressure cuff.

"A pain that's been getting more intense by the hour."

She pressed a stethoscope to Abby's chest and then to her belly.

"Hearing lots of strong heartbeats in there. Let's get you to the clinic and see what's going on."

Though she'd felt the babies moving all night, Abby was relieved to hear their heartbeats were strong, although Mallory probably couldn't tell if that meant they were all healthy. Victoria would be able to further evaluate her at the clinic.

Mallory and the other two paramedics gently and efficiently moved her to a stretcher and strapped her in for the ride downstairs.

While they tended to her, Adam quickly got dressed in their bathroom and followed them down to the first floor and into the back of the ambulance.

"Shouldn't you take a car to get us home?"

"I'll worry about getting us home later. I want to be with you."

She squeezed the hand he'd wrapped around hers.

"What're you thinking, Mallory?" Adam asked his sister.

"Hard to say without a lot more info. Her BP is good, and I heard a bunch of heartbeats in there. Both of those things are great news."

Abby winced as the pain stole her breath. She'd never experienced labor pain, but she couldn't help but notice the spasms of pain were coming closer together and were getting more intense. She could not be in labor at twenty-two weeks. She just couldn't be.

They arrived at the clinic within minutes and were met by Victoria, the nurse practitioner-midwife, and Dr. David Lawrence, the attending physician.

She was whisked inside, quickly attached to a fetal monitor as well as other machines and monitors—all that before anyone asked her a single question.

"She's in labor," Victoria said.

Adam gasped. "What do we do?"

Victoria quickly inserted an IV needle that barely registered with Abby because she was trying so hard not to panic. "We can try to stop it with meds."

"Try to?" Adam asked. "What if it doesn't work?"

Victoria looked him in the eyes. "We'll do everything we can."

Mallory stayed with them, holding one of Abby's hands while Adam had the other.

"I'm scared," Abby whispered. "I can't lose them. I just can't."

"Let's not think the worst," Mallory said. "There's a lot that can be done. The best thing you can do is try to stay calm."

Abby hung on Mallory's every word, knowing she was an experienced nurse who'd seen all the scenarios during a career working in a Providence emergency department.

"Just focus on breathing for now," Mallory said. "Nice deep breaths, in and out."

Abby did the breathing and focused on the movement of the babies, proof that they were still there, still with her, still in the fight. She vowed that if they could get through this, she would never again complain about the discomfort of carrying quads or bemoan the fact that she had to pee every two seconds.

She'd do whatever it took to safely deliver her baby boys.

LINDA MCCARTHY DROVE her bright yellow Volkswagen Bug into the driveway at her son Mac's home as her grandson Liam chattered in the back seat. His sweet, cheerful presence was keeping Linda from going crazy wanting to know what was happening with Abby.

If they lost those babies...

No, she couldn't even consider the possibility. That couldn't happen, not after everything those two kids had already been through trying to have a family after Abby was diagnosed with polycystic ovary syndrome, which, among other things, made pregnancy difficult to impossible to achieve. That she'd somehow conceived the quads naturally considering her condition was nothing less than a miracle. Linda refused to believe they wouldn't see that miracle all the way to the finish line.

She wished she had the power to make it so her kids could have anything and everything they wanted and needed, but alas, even Voodoo Mama didn't have that kind of power. As much as she pretended to despise the nickname bestowed by her beloved kids, she secretly loved that she'd intimidated them enough as youngsters to give her that name.

"Come on, my sweet boy. Let's go see what the cousins are up to."

"Cousins!"

Liam held her hand as they walked up the stairs to Mac and Maddie's deck and stepped into the kind of madness only five young children could create. Toys were strewn about, baby Mac was wearing only a diaper, one of Hailey's pigtails had fallen out, Evie was crying, while Emma sipped from a bottle that her mother held for her.

"Grammy!" Her eldest grandchild, Thomas, ran over to greet her. "You brought Liam!"

"I sure did."

Liam tugged his hand free of hers and took off with Thomas to check out his older cousin's extensive truck collection.

"How goes the battle?" Linda asked her daughter-in-law.

"Business as usual in the madhouse. How'd you end up with Liam?"

"They took Abby to the clinic with some pain."

Maddie's smile turned to a frown. "Oh no. What're you hearing?"

"Nothing yet, and I'm trying not to blow it up in my mind until we know more."

"How's that going?"

"Not so well."

Maddie winced. "I can't bear to think of anything happening to those babies."

"I know. Same."

"Poor Abby has been through more than enough."

Linda picked up baby Evie and took the second bottle Maddie had ready to feed the other twin.

"Grammy to the rescue," Maddie said. "What would we do without our grandmas?"

"We'd probably die," Hailey said with a seriousness that had her mother and grandmother laughing.

"I don't think it's quite come to that," Maddie told her daughter.

"But it's close," Hailey said before she ran off to play with Thomas, Liam and baby Mac.

After she was gone, Linda shook her head in amusement. "She's full of beans."

"She gets that from your people."

"I can't even try to deny that. My people are nothing if not full of beans, especially the one who fathered her."

"You said that, not me."

Linda and Maddie fed and burped both babies, who dozed off once their bellies were full.

"Thank goodness these two can sleep through anything," Maddie said, snuggling with Emma as the four older kids ran around the room, laughing and screaming.

Linda kissed the top of Evie's head, her wispy blonde hair tickling Linda's nose. "They learned that in utero, listening to their siblings long before they were born."

"I guess I need to be grateful for the never-ending chaos, then."

"It's hard to believe how quickly chaos will turn to moody, sullen teenagers who'll grow up and leave you just when they're becoming interesting people."

"When will that be exactly?" Maddie asked with a smile.

"Long before you're ready."

"I like that expression you shared with me. 'The days are long, but the years are short.' It's so true. I'm already seeing that with Thomas. How is he almost *seven*?"

"I have no idea where all the time goes. I look at my kids... Mac will be *forty* soon. How?"

"We have to plan something for that, and it must be a roast."

"Of course it will be. Who deserves that more than he does?"

"Absolutely no one."

"What are you hearing from Tiffany?"

"Nothing new."

Linda's deep sigh said it all.

. . .

113

WHILE THE GIRLS played a game with Blaine, Tiffany had cleaned everything she could reach without having to get on the step stool, which would've sent her husband over the edge since pregnancy had her balance out of whack.

Even as Blaine played with the girls, he kept one eye on her, making sure she wasn't overdoing anything.

The activity didn't help.

Nothing helped to ease her mind as she contemplated having to share heartbreaking news with Ashleigh.

How did one say such a thing to a precious six-year-old who loved her daddy with all her heart? Ashleigh had no clue what a jerk he could be, and if Tiffany had her way, she'd never know that stuff. What difference would it make now? No, she'd allow her baby girl to keep every illusion she had about the man who'd fathered her, even if Blaine would be the one to raise her.

He would show her everything she needed to know about men and how they treated their loved ones and what to look for in a potential partner.

She was grateful for her wonderful husband all the time, but knowing he'd be there for her and Ashleigh if the worst came to pass was a source of tremendous comfort to Tiffany as they waited to hear what'd become of Jim and his friend Billy.

Every time the phone rang, she jumped out of her skin, wondering if this would be the call to confirm what they already knew. She saw it was Maddie and exhaled. "Hey."

"I'd ask how you're doing, but..."

"Trying to stay busy. Not sure what else to do."

"Is Blaine still home?"

"Yep. He went to the office for a short time before he came back. He's been taking calls and giving orders from here."

"I'm glad he's with you."

"Me, too. I wish they'd find them. One way or the other. The not knowing is hard."

"I can only imagine. You want to talk about it?"

"You've got enough going on over there."

"The twins are down for a nap, and Linda is making lunch for Thomas, Hailey, Mac and Liam, who's hanging with us today while Abby is at the clinic. I guess she woke up with a pain."

"Oh no. No, no, *no*."

"We're hoping for the best."

"God, me, too. Poor Abby—and Adam. They've been through enough."

"I know. Linda and I were just saying that. But back to you... Talk to me, Tiff. What's going through your mind?"

"So many things, but ironically, I find myself thinking about the good times and not how it all went so very wrong."

"It's good to focus on the positive."

"I guess, but it makes me even sadder to think about how he let his perfectly lovely life go completely off the rails."

"He did that to himself."

"Yes, he did. I was hoping he might get a more positive second act at some point, you know?"

"Yeah, I get that."

"I wanted that for him and for Ash. And now... The not knowing is the worst part. I want them to find him—and I don't want them to find him."

"Both those things can be true."

"I suppose so."

"Why don't you lie down and try to get a little rest?"

"I feel like I'll go crazy if I stop moving."

"You won't. I promise. You and the baby need rest. As long as Blaine is with the girls, you should try to take a nap."

"I'll try."

"Big Mac and Linda are having everyone to the marina for dinner. Stephanie is over there helping him set up. I know you're probably not in the mood for a big gathering, but you're more than welcome to join us if you feel up to it."

"I might like to do something like that. I'll see how I feel later on."

"No pressure. Come if you feel like it."

"Thanks for the invite and the talk. It helps that you get it."

"Oh, honey, of course I do. You once loved that man with all your heart. Even if you wanted to punch him half the time lately, you'd never want this."

A sob came from the deepest part of her. "No, I wouldn't. How will I ever tell Ash?"

"You'll find the words you need when the time is right."

"It'll break her little heart. How do I do that to my precious girl?"

"We'll all be there to support her."

Tiffany heard the tears in her sister's voice. Maddie loved her girls as much as Tiffany did. This would break the hearts of everyone who loved Ashleigh.

"That helps. I just can't believe this is happening. As much as I wished at times that he'd just go away and leave us alone, I never wanted this."

"I know, sweetie. None of us wanted this."

"I'll let you know about dinner. The change of scenery and time with friends might do me good."

"I think it would. Everyone wants to hug you."

"Thanks for checking on me. Call me any time you need to talk. Don't worry about waking up the babies. They sleep through the madness around here."

"What are you hearing about Kelsey and Jeff?"

"They're moving him to rehab soon, and she's feeling a little better. The broken arm is still giving her a lot of pain, but it's less every day."

"Those poor kids."

"Big Mac is sick over it. Mac told me his dad is going to deposit money into their accounts, so they have everything they need."

"Of course he is."

"He feels responsible for what happened."

"It wasn't his fault. Ethel is the one to blame."

"That's what Mac tried to tell him, but he wasn't hearing it."

"It doesn't surprise me that he wants to take care of everything for them."

"Me either. He's the best. Check in with me a little later?"

"I will. Thanks for everything. Love you."

"Love you, too."

CHAPTER 13

"**W**as that Maddie?" Blaine asked when he came into the kitchen, holding Addie, who was asleep on his shoulder.

"Yes, she was checking on me. She said Big Mac is having dinner for everyone at the marina tonight."

"That sounds fun, but only if you're up for it."

"I told her I'd decide later."

He used his thumb to brush away a tear from her face. "Your tears break my heart, sweetheart."

"I know. I'm sorry."

"No need to be sorry. Let me go put this angel down for a nap. I'll be right back."

"Okay."

She got glasses of ice water for them and was seated at the table when he returned to the kitchen.

His phone rang with a call from Linc Mercer. He did more listening than talking and then thanked him for the update.

"What did he say?" Tiffany asked.

"They found a body. They think it's Jim, but they can't be certain until the coroner performs an autopsy."

"Oh my God."

Blaine reached for her, brought her onto his lap and held her while she sobbed.

"I was so hoping..."

"I know, honey. I was, too."

"We have to tell Ash."

"I know."

"I don't want to tell her this."

"I don't either."

"Should we wait until they know for sure?"

"They know for sure, or they wouldn't have called me. The coroner and the autopsy are formalities."

"Oh." She took a sip of the water. "We can talk to her later if that's better. You need to go back to work. I heard you on the phone with the mayor."

"The mayor can kiss my ass. My wife needs me, and I'm not going anywhere. My team has everything covered, and I'm in regular touch with them."

"I don't want you to get in trouble."

"I won't. He needs me more than I need him, and he'd better not forget that."

His vehement support of her triggered more tears. She was getting sick of them, but damn if she could stop them.

"Should we tell her now, then?" she asked.

"I suppose it won't get easier later."

"No, it won't."

Tiffany got up and held out her hand to him. "Let's get this over with." She'd never dreaded anything more than she did having to tell her sweet girl that her daddy was dead.

They went upstairs to Ashleigh's room, where she was playing school with her dolls and stuffed animals.

Tiffany stopped him in the hallway so they could listen.

"If you get all your work done before recess, there'll be a surprise snack for everyone. But you all have to get your work done, or there's no snack for anyone."

Tiffany placed her hand over her heart as more tears filled her eyes. She was one big pregnancy hormone on a good day, crying as easily as she breathed. This was most definitely not a good day.

Blaine's hand on her back gave her the strength to wipe away her tears, put a smile on her face and step into Ashleigh's room, bringing the weight of what she needed to tell her daughter with her.

"Hey, sweetie."

Ashleigh smiled as she looked up at them. "We're playing school."

"We see that. You're an excellent teacher." Tiffany sat on the bed next to Blaine. "Can we talk to you for a second?"

"Sure."

"Come here, will you?"

Ashleigh got up and crawled onto Tiffany's lap. "Are you sad, Mommy?"

"A little."

"Is the baby okay?" She placed her warm little hand on Tiffany's belly. "I think he's a boy baby."

"I think so, too, and he's fine." Tiffany took a deep breath and forced herself to say the words that would change Ashleigh's life forever. "So after the hurricane..."

"We couldn't watch TV. I'm so glad the power came back on. I missed watching Bluey."

"I'm glad it came back, too. Remember how the storm was so loud and the wind was so strong?"

Ashleigh nodded. "It was scary."

"I have to tell you something about the storm that will be hard to hear."

Her little dark brows knitted in confusion as Tiffany's heart shattered into a million pieces.

"What is it?"

"Since the storm ended, honey, no one has heard from your daddy. They've been looking for him and his friend Billy."

"Billy from the gym?"

"Yes, that's him."

"He gives me candy when Daddy takes me to the gym."

"The Coast Guard and the fire department have been looking for them since the storm ended, and today, we heard that they've found your daddy."

"Can he come home now?"

Tiffany shook her head as tears spilled down her cheeks. "He's gone to heaven, honey."

Ashleigh's little chin began to tremble. "Like Kyle and Jackson's mommy?"

"Yes."

"But their mommy won't ever come back. I don't want my daddy to go to heaven."

"I know, baby. I don't either."

"Daddy wouldn't leave me," she said, sobbing. "He'd never leave me."

Tears ran down Tiffany's face. "No, he wouldn't, but sometimes things happen that we can't help."

"Like a hurry-cane?"

"Yes, baby, just like that. The storm was so powerful."

"It made the house shake."

"That's right."

Ashleigh looked up at Blaine, who also had tears in his eyes. "I want Daddy to come home."

"I'd do anything to make that happen for you, sugar," Blaine said. "Anything in this world."

Tiffany wiped the tears off Ashleigh's face. "We wanted that more than anything."

"Even though you were mad at Daddy?"

Tiffany was momentarily speechless by Ashleigh's insight. Of course she'd known that. How could she not? "Your daddy and I had our differences, but I'd never want anything bad to happen to him. I know how much you love him, and no matter what, you'll always love him, and he'll always love you. He used to say you're the best thing in his whole life, just like you are in mine."

"Addie is, too."

"Yes, both of you."

"We're so sorry to have had to tell you this news, honey," Blaine said. "If you want to talk about anything any time, you can come to your mom or me. We're right here for you."

"I know. Thank you. I think I'd like to play with my toys now."

"Okay." Tiffany helped her get down.

They stayed for a few minutes, keeping watch over her.

Tiffany wished she could know what Ashleigh was thinking or whether she'd truly understood what they'd told her. Only time would tell on both of those things.

She tipped her head to tell Blaine that she felt like it was okay to leave the room. She knew Ashleigh would come find them when she was ready to talk. For now, she decided to let her daughter lead the way through this nightmare.

In the hallway, she turned to him and held on tight to his love and support.

"You were great with her, babe."

"So were you."

"We'll get her through this."

"I'm so glad you're here with us."

"There's nowhere else I'd ever want to be."

McKenzie carried Jax next door to meet the insurance adjuster, a man named Rob Kelly, who'd come from the mainland to view the damage to her place and several others.

He was about sixty, with thinning gray hair and a friendly smile.

"Ms. Martin?"

"Yes, that's me." She shook his outstretched hand. "I'm McKenzie, and this is Jax."

"Nice to meet you both. Sorry for what happened to your home."

McKenzie still found it difficult to look at the splintered remains of the cabin. "Me, too. I inherited it from my grandmother. We had a lot of good times here."

"I'm sure you will again. Easy enough to justify declaring it a total loss. It was fully insured along with clauses for replacing furnishings and personal possessions up to fifty thousand."

"Oh wow. I had no idea." Her mind raced as she imagined the shopping she could do for herself and Jax to replace the items they'd lost. They wouldn't need anywhere close to fifty thousand dollars' worth, but she could only imagine what it cost to get items such as furniture and appliances shipped to the island. It would be fun to pick out new things and design the house to her taste.

"I met your grandmother once when she came into the office. She left nothing to chance."

"Maybe she knew that someday her careful planning would make all the difference for me."

"Possibly. You'll be able to build to your specs and have everything you need. Let me just get some pictures for the file. Have you spoken to a contractor?"

"Yes, Mac McCarthy."

"He's great. We've worked with him before. I'll get this expedited for you. I'm sure you want to get settled back into your home with the little guy as soon as possible."

"That'd be wonderful. Thank you."

"No problem."

He photographed the pile of rubble from every angle, took some measurements and made notes on an iPad. Then he handed her his card and typed in her email address. "I'll send over your estimate and authorization to proceed with repairs to you and Mac later today or tomorrow morning at the latest."

"I really appreciate you coming over and taking care of this so quickly."

"My pleasure. Hope you two are settled back in your home again very soon."

After Mr. Kelly left, McKenzie walked back along the path toward Duke's just as he pulled into the drive on a gigantic motorcycle that was so loud, Jax whimpered from the noise.

McKenzie covered his ears. "It's okay, sweetie."

As Duke cut the engine, she noticed he wore black leather pants and a matching vest that put his colorful, muscular arms on full display. His long hair was held back in a ponytail. Holy hotness. The biker type had never done it for her until now.

"Sorry about that. Did I scare him?"

"A little, but he's fine. Where did that thing come from?"

He grinned at her use of the word *thing* to describe his bike. "The garage. Surprised you didn't hear me leave earlier."

"I heard something, but I thought it was out on the road."

"That'd be me, making a ruckus everywhere I go on this *thing*."

"Where's your helmet?"

"Oh damn, I knew I forgot something."

"Don't tell me you ride that beast without one."

"Okay, I won't."

"Duke! That's not safe!"

"It's fine. I don't go far. Just a couple of laps around the island to take in the scenery."

"Don't you know that the worst accidents happen within a mile of home?"

He got off the bike. "Been doing it for years. Never came close to having an accident."

"Yet."

"Aw, are you worried about me?"

"What if I am?"

"That's very nice of you, but there's no need to worry. I'm super careful."

"I'm sure you are, but you told me yourself that people drive crazy on the winding island roads. You don't want me walking on them with Jax. I don't want you driving that monster of a motorcycle on them without a helmet."

He gave her a side-eyed look that was equal parts amusement and aggravation. "If I agree to wear a helmet, do you promise to never walk into town?"

"Fine. I promise. You'll start wearing the helmet immediately?"

"Yes, ma'am."

"Do you even own one?"

"I've got one kicking around here somewhere."

"Find it."

He grinned as he came over to tweak Jax's bare foot, making the baby giggle. "Better watch out, pal. Your bossy mom is gonna be a big problem when you're a teenager."

"That's right, and he'll toe the line or else."

Duke's laughter made his eyes twinkle. "Hope I'm around to see that."

"Where else would you be?"

"Nowhere. I wouldn't be anywhere else."

CHAPTER 14

*A*dam McCarthy was having trouble breathing as he stood outside the cubicle while David and Victoria tended to Abby.

They'd begun an IV that was intended to stop her early labor, but what if it didn't work?

Twenty-two weeks was a long way from viability.

Could the babies survive at that age? A quick web search had answered the question he didn't want to ask in front of Abby when she was trying so hard to remain calm. Yes, the babies could survive, but it would be a roller-coaster ride of probably months in the neonatal intensive care unit with no guarantee of a happy ending. It was also possible that the babies could endure life-long challenges as a result of their early births.

He struggled to hold back the anger that threatened to boil over. She'd been through so much already. How much more could she endure before she cracked under the weight of despair?

At first, the news they were expecting quads hit like a tsunami, overwhelming them with the implications of having *five* sons under the age of two. But over time, they'd begun to excitedly anticipate the babies' arrival. The pregnancy had been rough on Abby, and it'd been getting more difficult with every passing day. But she'd been determined to see it through, to get the babies to the latest point she possibly could.

He'd never loved or admired her more as he watched her soldier through, despite her increasing discomfort as the babies grew.

If they lost them, he wasn't sure how they'd go on.

David came to the door. "A word in private?"

Adam glanced at the man who would've been his brother-in-law once upon a time. Now he was a trusted friend who'd saved the lives of several people Adam loved, including his sister Janey and her son, PJ. He nodded in response to David's question and followed him and Victoria into David's office, closing the door behind them.

David glanced at Victoria.

"We want to be straight with you," she said.

"I wouldn't want anything else."

"We were able to stop the labor. For now. But the situation is precarious. We want to get her to Women and Infants in Providence as soon as possible. It's very likely they'll admit her for the duration of her pregnancy."

Adam felt like the breath had been knocked out of him as he processed what Vic was saying. "She's got eighteen weeks to go."

"I know, Adam, but this just became an even higher-risk pregnancy than it already was, and we want her carefully observed. The longer we can keep the babies in utero, the better the chances are that they all survive without complications."

Adam ran a hand through his hair as frustration and despair overtook him. "How soon do you want to transfer her?"

"Immediately. We wanted to talk to you—and then to her—before we call for a Life Flight."

His heart sank as it became clear the situation was far more serious than he'd thought—and that their lives would be upended for the foreseeable future. "Yeah, okay. Let's talk to her." He glanced at David. "Could I borrow your car to run home to grab a few things?"

David nodded. "Of course."

They walked together to Abby's room.

Her eyes were closed, but opened when she heard them come in.

Adam forced a smile for her. "How're you feeling, hon?"

"Better. The pain has stopped."

"That's good news. David and Vic want to talk to us about what happens next."

Abby's gaze shifted toward Victoria. "Are the babies okay?"

"They're doing great," Victoria said, "but the early labor has me concerned enough that I'd like to get you to Women and Infants as soon as possible so you have the highest-level of care going forward."

"Oh." She looked at Adam and then back to Vic and David. "So, like I have to go there now?"

"That'd be our recommendation."

"We'd have to get Liam and get a car on the boat and..."

"We'd call a chopper for you."

Her entire body became tense as the implications of that registered with her. The words *Life Flight* were synonymous with *emergency* to the island's residents. "Is it... I mean, it's that serious?"

"You and the babies are stable right now," Victoria said. "We want to keep you that way, and to do that, we need to get you to Providence as soon as possible."

Abby's chin quivered as she listened to Vic. Then she looked to Adam for his take.

"I think we should do what Vic and David are advising and get to Providence right away."

"Wh-what about Liam?"

"My mom will keep him for as long as we need her to, and they'll bring him to us when you're ready for visitors."

"I... I don't want to be away from him."

"Neither do I, but he'll be very well cared for while we're gone."

"He'll be scared if we just disappear."

"We won't disappear. We'll FaceTime him later. Vic will call for the chopper. I'll run home and get some clothes for both of us and be back before it gets here. All right?"

She nodded as she wiped away tears.

He leaned over the bed rail to kiss her. "Everything will be okay. I promise."

"You can't promise that."

"I can promise we'll do everything we can to make it so." Adam kissed her one more time. "I'll be right back."

"Okay."

To Vic and David, he said, "I need fifteen minutes."

David handed him his keys. "Sounds good."

Adam ran out of the clinic and called his mother as he drove David's car faster than he should've.

"Hi, honey. How's Abby?"

"She went into early labor, which they were able to stop with meds. Vic and David want her in Providence right away. They're calling for Life Flight."

"Oh my goodness. Adam…"

"I know."

"How's she taking it?"

"She's worried about Liam."

"We'll keep him with us for as long as you need us to."

"I was hoping you'd say that."

"Of course we will."

"If it's easier for you to stay with him at our house, make yourselves at home."

"I'll talk to Dad about it, but don't worry about anything."

"I don't know how this'll go, Mom." His voice broke a little. "If something happens to her or the babies…"

"She's going to the best possible place to ensure that nothing happens. I know it's so hard not to think the worst, but don't do that. You must stay positive for her."

"You're right."

"What else can we do for you?"

"Pray?"

"Already doing that, honey. Keep me posted?"

"I will. I'm running home now to get some clothes for both of us and then going right back to fly over with her."

"We love you both, and we'll take very good care of your sweet little boy. Don't worry about a thing. He's having a great time with his cousins."

"Glad to hear it. We'll call him later, so he doesn't worry about us."

"That'd be great. Are you all right, Adam?"

"As long as she and the babies are, I am, too. I'll check in as soon as I can."

"We'll be here."

"Love you, Mom."

"Love you, too. Please give Abby all our love."

"I will."

After ending the call, Adam used his sleeve to wipe away tears as he rounded the last corner before his driveway. He ran into the house and up the stairs to grab a bag that he filled with essentials for both of them, including toothbrushes, his laptop so he could attempt to do some work and the maternity clothes Abby had been living in lately. Whatever else they needed he'd get on the mainland.

He was on the way back to the clinic three minutes after he entered the house.

As he drove, he thought about the shock of learning they'd conceived quads naturally after being told that Abby's chances of conceiving at all were low due to the PCOS.

That they could lose their miracle babies was impossible to fathom.

He'd set his heart on those four little boys, and Abby had gone through so much to get past the halfway point of her pregnancy. It couldn't end like this.

It just couldn't.

She'd never survive it. *They'd* never survive it.

Adam had to get himself together so he could be strong for her.

"Whatever she needs. That's all that matters."

He pulled into the parking lot of the clinic as the helicopter appeared overhead. The last time he'd seen that chopper had been when Maddie went into labor with the twins during Mallory's wedding.

This time, his wife and babies were the ones in trouble.

Panic threatened to consume him as he ran inside before the helicopter touched down in the parking lot. He was relieved to find Abby right where he'd left her. Big brown eyes gazed at him with the same fear he felt. "Ready to go for a ride, honey?"

"As ready as I'll ever be. Did you talk to your mom?"

"Yes, and she's happy to have Liam for as long as we need her and Dad to watch him."

"It feels so wrong to leave him here."

"He'll be fine. Mom said he's having a great time with the kids. She said not to worry about anything."

The Life Flight crew came into the clinic to collect Abby, who was transported on a rolling gurney along with the IV that Victoria had started.

David and Vic consulted with the chief EMT while the others got Abby settled inside the helicopter.

"You can sit right there," one of them said to Adam.

At any other time, he would've enjoyed the helicopter ride. But there was nothing cool about this. As they lifted off, he was terrified of where this journey might take them.

While he watched the island disappear from sight, he prayed they'd return with four healthy baby boys.

MCKENZIE WORE an olive-green tank top and cut-off denim shorts that put miles of creamy white skin on display that made Duke want to swallow his tongue. He'd love to put the most stunning flowers on her gorgeous skin, not that she needed any enhancements. But he couldn't look at skin like hers and not dream of the art he could create on such a perfect canvas.

And then she smiled.

Was it possible to swallow a tongue?

They hadn't gotten around to her looking at his QuickBooks yet, but she'd promised to do it as soon as she could. She'd spent the afternoon completing a questionnaire Mac had dropped off to outline her wishes for the cabin reconstruction.

Her dark hair was piled on top of her head, and she'd done something with her brown eyes that made them stand out even more than they usually did.

She was drop-dead gorgeous, and he was suddenly concerned about taking her to an event where she'd meet other guys better suited for someone like her than he'd ever be.

"Duke? Is everything all right?"

"Uh, yeah, all good."

"Are you sure you want us to go with you? Wouldn't you rather hang with your friends without having to worry about us?"

"No, not at all. I want you to come. If you're up for it, that is."

"I'd love to."

"All right, then."

"All right, then. You're sure you're okay?"

He was about to say what she wanted to hear so they could get on with their outing, but when he opened his mouth, the truth came spilling out. "I was okay until I saw you all..." He waved his hand in her direction. "You look beautiful, and you took my breath away for a second. Or two."

She stared at him long enough that he wasn't sure if he'd made a huge mistake telling her the truth. "That's very sweet of you to say."

"It's the truth. You're gorgeous, and the last thing I want to do is prove your mother right about anything..."

She came over to him and placed a hand on his chest.

Her touching him that way nearly stopped his heart.

Then she went a step further by going up on tiptoes to kiss his cheek. "You're nothing like the kind of men my mother described, and for what it's worth, I think you're rather beautiful yourself."

He snorted with laughter and embarrassment. "Sure, I am. I'm a freaking wildebeest next to you."

"You're beautiful inside and out, and I don't want you saying mean things about my friend Duke. Do you hear me?"

"Yes, ma'am."

Her smile... Goddamn if it didn't turn him inside out, especially when she directed the full force of it in his direction.

While she gathered sweatshirts for herself and Jax, he stood perfectly still, overwhelmed by the last five minutes in which it seemed like everything in his life had changed for the better. She thought he was beautiful—inside and out. What did that mean? How should he proceed from here?

He felt less certain of himself with her than he had with any other woman he'd ever spent time with. He'd had his share of girlfriends, dates and hookups, but no other woman had ever left him as dazzled as she did, even the one he'd thought he might marry.

As he carried Jax in his car seat down the stairs to the truck, he was as tongue-tied and flummoxed as he'd been in years. His heart hammered in his chest, his mouth had gone dry, and his palms were sweaty.

Christ have mercy. He was a grown man in the throes of the deepest crush of his life, and if he wasn't careful, he'd scare her away by being a weirdo.

While she secured Jax to the base of the child seat, he got in the driver's side to wait for her to be ready to go.

They pulled out of the driveway and headed for North Harbor.

After a couple of miles passed in silence, he felt her looking at him. "What?"

"Is everything going to be different now?"

He glanced over at her. It was a lot like looking directly into the sun. "What do you mean?"

"You said nice things about me. I said them about you. Does that change everything?"

"What if it did?"

"I'd be sad if we were awkward with each other. I thought we were becoming friends."

"We are friends. I don't want to mess that up any more than you do, but I can't help that when I look at you, I just..."

"What?" she asked, sounding as breathless as he felt.

He tightened his grip on the steering wheel. "It's important to me that I not take advantage of your need for the apartment or our proximity or anything that would be inappropriate."

"That's the last thing you could ever be."

"How do you know that?"

"I just do. That's not how you roll. You're a gentleman, or my grandmother wouldn't have given you the time of day."

"Oh, well... I was kinda rough around the edges when she met me."

"You're not anymore."

"Sometimes I am."

"Well, I haven't seen that. I've seen a kind, generous, sweet man who helps people without expecting anything in return other than friendship. I see someone who goes out of his way for me, which is something I've never had before."

"I like helping you."

"I know you do, and that makes you the sweetest man I've ever known."

He scowled. "I'm not sweet. Quit saying that shit."

"It's the truth, so don't be grumpy about it."

"You're supposed to think I'm tough and intimidating."

"Oh, didn't realize that. Sorry." Under her breath, she added, "Not sorry."

"I heard that."

Her laughter was almost as captivating as her smile.

"The mood's apt to be a bit somber tonight. Heard they found Jim Sturgil's body."

"Oh no. That's so sad. Poor Tiffany and Ashleigh. And his parents..."

"I know. He could be an SOB, but you'd never wish something like this on him."

"No, never. Even Tiffany said that." McKenzie pulled out her phone. "I texted her to tell her how sorry I am about the news and to let me know what I can do for her this week."

"I'm sure she'll appreciate the support. She may even be there tonight."

"I feel so bad for her. What a tough thing to see a child through."

"For sure. But she and Blaine are a strong couple. They'll love her through it."

"Love her through it. What a sweet way to put it."

"Cut it out with that sweet crap."

McKenzie laughed. "Sorry, but I only speak the truth."

"Maybe I should finally get some tats on my face to make me look tougher."

"Even if you do that, I'll still think you're sweet."

"Damn it. Clearly, I've played this all wrong."

"From where I'm sitting, it seems like you've played it all right."

"You really think so?"

"Uh-huh."

"So, like, if I was to say, 'Hey, McKenzie, you want to go out to dinner with me sometime?' you might actually say yes?"

"Ask me and find out."

"Oh, um, so, like... I should ask you now?"

"Were you doing something else?"

He gave her a side-eyed look. "You're enjoying this, aren't you?"

"Very much so. Aren't you?"

"Not as much as you are."

That only made her laugh harder.

"Keep laughing at me, and I might not ask you anything."

"You will."

If only he still couldn't feel the exact spot where she'd kissed his cheek. He would never wash that spot again. *Now you're just being ridiculous.* That might be true, but not even his internal narrator could ruin the euphoria of realizing that she liked him as much as he liked her and if he asked her out, she'd say yes.

Since they were approaching the marina, he decided to save that question for later.

When they were out of the truck, he took the baby seat from her and carried it toward the pier, where a crowd had gathered inside the restaurant and around the picnic tables outside.

Evan McCarthy and Owen Lawry were seated on stools outside with their guitars.

"You're in for a treat. Those two are great together."

"Who are they?"

"Evan McCarthy and Owen Lawry."

"Evan McCarthy who sings 'My Amazing Grace'?"

"Yep, that's him. His folks own the marina."

"I had no idea! I love that song. I saw him with Buddy Longstreet and Taylor Jones last summer."

"He's become a big deal over the last few years, but he still pops in to play here any time he's home."

"Wow. You never know who you're going to meet on Gansett Island."

"That's very true." Duke hoped with everything he had that she didn't meet someone she liked better than him.

CHAPTER 15

*E*ver since Duke had arrived at her door and said the things he did about her, McKenzie felt like her insides were made of champagne bubbles or something equally silly. Everything had changed during those two minutes. If someone had told her that might happen, she would've said there was no way she wanted that. But after having experienced it, she couldn't deny the euphoria he'd stirred or the feelings she had for him.

Or that he apparently had for her.

What a delightful and unexpected development.

Gran used to tell her that when people showed you who they really were, you should believe them. Usually, she meant that in the negative sense. Such as when someone showed you they were an asshole, don't go around thinking you were the one who could change them or make them better. "People are who they are," Gran would say.

Duke had shown her repeatedly who he really was, from checking on her after the storm to retrieving some of her belongings from the cabin, to making a special trip to Tiffany's to bring Mr. Bear to Jax, after having cleaned him up, to offering her a place to stay, to putting her in touch with Mac. He'd been rock solid and respectful and all the things that Gran had told her to look for in a man.

And he was flat-out adorable, regardless of his desire to be seen as menacing. Despite his tough exterior, he was a mush on the inside, and she liked that about him.

As they approached the group outside the marina restaurant, Duke introduced her to Alex and Jenny Martinez and their son, George.

"What a cutie," McKenzie said of George, who was in his father's arms. The baby was the picture of his dark-haired daddy. "How old is he?"

"He's two going on twenty," his mom said. "How old is Jax?"

"Nine months and soon to be too big for the baby carrier."

"I miss that thing." Jenny tucked blonde hair behind her ear. "George is a load to carry around when he refuses to use his feet for what they were made for."

They were joined by Alex's brother, Paul, his wife, Hope, and their daughter, Scarlett.

McKenzie was introduced to so many people that her head began to swim with names and faces. They enjoyed a delicious buffet dinner that included clam chowder and other seafood dishes, delicious roast beef, salads of all kinds and yummy desserts.

McKenzie was delighted to meet so many young children, who might become friends with Jax. How nice would that be?

Duke introduced her to everyone, helped her find a seat at a table and got her a plastic cup of ice water. "You want a drink drink?"

"No, thank you. I'm not back to drinking yet." She could tell he didn't understand what she meant. "I'm still feeding Jax. What I get, he gets."

"*Oh*, right," he said, adorably flustered. "Don't laugh at me."

Her lips quivered from the effort to hold it back. "I never would."

"That's a lie, and you know it."

McKenzie was trying not to laugh when she looked up and saw Tiffany, Blaine, Ashleigh and Addie outside. "They did come."

Duke turned to see who she was talking about. "Oh good. I'm glad. It'll do them good to be with their people."

Everyone wanted to hug Tiffany and Ashleigh.

McKenzie waited patiently for her new friend to greet the others before she, Duke and Jax went to say hello.

"I'm so sorry." McKenzie and Duke hugged Tiffany and then Ashleigh. "I wish there was something else I could say."

"It's okay." Tiffany's eyes and face were red and puffy from crying. "Ash wanted to come to see everyone, and we're following her lead."

"I'm glad you came. What can I do for you this week?"

"I'm going to keep the store closed for a few more days. Sorry for the delay in getting you started."

"Don't be. Do whatever you need to right now."

"Thank you for understanding. Strangest thing I've ever been through, that's for sure."

"I can only imagine."

"I was thinking about what you told me last week about Jax's father. I promised to call Dan for you."

"Oh please, Tiffany. Don't worry about that now."

"I am worried about it. Dan has gone to Maine with his wife, Kara. I'm not sure how long they'll be gone. He was the one I wanted to talk to about your situation. I texted him about it and to tell him about Jim. He told me that Jared James's attorney sister Kendall is on the island, and you might be able to talk to her."

"There's Jared right there," Duke said. "I bet that's his sister with him."

"I'll find out," Tiffany said.

She was gone before McKenzie could tell her again not to worry about her problems when she had more than enough of her own to contend with.

"It helps her," Duke said. "To focus on your thing rather than hers."

"What're you, a mind reader now, too?"

Grinning, he shrugged. "I figured that's what you were thinking."

"You figured right. I told her about his dad saying he'd had a vasectomy so Jax couldn't have been his, even though he knew full well I hadn't been with anyone else."

"Is it okay to say I can't stand that guy?"

"More than okay. Tiffany said his bullshit doesn't excuse him from his obligation to care for Jax, and she wanted me to talk to her friend Dan about it."

"She's right. You should talk to someone about it. Dan's a great lawyer, but I'm sure Kendall is, too."

"I'm afraid of stirring that hornet's nest."

"Don't be. You haven't done anything wrong. I hate when people don't care for their kids, who never asked to be born."

"I'm sorry if that strikes a nerve."

"One of those things I try not to think about."

She gazed up at him, wishing she could take away all the hurt he'd experienced in his life, which was a truly overwhelming thought to have about someone she hadn't known all that long. "I understand."

"Talk to the lawyer. You and Jax deserve the best of everything. Why should you have to struggle while he pretends he wasn't there when that little guy came to be?"

"Thank you for the support."

"Of course."

"So wait... You said that's Jared James, as in Jared James the billionaire?"

"The one and only. Nicest guy you'll ever meet. We love him around here."

"Wow, music stars and billionaires."

"We like to keep things interesting on Gansett. You know Jordan Stokes?"

"As in Jordan and Gigi?"

"One and the same. She's engaged to and expecting a baby with our fire chief, Mason Johns, and Gigi's madly in love with the billionaire's brother Cooper. They filmed a season of their show here. Should be on TV soon."

"Stop it. No way."

"Way."

"I love them. They're so funny. How did they end up here?"

"Jordan's grandmother has owned a house here for like fifty years. She and her twin sister, Nikki, who's engaged to Riley McCarthy, spent summers here when they were kids."

"Ah, I see."

Tiffany returned with another woman, who was probably in her early forties. She had reddish-brown hair and brown eyes.

"Kendall James, meet McKenzie Martin."

McKenzie shook hands with the other woman. "Nice to meet you."

"You as well."

"This is my friend, Duke Sullivan."

Duke shook hands with Kendall. "Nice to meet another James sibling."

"I'm the classy one of the bunch."

Duke and McKenzie laughed.

"I understand you're in need of some legal assistance."

McKenzie looked at Duke, who nodded in encouragement. "Yes, I am, but I don't want to bother you at a party."

"It's no bother. My brother and his wife are entertaining my sons, so this is as good a time as any."

"Let me take Jax and show him the boats," Duke said.

"Are you sure you don't mind?"

"I'm sure."

After Duke walked away with Jax in his arms, McKenzie sat next to Kendall. "Thank you for this."

"It's no problem. I'm planning to work from here, anyway. I'm the general counsel for my brother's business, which is mostly on paper these days. So I have time for other stuff. Tell me what's going on."

"Well, there was this guy..."

"Why does it always start that way?" Kendall asked, smiling.

"Right? This one was charming and said all the right things. We were together for a year. I thought he might be the one, only to find out he was married with two kids. I found that out after I told him I was pregnant. Then he said he'd had a vasectomy, so there's no way my baby was his." McKenzie couldn't believe that she could still be so outraged after all this time. "That was a lie. I hadn't been with anyone but him, and he knew it."

"Ugh, what an asshole."

"Totally. Part of me wants to leave it alone, but the other part, the one that's struggled to make ends meet and pay for everything Jax needs, wants to make him do his part."

"I understand that. Better than you might think. I have to warn you, though, it could get ugly. There's probably a good chance his wife doesn't know about you or Jax, and once she finds out, the shit will hit the fan for him. He's apt to turn that around on you."

McKenzie swallowed the lump of fear that landed in her throat. "I'm not afraid of him," she said with more conviction than she felt. "And I'm one hundred percent over him. The minute he lied and said he'd had a vasectomy, I knew he'd never been the person I thought he was."

"Takes a special kind of guy to be that kind of deceitful. You may be doing his wife and kids a favor to blow the lid off his game."

"I feel bad about the possibility of hurting innocent people, but I want Jax to have everything he needs. That would be a lot easier with financial help from his father."

"You're owed that by law. Let's remind him of that, shall we?"

"Yes, please."

Kendall withdrew her phone from her purse. "Give me your number." She punched it into her phone as McKenzie recited it. "Tomorrow, I'll reach out to get his name and anything else you know about where we might find him, such as an office or somewhere he might be during the day. I'll put together a letter that I'll run by you and then have delivered to him by certified mail. That'll get his attention. He may propose a settlement that'll allow him to keep you and Jax a secret from his wife. I've heard of that happening in cases like this."

"I suppose it might be for the best if it worked out that way."

"We'll see what happens. I'll reach out tomorrow about the letter, and we'll go from there."

"Let me know how much I owe you."

"We'll worry about that if we're successful. I'll send you a retainer letter by email and will be in touch."

"Thank you so much."

"Happy to help if I can." She stood to rejoin her family. "More to come. It was nice to meet you."

"You, too."

A few minutes after Kendall had left the table, Duke returned with Jax. "How'd it go?"

"Great. She's going to work on a letter to send him."

"That's good news. Sometimes all it takes to get someone's attention is a letter from a lawyer."

"Tiffany said the same thing the first time we talked about this."

"How do you feel about it?"

"Kind of nervous. I hope it doesn't get ugly."

"If it does, he won't have any idea where to find you."

"That's true."

"Try not to worry. You're doing the right thing for Jax by forcing him to step up. It's the very least he can do."

They were joined by Sierra and some of her colleagues from the massage studio, whom she introduced to McKenzie and Jax.

Like before, McKenzie had the same odd reaction to the sexy woman who was obviously close to Duke. She'd never been big on jealousy, as it seemed like a waste of time to want what other people had. But there was no way she could deny that Sierra got to her the way no other woman ever had.

It was so weird to be experiencing a brand-new emotion as she watched Duke chat with his friends.

Sierra was perfectly nice and friendly to everyone, so McKenzie couldn't explain her reaction to the other woman.

"Are you okay?" Duke asked McKenzie.

"Yes, of course."

"Where are you from, McKenzie?" Sierra asked.

"Coventry. It's up by Providence."

"Oh, I know. I grew up in North Kingstown."

"Ah, okay. We probably played each other in sports."

"Maybe. I did basketball and lacrosse. How about you?"

"Soccer."

"I bet you were good at that," Duke said.

"I did okay." When Jax started to get fussy, she put some new toys on the table for him.

Duke stood to greet an older couple with a handshake for the man and a hug for the woman. "Big Mac and Linda McCarthy, meet McKenzie Martin, Rosemary's granddaughter, and her son, Jax."

McKenzie, who'd also stood, was surprised when Linda hugged her.

"It's so lovely to meet you. MK, right?"

"That's me."

"Rosemary talked about you all the time. You were the light of her life."

"Thank you for telling me that."

"Of course. She'd be delighted to know you're here."

"I hope so. She'd be upset about the cabin, though."

"That can be fixed. I understand you've spoken to our Mac about that."

"I have, and he's wonderful."

"He'd better be."

"He'll fix you right up," Big Mac added.

"Everyone has been so nice and helpful here, especially Duke. He's given us a place to stay while the cabin is repaired."

"Duke's one of the good guys," Big Mac said with a warm smile for Duke. "We love him around here."

"Aw shucks," Duke said, seeming embarrassed.

"I only speak the truth."

"Heard they took Abby to the mainland today," Duke said. "Any word on how she's doing?"

"She and the babies are stable and in the best place they could be right now."

"I'm so glad to hear that."

"We've got their Liam for the time being," Linda said. "He's with our daughters-in-law Grace and Stephanie. We should probably rescue them. It was such a pleasure to meet you, McKenzie and Jax."

"You, too. My grandmother spoke so highly of you and your family. Now I see why."

"We live in that white house at the top of the hill." Linda pointed to it. "If you ever need anything, our door is always open."

"Thank you so much."

They returned to their seats at the table.

"Such nice people," McKenzie said.

"They're the backbone of this island."

"So Abby is their daughter?"

"Daughter-in-law. She's expecting quads and went into early labor. They sent her to the mainland by Life Flight."

"Oh wow. Quads. Gulp."

"I know. From what I heard, it came as a huge shock to them. They'd been told they wouldn't be able to have babies, and then pow."

"Yikes. I sure hope they're okay."

"You and me both."

CHAPTER 16

*W*ith Abby settled into her room and attached to a bunch of monitors, all of which indicated she and the babies were doing well, Adam finally exhaled after the long, stressful day.

Since the Lawrys were staying at his uncle Frank's house, Adam had booked a room at a nearby hotel. But he was reluctant to leave Abby alone in the hospital.

They were still waiting for the neonatal specialist to come by to check in with them. After that, he'd think about going to get some sleep. He knew he had to pace himself to support her over the finish line of a complicated pregnancy. Burning himself out now wouldn't help anyone, but he'd more or less accepted the state of hypervigilance he'd fallen into weeks ago as her pregnancy became more difficult by the day.

"How're you feeling, hon?" he asked her.

"As fine as I was when you asked me that ten minutes ago."

"Sorry."

"Don't be. I know it's super stressful for you."

"It's not about me. It's about whatever you and the boys need."

"It's about all of us, and it's okay to admit you're stressed. Anyone would be after the day we've had."

"I'm definitely stressed, but I'm so glad you're here where you can get the best possible care."

Abby's chin quivered. "I miss Liam."

"I do, too. I keep looking around for him."

"Do you think we could call him?"

"Sure. My parents were at the marina earlier, but they should be home by now." Adam put through the FaceTime call.

Liam's little face filled the screen. "Dada!"

"Hey, buddy. It's me and Mommy. We wanted to say good night."

"Home."

"Soon. We'll be home soon. Are you being a good boy for Grammy and Pop?"

"Pop!"

"Pop is his favorite," Linda said with a smile.

"Pop is everyone's favorite," Adam said.

"Indeed. How's the patient?"

Adam shifted the phone so his mother could see Abby.

She gave a little wave. "Hanging in there. The babies are busy, so that's a good sign."

"Indeed it is. We're so proud of you, Abby. You're doing great."

"Thank you. That means a lot."

"Is Liam still there?" Adam asked.

"Liam, come say good night to Mommy and Daddy."

He let out a squeal and nearly knocked the phone out of Linda's hand.

"Easy, buddy."

"Easy."

"That's right," Adam said. "Be gentle with Grammy. We'll talk to you tomorrow, okay? Sleep tight."

"K."

"Love you so much."

"Love."

Adam and Abby made kissing noises.

Liam kissed the phone.

Big Mac took it from him. "How're you kids holding up?"

"We're doing okay," Adam said. "We miss our buddy."

"He had a great day full of cousins. Try not to worry."

"We know he's in good hands with you guys."

"We love you both. We'll talk to you in the morning."

"We love you, too." Adam ended the call and sat on the edge of Abby's bed, taking her hand.

"I miss Liam so much," Abby said. "How will we spend weeks here when he's on the island?"

"Mom and Dad will bring him over, and we'll figure something out. There's no way we'll be without him for weeks."

"I couldn't do it. I'd go mad."

"So would I. Don't worry about anything, sweetheart. I'll take care of it."

"What would I do without you?"

"You'll never have to find out."

Fifteen minutes later, the specialist came in, apologizing for making them wait. Wearing light blue scrubs, she was tall and pretty, with light brown skin and long, curly hair that was contained in a ponytail. "I'm Dr. Isabella Connors, but you should call me Izzy. We'll be seeing a lot of each other."

"I'm Adam McCarthy, and this is my wife, Abby."

She shook their hands and then took a seat on the other side of Abby's bed. "I've reviewed everything that happened today. Your doctors on Gansett did a great job, and things are looking much better tonight. How're you feeling, Abby?"

"Tired, but relieved that the medication worked to stop the labor."

"Me, too. The babies look great. I saw that you're expecting two sets of identical twins?"

"That's what we were told."

"They're my first quads. Were you told how rare it is to have two sets of identical twins?"

"We were," Abby said. "And how rare it is to conceive quads without fertility treatment, especially with PCOS."

"You're a special case, my friend, and I'm going to do everything I can to get you and your boys over the finish line."

"We're wondering what's going to happen now," Adam said as he clung to Abby's hand.

"I'd like to keep you as our guest until the babies come." She quickly added, "I know that's not what you wanted to hear, but I think it's for the best. While I'm giving you the bad news, I'd also like you to be on complete bed rest for the remainder of your pregnancy."

Abby teared up.

Adam couldn't get past the words *complete bed rest.*

"I'm so sorry to have to do this, but if we can just eke out ten to twelve more weeks with the boys inside, it'll greatly reduce the potential for challenges after they arrive. While they continue to grow, we can give you meds that'll strengthen their lungs so they're ready for life on the outside."

Ten to twelve weeks of complete bed rest. Possibly longer. Dear God.

"I... Of course I want to do what's best for the babies." Abby used the tissue Adam handed her to wipe up tears. "We have a young son at home..."

"We'll bring him here to be with us," Adam said.

"That'd be great," Izzy said. "Whatever it takes to get his mom and brothers to the finish line."

"We can do this, Abs. I'll be right there with you the whole way. Your family will come over and my parents. We'll have tons of visitors. We'll get you through."

Abby nodded as she continued to mop up tears. "Can I get up to shower?"

"Every other day for a few minutes."

"I have to pee constantly."

"The nurses will help with that."

As Abby groaned, Adam's heart went out to her. This was going to be one hell of an ordeal for her. He'd go mad if he had to spend months confined to a bed. How would she bear it?

"I'll check on you guys tomorrow." Izzy placed a business card on Abby's table. "That's got my cell number and pager info. Call me any time you need me. We're in this together now, and I'll do everything I can to send you home with four precious baby boys."

"Thank you," Abby said.

"You got it. Sleep well."

"She seems great," Adam said after the doctor left.

"Yeah, she's so nice and upbeat. But, Adam… ten or more *weeks* or more of full bed rest… My God, how will I do that?"

"We'll do it one day at a time. I'll be right here with you."

"My store and the house and Liam…"

"I'll take care of everything. You won't have to worry about a thing."

"If you bring him here, you'll have to take care of him by yourself."

"That's no problem."

"How will you work?"

"At night after he's in bed. I'll make it happen. I don't want you to worry about anything other than taking care of yourself and those babies. That's your only job."

"I'm so thankful they were able to stop the labor and that the babies are okay… But the thought of what's ahead is overwhelming."

"I know, honey, but you're the toughest person I've ever met. I have no doubt you'll slay bed rest and deliver these babies when they're good and strong."

"What if we don't make it to good and strong?"

"We'll cross every bridge if we come to it. There's no sense worrying about things that might not happen."

"Do you think you could snuggle with me for a minute?"

"I'd love to." Adam moved carefully so he wouldn't jostle any of the monitors she was attached to as he curled up to her and put his arm around her. "How's that?"

"Much better."

"I'm available for bed rest snuggling on demand."

"That's good. I'm going to need a lot of it."

"I got you, babe. Whatever you need."

"Be careful what you wish for, huh?"

Adam grunted out a laugh. "That needs to be our family motto."

"For sure."

"Tell me you know that we've got this, and we'll get through it, and everything will be fine."

"We've got this. We'll get through it. Everything will be fine."

"That's the way."

DUKE WAS quiet on the ride home, which had McKenzie wondering what he was thinking about. Naturally, that had her also wondering when he'd become the most interesting person in her world. It'd happened over a series of surreal days after her island home was destroyed and the kindness of strangers, especially him, had shown her a sense of community she'd never experienced before.

She'd known her grandmother had loved the island for many reasons, including the rugged coastline, the pristine beaches, the excellent restaurants and the many other selling points that had Rosemary rushing to the island the minute spring had sprung and staying until the trees were dropping their leaves.

But after a couple of weeks there, McKenzie understood that her grandmother's love for the tiny island was due more than anything to the people who lived there. She'd seen that tonight as she met countless people who'd been friendly, welcoming and supportive of her and Jax and their goal of rebuilding the cabin to live on Gansett Island going forward.

She was more excited than ever about the prospect of that after having met so many other moms with young children.

"Hope you had a nice time tonight," he said as they took one of the last turns before home.

"It was great. I'm so glad I went. Everyone is so nice."

"They really are."

"I can see why you wouldn't want to give up this place, even for love."

"I suppose it wasn't really love if there was a choice."

"You love your home more than you loved her. That's the choice you made."

"And I've never regretted it, even if it gets a little quiet after the tourists go home and people hibernate for the winter."

"Do you get lonely?"

"Not really. I'm with people all day, and I've got friends I see outside of work. It's just, you know, you go home alone. That's the only time of day that I wonder whether I did the right thing."

"You did. You'd have yearned for everything you gave up here, because you'd lived long enough by then to know what you found here doesn't come along every day."

"Neither does a relationship that makes you happy."

"True." She looked over at him. "Were you happy with her?"

"Most of the time, other than that one major bone of contention."

"When I was with Eric, I thought I was happy, even though I could tell he was holding back. I thought maybe he was protecting himself from getting hurt, but it turned out he was holding back because he had a wife and kids."

He took a left turn into the driveway. "I'll never understand why people get married if they don't intend to be faithful."

"I know. That's why I'm sort of anti-marriage. I never want someone to feel like they *have* to stay with me if they'd rather be somewhere else."

As he put the truck in Park, he said, "Anyone would be lucky to get to stay with you. And Jax."

Taken aback by the emphatic way he said that, McKenzie stared at him.

"Sorry to be so blunt, but it's true. That guy was a fool and a dick to lead you on and then walk away when you got pregnant."

"You're very cute when you're indignant."

He scoffed. "I'm never cute."

"Yeah, you are. Quite often, in fact."

"Stop that. You should be running for your life away from me."

"Why would you say that?"

"Because."

"You're going to have to do better than that."

"You're too young for me, for one thing."

"I'm a fully grown adult with a mind of my own, and besides, age is just a number. You're thirty-six, not sixty-six."

"Sometimes I feel sixty-six."

"But you're not, so what else have you got?"

"You're a beautiful woman who could have anyone you want."

"Okay…"

"You could do much better than me. You're probably looking at me differently because I helped you out during a tough time, but once you get back to reality—"

"I'll always look at you differently because no one has ever been kinder to me than you've been."

He shrugged that off. "I just did what any decent person would do."

"No, Duke. You went above and beyond to make sure Jax and I were taken care of during a difficult time. That makes you a unicorn of the highest order."

"Don't make it out to be more than it was."

McKenzie was trying hard not to get mad—and not to cry—at the gruff way he was suddenly speaking to her. "Can I ask you something?"

"I guess."

"Why are you trying to talk me out of liking you when earlier it seemed like that was what you wanted?"

He stared straight ahead for the longest time, so long she'd begun to think he wasn't going to reply. "It doesn't feel right."

"What doesn't?" Her heart had begun to beat in an erratic staccato as she realized this conversation could turn out to be one of the most important she'd ever had.

"To like you this way."

"Why?"

"You're Rosemary's granddaughter. You're younger than me. You're… you, and I'm…"

"You're *wonderful*. How can you not see that?"

He shook his head. "My life is boring and small compared to what you could have with someone else. You could have anyone you want."

"And yet, the only man who has my attention is the one who's been kinder to me than anyone I've ever met."

"I'm sure you'll get over that when things return to normal."

Now he was just being mean in his attempt to talk her out of liking him. She didn't understand where this was coming from, so rather than continue to make her case, she unclipped Jax's seat belt, got out of the truck and reached for the baby carrier. "Thank you for taking me tonight. I had a great time. Tomorrow, I'd be happy to help with your books, if you'd still like me to."

"Sure."

"All right. I'll see you in the morning, then."

"McKenzie."

She stopped walking but didn't turn back.

"I'm sorry."

"For what?"

"I just think you can do better."

"We'll have to agree to disagree about that. Good night, Duke."

She kept her head held high as she walked away, even if she was crushed on the inside. Why had he taken a step toward her only to take two steps back a short time later? Had something happened while they were at the marina? Had someone like Sierra warned him off her or made him feel that his interest in her was wrong?

McKenzie wouldn't put it past her.

Which wasn't fair, and she knew that. She'd barely met Sierra and had no reason to believe her capable of anything like that.

But something had happened, and she had no idea what.

CHAPTER 17

cKenzie went through the motions of getting Jax changed into pajamas, reading him a story and nursing him one last time while ignoring the ache in her heart. How was it possible that this felt even worse than everything that'd happened with Eric?

Probably because Eric wished he could be half the person Duke was.

After she'd tucked in Jax and wished him the sweetest of dreams, she went to the living room and sat on the sofa, staring into the dark while trying to figure out what'd gone so wrong. She hadn't noticed anything, but then again, she'd missed the signs with Eric, too. With hindsight, she'd realized there'd been clues she'd failed to pick up on, but she'd been so happy and so in love she hadn't paid them enough attention.

Was she making the same mistake again? Was she failing to notice the signs?

"No, damn it. There were no signs. Everything was fine—better than fine—and then it wasn't."

When her eyes filled with tears, she closed them tightly, refusing to shed another tear over a man. She was done with that nonsense.

Whatever had been developing with Duke wasn't going to happen now, and she'd have to accept that and move on. There was no sense losing sleep—or tears—over a man who felt like he wasn't good enough for her or whatever other nonsense he'd told himself.

McKenzie was still sitting in the dark, trying not to cry, fifteen minutes later, when a soft knock sounded at the door.

Her heart lurched. It would be him. Who else could it be? Had he come to tell her more about why she was too good for him or too young for him or whatever bullshit he'd cooked up since she came upstairs?

She took a deep breath for fortitude and released it before she got up to open the door.

"Hey," he said.

"Hey."

"So... I'm sorry."

"For what?"

"Sending mixed signals and being weird and, well... all of it. It's... um, been a while since I was, you know, interested in someone this way."

"And what way is that?"

"The, um, well... you know..."

Had he ever been cuter than when he was trying to tell her how he felt? Nope, but she refused to make this easy for him.

"I'm not sure that I do."

The low growl that came from deep inside him almost made her laugh, but she wouldn't do that to him when he was clearly suffering. He deserved to suffer a little. But not too much. "Would you like to come in?"

"Yeah, I would."

McKenzie stepped back from the doorway to let him in and then returned to the sofa, curling her legs under her.

"Why are you sitting in the dark?"

"Because I felt like it."

"Okay." He sat on the edge of the sofa, as if he wasn't sure he was truly welcome.

She turned on a lamp so she could see him and then blinked several times as her eyes adjusted to the sudden burst of light. "Have you come to tell me more reasons why you could never be right for me?"

"I... uh, no."

"Then what?"

"I wanted to say I was sorry. I'm not even sure where all that came from in the truck just now. I think maybe I was a little... scared or something."

"Scared of what?"

"Liking you so much."

"Why would that be scary?"

"Um, well... It's you, and you're..."

"What am I?"

"You're special. Very, very special."

"So are you."

"That is nice of you to say, but—"

"No buts, Duke. It's true. You're a special person who's become very important to me, and it hurts me to hear all the reasons why you think I'm too good for you. I'm not. Maybe I might turn out to be just right for you. Did that ever occur to you?"

"Ah, yes, it did, and I believe that might be why I behaved badly."

She had to hold back the need to smile. "You didn't behave badly."

"Then why do I feel terrible about it?"

"I don't know. Why do you suppose that is?"

"I think I hurt you, and that was certainly not my intention. That's the last thing I'd ever want to do."

"Do you hear yourself? Did you hear what you said about how hurting me is the last thing you'd ever want to do?"

His brows furrowed in confusion. "What about it?"

"That, right there, is what makes you special, Duke, and you can't even see it. Most of the guys I've met, and most of the ones my friends have met, don't care whether they hurt us. They want whatever they can get from us without a single thought about anyone getting hurt. You care. That makes you different."

"I don't want you putting me on any kind of pedestal. I've lived a rough-around-the-edges kind of life. I'm not even sure I know how to do..." He rolled his hand to gesture between them. "This."

McKenzie's heart was fully engaged as she moved closer to him.

Duke seemed to stop breathing altogether while he waited to see what she might do.

"I think you know exactly how to do this."

He shook his head.

"Yes," she said softly as she placed her hand on his face.

She held back a gasp when he pressed a kiss to her palm.

"You could do better."

"No, I couldn't, so shut up with that." She applied gentle pressure to his face, encouraging him to look at her.

When his gaze collided with hers, she could see how much he cared, how badly he wanted her and how worried he still was about making a mistake that would hurt her.

She saw things she'd never seen in the eyes of any other man, which had her leaning in to press her lips to his.

For a hot second, she didn't think he'd kiss her back.

But then his hand encircled her neck and his lips moved against hers and everything went quiet and still, as if the whole world had paused in honor of this moment. She was kissing Duke, and he was kissing her back, and it was the best thing *ever*.

For the longest time, the kiss was nothing more than lips sliding over lips, but somehow, that was *everything* she hadn't known she needed.

"McKenzie..."

"Yes?"

"You're really sure about this?"

She moved quickly, before he could talk himself out of it, straddling his lap and putting her arms around his neck as she kissed him again. "I'm sure."

"Jeez. Are you trying to give me a stroke or something?"

"Not at all," she said, laughing. "I'm just trying to get you out of your own way."

"I'm trying to be respectful of you. And Rosemary."

"You've been nothing but respectful, but now it's time to be a little less... proper."

He sputtered with outrage. "I'm not proper."

"You're like an old cross-stitching church lady."

"Are you trying to piss me off?"

"Is it working?"

"Nah, takes more than that."

Smiling, she said, "I like you, Duke. I really, really like you."

"It's your funeral."

McKenzie laughed. "Drama queen."

"What's a sexy woman like you want with a guy like me?"

"Everything. I want everything with you."

He placed his hand on her forehead. "You running a fever or something?"

She swatted his hand away. "I'm perfectly healthy."

"Then you've lost your marbles."

"Nope. All my marbles are perfectly fine."

"Did you see the way those fire department guys and Coasties were looking at you earlier?"

"What? No."

"They were checking you out."

"Is that why you got so weird on the way home? Because you think I belong with one of them?"

"It would make far more sense than this does."

"I don't even know them."

"You barely know me."

"That's not true. You've shown me your heart from the first time you arrived at Tiffany's with the things you rescued from the cabin, and then again when you brought Mr. Bear and offered us a place to stay. You've shown me every time I've seen you or talked to you since then, and guess what?"

"What?"

"I like what I see." After a pause, she added, "I've had my share of boyfriends."

He frowned. "I'm sure you have."

She dropped her forehead to rest against his. "You know what I'm ready for now?"

His muffled grunt served as his reply.

"I want a *man*, Duke. I want someone who knows how to treat a woman, who takes care of the people he cares about, who steps up for a stranger because he wants to, not because she can do something for him. I want a grown-ass adult *man,* and if you think any of those guys who were supposedly checking me out earlier would do the trick, you're dead wrong. I promise you most of them are probably more of the same."

"How do you know I won't turn out to be, too?"

"I don't know for sure, but the other thing Rosemary taught me that I've never forgotten is that when someone shows you who they really are, you should believe them. You've already shown me who you really are. I believe you." She kissed him. "I believe you, Duke."

His arms tightened around her as he stared at her intently. "I can't believe you're here with me like this."

"Why not? And *do not* say I could have anyone."

"Okay, I won't say that."

"Now we're getting somewhere."

DUKE COULDN'T BELIEVE the series of events that'd brought McKenzie to his lap with her arms wrapped around his neck and her tongue rubbing against his in the sweetest, hottest, sexiest kiss of his whole damned life.

He still felt guilty for doing this with Rosemary's precious granddaughter, but he had to hope she'd approve. She'd loved him as much as he'd loved her. Had she loved him enough to want him making out passionately with her granddaughter?

He'd never know.

He could only hope so.

His head was spinning, and he was hard as stone by the time she pulled back to look at him, smiling as if she saw something she liked.

He still couldn't believe that was possible.

She twirled a length of his hair around her finger.

"Do you hate my long hair?"

"Not at all. It's part of who you are." She leaned in to kiss the side of his neck. "Just like your beautiful ink is."

He shivered from an almost painful need for more. "You're driving me crazy, but of course, you know that."

"Do I?"

Duke could barely speak or breathe or think for wanting her. "I've got to tell you something."

She continued to kiss his neck, making a red-hot mess of him. "What's that?"

"Remember when I told you about that fiancée I had for a second?"

"What about her?"

"I never once felt like this when I was with her."

"Like what?"

"Like I might die if you ever stop kissing me."

CHAPTER 18

*A*shleigh had cried herself to sleep in Tiffany's arms while Blaine held them both. In his entire life, he'd never been more heartbroken for anyone than he was for his sweet little Ashleigh. He wished he had a magic wand that could take away her pain and return her to the happy, smiling child she'd been before real life interrupted her childhood.

He couldn't imagine loving Ashleigh more if he'd fathered her himself, and it wasn't lost on him that he would now be the only father in her life. He'd be the one to raise her and nurture her and teach her to drive and holler at her when she missed curfew.

His heart ached for Jim Sturgil, a man he'd despised and, at times, feared due to the sometimes-violent way he reacted to Tiffany. The last few days had wrought some of the most intense emotions Blaine had ever felt. If he'd been asked before Jim went missing if he'd ever mourn for that guy, he would've laughed. But now... He ached for what Jim would miss with Ashleigh. He ached for a man who'd had it all and let it get away. And he ached for his sweet little girl, who would mourn her father for the rest of her life.

Her heartbroken sobs at bedtime had gutted him. She'd held up well all day, but reality hit when it was time to close her eyes and rest.

Tiffany was so great with her, reminding her that her daddy would always love her no matter where he was and that so many other people loved her, too.

Blaine loved her.

He'd take a fucking bullet for her if it ever came to that, which he prayed it never did. But God, he loved her, and his heart was crushed by her grief.

He couldn't remember the last time he'd cried. Not even when his brother was missing during the storm, but his eyes ached from silently weeping through the storm of her sorrow. Ashleigh didn't cry much either. She never had. Not as long as he'd known her, anyway, so that made it even harder to witness.

"I think she's finally asleep," Tiffany whispered.

"Are you okay, babe?"

"I'm broken inside for her."

"I am, too."

"I'd do anything to fix this for her."

"I was just thinking the same thing."

"I guess all we can do is love her through it."

"And we will. We'll love her so hard."

Tiffany turned over and into his arms.

He held her as tightly as he could, feeling the heat of her tears on his chest and hating every one of them because they represented such deep hurt for herself and Ash.

"I'm so sorry, Tiff. I'd do anything to make this better for you both."

"I know, and that helps. We'll be okay."

"Promise?"

"Yeah. What choice do we have but to go on and to help her remember him with love?"

"No choice, and that's what we'll do. Of course we will."

"This is the most confusing and painful thing I've ever been through." She lowered her voice even more. "How can I be so heart-broken over him of all people?"

"I know it seems strange, but you're grieving for the man you once loved and the man who always loved Ashleigh."

"Yeah, I guess. Thank you for understanding and for being there for us."

"Where else would I be but wherever you are?"

"I feel so lucky to have you every day, but never more than I have this week."

"I'm the lucky one, and I know it. I'm here for whatever you guys need for as long as you need it." He kissed the top of her head and caressed her back. "Why don't you try to sleep while she does?"

"Yeah, I should, but every time I close my eyes, my mind races. I keep picturing him in the water…"

"Don't do that."

"I'm trying not to."

"Think of happier things, like Ash and Addie and names for our new little person. We need to think of something. Let's focus on the joy as much as we can. It'll help."

"You're right. I have some names in mind."

"You need to sleep."

"I'm wide awake."

"Close your eyes and think about our sweet girls. Think about the way Ash takes care of Addie and calls her honey the way you do."

"I love that," Tiffany said.

"I do, too. Think about how Ash knows what her baby sister wants before she wants it and tends to her every need like a little mommy."

"It's the cutest thing ever."

"It sure is," Blaine said. "Soon, she'll have another baby to take care of, which will make her heart happy again."

"Yes, it will. Can I tell you my names?"

"If you must."

He felt her smile against his chest and notched that as a victory. Anything to keep her from thinking about Jim in the water.

"I figured we should try to come up with another A name."

"We don't have to."

"I know, but it's kind of cute that they'd all have A names," Tiffany said.

"If you say so."

"What do you think of Archer for a boy?"

"Hmm, I like it, but not sure I like it with Taylor. Archer Taylor."

"That's cute."

"There's too much R at the end."

"We'd probably call him Arch. Arch Taylor has a nice ring to it."

"I like that better. What are my other choices?"

"Axel, Atlas, Austin."

"I like Austin, but I don't love it."

"I don't either."

"My grandfather was Augustus," Blaine said.

"Really? How did I not know that?"

"I told you that."

"No, you didn't. I like that. We could call him Auggie."

"People called my grandfather Gus."

"That I've heard, but I didn't know it was short for Augustus."

"Yep."

"What do you think of Auggie?"

"It'd be cute when he's a toddler. Will it still be cute when he's an actual man?"

Tiffany's giggle was the best thing he'd heard from her in days of sorrow and worry. "Not as cute."

"Right. He could decide to go by Gus when he gets older."

"That's an old-man name."

"Are we back to square one?"

"We might be."

"What've you got for a girl?"

"I'm almost certain he's a boy."

"Oh yeah?"

"Uh-huh."

"That'd be nice. I could use some help around here, not that I don't love being a girl dad."

She laughed again, which made him so damned thankful. He

wanted her laughing and happy all the time, which he knew wasn't possible, but that didn't mean he wouldn't try with all his might to make it so.

BLAINE'S BROTHER Deacon was also wide awake in the middle of the night, tormented by the same images that were haunting Tiffany. Except, as the one who'd found him, he'd actually seen Jim Sturgil in the water.

He'd spotted a bare foot that'd turned out to be him.

It would take years, if ever, before he'd get that image out of his mind.

Yes, he'd been involved in searches for people who'd disappeared on the water before, and yes, he'd assisted in recovering bodies. But something about this one had affected him deeply, maybe because it could've been him if Joe and his crew on the ferry hadn't spotted him on top of his overturned boat during the storm.

He dropped his head into his hands, trying with all his might to focus on the many good things in his life rather than the sight of that goddamned foot underwater, but that was easier said than done.

Deacon smelled her distinctive scent before he felt her next to him on the sofa. He raised his head to look at his wife, Julia.

His *wife*.

Days after they'd secretly tied the knot, he was still amazed at how exchanging vows had made that which was incredible to begin with even more so. "Did I wake you?"

"No, but I woke, and you were gone, so I came looking for you. Are you okay?"

He hadn't told her he was the one who'd found Jim. She'd been fragile since he'd gone missing during the storm. "Yeah, babe. I'm okay."

"You've been upset since you got home. Are you going to tell me why?"

"I don't want to."

"How come?"

"It's upsetting."

"I don't want you to be upset alone."

"It might be for the best in this case."

She put her arm around him and leaned her head on his shoulder. "Tell me."

He gathered her into his arms and reached for a blanket. She was always cold. It was one of the things he found so adorable about her—that she was always looking to him to warm her up. There was nothing he'd rather do than keep her warm.

"I was the one who found Jim Sturgil."

"Oh. That must've been awful."

"It was."

"I'm sorry you had to see that."

"Part of the job."

"People think being the harbor master is such a fun job."

"Most of the time, it is."

"You're probably also thinking about how close you came to a similar fate."

"That's crossed my mind."

"It's all I can think about."

"Don't do that. Everything is fine."

"It's going to take me a while to get over the terror of those hours when you were missing in a hurricane."

"I'm sorry I did that to you."

"I'm sorry it happened to you."

"All I thought about the whole time was you. I swear you kept me alive out there."

"I'm glad I was there with you to keep you safe."

"You're always with me. Every minute of every day. If Blaine knew how much time I spend dreaming about you, he'd dock my pay."

Julia laughed as she tightened the arm she had around him. "Being married is the best thing ever, isn't it?"

"Hell yes. It's better than anything."

"Maybe it would get your mind off things if you took your new wife to bed and reminded her how much you love her."

"Does my wife need reminding?"

"Your wife never says no to reminders from her husband."

"In that case..." He scooped her up and was on the way to their bedroom before she figured out what he intended to do.

"How about some warning next time?"

"What fun would that be?"

Their dog, Pupwell, looked up from his bed and let out a sound that indicated his annoyance at being disturbed in the middle of the night.

Deacon helped her out of the T-shirt she'd worn to bed, dropped his own shorts, settled her on the bed and then came down on top of her, holding himself up on his arms.

Julia loved to comment on the muscles in his arms, and as she caressed them, he decided that this would be the memory he'd refer back to any time something more disturbing tried to take over his thoughts. Her gorgeous face was illuminated by the night-light they left on so they wouldn't fall over the dog, who liked to "sleep around," as they put it.

"After all this time, I still can't believe that the prettiest girl I've ever met in my whole life loves me."

"Stop that. There's no way that's true."

"Oh yes, it is most definitely true." He lowered himself to kiss her as her fingers tightened around his biceps. Something about that drove him crazy every time she did it.

"Thank you for coming home to me," she said as she looked up at him with her whole heart in her eyes.

"Thanks for having me." He flashed a dirty grin as he pushed into her. "Mmm, so good."

He loved the way her arms and legs entrapped him in the best kind of web, the one he wanted to be "stuck" in for the rest of his life.

"Love you, sweet Julia, more than anything in the whole wide world."

"Love you more than that."

"It's not possible."

"Yes, it is."

Shaking his head as he smiled, he kissed her, amazed at how she'd succeeded in taking his mind off the thing he most wanted to forget. He'd never had anyone who could do that for him the way she did. Loving her was the best thing to ever happen to him, and he'd be thankful for her for the rest of his days. He was also thankful to Blaine, who'd made him come to the island where he'd found his precious Julia.

After surviving the ordeal at sea, he was thankful for everything, even his ass-pain older brother.

He buried his face in the curve of her neck, breathing her in as they strained for the release that had them clinging to each other as they gasped with pleasure.

"How soon will we know?" he asked after a long period of silence.

"Know what?"

"If we made a baby."

"In a few weeks."

"Not sure I can wait that long."

"You're going to have to get some patience. Having a baby takes months."

"No way. When were you going to tell me that?"

She pinched his rear, making him startle as he laughed.

"Will you take good care of me while I drive you crazy wanting our baby here right now?"

"I'll do what I can with you."

"I can't wait."

"For what?"

"Everything. Every single damned thing with you."

"I can't wait either."

CHAPTER 19

ike I might die if you ever stop kissing me.

McKenzie revisited those words as she fell asleep and then as she awoke to a new day full of exciting possibilities.

Duke Sullivan.

She smiled so big, it was a wonder her face didn't break.

The thing with him wasn't without risks, especially after the ordeal Eric had put her through. But she wasn't thinking of him or his lies as she lay in bed for a few more minutes before beginning another day. No, she was thinking of Duke and how cute he'd been coming to her door last night to apologize for being weird.

Of all things, he'd been jealous of the way the guys from the fire department and Coast Guard had looked at her.

How silly and sweet.

She hadn't noticed a single one of them. Why would she bother with them when she had the full attention of a man like Duke, who knew how to treat a woman with respect and kindness?

A loud crash followed by beeping outside had her getting up to see what it was. Nothing was happening out front, so she went into the kitchen to look out the other side. Through the trees, she could see equipment and men working on the cabin.

Filled with excitement, she went to get Jax from his crib, then got him changed and fed so they could walk next door to check out what was going on.

Mac was standing in the yard with another man, who looked like a younger version of him. "Oh, hey, McKenzie, this is my cousin Riley. He'll be supervising things here."

McKenzie adjusted Jax on her hip so she could shake hands with Riley. "Nice to meet you."

"You, too."

"This is Jax."

"Hey, Jax. Nice to meet you, too."

Jax was dazzled by the orange machine that was pulling pieces of busted wood and other materials off the pile that had once been the cottage.

"Hope we didn't wake you," Mac said.

"No worries. We're thrilled to get started on the repairs."

"I received your questionnaire, and I'd like to meet with you in the next few days to go over some basic plans to make sure we're on the same page."

"Sure, I'm around whenever you have time. I'm going to be working with Tiffany at her store, but she's closed this week."

"Yeah, I heard that."

"Have you heard how they're doing today?"

"My wife, Maddie, talked to her this morning. She said they managed to get some sleep, but Ashleigh has a lot of questions for which there're no easy answers."

"I don't envy her that."

"None of us do, but Ash will be very well loved through it. I'm leaving you in Riley's capable hands. If you need me for anything, you've got my number."

"Thank you again for jumping on this so soon."

"Glad to help."

After Mac left, Riley asked for her phone number and punched it into his phone. "Where are you staying while the house is being rebuilt?"

"Next door at Duke's. He was nice enough to loan me his garage apartment."

"Oh great. I'll keep you posted on things here, or pop over here any time to check in. Mac said you'll be meeting with him to go over the floor plan and other details?"

"Yes, in the next day or two."

"Excellent."

As she was about to walk back to Duke's, a large truck pulled in with a dumpster that was deposited in the yard.

McKenzie was excited to watch the construction progress and was thrilled by how quickly things were moving.

Duke was rolling his big motorcycle out of the garage as she came into the yard. "Are they working over there?"

"Yep."

"Nice."

"Mac put his cousin Riley in charge of the project. They sure do make those McCarthy boys handsome, don't they?"

He grumbled out an inaudible response and then tilted his head, giving her a look that set her blood on fire. That'd certainly never happened before. "How you doing this morning?"

"Good. You?"

"Excellent."

"Did you sleep well?"

She gave him a coy look. "I was a little tossy-turny. Can't imagine why."

"Probably for the same reason I was."

"Maybe."

"Any regrets this morning?"

"Not a single one."

"You should be dating one of those handsome McCarthy boys."

"Are you really going to start that nonsense again?"

He shrugged. "It's true."

"I'll just go see if Riley is single, then." She spun around to walk away, but Duke was right behind her, reaching for her arm to stop her from getting away.

"I'm sorry. I shouldn't have said that."

"No, you shouldn't have."

"I suck at this."

"Yes, you do."

"I just can't for the life of me figure out what a goddess like you wants with me."

"Until you figure that out, maybe we should press Pause on the kissing and stuff."

"I don't want to do that."

"Then you need to stop questioning what you bring to the table, because I've told you—repeatedly—it's more than anyone has ever brought to any table in my entire life."

"That's a damn shame." He tucked a strand of her hair behind her ear and looked at her with such tender affection that her knees went weak—another thing that hadn't happened before. "You ought to be treated like the queen you are."

"I don't want to be treated like a queen. I just want to be treated with care and respect, two things you've shown me time and again."

He enveloped her and Jax in a hug. "You two are turning my whole world upside down."

"Does that upset you?"

"Not in the least, which is rather incredible."

McKenzie had no idea how long they stood there, holding each other, before Jax began to protest being squeezed between them.

They pulled back, smiling as Jax blew spit bubbles that made Duke laugh.

"Everything he does is so damned cute."

She thought so, too. It was nice to have someone else around who agreed. "He's pretty cute."

"So's his mama." He reached into his pocket and withdrew a black key that he handed to her. "That's for the truck. Use it for whatever you need to do today. I'll ride the bike."

"Are you sure?"

"Positive. If you wanted to come visit me at the studio, I'd be happy to see you."

"I'll come by to look at your books."

He grimaced. "You're going to want to smack me around when you see the mess I've made of them."

"I'll be the judge of that. Thank you for loaning me your truck."

"No problem."

"Where's your helmet?"

"I was just going back for it when I saw you two coming."

She eyed him skeptically. "Lying is a deal breaker for me."

"I'm not lying," he said with a laugh. "I was about to go grab it when I saw you."

"Go on, then."

"Sheesh," he muttered as he walked toward the garage, returning a minute later with a helmet that had no face coverage. "Satisfied now?"

"No. It doesn't protect your face."

"My face is fine."

"Yes, it is, and I want it to stay that way. Don't you have one with the shield thing that covers your face?"

"I might."

"Go get that and quit playing games with me."

"Honestly," he said on a huff as he went back to the garage. "Never knew you were such a bossy thing."

"Excuse me?"

"I didn't say anything."

"Sure you didn't."

He returned a minute later with the requested helmet, which was covered in dust that he blew off as he walked.

"Looks like that one doesn't get used very often."

"It's collected some dust."

"It won't anymore, will it?"

"No, ma'am."

"Excellent."

"Are you quite pleased with yourself?"

"I rather am."

"You're awfully cute when you're bossy, but then again, you're cute pretty much all the time."

She made a face at him. "No woman wants to be called cute."

"Is sexy as f-u-c-k better?"

Flustered by the way he looked at her, she said, "Yes, that's better."

Duke dropped the helmet to the ground and closed the distance between them, placing his hands on her hips as he worked around Jax to kiss her. "Couldn't wait another second to taste those sweet lips again."

He kissed her three more times in rapid succession, until he had her head spinning and her breath caught in her throat. Then he kissed the top of Jax's head, stepped back and bent to retrieve the helmet. Turning to face her as he put it on, he held her gaze until he had it snapped into place. He flipped open the visor. "You might want to take him inside before I start this thing."

"Good idea. Be careful."

"Yes, ma'am."

"Stop making fun of me."

"I'd never do that."

"Now you're lying again," she shot over her shoulder as he laughed.

He waited until they were inside with the door closed before he fired up the loudest engine she'd ever heard.

"Roooooom," Jax said.

Startled by the noise, McKenzie sat on the sofa with him. "That's right, buddy. Is that really going to be one of your first words?"

"Rooom. Rooom."

Smiling, she clapped his hands together. "Room, room."

"Roooooom."

She couldn't wait to tell Duke that he'd inspired one of Jax's first words.

A DAY PASSED SLOWLY when you were waiting for something to happen. Duke caught himself looking toward the door every five or ten minutes as he applied the latest portion of a full-back tattoo he was doing for Kyle, who worked as a deck hand on the ferries.

Kyle had been given a few days off after helping take the boats out to sea during the storm and was spending one of them in Duke's chair.

As he filled in the detail on a set of wings on a raptor, Duke let his mind wander to the night before on the sofa in the apartment. Kissing her had been one of the most thrilling experiences of his life, and he couldn't wait to do it again very soon. Would she want to pick up where they left off later? Things had gotten pretty heated the night before, but they hadn't progressed beyond kissing. And why hadn't they, exactly?

He couldn't say, but something told him to take it slow with her and let her set the pace. She'd been through a rough ordeal with the last guy she was involved with. Duke didn't want to press her for more than she was ready for.

"Duke!"

He turned to see Sierra standing behind him.

The other guys were out to lunch, and Kyle, who was wearing headphones, was dead asleep.

"Where the hell were you zoned out to?"

"Nowhere."

"I said your name twice, and you didn't even react."

"Sorry, what's up?"

"That's what I was coming to ask you. What's up?"

"Uh, nothing. Why?"

"That's not true. You've got yourself a little family all of a sudden."

"What?" Her comment shocked him. "No, I don't."

"Sure looked that way to me last night at the marina."

"What is it that you want to say, Sierra?"

"I'm just wondering what's up with her. It's like she's cast some sort of spell over you or something."

"Don't be dramatic. We're hanging out. Is that okay with you?"

She shrugged, but he could tell by the belligerent set to her jaw that she had something to say. "Sure, it's fine with me."

"Thanks. Can I get back to work now?"

"It's just that this woman shows up out of nowhere, and now you're suddenly all domesticated."

"Are you *trying* to piss me off?"

"Not at all. I'm worried about you."

"I'm fine."

"I don't want to see you hurt again like you were the last time."

"Totally different situation."

"Is it? Is she here to stay forever, or is she going to get bored like the last one did and want something else in a couple of months?"

Sierra's question struck fear in his heart. McKenzie was having the cabin rebuilt. Would she do that if she didn't intend to stay? "Don't worry about it, okay? It's all good."

"If you say so."

"I say so. She's coming in later to take a look at my books. You want me to have her stop by next door?"

"Sure."

"Are you okay, Sierra?" It was wildly out of character for her to question his choices, so he felt the need to ask.

"Of course."

"I'm going to get back to work, then."

"Okay."

She started to leave, but then turned back. "I know she's Rosemary's granddaughter, and you feel loyal to her for being such a good friend to you. But you don't owe her granddaughter anything. Be careful."

With that, she walked out the door, leaving Duke wondering what the hell she was warning him about. He'd reached out to McKenzie before he'd known she was Rosemary's granddaughter. He'd invited her to use the apartment for as long as she needed. Before he'd gone to see her at Tiffany's, McKenzie hadn't known he existed or that he was a friend of her grandmother's. What sort of nefarious plot did Sierra think McKenzie had hatched?

She just needed to get to know McKenzie, and then she'd see what he did. That McKenzie was a good person, like her grandmother had been. She was also a wonderful mother and had been nothing but honest and open with him about her past. What did he have to fear from her other than a broken heart if things didn't work out between them?

He lost himself in the work, the way he always did, but Sierra's doubts crept in to make him question everything. He'd known her for years and had developed a brother-and-sister bond with her, or at least that's how he'd always thought of it.

Had she viewed their relationship differently? Was she interested in him herself but had never said so? Not once in more than twelve years of close friendship had that possibility ever occurred to him.

Ace came back from lunch, bringing takeout for Duke. He was bald, muscular and, according to several women on the island, sexy as hell. Ace was the only person Duke had ever met who had more tattoos than he did.

"Thanks, man."

"No prob." He leaned in for a closer look at the tattoo Duke was working on. "Looks great. How's it going?"

"Slow but steady."

"Funny how some of them sleep through it and others whimper like babies the whole time."

"I know." Since the question was eating at him, he looked up at Ace. "You ever pick up a vibe from Sierra toward me?"

"What kind of vibe?"

"The interested kind."

"Nah, not really. Always thought you two were buddies more than anything."

"Me, too, but she said something just now…"

Before he could tell Ace the rest, McKenzie came through the door with Jax in his seat. "Hi there."

"Hey, come in."

"Am I catching you at a bad time?"

"Nope. I was just about to take a break to eat some lunch."

Ace gave him a curious look.

"Ace, this is McKenzie and her son, Jax. MK, this is Ace."

"Nice to meet you," she said.

"You, too."

"She's staying in my garage apartment while her place is rebuilt after the storm."

"Oh, cool."

Duke took the bag Ace had brought to the sofa and sat next to her. "Hungry?"

"No, thanks. I had a PBJ at home."

He'd ordered a grilled chicken sandwich and fries. After squeezing ketchup packs into a corner of the container, he nudged it toward her. "Have some fries."

"Maybe one."

"Have as many as you want."

She dipped one in ketchup and ate it. "Those are good."

"I know, right? They're from the Wayfarer. Best fries on the island."

"Good to know."

He took a bite of his sandwich. "Laptop on the desk has the dreaded QuickBooks on it. Remember, you promised not to be appalled."

"I won't be. I'm sure I've seen worse."

"I doubt that."

Smiling, she said, "I need bank and credit card statements, too."

"Uh, I think I've got them around here somewhere."

"You want me to poke around for them?"

"You'll have a stroke when you see the drawers."

"I'm sure I'll survive." She got up to go to the desk, positioning Jax in his seat so he could see her while she worked.

"Let me know if you have any questions."

"You'll be the first to know."

Duke was wondering how he was supposed to concentrate on lunch or work or anything else while she was there, looking so pretty and kissable. "Sierra said to stop by to talk about her books when you get a chance."

"I'll do that when I'm finished here."

"That's apt to take a week or two." He'd never been particularly embarrassed by his recordkeeping until now.

"I meant done for today."

"Ah, okay. So..."

"Stop fretting, Duke. Everyone's books are a mess when they bring in someone who knows what they're doing."

When Ace's afternoon client arrived, Duke got up to show her to Ace's station.

"Can I get you anything to drink?"

"No, thanks," she said, running her eyes over him and seeming to like what she saw.

Where in the hell was all this female attention coming from now that he was interested in McKenzie? Had McKenzie noticed the way the customer had checked him out? He ventured a glance her way and determined that, yes, she'd definitely seen it.

Shit.

Why did this stuff have to be so goddamned complicated? He liked her. Based on how she'd kissed him the night before, she liked him just as much. So why were his insides tied up in knots thanks to Sierra and some other woman he'd never laid eyes on before five minutes ago?

He went back to work on Kyle's back, relying on nervous energy to finish the wings and start the next part of the design before this session ended.

But he kept stealing glances at the woman across the room as he tried to calculate how many hours it would be before he could be alone with her to continue what they'd started the night before. How was a man supposed to concentrate on anything when she was in the room?

He'd much rather look at her than Kyle's back.

CHAPTER 20

*D*uke was cute when he was flustered, and he was most definitely flustered after Ace's client had given him the once-over and liked what she saw.

McKenzie understood that. The woman was only human, after all, and Duke was sexy as hell. That he was also sweet and kind and thoughtful was a potent combination for a woman who'd sworn off men and romance after the disaster with Eric had made her question everything.

Eric had swept her off her feet, filled her head with platitudes and paid her more attention than any man ever had. He'd dazzled her with his good looks, sweet talk and sexiness. Who cared if his story didn't add up at times? Who cared if he "traveled" more than any computer programmer she'd ever met? What did she know about the demands of that career field?

She'd been so blind with love for him that she'd failed to see the forest even as she was sitting under the trees.

The metaphor made her chuckle to herself. She'd been an idiot. That was a far more efficient way to put it.

As she opened the top right drawer to Duke's desk, she had to bite back a groan at the chaotic mess that greeted her. He wasn't kidding.

Her first order of business was to organize the paperwork. She made piles of bank and credit card statements, receipts, other bills and a few things she wasn't sure about that she'd ask him about later.

Next, she put the statements in chronological order.

Then she opened the second drawer and found more of the same.

Sighing, she pulled the paper from the drawer and added it to her piles.

Her phone chimed with a text from Kendall James, whom she'd texted earlier to provide the information she needed to get in touch with Eric.

Hi there,

Please take a look at the enclosed draft of the letter I'd like to send to Eric to begin the discussion. Feel free to call me at your convenience (even at night is fine with me if that works better for you). Look forward to reviewing next steps.

Best,

Kendall

McKenzie clicked on the attached PDF to open the letter, which was on official-looking legal letterhead.

Dated September twenty-fifth, it included the address of Eric's employer in Warwick, Rhode Island.

Dear Mr. Norton,

I represent McKenzie Martin and her minor child, Jax Martin. This letter is to inform you of our intention to sue to establish your paternity of Jax. When paternity is proven, as we believe it will be, our next move will be to demand support for the minor child until such time as he graduates from college. We understand that your wife and other children stand to be adversely affected by this action. Thus, we are contacting you at your place of employment. Should you fail to respond within fourteen days, we will reach out to you at your residence.

We look forward to resolving this matter promptly.

Sincerely,

Kendall James, Esquire

Of counsel

. . .

"HOLY SHIT," McKenzie said under her breath. Imagining Eric receiving that letter filled her with elation and a giddy sense of retribution. Ms. Kendall James, Esquire, was not screwing around. She responded to the text from her.

That letter is perfect. You have my approval to send it. Please let me know what I owe you.

No charge until we recover some money from him. I'll keep you posted.

I can't tell you how much I appreciate this.

Happy to help!

"What're you all smiles about?" Duke asked. "It sure as hell can't be my bookkeeping."

McKenzie hadn't seen him coming. Nor had she noticed that his client had left. "Your bookkeeping needs my help, for sure. But I'm smiling because Kendall James wrote an incredible letter to Eric." She called it up on her phone and handed it to him.

While he read it, she took in every nuance of his expression, from the way his blue eyes narrowed to the purse of his kissable lips.

He made her not care about her resolution to avoid men and romantic entanglements forever. He made her want to take a wild chance. That thought alone should've been like a bitch slap to the head to get herself together, but she couldn't seem to care about such warnings when the masculine scent of him filled the air around her. She wasn't sure if it was body wash or shampoo or cologne. Whatever it was worked for her.

"Wow. A letter like that would make me quake in my boots, especially if I had a wife and kids at home who had no idea what I'd been getting up to on the side."

"I know, right? He'll shit himself."

"Least of what he deserves after the way he lied to you."

"I'm afraid he'll be angry more than anything. He doesn't expect me to do something like this."

"I assume he'd have no idea where to find you."

"I don't think so. I mean, I told him about my grandmother having a place out here, but not that she'd left it to me or that I wanted to come out here. That wasn't part of my plan when I was with him. I thought we'd end up together, you know?"

"Yeah, I do, and you had no reason to think otherwise at the time. Where would he look for you?"

"Probably at the apartment where I lived when we were together."

"Would they tell him where to find you?"

"I don't think so."

"Might be worth a phone call to put them on alert that you don't want them giving out any info about your whereabouts."

"Yes, you're right."

"Does he know where your mother lives?"

McKenzie shook her head. "I never took him there, but he knew I was from Coventry. She has a different last name than me, so it wouldn't be an obvious connection."

"You might also want to make her aware you're taking legal action. Just to be safe."

"Do I hafta?" The thought of voluntarily telling her mother anything went against everything she believed in.

"Yes, you hafta," he said, smiling, "because you'd feel awful if anything ever happened to her because of you."

"Why do you have to make so much sense?"

Jax let out a squeal and began to strain against the confines of the seat.

McKenzie reached down to release the straps and lifted him into her arms. "Someone has been a very good boy while Mommy was working."

"He's such a good boy. Want to come see Duke? I'll show him around the ferry landing."

"Do you have another client coming in?"

"Not unless I get a drop-in."

"Okay, then. Thanks." She handed Jax over to Duke. "Jax, what noise does Duke's bike make?"

"Room room."

Duke laughed. "That's right. I'll take you for a ride when you're a little bigger."

"No, you won't."

Grinning, he said, "We'll be right outside if you need us."

"Don't go too far."

"We won't."

As they went outside together, McKenzie was aware that there was no greater demonstration of trust than to let him take her child out of her sight. But she did trust him, and not just because her grandmother had. No, at this point, it was because he'd repeatedly shown her that he was worthy of her trust and respect.

She made good use of the time alone to finish going through the drawers and organizing a year's worth of paperwork into neat, chronological piles.

While Duke had Jax, she decided to run next door to check in with Sierra about her books. She loved the idea of running a business helping people with their bookkeeping and taxes while she also worked for Tiffany. She could tend to her own clients at night after Jax was asleep. Between those two things, she should be able to support them since she wouldn't have to pay rent or a mortgage.

"Thank you, Gran," she whispered as she stepped into the glorious September sunshine. Across the parking lot, she spotted Duke and Jax. He'd seated him in the driver's seat of one of the forklifts the ferry workers used to move pallets around. Jax had his hands on the wheel and was pretending to drive.

It was the sweetest thing McKenzie had ever seen, especially the way Duke was clearly enjoying it as much as Jax was. He looked up, saw her there and waved.

She waved back and then put her hand over her heart to let him know how much she appreciated him.

His smile warmed her all the way through.

She was in big trouble with this man, and it was getting "worse" by the minute.

CHAPTER 21

*A*s she stepped through the doors of the massage studio, which was called Refresh and Renew, a warm, earthy scent greeted her. Whatever it was made her want to settle in for some relaxation of her own. As if that was going to happen any time soon.

Sierra was at the reception desk, chatting with a blonde woman who handed over her credit card.

"That was amazing," the client said. "Thank you so much for squeezing me in."

"My pleasure. I'm glad it worked out. Your hubby is the best for setting it up."

"You know it. After being marooned for days with three little ones and no power, he knew I needed it."

Sierra returned the credit card with a receipt to sign. She leaned around the client to say hi to McKenzie. "Be right with you, McKenzie."

"No rush."

"McKenzie has come to save my ass. She's a whiz with QuickBooks."

McKenzie would never use the word *whiz*, but before she could say so, the blonde woman at the desk turned to her.

"I'm Laura Lawry, owner of the Sand & Surf Hotel, and if you know QuickBooks, I want you to work with me like yesterday. Or actually more like last year..." She added a sheepish grin that made McKenzie laugh.

"Nice to meet you."

The two women shook hands.

"Will you help me? *Please?*"

"Of course. I'll stop by in the next few days if that works."

"That'd be perfect. This is truly turning out to be the best massage I've ever had."

"We aim to please," Sierra said.

"I have two friends who work out of the hotel who will want you, too. Is it okay to tell them about you?"

"Sure, thank you."

"No, McKenzie, thank *you*. This will change my life! Give me your number."

As McKenzie recited her number, Laura punched it into her phone.

"You'll definitely hear from me."

"Sounds good."

After Laura left, McKenzie stepped up to the reception desk. "This must be what it feels like to be the Good Witch of the North."

Sierra laughed. "For sure. It's something we're sorely lacking here, and everyone runs small businesses. Once the word gets out, you'll have more business than you can handle."

"That'd be incredible. It never occurred to me that I might be able to do something like this here."

"Well, now you know. Let me show you my setup, and we'll see if you can straighten me out."

"Sounds good."

KELSEY WAS LATE GETTING to the hospital to see Jeff. The bulky cast on her arm made everything take twice as long as usual, especially showering and attempting to dry her hair. She'd been so frustrated by trying to blow-dry with her left hand that she'd given up and let her curls take over.

When she walked into his room, she was surprised to find Jeff sitting up in the chair next to the bed. He had a blanket over his lap, and his face was pale and pinched with pain.

"Look at you out of bed!"

"And what a treat it was getting here."

Kelsey winced. "Are you okay?"

"I'm told I will be, eventually, but the pain is pretty tough."

Her heart ached for his suffering. As a recovering addict, he'd refused all narcotics, which had him relying on Tylenol and Motrin, which barely made a dent.

"I wish there was something they could do for you."

"There's plenty they can do, but I'm not willing to risk it." He held out his hand to her. "Come sit next to me and tell me why you looked annoyed when you came in."

"I did?"

"Uh-huh. What's up?"

"This stupid cast is a pain. I can't dry my hair, so it's gone wild with curls. I look ridiculous."

"You look beautiful, as always."

"You have to say that as my fiancé."

"I don't have to say anything, and I only speak the truth."

Kelsey moved her chair to his right side and then took a seat, reaching for his hand.

He kissed the back of her hand. "Hi there."

"Hi."

"I'm sorry your arm is making everything harder."

"Oh please, it's nothing compared to what you're dealing with."

"It's not nothing, so don't say that."

"It's a nuisance more than anything. I tell myself it's temporary and to get over it."

"My mom would've helped you with your hair, you know."

"I didn't want to ask her for that."

"Why not, hon? She'd have been happy to do it. She's a professional mom."

"I know. It just feels weird. I mean, I wonder if she's mad at me that you're so badly hurt."

"What? Of course she isn't."

"You got hurt protecting me."

"Which I'd do again in a hot second, and she knows that. She's not upset with you. She's incredibly thankful we both survived. She wouldn't have wanted to deal with me if something had happened to you."

"You're very sweet."

"It's the truth. You said I jumped on top of you without thinking. I don't remember that, but I want you to know that I'd do it again a thousand times if it meant keeping you safe."

"Let's hope this is the only time you'll ever have to protect me that way."

"I'll do it any time it needs to be done."

"I can't bear that you got so badly hurt."

He squeezed her hand. "I'll be okay."

Kelsey's phone chimed with a text. She took back her hand so she could check it. When she saw it was about her overdue cell phone bill, she frowned. She opened her bank app to see how much she had left and whether she could pay at least half the outstanding balance on the phone bill.

She saw a lot of zeros.

What the hell?

After blinking a few times, she saw there was one hundred thousand dollars in her checking account. "Oh my God," she said softly.

"What?"

"Look." She showed him her phone with the bank info on the screen.

"Whoa. Where'd that come from?"

"I have no idea. Where's your phone?"

"On the charger."

MARIE FORCE

She got up and went around the bed to retrieve the phone from the charger and brought it to him. "Check yours."

He clicked around on his phone and then looked up at her. "I have the same in my account."

"What the heck?"

"It's Mr. McCarthy," Jeff said. "He would've done that. He feels responsible for his building falling on us."

"But that's insane. He can't just give us two hundred thousand dollars!"

"It looks like he already did."

"That's crazy. We have to give it back."

"Before you go sending it back, stop and think for a minute. We're going to be out of work for a while. Months, in my case. We both have car payments, insurance, cell phones and other bills to pay while we're laid up."

"Not two hundred thousand dollars' worth!"

"It'll add up, Kels. Who knows what co-pays and other fees we'll have to pay from being hospitalized? Mr. McCarthy—and Mac— know all too well how expensive something like this can get. I have no idea how much of the rehab will be covered. They wanted us to have what we need."

"Jeff... We cannot accept this. It's not right."

"We could've sued them, and they know it."

"We'd never do that!"

"They know that, too, which is why they wanted to help us while we recover."

"I need to call Mac."

"Go ahead, but don't tell him we're giving it back."

Kelsey found Mac in her contacts and made the call.

"Hey, Kels. How's it going there?"

"We're doing well, but we're in total shock after seeing what's in our bank accounts."

"That's compliments of my dad. He wanted to make this time easier for you guys."

"We're shocked, Mac. It's too much."

"He doesn't see it that way. He feels terrible about what happened and is very thankful you both survived. He wanted to do it."

"I don't know what to say other than thank you—and please tell him…" Her voice broke. "We have no words."

"All we want is both of you returned to full health and back on the island where you belong."

"It's so incredibly generous."

"I'll let him know you got it."

"Tell him we said…" She glanced at Jeff. "Tell him we're so very, very thankful for his kindness and incredible generosity."

Jeff nodded in approval.

"I'll do that. Don't worry about anything, okay?"

"You just took care of our biggest worries."

"I'm glad to hear that."

"How're the kids and Maddie?"

"Everyone's doing well, but we miss you."

"Maybe I could FaceTime with the kids later?"

"They'd love that."

"I'll do it. I'll text you to make sure it's a good time."

"That sounds good. Take care, Kelsey, and hurry back. We all miss you."

"That's nice to hear. Thank you again, Mac. Thank you so much."

"You got it."

Kelsey realized she had tears on her face after she ended the call. She wiped them away with her sleeve. "I still can't believe they did that. Can you imagine having that kind of money to just give away?"

"Mr. McCarthy has worked hard for decades at the marina."

"And the hotel."

"That, too. I'm sure they've made a bundle over the years."

"Still… I just can't wrap my head around having money like that."

"You never know what might happen if we work hard. We could end up like them someday."

"That'd be something."

"Sure would. As long as we have each other, I bet there's nothing we can't do."

Kelsey leaned in to kiss him. "What a relief it is to be able to pay the bills."

"I didn't realize you were stressing about that."

"Of course I am. We're both out of work, and I had fifty dollars left in my account before our fairy godfathers intervened."

"You should've said something. I have some money saved. I could've taken care of whatever you were worried about."

"You have enough to deal with without worrying about my cell phone bill."

"Keeping your cell phone on is critical to me."

Kelsey rolled her eyes at him. "You're being dramatic."

"Hardly. If I can't talk to you any time I want, that'll set back my recovery drastically."

"Drastically, huh?"

"Yep. So to sum up, I would've happily paid your cell phone bill."

"Well, thanks to Mr. McCarthy, you don't need to."

"Do me a favor, will you?"

"What's that?"

"Don't stress about stuff on your own. Let me know what you're thinking. I can't help if I don't know."

"I will."

A knock on the door was followed by Sarah poking her head in. "Is it safe to come in?"

Jeff waved her in. "Why wouldn't it be?"

"You kids are madly in love. I don't want to see anything that can't be unseen."

"I think you're safe in that regard," Jeff said. "Since I can barely move at the moment."

Sarah and Kelsey laughed.

"Mom, Kelsey needs some help with her hair. You'd be willing, right?"

"Jeff!"

"Of course I would!"

"Oh my God. I didn't want him to just blurt that out."

"Why not?" he asked. "You need help, and my mom is right there. Now you're all set."

"What am I going to do with him?" Kelsey asked.

"He's always been unmanageable," Sarah said. "It's a baby-of-the-family thing."

"Hey! That's not true."

"Oh please," Sarah said. "You had every one of us wrapped around your little finger from the minute you were born."

"It's not my fault I was impossibly cute."

"Yes, you sure were, and you still are."

"You're only saying that because you're thankful I didn't die."

"That's right. And, Kelsey, honey, anything you need, just let me know. You're part of our family now."

"Thank you, Mrs. Grandchamp. It's really nice of you to say that."

"My name is Sarah, and I mean it. You're family. It would be my pleasure to help you with your hair."

"I'm a mess today," Kelsey said as new tears leaked from her eyes.

"What else happened?"

"Mr. McCarthy, Big Mac, deposited a shit-ton of money into both our accounts," Jeff told his mother.

"Oh wow. How lovely of him!"

"That's what I said, too. Kels thought it was too much."

"It's way too much," Kelsey said.

"Things like this can get crazy expensive very quickly. Charlie asked me this morning if you kids were doing okay for money. I was going to try to find a way to bring that up with you today."

"It's so nice of him to think of that," Jeff said.

"Just like Kelsey is family to me, you're family to him. That's how this works."

"Kinda nice to have a dad who cares. That's a first."

"You definitely have a dad who cares now."

Kelsey reached for his hand. "We have a lot of people who care."

"We sure do."

CHAPTER 22

y the time McKenzie brought Jax home to nap that afternoon, she had three new clients. Laura had texted her to say that Stephanie McCarthy, owner of Stephanie's Bistro, as well as the woman covering for Abby McCarthy at Abby's Attic 2, were both interested in retaining her bookkeeping services.

She'd no sooner put Jax down to play with his toys than the phone rang with a call from Martinez Lawn & Garden.

"Hello, this is McKenzie."

"Ah, yes, the goddess of bookkeeping who's come to our fair shores to save us all from ourselves."

McKenzie laughed. "That'd be me."

"This is Jenny Martinez, we met the other night, and we need you desperately. Did I mention the need is *desperate*? As in we have no idea what we're doing, and we're one hundred percent sure we're doing it wrong and going to be jailed by the IRS at any moment."

"I've got you covered. No worries. Let's set up a time when we can meet to go over your books."

"You tell me when. I'll take whatever I can get. Alex and Paul's mom took care of the books for years and did a brilliant job. Since she's been ill, none of us has been able to fill the void."

"I'm sorry to hear she's ill."

"Yeah, it's been rough. She has dementia."

"I'm so sorry. My friend's mother has that. It's awful."

"It sure is."

"Jax and I will come by in the morning."

"We'll see you then. And thank you so much. I can't tell you how exciting this is."

"Said no one ever about bookkeeping."

"Oh, girl, you have no idea how many of us need you."

"I'm starting to get an idea. I've landed four new clients today alone."

"I have a feeling it's just the start. I'll look forward to seeing you tomorrow."

"Same. Thanks for calling."

"Thanks for answering!"

McKenzie was laughing as they said their goodbyes. She liked feeling as if she had something meaningful to offer her new community.

"I think we're going to be happy here, buddy," she said to Jax when she sat with him on the floor where he was surrounded by his favorite things.

"Hap, hap, hap."

"That's right. We're going to be happy, and we're going to make lots of new friends."

While he was occupied, she sent a text to check in with Tiffany. *I hate to ask how it's going, but... I'm thinking of you and wishing there was something I could do for you. I'm here if you need anything.*

Tiffany wrote back when McKenzie was feeding Jax his dinner of sweet potatoes and cereal. *Thank you so much for checking on us. We're doing okay. Ash has her teary moments and lots of questions, of course, but I think she understands for the most part. Jim's parents are planning his funeral for this coming weekend. It's all surreal. I wanted him to go away and leave us alone for years, but now that he has...*

I'm sure your emotions are all over the place. Understandably so.

Everyone is being super nice to me, which is also weird. I'm not his widow.

No, but you were his wife, and I'm glad you're getting the respect you deserve as the mother of his child.

You're a very nice person. I'm glad we've become friends.

Me, too! You won't believe what's been happening.

McKenzie filled her in on picking up a bunch of bookkeeping clients.

Wait. When were you going to tell ME that you know QuickBooks? HELLO!? I was your FIRST FRIEND HERE!

McKenzie replied with laughing emojis. *I owe you at least a year of free bookkeeping for rescuing me during the storm.*

You owe me no such thing, but it looks like I'm going to need to find someone else to replace Patty.

No! I said I'd help you, and I intend to do that.

Don't be silly! You have the chance to be self-employed, woman.

I'd never want to leave you shorthanded.

You're not. I'm firing you before you ever started.

OMG, I've never been fired!

Don't worry, I'll give you a good reference if you wrangle my bookkeeping. That'd be HUGE for me.

Deal. Thank you for everything. If I hear of anyone looking for work, I'll send them to the store.

You're the best. Thanks!

Let me know when you're ready for bookkeeping.

You will be the first to know!

McKenzie took a deep breath and then released it.

Self-employed.

What the hell? She'd never in her wildest dreams expected anything like that to happen to her. Would she make enough without also working at Tiffany's store?

"Yes, you will. You'll charge hourly, work hard and make this work."

Jax clapped his hands, splattering sweet potatoes on her and the wall.

"We're going to work very hard, aren't we, Jaxy?"

He squealed and smacked his hands on the tray, compounding the mess.

The most curious feeling of joy and contentment came over her. She'd figured out a way to support herself and Jax, she'd made a bunch of new friends and had the sweetest, sexiest man ever interested in her—and vice versa.

Even though her house had fallen down, she couldn't recall a time when she'd been happier than she was at the end of this remarkable day—and she had a feeling it might get even better before it was over.

DUKE MADE TWICE the usual amount for dinner, planning to feed his neighbor, too, if she was interested. He waited until he saw the light go off in the bedroom before he texted her.

Hungry?

Ten very long minutes passed before she finally replied. *Starving!*

You want a delivery?

Are you the deliveryman?

Duh, who else would I send over there? One of those Coasties who checked you out?

LOL, yes, please (to the delivery, not the Coastie)!

GRRRR. Stand by...

Standing by...

Was he the deliveryman? She enjoyed messing with him, but he was willing to put up with it coming from her. Hell, she had him wearing a freaking helmet on the bike for the first time in twenty years. That was a miracle in and of itself. In the years since his last relationship had ended in dramatic fashion, he'd gotten accustomed to doing his own thing, making his own decisions and not considering what anyone else wanted, except his employees and close friends, of course.

So it was kind of amazing to him that he'd willingly stepped into her web, fully aware of what he was doing and happy to be ensnared by her and her baby son.

A month ago, the thought of being involved with a single mom would've been ludicrous. He'd begun to believe that he'd had his one go-round with true love, and that would be that. When he looked back now at that earlier relationship, he could barely remember the details of her face or the sound of her voice or why he'd been so enthralled.

He already knew that if McKenzie left tomorrow, he'd never forget the fine details that made up her unforgettable face or what she sounded like telling him to go get his helmet and to hurry up about it. Recalling that made him smile like a fool. For a guy who hadn't been bossed by anyone in longer than he could remember, he was sure enjoying being ordered around by her.

Funny how that'd happened—and how he'd let it—knowingly, willingly, eagerly.

As he packed up chicken, potatoes, green beans and salad into containers for transport, he hoped she liked what he'd cooked. If she didn't, he'd order her some takeout. Whatever it took to make her happy.

That last thought should've been enough on its own to send him running for his life from the sort of commitment that would be required to date a single mom—and her son. He ought to talk to Mac about that since he'd had a similar journey with his now-wife and son. He'd do that the next time he saw him.

He hoisted the tote containing dinner over his shoulder and grabbed the bottle of white wine he'd bought for himself since she wasn't drinking and strolled across the yard to the garage apartment, whistling a catchy tune as he went.

McKenzie came to the door, looking like a sunny spring day as she waited for him, wearing those sexy cut-off denim shorts and a sleeveless top with flowers on it.

Now she had him waxing poetic. If that didn't beat all. Maybe Sierra was right that she'd cast a spell over him. How else to explain the gallop in his heart and the heating of his blood as he went up the stairs to her?

She opened the door for him and stepped back to let him in.

The scent of something cooking had his mouth watering.

"What did you make?"

"Gran's banana bread that I promised you and Sierra."

"Oh damn. It smells incredible. My mouth is watering. Am I drooling?" He stuck his chin out so she could get a good look at him.

McKenzie gave him a close inspection that set his heart to racing again. "No sign of drool."

"That's surprising. You and Rosemary's banana bread are a potent combo that would usually cause copious drooling."

She laughed as he deposited his bag on the counter and began unpacking their dinner. "What did you make?"

"Chicken, potatoes, green beans and salad."

"And you made enough for me?"

"Yeah."

"That's very sweet of you."

He gave her his trademarked side-eyed look as he released a low growl.

"What?" she sputtered on a laugh. "It is sweet!"

"It's food. Don't be a doofus about it."

"It's food that you made for *us*."

"You're still being a doofus."

"I appreciate it, Duke." She took him by the chin and kissed him. "I really do."

He was far more undone by a chaste kiss than he should've been. "You're welcome. Grab some plates."

She collected plates and silverware and brought them to the small table with two chairs.

Then she went back for glasses and deposited a lit candle on the table.

While wishing he'd thought to buy some wineglasses for her, he glanced up at her, brow raised at the romantic gesture.

She shrugged. "I found it in the closet."

"It's nice."

"I'm glad you think so."

"Never had dinner with a candle on the table."

"No?"

He scooped potatoes onto both plates. "Nope."

"Well, you've been missing out."

"I can see that. Also never seen anything prettier than you are in candlelight."

As soon as he said the words, he felt like a fool.

"That's the most romantic thing anyone has ever said to me."

He scoffed. "Come on. No way."

She looked at him with those big brown eyes gone liquid with emotion. "Way."

"Well, that's a crying shame, because you deserve it all."

After that, he focused on the meal because it was far too overwhelming to focus on her when she was looking at him like he hung the moon or some other such bullshit. What did he know about hanging moons or waxing poetic?

He stabbed a bite of chicken and chewed it roughly. She was making him into a goddamned fool, and that wouldn't do. After they ate, he was going home to where things made sense. If he tried really hard, he might be able to forget the goddess occupying his garage apartment.

"Why do you seem mad all of a sudden?"

"Huh?" Duke looked up at her, feeling exposed, as if he were sitting there stark naked. He might as well have been. "I'm not mad."

"Yes, you are. It's because you said stuff to me that made you uncomfortable after you said it."

He paused, fork halfway to his mouth. "What's that you say?"

"You said something sweet and romantic, and then you decided it was stupid, so you got mad at the chicken. But it wasn't stupid. It was... It was one of the best moments of my life, and you can't take it back because that would break my heart."

"Goddamn it," he muttered as he let the fork fall to his plate with a loud clank. "Why you gotta put it like that?"

"It's true. No one's ever said anything like that to me before."

"Well, that's a crying shame."

"Don't be mad at yourself for being the first."

"I'm not."

"You are. Why?"

"You freaking undo me with the way you look at me and how open and honest you are about everything."

"Oh, well… I suppose that's not a *bad* thing, right?"

"I'm still trying to decide."

Her face shifted into a sexy little smile. "Let me know when you do."

"Quit enjoying this so much."

"You can't make me, so stop being grumpy and finish your dinner."

"Bossiness turns me on. Never knew that before."

"Is that right?"

"Uh-huh. Don't use that against me."

"Why wouldn't I if it turns you on?" She got up from her seat and came around to his side of the table. "Make room."

"For what?"

"For me."

He scooted his chair back and tried to hang on to some semblance of control when she straddled his lap and wrapped her arms around his neck.

"Hey."

"What's up?"

"Ummm…" She shifted to press her heat against his hard cock.

He grasped her ass and pulled her in tighter against him, nearly giving himself a heart attack in the process. "You're quite pleased with yourself, aren't you?"

"I am. This has been the best day *ever*."

"What else happened?"

"Including you and Sierra, I now have *seven* new clients."

"Wow. That was fast, but I'm not surprised. Everyone needs you. But what about your job with Tiffany?"

"I got fired."

"What?"

"When I told her what was happening with the bookkeeping busi-ness, she hired me to do hers and fired me from the shop. She said being self-employed is the best and that I'll have more business than I can handle."

"She's right."

"First time I ever got fired," she added with a big goofy grin that made everything inside him go soft with affection for her, except for the one part of him that was most definitely *not* soft.

His insides had never gone soft over anyone like they did for her. "You're really making a mess of me, MK."

"A good mess?"

"I think so."

"You're not sure?"

"It's all so unprecedented, I don't know what I am."

"Are you happy?"

As he looked up at her gorgeous, sweet, sexy face, he realized he'd never been happier than he was right in that moment. "Yeah, I'm happy."

And then she kissed him and made it even better.

CHAPTER 23

*M*cKenzie loved kissing him. She loved the way his beard rubbed against her face and how he held her so close. She loved the tenderness, the barely contained desire and the sense of wonder that came over her every single time her lips connected with his. In her former life, she would've looked right past the long-haired, bearded man wearing a leather vest that put full-sleeve tattoos on display.

A lot of women went wild for ink on a man. She'd never been one of them, until now. Until him.

Until Duke.

"What's your real name?" she asked between tongue-twisting kisses.

"Duke."

"No way."

"Way."

"That's not a nickname?"

"Nope."

"Who named you that?"

"No idea."

"You've never asked your mother where the name came from?"

"Nope. More kissing, less questions."

"Not until I finish asking my questions."

He groaned and dropped his forehead to her shoulder. "What else you want to know?"

"Why haven't you asked her that?"

"I've seen her five times in my whole life. It's never come up."

"Duke…"

"Don't do that pity thing. I'm totally fine with it. She is who she is, and I'm not trying to make her into the mother of my dreams. Already had that with Rosemary."

"Oh, I love that."

"Don't do that eye thing again. Once in a day is all I can take."

"What eye thing?"

"When you use them as the most powerful weapon in your considerable arsenal."

"I do that?"

"Yeah, you do, and it works, so cut it out."

"What does it do to you?"

"I'm not telling you out of self-preservation."

"Come on! I want to know."

"No."

"I could get it out of you."

"You think so?"

"I know so."

"Now you're just getting full of yourself."

"I'd rather be full of something else."

"McKenzie…"

"Yes, Duke?"

"I feel like this is getting way out of control before we're ready for that."

"You're not ready for it?"

"I want to be, but…"

"But what?"

"You're a lot younger than me."

"I know."

"You're a single mom."

"I also know that."

"You're Rosemary's granddaughter, and she meant the world to me."

"She did to me, too. Isn't that a nice thing to have in common?"

"It is, but…"

"Duke?"

"What?"

"Do you want to have sex with me?"

"Holy hell, woman."

"Well, do you?"

He pressed his hard cock against her and nearly whimpered from the jolt of pleasure. "Isn't it obvious?"

"Yeah, it is, so why are you trying to come up with a million reasons why we shouldn't?"

"I don't want to mess this up."

"You couldn't."

He laughed—hard. "Sweetheart, there are a million *bazillion* ways I could mess this up."

"You won't."

"How can you possibly know that?"

"It's the weirdest thing…"

"What is?"

"That I feel like I know you better than I've ever known anyone, even though we haven't known each other that long."

"How is that even possible?"

"It's all the little things… How you went to the police station to ask about us after the storm. You brought as much of our stuff as you could rescue from the cabin, and then you went back and got Mr. Bear and cleaned him up for Jax. It was how you drove us around and showed Jax the flowers in your garden, and don't get me *started* on the cross-stitching." She fanned her face. "Sexiest thing I've ever seen."

"You gotta be freaking kidding me," he said, even though he was deeply moved by her recitation of the facts of their story thus far.

"I'm so not kidding. I've never been more surprised by anything."

"Not even Eric's wife and family?"

"That's got nothing on you cross-stitching."

"Something is wrong with you."

She tossed her head back and laughed as hard as he'd seen her laugh yet.

He took full advantage of the opportunity to nibble on her glorious neck.

She gasped and shuddered, and he was fucking done.

Done.

How had he lived for thirty-six years without *craving* someone like this?

It was hard to hear any other thought in his head around the drumbeat of desire, but one kept creeping through:

Too much. Too soon.

Too much. Too soon.

He wanted to ignore it, but he'd learned to trust his instincts in all things. That's what'd allowed him to have a successful life without much help or guidance. With something this important, he couldn't ignore the voice that had never steered him wrong.

"MK," he whispered against her lips.

"Hmm?"

"I want what you want."

"I like when that happens."

"Me, too. It's just that… I want to do this right, and knocking one out on the sofa while your baby sleeps in the next room isn't right."

"It could be."

He shook his head. "I want you to take a beat and think this through. We both know everything changes after that happens, and I like this a lot the way it is now. I don't want it to become something different."

"It'll become something better."

"You're very certain of that."

"I am, but I want you to be, too."

"I'm very certain that you've turned my whole life upside down in the best way possible." He kissed her because he couldn't resist her plump, swollen lips. "I'm very certain that you're the most beautiful woman I've ever laid eyes on."

When she would've protested that, he kissed her again. "I get to say who that is for me, and it's you. Three hundred thousand percent you."

Her little whimper nearly broke the fragile hold he had on his control.

"But I want you to consider the other stuff I said. I want you to be totally sure."

"I am."

"McKenzie..."

"Duke." She leaned in and took his earlobe between her teeth and nearly made him come in his pants when she bit down on it. "Maybe I'm a bit younger than you, but I'm a fully grown woman who knows the difference between a guy who'd make for a fun one-night stand and one who could go the distance. I'd never have let you anywhere near my son if I wasn't one hundred percent sure you're in the latter category."

"I never should've let you catch me cross-stitching."

Her husky laughter was the best thing he'd ever heard. "That was an error of epic proportions."

"I'm beginning to see that."

"I want to be with you. I want to end the best day I've ever had with you."

What in the world could he say to that? "Can we bring Jax over to my place?"

"Uh-huh."

"He won't wake up?"

"If he does, he'll go right back to sleep."

"Okay, then..."

"Should I get him?"

Duke felt good about having tried to do the right thing, but the time for talking was over. "Yeah, I think you should."

. . .

JACK DOWNING FOUND Billy Weyland floating in about six feet of water in the southern corner of the Great Salt Pond.

"Son of a bitch," he whispered upon realizing what he was looking at. He'd met Billy a few times at the gym and had liked talking to him while he worked out.

He reached for the handheld radio to call in the grim discovery. "Downing to base. Come in."

"This is base. Go."

"I've found Weyland in the southeast corner of the pond."

After a long pause, the dispatcher said, "We're sending additional resources. Please stand by."

"Copy."

While he waited, Jack never took his eyes off the body. Other people would be in charge of retrieval, thank goodness. After his brother was notified, word would ricochet through the island community that the second missing man had been found dead. He hurt for Morgan, who'd held out hope even in the face of grim odds.

Billy and Jim had taken a foolish risk and had paid for it with their lives.

In a contest of man versus Mother Nature, she almost always won. After growing up on an island, Billy and Jim should've known that.

Blaine and Deacon Taylor were in the first boat to pull up next to Jack's.

He pointed.

"Damn it," Blaine said. "I was so hoping."

"I know," Jack said. "Me, too, but at least Morgan and Billy's friends will get closure." He surprised himself with the statement as he rarely used that word and seriously doubted such a thing even existed. He knew all too well how elusive a concept *closure* was after having lost his wife to breast cancer when she was only thirty-five.

The fire department boat joined them next and took command of the scene.

Blaine transferred to Jack's boat since Deacon would be assisting in the recovery. "Give me a lift back to the dock?"

"Sure."

Jack turned the boat toward McCarthys', thankful to be leaving the scene before he had to see more of Billy.

"Are you all right?" Blaine asked.

"Yeah, I'm glad we found him even if it wasn't the outcome we wanted."

"Agreed."

"How's Deacon doing after finding Sturgil?"

"He seems okay."

"Keep an eye on him. After his own ordeal, that'll hit close to home."

"I hear you, and I agree."

"I've been thinking nonstop about Tiffany and sweet Ashleigh."

"Thank you for that," Blaine said. "They appreciate the outpouring of love and support."

"They deserve it."

"For sure."

"How're you dealing with it?"

Blaine looked over at him. "Me? Doesn't involve me, except for supporting them, of course."

"It involves you."

"How do you figure?"

"You just became that little girl's only father."

"Yes, I guess I did."

"That's kind of a big deal, no?"

"It only makes official how I already felt about her. I've always loved her like she was mine. How can you not?"

"Right? She's adorable and sweet. I love the way she takes care of Addie." Jack had spent a memorable evening with the Taylors recently and had fallen in love with Blaine's little girls.

"She's her second mommy. Cutest thing ever."

"She's a doll."

"I hated that son of a bitch Sturgil and what he put them through," Blaine said fiercely. "I fucking hated his guts."

"That's understandable."

"So why do I feel so bad that he ended up dead in the pond?"

"Because you're a decent kind of guy who wouldn't want that for anyone, even someone you hated."

"My mom used to tell us not to hate anyone, and I swear to God, I've tried not to. But that guy..."

"Yeah, I think your mom would give you a pass after some of the shit he pulled."

"She knew all about it and probably has her own opinions. Then again, she thought I should steer clear of Tiffany when we were first together."

"Really?"

"Oh yeah. You weren't around when Tiff first opened her store and was advertising her wares outside on the sidewalk, causing at least one accident a day."

"Come on," Jack said, laughing. "She did not."

"She absolutely did!"

"That must've been quite something."

"Stop imagining it, or I'll punch your lights out."

Jack howled with laughter. He laughed so hard he had tears in his eyes that made it difficult to drive the boat.

Blaine glowered at him.

Gasping for breath, Jack waved a hand in front of his face. "The best part is imagining you dealing with her when she was causing accidents in front of the store."

"We put on quite a shit show."

"Oh my God, this is the best thing I've heard in a long time."

"Stop trying to picture it. That's my fucking wife!"

Jack started laughing again and couldn't stop. He couldn't recall the last time he'd laughed like that. It'd been a long time. Since before Ruby died. "Feels wrong to be laughing my ass off shortly after finding Billy's body."

"It's okay. We're not being disrespectful. If we don't laugh, we might never stop crying with some of the stuff we see on the job."

"That's true." Jack brought the boat in for a smooth landing at a floating dock next to McCarthys' Marina. While Blaine secured the bow line, Jack took care of the stern. They went up the ramp to the main pier, where Mr. McCarthy was holding court with the usual cast of characters.

"How's it goin' out there?" Ned Saunders asked.

"We found Billy," Blaine said. "Heading into town now to find his brother to let him know, so keep it between us for now."

"Will do," Big Mac said. "Sorry to hear, but glad he's been found."

"Yeah, same."

"How's Tiffany and Ashleigh?" Frank McCarthy asked. "Been thinking about them."

"They're hanging in there. Tough thing to explain to a six-year-old."

"I can't even imagine," Dr. Kevin McCarthy said. "If they need to talk it out, you know where to find me."

Big Mac and his brothers, including their honorary brother Ned, were some of the finest men Blaine had ever known. "We do. Tiff and I were thinking about making an appointment with you for Ashleigh."

"Can't hurt," Kevin said. "I'd be happy to help in any way that I can."

"Thanks, Doc. Well, we'd better go get this done."

"Don't envy you that," Big Mac said.

"Part of the job," Blaine replied. "We'll see you later."

"Thanks fer what ya do, guys," Ned said. "It's appreciated."

"That's nice to hear," Jack said. "Thanks."

They walked to Blaine's SUV and drove into town to find Billy's brother, Morgan.

"I guess we should start at the gym," Blaine said. "From what I've heard, he's been hanging there and taking care of things in Billy's absence."

"Yeah, I heard that, too. Billy's pals have been rallying around him."

"Linc Mercer told me Billy and Morgan lost their parents and sister in quick succession a few years back. Was just the two of them left."

"Ah, crap. I hate to hear that."

"I know. I can't imagine being the last one left in my original family."

"Me either."

"The close call with Deacon, and now this thing with Jim, has me feeling extra thankful lately."

"I'm sure. Deacon got so freaking lucky."

"I know. Far too close for comfort. I wake up in a cold sweat thinking about what would've happened if Joe and Seamus hadn't taken the ferries out to sea to ride out the storm."

"Thank God they did," Jack said.

"Yeah, no kidding."

"How does Deacon seem after nearly being lost at sea?"

"Fine, which is a bit worrisome. I mean, how can he just pick right up and go back to work like it never happened?"

"Maybe the return to normalcy is what he needs more than anything."

"Yeah, I guess. And then he had to be the one to find Jim. It's been a lot for him."

"I'm sure his big brother is keeping a watchful eye on him."

"You know it."

Blaine pulled into the parking lot at the gym, across the parking lot from the ferry landing, about a block from the tattoo and massage studios. "Let's get this over with."

Jack followed Blaine inside, where the blast of rock music and metal connecting with metal greeted them.

Morgan Weyland, who was about thirty-five, with dark hair tinged with gray on the edges, was folding towels behind the registration desk. His expression went blank when he saw them coming. "You found him."

"We did," Blaine said. "Please accept our condolences on the loss of your brother."

Morgan's dark eyes were rimmed with red from a week of sleepless nights and unbearable stress. "Goddamn it, Billy."

"We're so sorry," Jack said.

"Thanks for all you guys and the others did to find him. That stupid son of a bitch." Morgan's eyes filled with tears. "How could he go and leave me here all alone?"

"Is there anyone we could call to come over and be with you?" Blaine asked.

Morgan shook his head. "It's just me—and him. Or it was."

"How about a friend?" Jack asked.

"Yeah, I'll reach out. Thanks for letting me know. Where are they taking him?"

"The coroner will be over from Providence," Blaine said. "They'll perform an autopsy and then release him to the funeral home of your choice on the mainland. We can give you some suggestions."

"Sure, that'd help. Thanks."

"When they're done, they can send him back over on the ferry if you want to bury him here on the island."

"There's nowhere else he'd rather be."

"I'll be in touch," Blaine said.

Jack handed Morgan his card. "Call if there's anything at all I can do for you."

Morgan shook hands with both of them. "Thanks again, you guys, and to everyone who was part of the search. Please tell them..." His voice broke. "Tell them I appreciate it."

"We will."

As they left the gym, Jack said, "I feel bad leaving him."

"I do, too, but we've done what we can for him."

"I wonder if he'll stick around and take over the gym?"

"I guess we'll see."

CHAPTER 24

$\mathcal{M}$cKenzie carried her sleeping son across the yard to Duke's house, expecting to have second or third thoughts or regrets or something that would stop her from taking a step that could never be undone.

The only thoughts she had, however, involved excitement, anticipation and relief at finally, finally, *finally* having found a truly decent man who was also sexy, thoughtful, funny and, much to his dismay, sweet. This must be what it was like to find a unicorn.

That thought made her laugh as she knocked on Duke's door.

He'd gone over ahead of her to set up a place for Jax to sleep.

"You don't have to knock here," he said gruffly as he opened the door for her.

"Yes, I do. It's polite."

"Don't be polite with me."

"Are we going to fight about me having manners, or was there something else you had in mind?"

"That sassy mouth of yours is going to get you in trouble."

"Promise?"

His low growl made her giggle.

"Laughing at me isn't exactly polite."

"Maybe not, but it's fun." If McKenzie had to choose one thing that she liked best about being with him, it was that she felt safe to be herself. There was never a time when she had to think about what she was going to say before she said it or need to worry that she might offend his delicate sensibilities. That'd been a huge challenge with Eric, who was easily offended and didn't take well to joking around.

Duke's home was warm and cozy and had framed cross-stitch samplers on almost every wall. She would take a closer look at all of them another time.

"I set him up in here." Duke led her to a smaller bedroom where he'd placed rolled blankets in a circle on the bed. "Will that work?"

"That'll be great, thanks. He hardly ever moves when he's asleep." McKenzie settled Jax in the center of the nest Duke had made for him and waited to make sure he'd stay asleep.

As she stroked his downy, soft hair and kissed his cheek, he never stirred.

"Mommy loves you," she whispered.

She got up to leave the room and found Duke leaning against the doorframe. "He's a lucky boy to have you as his mom."

"I'm the lucky one."

"As a boy who never once heard his mother whisper that she loves him, trust me. He's the lucky one."

She rested her hands on his hips as she looked up at him. "I'm sorry you didn't have that."

"You don't miss what you never had."

The way he said that indicated it was something he'd said—and thought—many times before. "How did you become this sweet, kind, loving man with no one showing you how?"

"I had people who showed me how I wanted to live, especially your grandmother."

"I love that she did that for you."

"She was my Yoda. She made me want to live the way she did."

"She'd be so, so proud of you."

"I hope so."

"I know so."

"Look at this." He took her hand and led her to the mantel over his fireplace, where he showed her a photo of him and Rosemary. "That's the Christmas I spent at her place on the mainland."

McKenzie picked up the framed photo to take a closer look. "I remember you now. You were sort of gruff and quiet."

"I was so nervous about saying the wrong thing or something."

She put the frame back on the mantel next to others of him with various groups of people. "That's so sweet."

"I didn't lure you over here to talk about your grandmother."

"No?"

He shook his head before he kissed her. "I can't think about her when I want to get you naked. It feels wrong."

McKenzie laughed. "She loved us both. I have to think she'd love us together."

"Maybe so, but if she's hanging around keeping an eye on things, this would be a really good time for her to get lost."

The comment had McKenzie howling with laughter that quickly turned into a moan when Duke kissed her neck. Just like that, her knees went weak, and only his arm around her waist kept her standing. How'd he do that with a simple kiss? That was just one more thing to add to his list of unicorn qualities—the ability to render her weak in the knees with a kiss.

"I was thinking about how you're a unicorn."

He tightened his arms around her, lifted her and carried her to the other bedroom at the far end of the hallway. "Huh?"

Impressed by the show of strength, she said, "You're all these things that most other guys will never be."

"I'm almost afraid to ask…"

"Sexy." She kissed his neck to return the favor. "Funny." More kisses and a bit of teeth tossed in to make him growl.

He didn't disappoint.

"Thoughtful. That's a big one." She dragged her tongue over the pulse point in his throat. "Kind. That one's *huge* and hard to find." More kisses, followed by more groaning as he pressed his erection against her abdomen. "You're also a loyal, dedicated friend." She bit his earlobe. "And you can cross-stitch."

He grunted out a laugh. "That's really your favorite thing, right?"

"You know it."

"Never gonna live that down."

"Not ever." She used her chin to gesture to his bed. "Did you do those pillows?"

"All of them except the big one in the middle. That was from Rosemary."

"Duke..."

"Yes, McKenzie?"

"You have *throw pillows* on your bed."

"So?"

"I'm ridiculously turned on by that."

"Are you making fun of me again by any chance?"

"Would I do that?"

"Yes, and you'd enjoy it."

She looked up at him, meeting his intense gaze, which was completely focused on her. "I enjoy everything with you."

"Yeah?" he asked, sounding surprised.

"Uh-huh."

"That's a heck of a nice thing to say."

"It's the truth."

"I enjoy every freaking second I spend with you—and Jax."

"Thank you for including him."

"Of course I included him. He comes with the sweet, sexy, funny, smart, bossy, sarcastic, gorgeous, smoking-hot package named MK."

"Smoking hot, huh?"

"*Girl...*"

She was falling in love with that growl—and every other thing about him. After Eric, she'd promised herself she'd never again give a man the power to break her heart—and she'd fully intended to keep that promise. Until Duke Sullivan sauntered into her life and showed her something she'd never had before. And now that she'd seen it, she wanted as much of it as she could get.

She wanted him. She wanted to love him and take care of him the way he cared for everyone in his life.

He tipped his head and gave her an intense look. "Did you have any second thoughts between your place and mine?"

"Not one. And don't tell me again that it's my funeral. I don't want to hear that."

The left side of his face lifted in an adorably crooked grin. "The bossiness is a massive turn-on."

"That ought to give you second thoughts."

"And yet... It just has me wanting more." His fingers slipped under her top and scorched her back.

Goose bumps erupted on every inch of her skin, making her shiver.

"Are you cold?"

"Not at all."

"It's like that, is it?"

"It is." She pushed the leather vest off his shoulders to reveal a T-shirt with a skull and crossbones prominently featured.

The badass persona on the outside was in sharp contrast to the softie on the inside. She suspected his tough outer shell had served as a defense mechanism to survive in the world on his own.

"Can we take this off?" she asked, tugging on his T-shirt.

He reached behind him and hauled it up and over, revealing a muscular chest and abdomen that had her licking her lips in anticipation of exploring every hill and valley.

"That time you spend at the gym?"

"Haven't been getting there lately."

"You need to keep that up," she said, dragging her fingertips over his ab muscles, which quivered under her touch.

"Yes, ma'am." He reached behind her to release the clasp on her bra and stepped back to let it fall to the ground between them.

McKenzie closed her eyes to absorb the wallop of emotions that raced through her as her breasts brushed against the soft hair on his chest.

"Damn," he whispered.

"Mmm, damn is right."

"What're you doing here with me? You're a fucking goddess."

"And you're a fucking unicorn, and don't you ever forget it."

"You make me feel ten feet tall."

"You don't have to be anything other than exactly who and what you are to make me happier than I've ever been."

"You sure know how to get to me."

"Do I?"

"Yes, and you know you do."

She flashed her biggest smile and then reached for the first of five buttons on the fly of his jeans, pulling them open one after the other and then pushing her hands inside the back to remove them.

"You forgot the boots."

"So I did." She could tell she surprised him when she dropped to her knees to untie them. When she looked up at him, the gaze he directed her way could only be called scorching.

"I want to remember this for the rest of my life."

"And you wonder what I'm doing here with you?"

He nodded as she sat up on her knees to press her face against his straining cock.

His fingers dove into her hair as he gasped. "McKenzie..."

"Yes, Duke?"

"I, uh..." His deep sigh amused her.

"You don't say?"

"Can't talk."

McKenzie laughed softly as she freed his erection from snug boxer briefs and took in the sight of him in all his glory. "I've got another thing to add to your list of unicorn qualities," she said as she ran her tongue over the piercing tucked under the broad crown.

"Fuck *me*," he said on a protracted hiss.

"Um, what's this I see?" she asked of the piercing.

"Can't talk right now."

"That must've hurt."

"Like fuck, but you'll like it."

"Mmm, is that right?"

"Uh-huh."

She decided to have some fun with him as she teased him with her tongue and the lightest of teeth before she took as much of him as she could into her mouth, loving the way he tugged at her hair while holding on for dear life.

"Hey, so, um…"

McKenzie doubled down and added the tight squeeze of her hand at the base.

"MK!"

She heard the warning but didn't back off until he'd shouted from the power of his release. Then she released him slowly, drawing out the pleasure for him as long as she could.

"Mother-effer." He helped her up and into his arms. "That was… *Wow.*" He fell backward, bringing her with him as he kicked off his boots and pants. "You're incredible."

"So are you."

"I've got nothing on you."

"Are you trying to make me mad right now?"

"Not even kinda."

"Then quit talking shit about my new favorite person."

"I like being your new favorite person."

"I like being yours." She raised a brow. "I am, right?"

His laughter was becoming one of her favorite things, mostly because she suspected he didn't let it loose that often. "Hell yes, you are, and you know it."

He rolled them so he was on top of her, gazing down at her with all the things she'd hoped to one day find in a man. He didn't look like the Prince Charming of her childhood dreams, but she'd learned that most of the men who looked like Prince Charming were frogs. This one had everything she could want or need, and she'd known that almost from the first time she ever saw him.

"What're you thinking about?" he asked as he laid soft kisses on her face, the tip of her nose and then her lips.

"How you showed me who you really are the day we met, and you've never deviated from that first impression. You know why that is?"

"Tell me."

"It's the truth of who you are. It wasn't a game you were playing to get me to notice you."

"Is that how it usually goes?"

"Always. It's all bullshit at the beginning until they get you where they want you and the ugly truth starts to emerge."

He used his thumbs to brush the hair back from her face. "And where is it that they want you?"

"Right where you have me."

"Just for the record, I love having you here, but I loved having you at the shop today, and I loved having you at my firepit and eating with you in the apartment and riding with me in the truck. I like having you everywhere else, too."

"I know you do, and that means a lot to me. That's a big part of why I invited myself into your bed."

"You have a standing invite."

"Good to know." She drew him into a kiss that went from soft and sweet to hot and bothered in about three seconds.

He settled between her legs, breaking the kiss only to move down to kiss her breasts. The feel of his mouth closing around her nipple made her crazy with desire and affection and something that felt an awful lot like love for this one-of-a-kind man.

She'd felt safe with him long before they'd gotten naked, and that allowed her to let go of the anxieties that were usually part of the first time with someone new and to relax and wallow in the pleasure.

A sound from another part of the house had her eyes opening while Duke went still on top of her.

"Duke! Wake up!"

Was that Sierra?

"What the fuck?" He pushed himself up and off McKenzie,

reaching for a pair of sweats from the foot of the bed. "Sorry. I'll be right back."

He put on the pants, left the room and closed the door behind him.

McKenzie pulled a throw blanket over her and tried to hear what they were saying as she hoped against hope that she hadn't misjudged him.

CHAPTER 25

"What the hell are you doing here at this hour?"

"It's only ten. Since when are you in bed by then?"

"Since now. Are you drunk?"

"Maybe. A little."

"How'd you get here?"

"Ned brought me."

Great, Duke thought. *Now someone else knows Sierra came to his house late at night and will jump to the usual conclusions.* Not that Ned would tell anyone, but still...

"Why didn't you text me?"

"I did. You didn't answer."

"That's because I'm busy."

Her eyes got wide. "Is she *here?* Now?"

Before he could reply, he was horrified to see tears in her eyes. What the hell was happening? "What's going on, Sierra?"

"Nothing. I'll go. I didn't mean to interrupt."

She was out the door before he could stop her, so he followed her into the yard.

"Sierra. Stop."

He honestly couldn't believe what he was seeing when she crum-

223

pled before his eyes, dropping into one of the Adirondack chairs near his firepit and weeping as if her heart had been demolished. "Did something happen?"

She shook her head as she continued to sob.

Duke sat next to her and put a hand on her shoulder. "Tell me what's going on."

The Sierra he knew and loved didn't cry. She made other people cry. He was truly unsettled to see her so upset, and he couldn't help but wonder what McKenzie must be thinking after another woman had come barging into his home like she lived there at the worst possible time.

"They found Billy."

Duke gasped. "Oh damn."

As a daily regular at the gym, Sierra had been closer to him than Duke was. "I'm sorry. I was so hoping he'd be found alive."

"I know. We all were. His poor brother. Did you know it was just the two of them? Their parents and sister all died young."

"No, I didn't. That's so sad."

A few minutes passed before Sierra had pulled herself together to the point where she could speak. "I'm sorry. I shouldn't have barged in on you like that."

"It's okay."

"No, it isn't."

"Is something else other than Billy upsetting you?"

"It's going to sound so stupid."

"Tell me anyway."

"You have better things to do than listen to me freak out."

They'd been friends for a long time, and he'd never seen her freak out, which was why it was so disconcerting to see her this way.

She wiped her face and seemed to force herself to look at him. "Remember that I told you this is going to sound stupid..." She took a deep breath and then released it. "As we get, you know, deeper into our thirties, I guess I had it in my mind that if it never happened for us, we might, you know, end up together."

Duke stared at her almost as if he were seeing her for the first time. Her confession shocked him.

"It told you it was stupid. Seeing you with McKenzie kind of forced me to confront some things, and... I'm sorry. I never should've come here and barged into your house like that."

"You're welcome here any time. You know that."

"I do. I know that." She glanced at him through the loose strands of her hair. "I've made everything weird between us now, haven't I?"

"No, but you've surprised me. I didn't know you thought of me as your backup plan."

"Don't put it that way."

"Isn't that what it would've been, though?"

"I guess, but I care about you too much to ever think of you in those terms."

"And I care about you, but not like that. Believe me, there've been times when I wondered what was wrong with me that I wasn't asking you out or trying to make something happen with you. But it was the word 'trying' that always stopped me. If it was going to happen between us, it would have. A long time ago."

"Yeah, I know, and you're right. My meltdown has nothing to do with you and everything to do with me realizing that time is moving on and my life isn't what I hoped it would be at this point. That's on me, not you." She stood. "I'll go. I'm sorry I interrupted your evening. McKenzie seems like a nice person. I hope you guys will be h-happy."

"I'll drive you home."

"Don't be silly. I can get myself home."

"I'll drive you. Just let me grab my keys."

She sighed. "Fine."

Duke went inside and directly to the bedroom, where McKenzie was stretched out on his bed under a blanket.

"Everything okay?"

"Yeah, she's... I don't know. She's upset. They found Billy, who was a friend of hers. I'm going to drive her home. I'll be back in twenty minutes. I'm really sorry about this."

"It's fine."

He leaned over to kiss her. "It's not fine, but I didn't know she was coming or that she was upset or any of it."

"It's not your fault. I think I'll go home, though."

"Please don't." He paused, feeling as torn as he ever had between where he wanted to be and what he needed to do for a longtime friend. "The only thing I want in this entire world is to be here with you. Please don't go."

She smiled, and some of the earlier warmth returned to her eyes. "Okay. I won't."

"I'll be right back."

"I'll be here."

He kissed her again before grabbing a sweatshirt and his keys and heading for the door. When he stepped into the cool autumn air, he unlocked the truck for Sierra.

She climbed into the passenger seat.

Duke backed the truck out of the driveway and headed for town, where Sierra lived above her studio.

"I feel like a total asshole. Is she mad?"

"Nah. It's fine."

"I'd never want to mess anything up for you. I hope you know that."

"I do."

"Can I ask you something?"

"Yeah, sure."

"What is it about her that does it for you?"

Duke huffed out a laugh. "Everything. Every fucking thing. She's smart, funny, sexy, practical and an amazing mother. She's bossy as hell and tells me to wear a helmet on the bike, and I do it because she cares. That's why she's making me do it."

Sierra turned toward him in her seat. "You're wearing a helmet?"

"Yep."

"Wow, this is serious."

"I think it could be."

"You really want to take on a woman with a kid?"

"If it's that woman and that kid, then yeah, I do."

"Huh."

"What does that mean?"

"I never pictured you as the domesticated family man."

He shrugged. "People grow up. They change. They want different things."

"I know they do. I just didn't think you would."

"Why?"

"I guess because you didn't have it growing up, so I figured you didn't want it."

"I didn't until I met someone who made me want it."

"And you already know you want that with her?"

"I know that for the first time since Lynn, I want to see what it could be." After a long silence, he added, "I hope you can be happy for me."

"I am! Of course I am."

Duke pulled up to a parking spot next to the stairs that led to her apartment. "I hope so. You know how important you are to me, and you always will be."

"I do know, and same goes. I'm sorry I made everything weird tonight. I had too much wine and…"

"No worries."

"I want you to know… No one deserves to be happy more than you do."

"That's not true—"

"It is, Duke. It's true."

Sierra was one of the few people who knew just how rough his childhood had been.

"Does she know?"

He shook his head. "There's no need to go there. It's all in the past now."

"It's a big part of your past, and if this thing with her is as serious as you say it is, you should tell her everything she needs to know."

"Thank you for your input. I'll take it under advisement."

She leaned over to kiss his cheek. "Thanks for the ride home and for not kicking me out of your life."

"I want you in my life. But you have to accept McKenzie to stay there. I won't have any drama where she's concerned. She's had enough of that to last a lifetime."

"I get it. No drama."

"Go get some sleep—and take a Motrin so you're not hurting tomorrow."

"Thanks, Dad. I will. Love you."

"Love you, too, kid."

Duke watched her go up the stairs and waited until the lights went on inside before he backed out of the spot and headed for home.

Freaking Sierra. Ugh. Not only had she arrived at the worst possible time, but she'd also filled his head with things from his past that he tried hard to never revisit. It'd taken years for him to not think about the bad stuff every day anymore, and now she had him wondering if he owed McKenzie the full truth about his past before he could expect to have a future with her.

He so, so, *so* did not want to go there with her or anyone.

Ever.

But was it fair to her for him not to give her all the information she needed to make decisions about whether she wanted to be with him long-term?

He'd never told Lynn, and he'd been relieved later that he hadn't reopened that wound for a relationship that hadn't lasted.

Today had been a really good day. Tonight had been a great night. He wished he could rewind to earlier to see Sierra's text so he could tell her not to come over. That way, he'd never have had to hear her tell him he owed it to McKenzie to fully share his painful past with her.

That was the last fucking thing he wanted to be thinking about as he headed home to her mostly naked in his bed.

He hoped they could pick up where they'd left off before they were interrupted, and more than anything, he hoped that Sierra's sudden appearance at his house hadn't given McKenzie doubts about him or his relationship with Sierra.

In the driveway, he applied the brakes impatiently and brought the truck to an abrupt stop. He jogged from the truck to the door and rushed to the bedroom to find her curled up in a ball, fast asleep in his bed, hands placed angelically under her face.

The sight of her sleeping in his bed came with an overwhelming feeling of rightness. As he got undressed, he hoped she'd make herself comfortable in his bed and his life. He went to check on Jax, brushed his teeth and took a leak before he crawled into bed next to her, putting an arm around her.

She sighed and relaxed into his embrace, as if she knew it was him and that she was safe.

This night hadn't turned out the way he'd thought it would, but she was sleeping in his arms while her little boy slept in the next room.

Having them there was like having a dream he hadn't dared to entertain come true. He wanted to close his eyes and dwell in that perfect place for as long as he possibly could.

CHAPTER 26

*E*arly the next morning, Tiffany told her mom and Ned, who'd brought coffee and doughnuts from the marina, that she wanted to go see Maddie.

"I'll drive ya over," Ned said.

"I can take the SUV," Tiffany replied, still mourning for her beautiful Bug.

"No need. I'll take ya."

She understood that the dear man who was now her stepfather, and truly the only father she'd ever known, wanted to do something to help. So she let him. "Thank you, Ned. That'd be great. Let me get the girls ready."

They set out fifteen minutes later, bringing the rest of the doughnuts for the kids to enjoy with their cousins.

Ashleigh had lit up with delight at being told she'd be seeing her cousin and best friend, Thomas. If anyone could make her feel better, Thomas could. With only a few months between them, they'd been raised like siblings from the beginning, and he was still her favorite person in the whole world. She also adored Addie, Hailey, Mac and the twin babies. But Thomas was her person, and their mothers loved the tight bond their children shared.

From the back seat of Ned's cab, with her girls strapped into the seats Ned always had handy for them, Tiffany watched the familiar scenery go by while feeling oddly detached from the place she'd called home most of her life. She'd left only to help Jim through law school. They'd returned to set up his island practice right after he graduated.

His discontent had set in soon after they came home to the island. She saw that now. For a long time, she'd tried to pretend that nothing had changed as she went through the motions of being a wife and mother, supporting his dreams the way she always had while fighting for a few of her own. She'd run an at-home daycare and a dance studio then, trying to do her part to supplement his income while he built the practice.

But nothing she'd done had been enough. After working multiple jobs while he was in law school and giving him a beautiful daughter, he'd simply checked out of their marriage right when they were on the cusp of finally realizing the life they'd envisioned for themselves.

Suddenly, he'd no longer wanted that life—or her.

Tiffany was amazed at how, even after all this time, after years of marriage to a man who worshipped the ground she walked on, that it could still hurt to think about the way Jim had discarded her.

Things had gone rapidly downhill between them, culminating in a messy divorce that had turned most of the island against him and his practice and led to him making a series of disastrous decisions, one of which had landed him in jail after he slashed Dan Torrington's hand open during Dan and Kara's engagement party.

Speaking of Dan, she'd gotten a text from him and Kara the night before that she'd failed to respond to.

She withdrew her phone and read it again.

Hey, Tiff, Kara and I were sorry to hear the news about Jim. Like you, I'm sure, we're shocked and saddened. We're thinking of you, Ashleigh and your family at this difficult time. Sending much love from Maine!

Thank you so much for your kind note. You're right that we're shocked and saddened, which is the ultimate paradox, right? I wanted him gone, but not like this. I'm sure you understand better than most. Everyone is rallying around Ash, and she's holding up as well as can be expected. It's a lot for a six-year-old to understand. We heard about why you went to Maine, and we're sorry to hear Kara's family is going through that. With you on their side, we have no doubt her brothers will be exonerated, and you'll be back here where you belong in no time. In the meantime, we'll miss you very much. Please stay in touch and let us know how you're doing. Much love back to you!

Two of Kara's brothers had been charged with murder. Tiffany didn't know the details, but she hoped that what she'd said was true and their friends would be back on the island soon.

Ned pulled into Maddie's driveway on Sweet Meadow Farm Road, where Linda's yellow Bug was parked next to Maddie's SUV.

Tiffany recalled being intensely jealous of her older sister after she'd fallen for Mac McCarthy and ended up in this palace of a home with him.

Those days seemed long ago now that she'd found her own prince and built a whole new life with him, but the loss of Jim had resurrected a lot of old and unwelcome emotions. She'd hated being jealous of Maddie and the rift her jealousy had caused between her and her sister for a time. They were long past that now, thank goodness.

Ashleigh was out of the car and up the stairs the second after the car came to a stop in the driveway.

Tiffany freed Addie from her car seat and gathered the big bag she took everywhere that had them covered for any potential disaster while away from home. As she shouldered the bag and followed her mom and Ned up the stairs to Maddie's deck, she realized how long it had been since anything that could be called a disaster had happened. There'd been a time when it seemed like a new disaster occurred almost daily.

Thanks to Blaine and their blissful relationship, she'd known a kind of peace and tranquility that had eluded her all her life before him. Unlike Maddie, she had no memories of their father living with them on the island. He'd been long gone by the time Tiffany was aware of his absence.

A shrink would probably have a field day with her latching on to her high school boyfriend, the first "man" to ever come close to filling the void her father had left. With hindsight that came from being in a loving relationship with Blaine, she could see that Jim had never been capable of giving her what she needed most.

So how was it possible that his death had left her feeling completely flattened by grief?

It made no sense.

They stepped into the usual chaos in Maddie's open-concept home, which was littered with toys and baby equipment and shrieks of excitement at the arrival of cousins.

Addie squirmed in her arms, wanting to be put down to join the fray.

"Welcome to Bedlam," Maddie said as she got up to hug Tiffany.

The sisters held on to each other for a long time while Linda, Ned and Francine tended to the kids.

"I'm sorry we didn't make it to the marina last night," Maddie said.

"Don't be. I can't get two kids out of the house. Not sure how you manage five of them."

"It's a s-h-i-t show."

"I know what that spells," Thomas shouted.

They laughed as they pulled apart.

Maddie put her hands on Tiffany's face. "How are you? Really?"

"I'm heartbroken, and I can't, for the life of me, understand why."

"Aw, honey." Maddie hugged her again. "Of course you are. You were with him for ten years, had a child with him. Despite how it ended, he was a big part of your life."

Tiffany hated that she was once again crying over the man who'd broken her heart plenty of times when he was still alive.

A tug on her leg had Tiffany pulling back from her sister's embrace.

Addie looked up at her. "Mommy sad."

Tiffany bent to pick up her little lady. "Mommy's okay. Don't worry."

Addie wiped the tears from Tiffany's face. "No sad, Mommy."

"No sad." She forced a smile for her daughter. "All better, thanks to Addie-pooh."

The little girl flashed a big, satisfied grin that reminded Tiffany of Blaine. People said she was another Tiffany mini-me, but at times she embodied Blaine's smug grin to perfection.

She put Addie down to go back to playing.

"Mommy is allowed to be sad," Maddie said.

"I know, but I gotta keep it together in front of the kids." Tiffany wiped the remaining dampness off her face, determined to stay focused on her children, nieces and nephews, the sources of so much joy. "What're you hearing about Abby?"

"Total bed rest for the remainder of her pregnancy."

"Damn," Tiffany said with a gasp as Liam ran past with baby Mac. "How's that gonna work?"

"They're trying to figure that out now."

"YOU SHOULD GO HOME to pack and get Liam," Abby told Adam after he'd slept curled up to her all night in the narrow hospital bed.

He'd gone to the hotel to shower and change and had returned an hour later with breakfast sandwiches for both of them.

"I don't want to leave you. I can ask the parents to pack for us and to bring Liam."

"I think you should do it. You know best what we need and what Liam will want. It's too much to ask of others, even the grandparents."

"When I think of leaving you here, going to that damned island and not being able to get back to you if something happens... I feel like I'm having a heart attack."

"Don't do that."

Adam finally cracked the smallest of grins, the few she'd seen since David and Vic had recommended the flight to the mainland.

Abby reached out to him.

He took her hand.

"This is going to be a long slog for both of us. You're not going to be able to be here every second of the day and night. You can't run yourself ragged worrying and not sleeping or eating right or working out. We have to manage your stress as much as mine."

"Yours is what matters most."

"No, Adam, that's not true. I can't do this without you, so please... I need you to promise me that you'll take as good care of yourself as you are of me and Liam."

"I hear you. And I promise."

"If you leave now, you can grab an Uber to the ferry and be back on the last boat tonight. Call Seamus. They always save a spot for emergencies. He'll get the car on for you."

"Are you sure you won't do something dramatic, like have four babies while I'm gone?"

"I'll do everything in my power to keep that from happening. But if it does, no matter what, I'd never blame you for not being here when I was the one who sent you."

"Okay, then," he said with a deep sigh. "I'll go, and I'll be back as fast as I possibly can."

"Kiss me and make it a good one to tide me over until you get back."

Smiling, he leaned over the bed rail and laid a hot, sexy kiss on her.

"Now that is what I'm talking about."

"Text me a list of what you want from the house and what I should bring for Liam, so I don't forget anything."

"I will. It'll give me something to do while you're gone. One more kiss, and then I'm kicking you out."

His kisses were always the best, but they were extra special today.

"While you're on the boat, think about that first day and how far we've come from there and how much we have to look forward to."

"Where's Zen Abby coming from today?"

"I'm trying to stay focused on the gratitude. Remember when we thought we'd never be able to have one baby? Now we have our precious Liam and four more on the way. All that matters is getting them to the finish line. I don't care what I have to do to make that happen."

"I'm so freaking proud of you."

"Aw, thanks. That means everything to me."

"I guess if I leave now, I can catch the one o'clock boat to the island."

"Don't forget to call Seamus about getting the car on later."

"I won't."

He kissed her one last time. "I love you. Behave while I'm gone."

"I love you, too. Hurry back and bring me my son."

"Will do."

After he left, Abby rested against the pillows and released a deep breath full of angst and worry and stress that she'd had to put aside so she could convince him she'd be okay without him for a few hours. Since yesterday, she'd talked to everyone she knew—or so it seemed—as they'd called and texted with support and encouragement and plans to visit.

Despite the amazing outpouring and the best husband any girl could ever hope to have, she was scared and intimidated at the thought of being in bed for months. She was terrified of how much weight she'd gain that she might never lose again and whether she'd be up to caring for four babies after all that inactivity.

Izzy had told them that physical therapy would be brought in to keep her muscles from atrophying, but she wondered how effective that would be.

Her phone rang, and she took the call from her mother. "Hey."

"How're you doing, honey?"

"Hanging in there. Adam just left to make a quick trip home to grab Liam and pack up what we need for the long haul."

"Are you sure you want to bring Liam there? I talked to Linda this morning and told her we're available to help, too."

"I know you are, and we so appreciate that and what Adam's parents have already done. But we don't want to be away from him for weeks."

"I get it. You waited a long time to be a mommy. You don't want to miss anything."

"Yes, exactly. Adam is great with him. He can handle taking care of him on his own."

"I have no doubt you two can get through this."

"Thank you for the vote of confidence. It's feeling a bit daunting now, but I'm trying to focus on the goal of bringing these four little boys into the world as safely as possible."

"Four more McCarthy boys. Is the world ready?"

Abby laughed. "Probably not, but here they come, ready or not."

"I'm proud of you, sweetie. You've had more than your share of upheaval and drama, and you're handling this latest challenge with aplomb."

"That's nice of you to say."

"I mean it, and Daddy feels the same way. You're amazing, and we can't wait to meet those babies."

"I can't either."

"You and Adam will have plenty of time to figure out what you're going to name them."

"That's true. We've gone in circles on that, but it's probably time to start making some decisions."

"Yes, embroidery needs to begin soon to ensure they have the most stylish going-home outfits."

"As always, your priorities are straight."

"You know it, honey. Call me later?"

"I will."

"We'll be over to spend some time with you this weekend. Daddy booked a room at the Westin."

"I can't wait to see you."

She took calls from both her sisters as well as a cousin before she received a text from Adam that he was on the ferry and awaiting her packing list.

Sorry, I've been busy since you left!

Tell me the truth — are you having a fling?

HAHAHAHAHAHAHAHA. No.

What kept you busy?

Phone calls from Mom and the girls. I'll make the list now.

K.

Having a fling? Was he out of his mind? She could only imagine her online dating profile: BEDRIDDEN MOM PREGNANT WITH QUADS

SEEKS A NICE, STABLE, HANDSOME MAN TO TAKE ON HER AND HER FIVE BABY SONS. They'd be lining up at her door!

As she cracked up at her silliness, she gave Adam credit for making her laugh when she needed that more than ever. She couldn't wait to see him and Liam in a few hours.

ASHLEIGH FOLLOWED Thomas upstairs to his room. He wanted to show her the new truck he was keeping hidden from his baby brother, Mac, who liked to break things. That's what Thomas thought anyway.

Mac didn't really know better yet, so he was always throwing toys around, which made his brother mad.

"Daddy told me to keep it up here if I want it to be safe," Thomas told his cousin.

Ashleigh wasn't all that interested in trucks, but Thomas was her best friend, so she pretended to be fascinated with the things the truck could do. He used the remote to show her the lights and the beeps and how he could raise the bed to dump a load of Legos onto the floor.

"That's super cool."

"I know, right?" He looked over at her. "I'm, um, really sorry about your daddy."

"Thank you."

"Are you... Are you sad?"

Ashleigh nodded. "I'm so sad."

"I'd be so sad if my daddy died. I wish it hadn't happened to yours."

"I do, too."

"Can I give you a hug?"

"Sure."

Thomas came to her and held out his arms.

Ashleigh hugged him back.

"Does that help?"

"So much."

"I wish you weren't sad."

"Blaine told me I won't be this sad forever, but I'll always miss my daddy."

"That's probably true. I was sad when Mommy and Daddy told me the twins were girls. But I'm not sad about that anymore. They're kinda cute."

"They're *so* cute."

"I hope happy lasts longer than sad, because sad is no fun."

"Nope."

"Will you come back to school soon?"

"Mommy said I can go back whenever I feel ready."

"I hope it's soon. I miss you there."

"I miss you, too."

Thomas told her all about what'd gone on at school while she'd been out. One kid had thrown up during lunch, and another had broken his little finger at recess. "It was so gnarly." He showed her what Anthony's finger had looked like after he fell off the swing.

"Ew. I bet that hurt."

"He was screaming."

She giggled at the face Thomas made as he pretended to scream like Anthony had.

"I like it when you laugh."

"I do, too. Crying makes my eyes hurt."

"If you ever feel sad, you can call me."

"I will."

"Tell your mommy to call my mommy."

"Okay."

"I'm hungry. Do you want another doughnut?"

"Yes!"

Thomas took off toward the stairs.

Ashleigh ran after him, yelling at him to wait for her.

CHAPTER 27

*T*he strong, rich scent of coffee dragged McKenzie out of a sound sleep. She opened her eyes to find Duke, fully dressed and seated on the edge of the mattress, holding a mug of steaming coffee.

"I went over to your place to get that froufrou stuff you put in it."

"Do you mean my French vanilla creamer?"

He pulled a face. "Yeah, that. Also grabbed a couple of diapers and some clothes for the little mister, who's sleeping in."

McKenzie tucked the covers under her arms and sat up to take the coffee from him. "He does that when he's growing." She took a sip of the coffee and sighed with pleasure. "That's really good coffee."

"One of my specialties."

"This is the first time anyone has ever brought me coffee in bed."

His face lit up with an adorable smile. "Is that right?"

"Yep."

"Well, stick around, and it could become part of your daily routine."

"That's quite an incentive package when added to all the other things that led to me sleeping in your bed last night."

"I'm really sorry our evening got interrupted."

"I'm sorry I conked out while you were gone. That's how I am. When it's time to sleep, there's no keeping me awake."

"Good to know."

"Is Sierra okay?"

"She will be. Billy was a friend of hers."

"And yours."

"Yeah, but she was closer to him. Hit her hard."

"Does she regularly pop by unannounced?"

"That was the first time ever."

"Interesting timing. Does she have the place bugged or something?"

"Not to my knowledge. I want you to know… She's my very good friend, but that's all she's ever been or ever will be."

"She's drop-dead gorgeous."

"So are you."

"Not like her."

"No, you're drop-dead gorgeous like you, and I like you and your gorgeousness. I like being with you and kissing you and laughing with you, and I will never, for the rest of my life, forget the vision of you on your knees with my—"

Smiling, she held up a hand to stop him. "No need to finish that sentence."

"Why not? It was one of the most amazing things I've ever experienced, and I'm very eager to return the favor, which is what I would've done next if we hadn't been interrupted."

"Very eager, huh?"

"You have *no* idea."

"What time do you have to work?"

"First client is at nine."

"Then I guess we'll have to pick up this conversation at another time."

"Tonight. We'll pick it right up tonight. I'll bring dinner."

"I'll make dinner. You made it last night."

"I want to take you out. I want to give you romance and flowers and candles and all the things you deserve."

"I don't need the frills. I'm very happy with dinner at home and time to ourselves."

"Then that's what you'll have. For now. But I still plan to give you the rest, too."

"Thanks for letting me know."

"No problem."

"Thank you for bringing me coffee and going to get my special creamer."

"My pleasure. I might've stolen a piece of banana bread while I was there. Rosemary would be very proud. It's as good as hers."

"I'm glad you liked it."

"I loved it. Felt like coming home."

"I want you to know… I was a little rattled when Sierra showed up here last night, but I also got to see another example of what a great friend you are."

"Well, I try to be."

"Your friends are lucky to have you."

"I'm lucky to have them. They're my family."

"Mine are, too. Thank goodness for them."

"Are your sisters like your mother?"

"More so than I am. We get along, but we're not super close. They're always stirring up some sort of drama, which is just so not my thing."

Jax let out a cry to let her know he was awake.

She put the coffee on the bedside table. "Duty calls."

He handed her shirt to her.

"Thanks."

"Don't feel like you to put that shirt on on my account."

Laughing, she pulled it over her head and took the hand he offered to help her up.

Before she could go get Jax, he leaned in to kiss her.

"Morning," he said.

"Morning."

"Best one I've had in a very long time."

"Same."

He released her to go fetch Jax, but she felt his eyes on her as she left the room. He'd brought her coffee in bed.

Swoon.

Jax squealed when she walked into the room, kicking his feet with the usual morning enthusiasm.

"Good morning, my pumpkin pie. Did you sleep well?"

Duke had left the diapers, a package of wipes and a change of clothes for Jax on the foot of the bed. What a guy.

She changed Jax's heavy overnight diaper, washed him up and got him dressed. When she carried him out of the bedroom, she found Duke in the kitchen, standing over the stove.

"What does he like for breakfast?"

"Usually some mommy milk and cereal."

"Why don't you take care of that while I cook some eggs for us?"

"Are you for real? Coffee *and* breakfast?"

He flashed a dirty grin over his shoulder. "I'm as real as it gets, baby."

"THIS IS JUST WHAT ASH NEEDED," Tiffany told her sister, parents and Linda after lunch. "Some time with her best pal."

Thomas and Ashleigh were on the floor, reading out loud to each other while Hailey and Addie played with Hailey's dolls. Liam and Mac were joined at the hip as they toddled around, getting into everything. The twins were down for their afternoon nap.

"You needed it, too, doll," Ned said.

Tiffany, who had her head resting on Maddie's shoulder, smiled at him. "You're right, as always, Dad."

Ned's eyes went very wide and then got very shiny. "Sheesh, how about a warnin' before ya go sayin' somethin' like that?"

"What fun would that've been?" Tiffany asked, smiling.

"Not as much fun as this," Maddie said. "Dad."

"For God's sake, you two. Yer gonna make me bawl."

Francine, who had tears in her eyes, took his hand. "You've earned it, my love. Every day for years, as you've shown up for all of us."

"Agree wholeheartedly, old pal," Linda said. "If you're not their dad, I don't know who is."

"For the love a God…"

Ned's muttered words made the women laugh.

He was so damned cute, and they were lucky to have him in their lives. She and Maddie had a better-late-than-never feeling toward having a wonderful father. He was a devoted, loving, generous husband, father and grandfather, and he deserved the title of Dad.

"Don't tell my best buddy that you crazy ladies made me weep," Ned said to Linda.

"I never would, but I bet you'll get weepy when you tell him about it yourself."

"Don't get sassy with me."

"I don't know how to be any other way with you after all these years."

The laughter, the love, the friendship, the support… It was everything Tiffany and Ashleigh had needed.

NIALL HAD GIVEN John a few days before he went looking for him at the Wayfarer, where he was the director of security. The season was winding down, but the beaches were still busy with day-trippers and partiers who kept the Wayfarer hopping into October. For the tourists, it was as if the storm had never happened, even as the island continued to clean up and get back to normal.

What was normal anyway? How did anyone define that concept? Sometimes Niall wondered if he wasn't descended from ancient philosophers who were constantly questioning the meaning of life the way he did.

For instance, what did it mean that he and John had spent a hot night together during the storm? What did it mean that other than a few texts, he'd barely heard from John since he accompanied his injured brother Jeff and Jeff's girlfriend to the mainland after the storm? What did it mean that he'd gone silent all of a sudden or that

John's sister Cindy said he'd been back on the island for a couple of days but hadn't reached out?

What did any of it mean?

That's what he was determined to find out with this mission to the Wayfarer. Confronting a guy at work wasn't ideal, but desperate times called for desperate measures. And really, this couldn't be called a confrontation so much as a visit.

At the reception desk, he asked where he might find John Lawry.

"I believe he's upstairs doing a fire safety check." The young woman pointed to the staircase that led to the second-floor hotel rooms.

"Thank you."

Niall went upstairs and poked his head into three open doors before he found John in the fourth room, clipboard in hand as he gazed up at something in the ceiling.

John's dark blond hair was shorter than it had been the last time Niall had seen him. He'd probably had Cindy give him a trim when he got back to the island. Funny that he had time for a haircut, but not a text or a phone call to check in with Niall.

He stood in the doorway for a full five minutes before John noticed him there.

"Some security director you are," Niall said in a teasing tone. "I could've murdered you six times by now."

John smiled, but Niall couldn't miss the troubled furrow of his brow or the tick of tension in his jaw. "I'm not expecting to be murdered at the Wayfarer."

"Have you lost all your cop instincts during your stay on our fair island?"

"I guess so. What brings you by?"

"Gee, I wonder. Could it be the radio silence from someone I thought was becoming more than a friend?"

"I'm sorry. Things have been crazy since I got back."

"I kind of thought I might hear from you that you were back, not from your sister and Jace."

John winced. "I'm sorry."

"Quit apologizing and tell me what's going on."

"It was a lot in Providence. Jeff is in rough shape and refused narcotics. He was in so much pain. I guess I'm still processing everything that happened."

"I'm sorry that happened to your brother. He's lucky to have you and your family rallying around him. He'll make a full recovery, won't he?"

"Yeah, in time. Thankfully, he's young, strong and stubborn. He's a survivor."

"So are you."

John shrugged. "Not like him."

"You've survived your own stuff, and done so quite admirably, if you ask me. I thought maybe you were starting to embrace who you really are and to live your truth."

"I was. I mean... I am."

"Then what's wrong?"

"I... I don't know."

"You want me to go away and leave you alone?"

"No."

"Then I'm afraid you're going to have to talk to me so we can figure out where we go from here."

"That night... During the storm."

"That was a great night."

"Yeah, it was."

"Are you freaked out about what happened that night?"

"I've thought about it a lot."

Niall took a step into the room. "So have I. I've thought about it nonstop, actually."

"Yeah, me, too." John looked directly at him. "It got kind of intense."

"Yep."

"I'm not sure how to feel about that."

"You should feel good about it. This kind of connection doesn't come along every day, you know."

"I do know that."

246

"Are you not ready for it?"

"I'm not sure."

Disappointment filled him with a sinking feeling. "How about you let me know when you figure that out, huh?"

"I just need some time."

"Fair enough."

"Thanks for coming by."

"No problem."

As Niall turned to leave, he wished he hadn't sought John out. It was much better not knowing what he was thinking than to hear he might be pulling back from the best thing to happen to Niall in, well, ever.

CHAPTER 28

*W*as it possible to float through a day? If so, that's what McKenzie did after the lovely wakeup at Duke's house. Once again, he'd insisted she use his truck while he took the bike to work. If her bookkeeping business continued to grow like it had this week, she'd be able to afford a car of her own in no time.

After Eric had walked away from her and the baby she was expecting, she'd sold her car to cover a few additional months of rent when she wasn't able to work as much due to relentless morning sickness. By the time that unpleasant phase had passed, she was already low on money and had made the painful decision to move back to her mother's house temporarily.

Talk about a worst-case scenario: abandoned by the man who made her pregnant and forced to live with the mother who drove her crazy.

But she'd done what she had to for Jax.

He was buckled into his car seat in the passenger seat of the truck as she drove toward her first stop of the day at Sierra's massage studio to drop off the banana bread she'd made for her. She also wanted to get a sense of whether Sierra was going to be a problem for her with Duke.

She found Sierra at the reception desk when she entered the studio, carrying Jax. "Morning."

"Hey, what's up?" Sierra asked with a guarded expression.

She placed the plastic bag with the banana bread on the counter. "As promised."

"Oh damn. Thank you. I'm so excited. I've missed Rosemary's."

"Duke says it's just as good as hers."

"Well, that's a heck of an endorsement."

"Is everything okay?" McKenzie asked.

"Of course."

"Call me crazy, but I'm picking up a vibe, especially after last night."

Sierra took a deep breath and released it before she glanced up at her. "I'm sorry about showing up unannounced. It's just that... He means a lot to me."

"I know."

"It would hurt me to see him hurt—again."

"The last thing I'd ever want to do is hurt him. He's the best thing to happen to me in... well... ever."

Sierra nodded. "That's who he is. When he cares, he cares with his whole heart."

"We're both lucky to be cared for by him, right?"

"Right."

"I hope we can be friends, Sierra. It would mean a lot to him."

"I hope so, too. Thanks for the banana bread."

"Any time. Have a great day."

She turned to leave.

"McKenzie?"

She turned back toward Sierra.

"Thanks for coming by. I'm glad we got the chance to talk."

"Me, too."

McKenzie was relieved to have cleared the air with Sierra as she drove to Martinez Lawn & Garden on a gorgeous fall morning. The cloudless sky was a vivid cornflower blue, the air cool and crisp, and the first hints of foliage were beginning to appear in the trees.

McKenzie loved autumn and all things pumpkin and pumpkin spice, so when she spotted the sign for Martinez Lawn & Garden and pulled in, she was thrilled to see pumpkin patches on either side of the long driveway that led to the retail store Jenny had told her to look for. She was still getting used to parking Duke's huge truck. This time, she succeeded on the second attempt, which was an improvement from the day before.

She retrieved Jax from his seat and put him into the stroller, which she was relieved to have again with him getting too heavy to haul around in the seat.

The retail store was made of a light-colored wood with dark green shutters and window boxes decked out with colorful chrysanthemums mixed with purple and green cabbage. She stepped into a shop full of brightly painted pots, gardening tools, wind chimes and other fun things.

Jenny came out to meet her carrying George.

"Hi there, welcome! Come on back to the office."

She followed Jenny. "The shop is so pretty."

"That's been my personal passion project. Took some doing to convince the guys that it could be profitable, and now they're eating all kinds of crow, which I enjoy."

McKenzie laughed.

"That's what happens when you work with your husband and brother-in-law. There's often bickering involved." She gestured for McKenzie to take a seat.

She released Jax from the stroller and gathered him into her arms.

"If he wants to play with George, he's welcome to join him on the mat." Half the office was devoted to George and his toys.

"He'd love to." McKenzie settled Jax on the mat, close enough to George that they could see each other, but not so close that they could pull hair or pinch each other.

"George loves other kids, but he hasn't quite worked out how to play with them yet. His older cousin, Ethan, has been great with him, but he's a work in progress."

"I read about a thing called parallel play, where they like to know another child is there, but they don't want to play with them. They want to play *near* them."

"Yes, we're in that stage now."

"Jax is about sitting up and throwing things."

"Ah, yes, I remember that. While they're calm, let me show you what I've done in QuickBooks, and you can tell me everything I've done wrong."

"I'm sure it's not that bad."

"I'm sure it's worse than you think."

Over the next hour, McKenzie reviewed the balance sheet and income statement, the credit card statements for the last six months and took a look at the payroll account.

"How bad is it?" Jenny asked when she returned from waiting on a customer.

"You've made a great start. Way better than most."

"May I quote you on that when I brag to Alex about how smart I am?"

"Absolutely."

"Here comes one of them now. You can tell by the clomp of boots on the concrete floor."

"Good to know what the bosses sound like."

"Don't let on to them, but I'm the real boss around here."

McKenzie was still laughing when Alex came into the office, his entire countenance softening at the sight of Jenny and George.

"Hi, family."

"Hi, Daddy."

George let out a happy cry at the sight of his dad. "Da!"

Alex leaned down to pick up George from the floor and swung him over his head, to the delight of his son. "What goes on around here?"

"You remember McKenzie Martin and her son, Jax, from the marina the other night. She just said that I'm way better at book-keeping than most people are."

"How much did she pay you to say that?" Alex asked. "Oh, and it's nice to see you again."

"Nice to see you, too, and I told her that for free because it's true."

"That doesn't mean I don't need you," Jenny said. "I'd like very much to turn the bookkeeping over to someone who actually knows what they're doing."

"Bookkeeping makes my beloved grumpy," Alex added, "so I'm all for getting some help."

"I can't even deny the grumpiness," Jenny said with a sheepish grin.

McKenzie's phone rang with a number she didn't recognize. In case it was another potential client, she excused herself to take the call.

Jenny gestured for her to go into the store and pointed to Jax to tell McKenzie she'd watch him.

"What the fuck are you doing?"

At first, McKenzie didn't realize who she was talking to.

"Sending me a letter at work, threatening to tell my wife about us?"

Eric.

"Are you out of your fucking mind?"

"Not at all. I'm finally in my right mind about you getting me pregnant and then walking away from your obligations."

"I have no obligations to you!"

"No, but you have them to your son. He deserves to have everything your other kids have."

"That's not going to happen. There's no way I can pay child support without people finding out about him."

"That's your problem, not mine. He's your son. You know that as well as I do, and I'm prepared to take you to court to get what's coming to him."

"This is about revenge, right? I left you, so you're going to ruin my life."

"Don't give yourself too much credit. I've barely given you a thought. This is about our son and doing what's right for him."

"I told you I can't have any more kids."

"Tell it to the court. My attorney says the next step will be a paternity test that'll prove that in addition to your other charming qualities, you're also a liar. Oh wait, we knew that already."

"McKenzie, please... Don't do this to me. You don't understand what's at stake."

She released a harsh laugh. "That's rich coming from you. Guess what? I don't care what's at stake for you. All I care about is doing right by my son. We created him together, and we'll both pay for his upbringing. If you want to avoid a protracted public battle over this, make a settlement offer through my attorney."

"I don't have the money."

"Then I guess I'll see you in court."

When she went to end the call, she realized her hands were trembling—not with fear but with adrenaline. Damn, that had felt good. It also felt good to realize she had not a single feeling left for the man she'd once thought was her forever love.

Jenny poked her head into the store. "Everything okay?"

McKenzie nodded. "I'm so sorry about that."

"Don't be. You want to talk about it?"

Was it professional to share her personal drama with a new client? Probably not, but Jenny had felt like a new friend from the get-go. "That was Jax's dad, who just received the letter my new attorney sent him, letting him know we're suing for child support."

"Ah. I take it he wasn't pleased with this news?"

"Not at all. He's concerned about his wife and kids, the wife and kids I had no idea he had, finding out he's got another kid out there, and apparently, he doesn't have the money to support him."

"Well, that sucks for him, right?"

McKenzie smiled. "Sure does. I want you to know I'm not a drama girl. I'm so sorry to bring that into your workplace..."

"Don't sweat it. I just want to hear that you put the fear of God into him."

"I sure did."

"Good. I hope he's crapping his pants worrying about your next move."

Laughing, McKenzie said, "I think we're going to be very good friends."

"I'd love that."

. . .

SITTING at her brother's kitchen table, with a mug of coffee and the company of her sister-in-law and baby niece, Kendall exhaled a breath she'd been holding so long, it felt like she'd forgotten how to breathe normally.

The last few years had been a total nightmare as she'd lost her once-loving and devoted husband to pain medication addiction and alcoholism that he'd refused to deal with long enough that their marriage had been unsalvageable. Their divorce was now final. Their home had been sold, their possessions put into storage, and a whole new chapter had begun for her and her boys.

"Can I get you anything?" Lizzie asked as she fed Violet applesauce that the baby lapped up with enthusiasm.

"No, thank you. It's so nice to be here, away from everything."

"We're thrilled to have you and the boys."

"Said no new mom ever about having three unexpected houseguests."

"You're family, Kendall, and we are thrilled to have you here. Jared has been so worried about you guys. He slept much better last night knowing you were here. In fact, he hasn't slept this late in months."

"It's still early."

"He's usually been up for an hour by now."

"I'll figure out something for me and the boys and get out of your hair."

The boys had wanted to be near their beloved uncle and baby Violet, so the three of them had stayed at their house rather than in the garage apartment.

Lizzie reached over to put her hand on Kendall's. "Please don't worry about that or figuring out anything. Just relax and take a breath."

"I'm not sure I remember how to relax or breathe."

"Gansett is a great place to relearn an old habit."

"That's what my brothers tell me. All three of them are gone over the place."

"It's been good for each of them in its own way." Lizzie wiped Violet's face and put some dry cereal on her tray to entertain her. "I know we haven't gotten to spend a ton of time together since I married Jared, but I hope you know you've got a friend in me. If you want to talk or vent or rant or just sit and be silent together, I'm your girl."

"That's very sweet of you to say."

"I mean it. I can't possibly know what you and your kids have been through, but I'm here if you want to talk or if I can do anything at all for any of you."

"My brother is a lucky man."

"We're both lucky, and we know it."

"Thanks to him, I don't have to worry about the usual things that a newly single mother has to think about."

Years earlier, Jared had shared his fortune with his parents and each of his four siblings.

"I'm sure that's only one piece of a very complicated puzzle."

Kendall nodded. "I'm worried about the boys."

"You'd know much better than me, of course, but they seem to be happy, well-adjusted kids. Jared is crazy about them."

Kendall smiled. "And vice versa. He's always been great with them, giving them his full attention any time he's with them, no matter what else he had going on."

"That sounds like him. He's smitten with our Violet. I swear he's barely thought about work since she arrived."

"He worked enough in his past life to take it a little easier now."

"That's what he says, too."

Kendall's phone buzzed with a text from McKenzie, who reported that Eric had received the letter and was none too pleased about it.

Let's talk this afternoon about what he had to say and our next steps. Text me when you're free to talk.

Sounds good.

"Everything okay?" Lizzie asked.

"That's my first island client updating me. I'm helping her with a situation involving her ex. He's a real piece of work."

"I'm glad she's got you to help her."

"She's given me something to think about besides my own problems."

"Our resident lawyer, Dan Torrington, will be in Maine for a while with his wife's family. I bet he'd appreciate you filling in for him when he's gone, if you're up for that."

"There're no other lawyers here?"

"One of the two men who was killed in the storm was an attorney, but his career was kind of over around here due to some poor decisions."

"That sounds like a story."

"And a half. He was awful to his ex-wife, who's very well loved, and blamed Dan for ruining his practice, which he did all on his own. He showed up drunk at Dan and Kara's engagement party and ended up stabbing Dan."

"Jeez... And here I thought this was a sleepy little place where nothing ever happened."

Lizzie's bark of laughter startled her daughter. "There's never a dull moment around here. Look at how we came to have our sweet Violet."

Lizzie had come to the aid of a single mom who'd later left the baby with her and Jared.

"I could tell you stories about what goes on here for days and days."

"I'll look forward to hearing all the gossip."

"Can I ask you..."

"Anything, Lizzie. I'm an open book."

"How's Phil?"

Kendall's deep sigh said it all. "He's in rehab—for the fourth time. He swears this'll be the time it takes. I hope for his sake—and the boys'—that's true, but I've learned not to get my hopes up."

"I have a friend from the city who's been through a similar ordeal with her brother. Their family has done everything they could think of and then some."

"None of it will matter until he makes the decision to help himself."

"Yes, for sure." She used a wet paper towel to wipe Violet's tray. "Do you want me to ask Dan about whether he has some work you could help with?"

"Sure, that'd be good. I've found it helps to stay busy and engaged in other people's problems. I turned over my New Jersey clients to my partners when things got crazy with Phil, so I'm ready to get back to feeling productive."

"I'll text Dan today. He's been great helping us with Violet's adoption."

"Where does that stand?"

"It'll be final in a couple of months."

"Are you anxious about it?"

"Not really. She wasn't planned, and Jessie was in no position to take care of her. We've barely heard from her since she agreed to the adoption."

"What's the story with the father?"

"From what I was able to piece together, it was a short-term thing before they went their separate ways."

"So he doesn't know about her?"

"I don't think she knows where he is."

"I see." That detail made Kendall nervous, but she'd never say so to Lizzie.

When Jared came into the kitchen, hair standing on end and his face flushed from sleep, Kendall was reminded of being home from college while he was in high school and laughing at his morning hair.

"What?" he asked when he saw her trying not to laugh at him.

"Some things never change."

"What does that mean?"

"You look exactly the same as you did first thing in the morning when you were fifteen."

"Thank you. I think?"

"Jared's morning hair is a thing of beauty," Lizzie said, smiling at her husband as he leaned in to kiss her and Violet.

"That's one word for it," Kendall said. "Good thing the editors of *Finance* magazine can't see their favorite whiz kid first thing in the morning, huh?"

Lizzie laughed at the face Jared made at his sister.

"And to think I woke up feeling glad you were here. That didn't last long."

"Haha." Kendall was delighted to be sparring once again with her little brother rather than fighting with her ex-husband. "All kidding aside, thanks again for having us. I slept better than I have in a long time."

Jared poured himself a cup of coffee and then topped off Kendall's and Lizzie's. "I'm glad to hear that, and all kidding aside, I hope you'll stay for as long as you want."

"Even if I make fun of your morning hair?"

He smiled warmly at his sister. "Even if."

CHAPTER 29

*A*fter McKenzie left Martinez Lawn & Garden, she made a quick stop back at Duke's to feed and change Jax before she drove to the Sand & Surf Hotel in town. There, she met with Laura and her manager, Piper, to go over the hotel's bookkeeping while Laura's husband, Owen, entertained Jax and their three kids in the main-floor living room.

"I can't believe how many new friends Jax has made in one day."

"We're very kid- and dog-friendly around here," Laura said.

"I love that. Getting a dog is on my to-do list once my cabin is rebuilt."

"I heard you've got my cousin Mac lined up to rebuild."

"I do, and he's been amazing."

"He's good at what he does, even if he's full of beans outside of work."

McKenzie glanced at Piper and then back to Laura. "Full of beans?"

"Always up to no good with pranks and other tomfoolery."

"I never would've guessed that. He's all business with me."

"Wait until you get to know him better," Laura said. "He's a lot of fun, although with five kids at home, he doesn't have as much time for foolishness as he used to, which is good for all of us."

"This place is so... fun."

Piper nodded in agreement. "*So* fun. There's always something going on, and everyone is so nice and welcoming."

"I love it," McKenzie said.

"Does that mean you're going to stay?" Laura asked.

"I wasn't sure what I was going to do when I first arrived to check out my grandmother's cabin after not having been out here in years. Then the storm hit, Jax and I were nearly killed, and the cabin was demolished by the storm. It seemed like I'd made a very bad decision. But everything—and everyone—since then has been wonderful. So yes, I'm planning to stay."

As she said those words out loud, she realized the decision had been made over the last week as she experienced the island community and the way people came together to support one another, not to mention a promising new romance.

Laura clapped her hands in glee. "Yay!"

"She's very excited to have someone who knows what they're doing taking over the books," Piper said.

"And I'm excited to make a new friend," Laura added.

"Everyone is thrilled about my bookkeeping service. I had no idea there'd be such a need for that here."

"You'll be very busy," Laura assured her. "Year-round. I've already told my cousin Evan about you, and he and his wife, Grace, want you for the Island Breeze Recording Studio and Ryan's Pharmacy."

"Wow. Word travels fast."

"It's lightning speed when someone shows up with a skill we all need desperately."

"I still can't believe Evan McCarthy is from Gansett and plays at family gatherings like he's not a superstar."

Laura laughed. "He'd better not act like a superstar around here, or we'll remind him that we knew him when."

They talked for another half hour about the routine at the hotel and went over some of McKenzie's questions.

"My cousin Adam designed our registration system, so that's custom," Laura said. "We have a lot of return customers who request certain things every year. Adam made it so that's an easy, online process."

"I'm sure it'll all make sense to me in no time. Are you okay with me bringing Jax with me when I have to be here?"

"Of course. That's never a problem."

"It'll be easy until he starts walking. After that, I might have to look for a sitter for him once in a while."

"I'm sure we can help you find someone," Laura said.

A woman with short red hair and a belly rounded with pregnancy came in through the main doors. "Oh good. I didn't miss you! I totally overslept!"

"This is Stephanie McCarthy, owner of Stephanie's Bistro and my cousin Grant's wife. Steph, meet McKenzie, who's here to save us from ourselves and the IRS."

As she shook hands with Stephanie, McKenzie asked, "How many cousins do you have, anyway?"

"A lot," the other three women said as one.

"Eight first cousins and a brother who's also a McCarthy," Laura said.

"There're McCarthys everywhere I look around here," McKenzie said.

"Adam's wife, Abby, owns the Attic." Laura pointed toward the lobby gift shop. "She's in Providence, now on full bed rest awaiting the arrival of quadruplets."

"Damn," McKenzie said. "Four of them."

"Right?" Stephanie patted her belly. "Thank God I'm only having one."

"I had twins and thought I'd die the first couple of months," Laura said. "I can't fathom four."

"I can't fathom months of in-patient bed rest," Stephanie added. "Ugh. Poor Abby."

"I know," Laura said. "But I'm relieved she's being monitored around the clock. I was worried about her being out here during such a high-risk pregnancy."

"Grant said the same thing last night," Stephanie said. To McKenzie, she said, "When you're done with Laura and Piper, come into the Bistro. Have I got a job for you!"

McKenzie laughed. "Everyone says that."

"Some of us really mean it," Stephanie said.

"We're all set for now," Laura said, "so Ms. McKenzie is all yours, Steph."

"Right this way, my new best friend."

DUKE FINISHED up early at the shop and headed home, hoping to spend more time with McKenzie and Jax. Normally, he'd go to the gym and then stop by the Beachcomber for dinner with his friends. But nothing was normal since they'd come into his life, and that was fine with him.

He was unreasonably disappointed that the truck wasn't in the driveway when he arrived. The letdown had him laughing at himself and how ridiculous he'd become over her and her little guy.

He'd found it hard to concentrate on anything with the vivid memories from last night running through his mind like the best movie he'd ever seen.

After he stashed the bike in the garage, he heard voices next door, so he took a walk over to check on the progress at the cabin.

Mac was there with a clipboard and iPad as he pointed to something on the screen while talking to his cousin Riley.

Since Duke had last been there, they'd cleared the debris from the site and had bagged up the items they'd found inside. When McKenzie got home, they'd bring the truck over to transport the bags to his garage.

"Hey, Duke," Mac said. "How's it going?"

"It's a good day to be alive."

"Ain't that the truth? I love this time of year."

"Me, too. Cool and sunny and quiet after the summer madness."

"Yep, that's it exactly."

"I'm heading into town to pick up supplies from the ferry landing," Riley said.

"Sounds good," Mac said. "See you after a bit."

"Later, Duke."

"Take care, Riley."

"Must be fun to have your cousins working with you," Duke said after Riley had left.

"It is. He and his brother, Finn, are a great asset to the company, and so's my other cousin Shane. Wouldn't be any fun without them."

"Nice to keep it in the family."

"For sure. We've got everything ordered to hit it hard here as soon as it arrives. That's always the complicated part—waiting for stuff from the mainland."

"McKenzie appreciates everything you're doing for her."

"I heard she's opening a bookkeeping business. I'm very interested in that for the marina and the construction company."

"I'll let her know. Everyone wants her."

"Not surprised."

"Do you have another second?"

"Sure. What's up?"

"I just… ah… I wanted to ask you…"

"What's on your mind?"

"What you said the other day about meeting Maddie when Thomas was nine months old."

"Best day of my life."

"I'm starting to understand how you felt."

"Oh… It's like that, is it?"

"Yeah, it is. And I'm thinking about the little guy and how to, you know, do that part right."

Mac's entire demeanor softened as he smiled. "The little guy I got out of my relationship with Maddie is one of the greatest blessings in my life. He's taught me so much more than I'll ever teach him."

"That's really cool."

"He's an incredible kid, and I'm lucky to have him as my son."

"How did you, like, bond with him at first?"

"I spent as much time with him one-on-one as his mother would allow. When I look back on it, it wasn't intentional at the time, but I formed my own rapport with him separate of what was happening with her. And then at other times, it was the three of us together. Not sure if that makes sense."

"No, it does. You treated them individually and as a unit."

"Right."

"That's very helpful. Thank you."

"It's always fun to think about those early days with Maddie and Thomas. Seems like such a long time ago now. It goes by crazy fast. They're little for the briefest time before they're bossing you around like they pay the bills."

Duke laughed. "Sounds like you've got your hands full."

"I sure do, and I love everything about it."

"I remember when you first came home. Everyone said you'd be out of here as soon as you could."

"That was the plan. Funny how plans change when the right one comes along."

"Yeah, for sure. Appreciate you sharing your insight."

"Any time. I hope things work out for you and McKenzie. She seems like a really nice person."

"She's great."

"I'm happy for you."

"Thanks. You won't, you know... say anything about it, will you? Early days yet."

"Of course not. I'm all too aware of how things spread like wildfire around here."

Duke chuckled. "I remember the buzz about you guys when you all but moved in with her after the bike accident."

"It was a five-alarm Gansett Island scandal, as my dad says."

"Sure was. Not looking for anything like that myself. We'll be over to grab the bags with the truck. Thanks for packing it up for her."

"No worries."

Duke returned home on the well-worn path between his home and Rosemary's. He missed her more than ever now that he was dating— or whatever you wanted to call it—her precious MK. More than anything, he hoped Rosemary knew that he'd take good care of

McKenzie and Jax and that she'd approve of his growing feelings for them.

He was about to start some yard work when the truck came into the driveway, and all thoughts of anything that wasn't her and them faded to the background as he walked over to greet them.

McKenzie put her finger over her lips as he approached the open driver-side window.

Duke leaned in and saw that Jax was sacked out in his seat. "Want me to carry him in for you?"

"Yes, please."

While he walked around to the passenger side, she released the seat belt and handed it to him so it wouldn't make noise retracting after he opened the door to retrieve the seat.

She followed him up the stairs to the apartment. "He can go right into the crib, seat and all."

As Duke carried the sleeping baby into the bedroom, he gazed down at his sweet face, noting how his lips were puckered as if he were having deep thoughts. A fierce feeling of protectiveness came over him as he placed the carrier in the crib. The realization that he'd do anything to keep the child safe was as profound as it was unexpected.

"All set?" McKenzie asked when he met her in the kitchen.

"Yeah, I was just watching him sleep. He's so damned cute."

"Aw, that's sweet."

He scowled at her.

"Easy, tiger. I already knew you were sweet."

Duke stepped closer to her, putting his hands on her hips as he leaned in to kiss her. "Missed you today."

"You did? Really?"

"I really did."

"I hate to tell you, but that, too, is sweet."

His low growl made her laugh, which he stifled with a kiss. "I have some news for you, but if you're going to keep up with that sweet nonsense, I might not tell you."

Who was this playful guy, and where had he come from? He'd

never been this way with a woman before and had to admit it was kind of fun.

"Tell me."

"Are you going to behave?"

"Absolutely not."

His huff of laughter took him by surprise. He also did a lot of that when she was around. "I saw Mac over at your place, and he said he'd like to talk to you about bookkeeping for the marina and the construction business."

"Wow."

"I think you have yourself a business, sweetheart."

"You called me sweetheart."

"So I did. Is that a problem?"

"Not for me. Is it for you? It contains the word 'sweet,' which you don't care for."

Smiling, he said, "You think you're very clever, don't you?"

"I am very clever. I've landed like *ten* new clients in two days, and I've got this sweet guy who likes to kiss me."

"No one deserves it more than you do."

"Plenty of people deserve it more, but I'm thrilled to be finding a way to make a life for myself and Jax here. That was my biggest concern—that I'd be able to make a living in the off-season."

Duke couldn't resist planting a kiss on the tempting length of her neck. He loved the way she shivered when he kissed her there. "They packed up your stuff in bags next door. We can go get it with the truck when Jax wakes up."

"Sounds good."

"How long will he nap?"

"A couple of hours probably."

"That long?"

"Uh-huh."

"There's a lot we can get done in a couple of hours," he said as he continued to kiss her neck.

"I was thinking about opening QuickBooks and getting some work done."

"That word is the ultimate cockblocker. Everything shrivels up and dies at the sound of it."

McKenzie rubbed up against his still-formidable erection. "Doesn't seem to have happened yet."

"Any second now."

She continued to rub against him. "Are you sure about that?"

"I might've found the QB antidote."

He loved the way her smile lit up her entire face, and more than anything, he loved being the one to make her smile like that. "Do you need to work now, or can you hang out with me?"

"I'd love to hang out with you, but I really do need to get some things done while Jax is sleeping."

"How about I figure out dinner, and you guys come over when you're ready?"

"You made dinner last night."

"I'm not keeping score."

"I'll make it up to you."

"I'll look forward to that." He kissed her once more and forced himself to let her go—for now, anyway.

As he left the apartment to return to his home, he realized he was looking forward to everything. Every. Single. Thing. And it was all thanks to McKenzie and her little boy.

Life was looking rather *sweet* lately, and it was getting *sweeter* all the time.

CHAPTER 30

$\mathcal{M}$cKenzie spent Jax's naptime completing her initial assessment of Duke's books and made a list of recommendations for streamlining processes. The good news was that his records weren't in terrible shape. The bad news was he owed estimated quarterly state and federal taxes that were overdue and accumulating penalties. He needed to take care of that as soon as possible, and she hoped that wouldn't be a problem for him.

Next, she spent an hour reconciling Sierra's bank statements and posting journal entries to her general ledger. She made a list of recommendations for her, which included separating her personal and corporate expenditures by procuring a corporate credit card that offered points or cash rewards. The commingling of personal and professional made for messy accounting, which she explained to Sierra in an email that included a list of credit cards that would suit her business.

The work made her feel useful and productive. When she was finished, she made notes about the time she'd spent on both accounts. She wouldn't bill Duke for any work she did for him, but she added an hour and a half to Sierra's tab for month-end billing. Figuring out her hourly rate was on her to-do list.

She stood to stretch just as the first squeak came from Jax.

Smiling, McKenzie went to retrieve him, freeing him from the car seat and lifting him into her arms. He was sweaty from sleeping and snuggled her as always when he first woke up. "How's my best buddy?"

"Bud."

"Yes, you're my bud!"

"Bud."

McKenzie put him on the bed to change him and took full advantage of the opportunity to place noisy kisses on his belly that provoked the laughter she loved so much. When she first realized she was pregnant with him, she'd been terrified. She and Eric hadn't spoken about having children and had been careful to prevent pregnancy. To this day, she had no idea what had gone "wrong," but once the fear had subsided, she'd been excited.

Until she'd told Eric, and all her excitement died a painful death. She'd been shocked, devastated and terrified after he left her to deal with the baby on her own. A few bleak weeks had followed, along with debilitating nausea that had made it nearly impossible to work. Moving back in with her mother had been a new low.

But a funny thing had happened as her baby had grown inside her. The excitement had come back, and then after he was born, she'd experienced the most profound feelings of pure joy that she'd ever known. Jax might've been "an accident," but he'd become the happiest accident of her entire life.

She gave him a quick bath and changed him into pajamas. Then she took a quick shower and packed up what they needed to spend the night at Duke's.

Spend the night at Duke's.

She had no doubt they'd pick up where they'd left off the night before, and the very thought of it made her scalp and various other parts tingle with anticipation.

Every minute they spent together took them a step down the path toward something significant. Was she ready for that? Was he? Before him, she would've said no way, no how. The last thing she needed was another man in her life. But this man… He was different. Her unicorn, her one-in-a-million.

She was so tempted to jump right in with both feet—case in point: packing a bag to spend the night—but they needed to have a conversation about where this was headed, because it wasn't just about them. Jax was part of the equation, too, and as such, she needed to make sure they were on the same page.

Carrying Jax and her backpack, she went downstairs and across the yard.

He had music playing, loudly, so he didn't hear her knock.

In the kitchen, she found him singing along to "Tennessee Whiskey" as he stood watch over something on the stove, his hips keeping time with the song.

For a moment, she was struck dumb by the realization that she was more than halfway in love with him—and that was before he sensed her there, turned and smiled with his whole face. Yeah, she was probably more than halfway in love.

He reached out to take Jax from her and continued to dance around the kitchen, delighting her little boy with his singing and his moves. "You gotta love Chris Stapleton. What a voice."

"I do love him." *And you. I love you, too.* But she couldn't say that. It was far too soon for such things, and besides, who knew if he even wanted a little insta-family?

The insecurities hit hard, one right after the other. Every man left. Her father had left. Eric had left. Others before him… How did anyone who'd been through that ever take a chance on someone new?

"Something wrong, sweetheart?"

His voice tugged her out of the deep thoughts.

"No, just thinking."

He turned down the music. "About what?"

"Everything."

"That's a lot of thinking."

"Yeah, it is."

"Look what I found sitting on the side of the road today." He gestured to a high chair in the corner that she hadn't noticed. "Cleaned it up and tightened the screws so it's safe for Jax."

McKenzie was so shocked, she could barely think, let alone speak.

"What do you say we give it a whirl, Mr. Jax?" Duke settled her son into the chair and put a couple of animal crackers on the tray that immediately grabbed the baby's attention.

With Jax occupied, he came over to McKenzie, singing along to Chris singing "Think I'm In Love With You." He held out his arms, inviting her to dance with him, and her heart was completely and absolutely lost to this dream of a man.

He held her close as he sang and moved her around the kitchen. "Whatever you're thinking or stressing about, knock it off. I'm here, and I'm not going anywhere as long as you and Jax want to be with me. I hope you want to be with me for a very long time, because I've never felt better than I do when you're in my arms."

McKenzie melted into him, swept away by his words, the song lyrics, the way they moved together like they'd been dancing forever rather than this being the first time. The high chair had been the kicker, she would decide later. The absolute send-her-over-the-edge kicker.

"How did you bring a high chair home on a motorcycle?"

"Carefully."

"You're too much."

"I saw the one from the cabin in the dumpster, so I thought it might help to grab that one."

"It's a huge help. Thank you for doing that and for cleaning it up and making it safe for him."

"I loved doing it." He pulled her in even closer to him, letting her feel what her nearness had done to him. "Tell me what you're worried about."

"I don't want to make another bad decision."

"Does this feel like a bad decision to you?"

She shook her head. "Not even kinda."

"And that's a problem?"

"Everything is perfect until it isn't."

"I can't promise it'll be perfect. Hell, what fun would that be? All I can tell you is I'm as into you as I've ever been with anyone. And yes, I know you and Jax are a package deal. If you'd asked me a few weeks ago if I was ready to be a dad, I would've laughed. What the hell do I know about being anyone's father? But now... Today, I saw a high chair by the side of the road and grabbed it for Jax because he needs one, and I'm sure they don't sell 'em on the island anywhere."

McKenzie looked up at him with the start of tears in her eyes. "That's literally the sweetest thing anyone has ever done for us."

"No way."

"Other than giving us a place to live, that is."

"Aw, that was nothing."

"It was everything to us."

He kissed away her tears. "I don't want you to worry about anything where I'm concerned. I'm right here, and I'm not going anywhere as long as you want me around."

"I want you around."

"Is it scary to admit that?"

"Not as scary as it would be with anyone other than you."

Jax started banging on the tray, demanding more crackers.

Duke laughed as he released her to go to him. "I like how he tells us what he wants."

"I hear we'll be wishing he'd hush up in no time at all."

"I can't wait to hear what he has to say."

"There you go again. Being sweet." As she fed Jax cereal and the peas he loved, McKenzie was awash in the strongest feelings she'd ever had for another human being—other than Jax, of course. But these were different feelings. These were full of giddy hope, sweet anticipation and excitement for a future that looked so much brighter than it had before Duke.

He served her a salad with an array of dressings. "Wasn't sure what you like."

"So you bought them all?"

"I bought three."

"I like them all."

"Then they won't go to waste."

"And you bought animal crackers."

"My buddy loves them."

"Yes, he does."

He went to the stove and returned with plates for each of them. "My own creation—seasoned ground beef, pasta, tomatoes and sauce."

"It looks and smells delicious."

"It always does when you don't have to make it."

"You're spoiling me."

"And loving every second of it. Oh, I forgot. There's bread, too."

After things blew up with Eric, she'd had to force herself to eat for her sake and the baby's. Even after Jax arrived, she'd still struggled to eat with her nerves in a constant uproar.

The second she caught a whiff of the meal Duke had made, she was ravenously hungry for the first time in longer than she could remember. She took a bite, and the flavors exploded on her tongue, making her want more. "This is so good."

"I'm glad you like it."

"I have news about your books."

"Ugh, is it gonna give me heartburn?"

"Not unless you don't have the money in an account I don't know about to pay your overdue estimated quarterlies."

"I've got the money."

"Then no heartburn. You should pay them tomorrow because you're accruing penalties with every day that goes by."

"I'll take care of it in the morning."

"I'll send you the info you need by email."

"Thank you. Can we not mention it again until then?"

She laughed as she nodded. "My lips are sealed."

"Well, don't do that."

She laughed again at the pained face he made.

They ate in companionable silence while she gathered her thoughts so she could tell him how she was feeling.

"When I said this is so good, I wasn't just talking about the food, which is delicious. I'm talking about all of it. You and me and Jax. *This.*"

"I think so, too. I couldn't wait to come home to see what you guys were up to."

"And then we weren't even here."

"You were at work. I liked knowing you'd be back before long."

"You've been the best friend I've ever had, Duke. You've been there for me more than people I've known all my life. You gave us a place to stay and let me borrow your truck and cooked for me and found a high chair and—"

His hand landed on top of hers. "I love having you guys here. If I had my way, I'd want you to stay forever."

"Forever is a really long time."

"I know." He leaned over to kiss her. "I hope it's a really, really long time. If I had you and Jax to come home to every night, I can't imagine ever wanting anything else."

"It's too soon for you to know that."

He shook his head. "I've known that for weeks."

"You've only known me for a few weeks!"

"It took about ten seconds to be nearly one hundred percent certain that I wanted you in my life. I had to talk myself out of running away from you because you're Rosemary's granddaughter, and I worried that she wouldn't approve. But then I thought maybe she'd been preparing me for you with all the time she invested in me. I know that sounds dumb, but I'd like to think it's possible."

"It's not dumb. It's very sweet."

"There's that damned word again," he said with an exasperated grimace.

"You'd better get used to it since you keep doing *sweet* things."

"I suppose I can live with that tag as long as I get to do sweet things for you and those sweet things make you happy."

"They make me very happy. Scary happy."

"Don't be scared."

"Can't help it."

"Any time you feel scared, you tell me, and I'll give you a hundred reasons why you don't need to be."

"A hundred, huh?"

"I can do a hundred without even breaking a sweat."

"Give me three."

"You're beautiful, smart and sexy as f-u-c-k. To start with. You make me laugh, you make me smile so much my face hurts, you care enough to make me wear a helmet, you've got me counting the minutes until I can see you again."

"You count the minutes?"

"I do. Five times sixty was three hundred minutes today. They went by *slow*."

"And then I wasn't here when you got home."

"Believe me, I noticed."

"You want my list?"

"You have one?"

"I sure do. First and foremost, you're sweet and kind and thoughtful. You're a hard worker, and you've built a life for yourself that you love so much you won't give it up for anything or anyone. You're a good friend to everyone in your life. You're an amazing artist, and you make cool things from nothing, including the most elaborate cross-stitch I've ever seen. You think of everyone else before you think of yourself, and you're sexy as f-u-c-k, too."

"All that, huh?"

"That's just off the top of my head."

Jax picked that moment to bang the two spoons McKenzie had given him on the tray like it was a drum.

"Someone's not looking too sleepy."

"Nope. Maybe some playtime will help." She used wet paper towels to clean him up and retrieved him from the chair while Duke carried their dishes to the sink. "I'll wash the dishes."

"No worries. I've got it."

"That's not fair. You cooked."

"Go play with your son. I've got this."

"And he does the dishes…" She waved her hand in front of her face. "So sexy and *sweet*."

His low growl made her laugh as she carried Jax to the living room and put him down to play with his toys for a bit. They rolled a ball back and forth until he got bored with that and turned his attention to a toy with lots of colorful buttons that made a variety of sounds. He loved that one, of course. The louder the better.

Duke joined them a few minutes later, bringing her a glass of water and his wineglass as he sat on the floor with them.

"Coffee and water. Such service."

"You know it."

He stretched out next to Jax and fiddled with the ball.

Jax crawled toward him, reaching for the ball, which Duke snagged before he could get it.

The baby laughed and lunged toward Duke, landing on him, which triggered a mini wrestling match that Jax thoroughly enjoyed.

Her heart was full to overflowing as she watched them play and laugh. How lucky were they to have such a good man in their lives? She'd been so heartbroken by the breakup with Eric, but she could now see that it'd been for the best. She never would've come to Gansett and found a whole new happy, satisfying life if he hadn't betrayed her.

When Jax began rubbing his eyes, McKenzie changed his diaper and sat in the rocking chair in Duke's living room with a light blanket over them to breastfeed him and rock him to sleep. "I can feel you watching me."

"I love watching you in mom mode."

"I love him so much. I never imagined I could love anyone the way I love him."

"He's a very lucky boy."

She used her free hand to run her fingers through his soft blond hair. "We're both lucky to have each other."

"He must look like his father."

"He does."

"Does that bother you?"

"Not at all. He's his own unique self."

"What'll you tell him about his dad when he asks?"

"I haven't really thought about that, but I suppose I'd tell him that his dad wasn't available to us. I hope he doesn't ask about that for a long time."

"Maybe by the time he gets curious, he'll have a dad who loves him and is there for him every day."

"Wouldn't that be something?"

"Sure would."

"Is that what you want?"

"It's funny... If you'd asked me a couple of months ago if I was jonesing for kids, I would've said not really. But now that I know him —and you—it doesn't seem so out there anymore. I keep thinking about all the things I could teach him. Like how to ride the Harley and how I could give him his first tattoo."

McKenzie gave him a withering look that made him laugh.

"What? I'd get him a helmet."

"No Harley and no tattoos."

"Looks like it'll be me and you against Mommy, Jax."

"I'll put you both in time-out."

"I love when you're bossy with me, babe."

"No tattoos, Duke. I mean it."

"Not until he's eighteen, of course."

"Not even then!"

His bark of laughter startled Jax.

"Hush. The baby is trying to sleep."

"Yes, ma'am." His eyes sparkled with mischief. "I'll hold off on the tattoos. For now, anyway."

"I'd rather you teach him things like cross-stitching, cooking, gardening."

"I'll add them to the list."

"And no Harley."

"Don't knock it until you've tried it."

"Nonnegotiable. My son will not ride on motorcycles."

"Said every mom everywhere. What else is a hard no?"

"Football." She shuddered. "The head injuries are terrifying."

"You can get head injuries playing any sport. Hell, you can get a head injury tripping down the stairs."

"Don't give me more things to worry about." She adjusted her top and her sleeping son so she could carry him to bed. As she tucked him in, she thought about how she ought to bring the portable crib to Duke's house since it seemed like they were spending more time there than at the apartment.

Everything was moving fast. Lightning speed, actually, but she couldn't seem to bring herself to slow it down. She didn't want to slow it down. She wanted to jump in with both feet to whatever this was and wallow in the nicest thing to ever happen to her. For a girl who'd been so badly burned in the past, alarm bells should've been sounding loudly. But there were no bells. Just lots of butterflies, excitement and anticipation.

She kissed Jax good night. "Mommy loves you to the moon and back." After adjusting the bumper that Duke had made from a blanket to keep him on the bed, she tiptoed from the room.

When she returned to the living room, Duke had moved from the floor to the sofa and was sipping amber liquid from a cocktail glass.

"Whatcha got there?"

"A little taste of bourbon."

"I've never had it."

"Want to try?"

"Sure." She sat next to him and took the glass from him, taking a tentative sip since she wouldn't feed Jax again until the morning. The liquor heated her from the inside as she handed the glass back to Duke. "Oh, I like it."

"I do, too."

"Hold that thought for a few more months, and then I'd like to try it again."

"You got it. Is the little guy down for the count?"

"Yep."

"He's such a good baby."

"He's the best. The first couple of months were rough. He barely slept and was a bit colicky, which is no fun at all. But thankfully, he's become super easy."

He twirled a strand of her hair around his finger. "I wish I'd been there then."

"I do, too." She ventured a glance at him. "This is starting to feel oh-so-serious."

"Is that okay?"

"I want it to be. It feels so good to be with you this way. It feels better than anything ever has. It's just…"

He reached for her hand and linked their fingers. "Tell me."

"I know I have nothing to be afraid of where you're concerned, but I feel like I'm tossing all caution to the wind and diving in headfirst, which would be totally fine if it was just me. But it's not just me. I have to think of Jax, too."

"I hear you, and I get why you feel the way you do. All I can tell you is I've never wanted anything more than to make the three of us a family. I hope you know that I'm already most of the way in love with both of you, and I want more nights like this one. I want a lifetime of nights just like this."

What could she say to that? How could she deny that was exactly what she wanted, too? She couldn't, so she took his glass, put it on the table and reached for him.

Their kiss was hot and desperate and full of longing.

"God, MK, what you do to me."

"What do I do?"

"You make me feel everything."

"Same." She put her hand on his face and drew him into another deep, sexy kiss. "Let's go to bed."

CHAPTER 31

*H*e must be living in a fever dream. That was the only possible explanation for how his boring, orderly life had become this intense, beautiful, wild adventure.

Standing next to his bed, McKenzie unbuttoned his shirt and pushed it off his shoulders as she nuzzled his chest hair and peppered him with little kisses that set him on fire.

"This time is all about you," he said.

"It's all about *us*."

"First, you." He pulled the formfitting tank top that'd been driving him wild all evening over her head and released the clasp to her bra. "I thought about you and this all day long," he said as he cupped her breasts. "It's a wonder I didn't ink a picture of you on my client's back instead of the dragon he asked for."

Her low chuckle made him smile. "That would've been quite a surprise for your client."

"Sure would, but that'd never happen because I don't want anyone else to see you the way I do."

He ran his hands over her back and down to tuck them inside the leggings that he pushed down, leaving her only in the tiniest pair of panties he'd ever seen. Christ have mercy, but she was the sexiest thing on two legs.

Duke eased her down to the bed and leaned over her to tease her nipples with his lips and tongue.

Her fingers tugging at his hair was like gas on an already out-of-control wildfire. He wanted to wallow in her sweetness, her soft skin, her scent, her very essence. If this was love, and he was pretty damned sure it was, he was glad he'd waited for her to come along. He knew now that no one else could've made him feel the way she did.

He removed her panties, dropped to his knees next to the bed and set out to drive her as wild as she'd driven him the night before. With tongue, fingers and lips, he teased her to a series of orgasms that had her crying out with abandon that had him reaching for a condom and rolling it on.

He leaned over her, kissing her until her eyes opened.

The way she looked at him…

"You're a unicorn in every possible way."

"Is that right?"

"Uh-huh." He pressed against her. "How about we see if we can add one more way to the list?"

She wrapped her arms around him. "I'm here for it."

Never before had sex felt like a homecoming, an arrival to the place he was always supposed to be, with the person who was meant to be his. The feeling of absolute rightness that came over him marked the first time he'd ever felt he was exactly where he belonged.

"God, MK. This is…"

"Amazing."

"Yeah. Totally." He held her close and loved her with all his heart and soul, giving her everything he had until they were clinging to each other and riding wave after wave of the most intense pleasure he'd ever experienced.

"Damn," he whispered after a long silence punctuated by deep breaths and contented sighs.

"Damn is right."

He rolled to his side, bringing her with him. "Are you okay?"

MARIE FORCE

She rested her head on his chest. "I'm much better than okay. And the piercing... *whoa.*"

"Told you you'd like it."

"I did."

"Remember how I chose Gansett over my ex?"

"Yeah."

"I'm so, so glad I made that decision. I can see now it was all leading me to you and this."

"It's funny how you can look back at something that was so awful at the time, but necessary to get where you were meant to be."

"Yes, exactly."

"I thought I'd never recover from what Eric did to me. The lies, the gaslighting, the deception, the abandonment. But now it just seems like a bad dream that happened to someone else, and I'm oddly thankful for what he did. It was leading me to you."

"I'm very glad your house fell down."

McKenzie laughed. "I guess I am, too. Not that I'd like to live through another hurricane any time soon, but we do have Ethel to thank for our current predicament."

"You said 'dick.'"

"I said predicament!"

He snorted. "I heard it. Both times."

"*Now* you're going to reveal your inner twelve-year-old boy?"

His hand made a lazy path over her back. "I kept him hidden until I had you right where I wanted you."

"I see how it is."

"I hope you also see how gone over you I am."

"I do see that, and I'm equally gone, even as my better judgment says, 'Slow down! Take a breath! Don't be crazy!'"

"Crazy ain't never felt so good."

"No, it hasn't."

His fingertips skimmed over her shoulder and down her arm, leaving goose bumps behind. "I could put the prettiest ink on this glorious skin."

"No ink. Mama doesn't do needles."

"You wouldn't feel a thing."

"That's a big fat lie!"

"No lie. I've got stuff to numb you up. You'd probably sleep through it."

"Doubtful."

"Keep it in mind."

"I'll do that."

"Are you lying to me?"

"Not at all. I will keep it in mind."

"I know a brush-off when I hear one."

"You might be the one person in the whole world who could talk me into a tattoo."

"Inking you would be the highlight of my entire career."

IN THE MORNING, after breakfast with Duke, McKenzie and Jax returned to the Sand & Surf to work with Piper in the office off the lobby. With Jax content in his seat with toys and several of his stuffed animals, McKenzie forced herself to concentrate on accounts receivable and payable when all she wanted to do was relive the romantic night she'd spent with Duke.

They'd made love a second time at three in the morning, and it had been even hotter than the first. How was that even possible?

He'd woken her with kisses down her back and coffee in bed. A girl could get used to that kind of treatment.

"McKenzie?"

She realized she'd zoned out of Piper telling her about the schedule for ordering supplies for the hotel. "I'm sorry. Say that again."

"Is everything all right?"

"Everything is great, and that's the problem."

"Um, okay…"

"New guy. Sleepless night. Scattered brain."

"Ah, I see how it is," she said with a knowing smile. "I've got a new guy, too, and am also suffering from sleep deprivation."

"I'm obviously a red-hot mess without a full night of sleep."

"You're fine. I totally get it, and it's for a good cause."

McKenzie laughed. "The best kind of cause. How long have you been seeing your guy?"

"A few weeks seriously. Lots of months of subtle flirtation before that."

"What's his name?"

"Jack Downing. He's the state police officer assigned to the island."

"Oh, I see."

"How about you?"

"Duke Sullivan, who owns the tattoo studio."

"I know Duke. He's a great guy."

"I think so, too. How do you know him?"

"He hangs out at the Beachcomber across the street. It's a fun group over there. You should come some night."

"I have Jax."

"It's Gansett. You can bring a baby to a bar here. No one would think a thing of it. In fact, Kevin and Chelsea McCarthy bring their baby girl, Summer, in all the time."

"Maybe I will some night."

"Everyone loves Duke. He'd give you the shirt off his back, even if it was the last shirt he owned."

"That sums him up rather nicely. He's been so good to me and Jax, and now we're just... I don't know what we are, but I'm sleep-deprived and looking forward to being sleep-deprived tomorrow, too."

"It's the best feeling, isn't it?"

"Yeah, it is, even though I keep telling myself to slow down and not get in over my head, but it's probably already too late for warnings."

"I totally get that! My fiancé called off our wedding earlier this year, and I keep thinking I shouldn't be ready for what's happening with Jack, but that doesn't seem to be stopping me from diving in headfirst."

"I'm sorry about your fiancé."

Piper shrugged. "I've come to realize he did me a favor. I would've hated to have missed out on what's happening with Jack."

"I'm starting to feel that way about what Jax's dad did—leading me on for a year and getting me pregnant when he had a whole other wife and kids stashed elsewhere."

"What? Are you serious?"

"Sadly, I am, and then he made it even better when he told me he couldn't possibly be Jax's father because he'd had a vasectomy years earlier. He knew full well I hadn't been with anyone but him."

"What an asshole. Damn. Just when I think I've heard everything..."

"I know, right? I'm working with Kendall James to go after him for child support."

"Good for you."

"He's not too happy with me."

"Whatever. He helped make the baby. He can help pay the expenses."

"That's how I feel, too. Anyway... Sorry to get sidetracked. Let's get back to debits and credits."

"Talking about our new guys is way more fun."

"It sure is."

They got back to work, but McKenzie left a while later feeling as if she'd made another new friend in Piper. Next, she was off to meet with Sydney Harris, who ran an interior design business on the island and had heard about her from Jenny Martinez. News of her business was traveling fast, and each day brought new clients and interesting challenges.

She yawned as she drove to Sydney's, thankful to have only one more meeting before she could head home to feed Jax and put him down for a nap. Maybe she'd take one, too.

Sydney and her husband, Luke, lived on an oceanfront parcel with stunning views.

McKenzie couldn't imagine what it would be like to look out at such a beautiful view every day.

"It still dazzles me, too."

McKenzie turned to find Sydney standing at the door with a baby in her arms. Both mom and daughter had strawberry-blonde hair. "It's stunning."

"You ought to see the sunsets. I'm Syd, by the way. And this is Lily."

"McKenzie and Jax."

"Pleasure to meet you both."

"You, too."

"Come in." Sydney stepped aside to welcome McKenzie and Jax into her home.

"This is lovely."

"Thank you. My first island decorating project. I say this to everyone, but can you believe there were walls where those windows are?"

"That must've been a crying shame."

"It was, but I fixed that and many other things around here."

She gestured for McKenzie to have a seat on the sofa. "Does Jax want to play with Lily?"

"He'd love to, although he's not very good at playing with other kids quite yet."

"That'll come. He'll be surrounded by a million kids here."

"Which is just another thing to love about Gansett."

"It's the best place ever to live and work, especially now that McKenzie has come to town, bringing her accounting know-how. It's all everyone is talking about."

McKenzie laughed. "I believe it, based on the way my phone is ringing nonstop."

While their little ones played on a blanket full of toys on the floor, Sydney explained how her business worked, showed her some of the jobs she'd completed, covered how she sourced and procured items for clients and went over the balance sheet.

"Are you sure you need me? Your books are already in great shape."

"We haven't told too many people yet, but I'm expecting another baby, so I'll need some help with the business. I want to be able to focus on the part that's fun for me while someone else makes sure the taxes get paid."

"I can certainly help with that, and congrats on the new baby."

"It's a very special time for me. I'm sure you'll hear this from someone before too long, but I lost my first husband and our two children in a drunk-driving accident several years ago."

"Oh my God, Sydney. I'm so sorry."

"Thank you." She reached for a framed photo on a side table. "That's Seth, Malena and Max."

"They were beautiful."

"Yes, they were, and it took me a long time to be able to even consider moving on with a new life, but then I came here, reunited with my first love, and now we've got our precious Lily with another on the way." She retrieved a second photo of a handsome dark-haired man holding Lily. "That's my Luke."

"I give you so much credit for what you've overcome."

"I survived the accident that took them from me. I had no choice but to figure out a new life for myself."

"A lot of people wouldn't have made the effort. I don't know that I could've." The thought of losing Jax was too big for her to even consider.

"It's amazing what you can do when life gives you no choice."

"I suppose that's true."

"Did Jax's dad come out to the island with you?"

"No, he's not in the picture." She shared the details of what'd happened with Eric.

"Come on," Sydney said. "What is *wrong* with people?"

McKenzie laughed. "So many things. But we're doing okay. My grandmother left me her cottage here, which is how we ended up coming to Gansett in the first place. Then the storm hit, the cottage collapsed, Blaine Taylor rescued me, and then Duke Sullivan offered me a place to stay in his garage apartment. And now I seem to be falling in love with him... So yeah, things happen for a reason, I guess."

"That's quite a story, and for what it's worth, I love hearing you're with Duke. He's the best."

"That's what everyone says. My grandmother adored him."

"Who was your grandmother?"

"Rosemary Enders."

"Oh, no way! I knew her back in the day when I scooped ice cream in town. She came in almost every day."

"That sounds about right. She used to say if only she could figure out which of her teeth was the sweet one, she'd have it pulled."

"Yes! I remember that. She used to say that all the time when she was justifying her 'daily scoop,' as she called it. She was a lovely lady."

"I miss her."

Sydney insisted she stay for lunch, which was a delicious salad with grilled chicken. She had cereal and baby food for Jax and fed Lily with cheese, crackers and apple slices while Jax ate in Lily's high chair.

"This was so nice. Thank you for feeding us. You didn't have to do that."

"We enjoyed it very much, didn't we, Lily?"

"Jax."

"Yes, that's your new friend Jax."

"We've made so many friends here. More than I've ever had in my life."

"Welcome to Gansett."

CHAPTER 32

cKenzie drove back to Duke's with the window down to let in the warm early autumn breeze. She picked up a hint of woodsmoke in the air, which only added to the contentment that she'd found on the island. New friends, new work, new love, a whole new life.

Pulling into Duke's driveway felt like coming home to the place she'd always been meant to find. She took Jax up to the apartment to change him and put him down for his nap. Even though she had a million things to do for several of her new clients, she stretched out on the bed and passed out.

She came to when she felt Duke snuggle in next to her.

He put his arm around her. "I hope that's Duke," she whispered.

"Who else would it be?"

He'd been there two seconds and already had her smiling like a fool in love. "I thought it might be my boyfriend."

"It is. Now go back to sleep."

"Let me turn over."

He raised his arm so she could turn to face him.

"Hi."

He kissed her. "Hi yourself. Missed you. It was a long two hundred and thirty-five minutes."

"Yes, it was, especially since I was trying to stay awake the whole time."

"Same. A wild vixen messed with my sleep last night."

"Right. Who messed with who?"

"That's my story. Sticking to it." He kissed her again and again until they were clinging to each other and straining to get closer. "We're supposed to be sleeping."

"But this is way more fun."

A loud car horn sounded from the yard.

"What the hell?" he muttered as he sat up.

"McKenzie! Come out here!"

"Who's that?"

"I... I think it could be Eric." She followed Duke off the bed and out of the bedroom to the window to look out at the yard. "It is." God, what was he doing there?

"Stay here. I'll get rid of him."

"Duke!"

"Stay here. I promise it'll be fine."

It felt wrong to let him go out to confront her ex.

"Can I help you with something?" Duke asked as he went down the stairs to the driveway.

"Where's McKenzie?"

"She's not here."

"Yes, she is. I tracked her phone. So go get her."

McKenzie's heart stopped when she heard that. He'd tracked her phone? Since when?

"What do you want?"

"That's between her and me."

"Not anymore it isn't. It's between you and me."

"Who are you?"

"That doesn't matter. State your business and then get off my property."

"I want to see McKenzie."

"That isn't going to happen. Do I need to call the police to get you to leave?"

"I'm not leaving until I talk to her."

Duke withdrew his phone and made a call. "This is Duke Sullivan. I have someone on my property who's refusing to leave." He paused. "No, I don't know him. Thank you." He put the phone back in his pocket. "The police are on their way."

"McKenzie! Call off your dog and get out here!"

"Shut your mouth. I know exactly who you are and why you're here, and let me tell you, there's nothing you can say or do to convince her to drop the case against you. This is a mess of your own making, so go home to your wife and kids, do the right thing by Jax and leave them alone."

McKenzie stepped out of the apartment. "You should listen to him, Eric. He's absolutely right."

"You don't know what you're doing!" He took a step toward the stairs.

Duke stopped him with a hand to his chest that Eric tried and failed to shake off. "Take one more step, and I'll end you."

As Eric looked up at her, McKenzie tried to remember what she'd ever seen in him.

"You're going to ruin my life!" he said. "Is that what you want?"

"I don't care about your life. I care about Jax's life. You don't get to lie and deceive and cheat and then walk away like none of it ever happened. It happened. We happened. He happened."

"I told you I can't have kids. He's not mine."

"And you felt like you had to come all the way out here to tell her that again?" Duke sounded fiercer than she'd ever heard him. "I hear sirens in the distance. If I were you, I'd get gone before they show up, and I'd stay gone. There's nothing here for you. Not anymore."

He pushed at Duke's hand, which was keeping him from getting any closer to her and Jax. "Who is this guy, anyway?"

"He's the best man I've ever known, so you'd be wise to listen to him. You're trespassing on his property."

"This is what you moved on to after me?" he asked with a sneer.

"That's right, and he's ten million times the man you'll ever be. Go home to your family, Eric. There's nothing for you here. That's how you wanted it, and PS, thank you for that, because what you did led me to where I belong."

A police car pulled into the driveway, lights flashing.

"This man is refusing to leave my property," Duke said when a young male officer got out of the car.

"I'm going." Eric shook off Duke. "But this is not over."

"If you ever step foot on my property again, I'll make you regret it. You hear me?"

"McKenzie, come on. Can't we at least talk about this?"

"I've got nothing to say to you. You can talk to me through my lawyer."

"Are you leaving?" the officer asked Eric.

"Yeah, whatever."

"Be on the next boat back to the mainland," the officer said.

Eric got into a silver sedan that McKenzie didn't recognize and made a cloud of dust as he reversed out of the driveway.

She breathed a sigh of relief.

"Sorry for the trouble," Duke told the officer.

"No problem. I'll make sure he gets on the boat."

"Thank you."

"I'd recommend coming in to file a report so there's a record of what transpired today, just in case there's any more trouble."

"We'll do that." Duke shook his hand. "Thanks again."

After the officer left, Duke came up the stairs to where she stood, frozen with shock over the entire incident. He put his hands on her shoulders. "It's okay. He's gone, and if he knows what's good for him, he'll stay gone."

"I... I can't believe he came here, that he tracked my phone. I didn't know he'd done that. I'm so sorry, Duke."

"For what? You didn't do anything."

"I brought this mess to your home."

"That's not all you've brought to my home. Please don't blame yourself for what he did."

"I... I didn't know he was tracking me. I don't even know how that works."

"I'll show you, and we'll make sure he can't do that anymore."

"That'd be good. Thankfully, Jax slept through it."

"Everything's okay. Take a deep breath."

She breathed in deeply and then let it out slowly. "Thank you for what you did. I never could've handled him as well on my own. I'd have been too shocked to tell him off."

"You would've kicked him in the balls and sent him on his way."

She huffed out a small laugh. "I would've wanted to. It means everything that you stuck up for me. You didn't even hesitate to go out there and confront him."

"Don't you know by now that there's nothing I wouldn't do for you and Jax?"

"I'm beginning to see that."

He put his arms around her and drew her into his embrace. "I'm here. I've got your back. You've got mine."

"No one's ever had my back before. Not like you do."

"Same. Never had someone who had mine. I love you, MK. I'll always have your back."

"I love you, too."

They were the biggest and yet also the simplest words she'd ever said to anyone, and as she stood in the arms of her love, she had no doubt at all that this leap of faith would turn out to be the one that made her life—and her son's life—complete.

OVER THE NEXT MONTH, McKenzie's new life fell into place in every possible way. She had more work than she could handle, with clients lining up for a meeting with her. She'd proposed group payroll and health insurance options to lower the cost many businesses were paying currently and had landed the McCarthy family and all their island businesses, which was almost a full-time job on its own. Her clients had insisted on paying her no less than fifty dollars an hour for her time, and she was amazed at how much money she was making doing something she loved.

She'd enrolled Jax in morning preschool three days a week that wasn't really preschool quite yet, but it gave him time to be with other kids his age while she got some work done. Their days had fallen into a lovely routine that included new friends for both of them and lots of time with Duke, their new best friend.

After Kendall heard about what Eric had done, she doubled down with his attorney and threatened to file a criminal complaint if he came anywhere near McKenzie or Jax again. They'd filed the police report, and Duke had taken care of making sure her phone wasn't trackable by anyone. He'd also installed cameras around his property so no one could take them by surprise again.

McKenzie was on her way home from delivering Jax to school on a Wednesday morning in early October when Kendall called.

"Am I getting you at a good time?"

"Yes, I'm driving."

"Great. I heard from Eric's attorney, and he's prepared to offer a one-time payment with the caveat that it's all he's willing to pay, and if you want more, you'll have to take him to court. Since I doubt he's told his wife about you and Jax, you do have leverage there. If you don't like the offer, we can tell him we'll see him in court. I have to believe he'll want to avoid that at all costs."

All it took to trigger the anxiety from that day in Duke's yard was hearing Eric's name. Her stomach instantly hurt, and the quiver in her hands made her angry. "What's the offer?"

"One hundred thousand."

"Well. That's not nothing."

"No, it isn't, but it's far less than what you'd get over the next seventeen years if you went to court and demanded regular child support payments. That would also make it a lot more difficult for him to keep you and Jax hidden from his wife."

"I'm not looking to blow up her life. I'm sure she'll find out eventually who he really is if she doesn't know already. That's not my goal. I want to make sure I have what I need to raise my son without him having to do without anything and to be able to help him with college later, if that's what he wants."

"Which is a fair request. If you want to think about it, there's no need to respond right away. My fee would be five thousand since this didn't take much time at all."

"That's totally fine. I'd like a day or two to consider it, if that's okay."

"Absolutely. Give me a call when you decide."

"Thank you for your help with this."

"No problem at all."

During an earlier call, Kendall had told McKenzie that she'd enrolled her sons in school and was looking for an island home to rent for the school year. After that, she wasn't sure of their plans, but she was taking things one day at a time. In the meantime, she'd taken over much of Dan Torrington's local practice while he and his wife, Kara, were in Maine. McKenzie had read about Dan's legal career and his innocence project and still couldn't believe he lived and worked on Gansett Island.

She and almost everyone else she knew on the island had attended a memorial service for Jim Sturgil, which had focused on his enduring love for his daughter. Tiffany told McKenzie later that Jim's parents asked to have Ashleigh sit with them during the service, but Tiffany had insisted on keeping her daughter with her and Blaine.

Some things were simply nonnegotiable. Doing what was right for your child was certainly one of them. How did any mother know for sure what was right? Would a hundred thousand dollars, combined with her income, allow her to give Jax the childhood she wanted for him? How in the world did anyone put a price on such a thing?

The day after Kendall's call, she and Jax were heading to Tiffany's store, and she hoped to get the chance to talk to her new friend about Eric's offer. She hadn't yet mentioned it to Duke. Before she did, she wanted the input of a more experienced mom to help her decide whether to take the offer or fight him for more in court.

The thought of an extended battle exhausted her, but she'd do whatever was necessary to advocate for Jax.

McKenzie parked the truck behind Tiffany's store and entered through the back door with work and diaper bags hooked over her shoulder and Jax in her arms. Her booming business was a huge relief, especially since none of her clients minded if she brought her son to in-person meetings. Not having to pay for daycare was another blessing in this new life she was creating for them. Every day, she gave thanks to her beloved grandmother for leaving her the cottage that had led to this lovely new stage for them. It was as if Rosemary had known that someday McKenzie would need a fresh start and had made sure she'd get it.

Next week, she would hold a meeting for sixteen clients to discuss the group payroll and health insurance options she'd researched. They'd been thrilled to hear that they could reduce their overall fees by banding together. The sense of accomplishment at having finally found her niche in life was profound. That, coupled with her blissful relationship with Duke, had made her happier than she'd ever been.

"Morning," Tiffany said when she spotted McKenzie and Jax.

"Morning."

"Addie is super excited to play with Jax this morning. Aren't you, sweetie?"

"Jax."

"That's right."

"Aw, he's excited, too." She plopped him into the gated play area where Addie waited for him.

He crawled over to hug his friend, which was the cutest thing their mothers had ever seen.

"They're adorable," Tiffany said.

"Truly. She's the one friend he responds to every time. He's always happy to see the others, but he keeps his distance from most of them."

"He'll grow out of that."

"Definitely, but for now, Addie is his bestie."

"She's very happy about that." They sat at Tiffany's small desk. "I got you a coffee."

"You're the best. Thank you."

"No problem."

"How's Ashleigh?"

"Doing a little better. Sleeping through the night again, which helps. She still has her moments, though. She decided to go back to school today, but she knows she can call me if she wants to come home."

"I'm glad to hear she's a little better."

"Tough thing to see your baby through, that's for sure."

"I can't imagine."

"Anyway..."

"Can we talk about something else before we work?" McKenzie asked.

"Of course. Is everything okay with Duke?"

Tiffany was the one friend who knew how serious McKenzie's relationship with Duke had gotten in recent weeks. "Everything is way better than okay."

"Yay, I love that! You two are such a great couple."

"Thanks. We're having fun."

"I remember those starry first days with Blaine, when I was so sleep-deprived and drunk on sex that I could barely function."

"I know that feeling."

They shared a laugh.

"It's the best," Tiffany said. "And when you're really lucky, the glow never ends."

"That'd be nice."

"What's on your mind?"

"Jax's father."

"Have you heard from him since the incident at Duke's?"

Like all juicy news did, word of Eric's "visit" had traveled around the island at lightning speed.

"Yesterday. His lawyer reached out to Kendall with an offer of a one-time cash payment. I'd have to sign away the right to ask for more."

"How much did he offer?"

"One hundred thousand."

"Hmmm."

"Is it enough?"

"That's hard to say. For most people, it'd be more than enough to raise a child comfortably, but it won't cover college."

"Right. I thought of that. He's trying to avoid me taking him to court since his wife and kids don't know about us."

Tiffany made a sound that was a cross between a groan and a gag. "If I were you, I'd want to blow the lid off his entire bullshit game."

"Part of me does, but honestly, what would I gain from turning their lives upside down? They haven't done anything to me."

"His kids are Jax's half siblings, who he'll never know if you accept this offer."

"I thought of that, too. Having them in his life would mean having his father in his life, and he's not a man I want my son to grow up emulating, you know?"

"Definitely. It's a tough call, for sure."

"What would you do if you were me?"

"Oh gosh, I don't know, McKenzie. It's such a big decision. On the one hand, you could accept this one-time payment and be rid of him forever. On the other, you take him to court, forcing him to come clean to his wife, which would make him angry and vindictive. After having been through something similar, I would add that peace of mind is underrated until you don't have it. Fighting with an ex is grueling and devastating and..." Her eyes filled. "It breaks your heart all over again, every time you realize he was never the man you thought he was."

McKenzie placed her hand over Tiffany's. "I'm sorry he hurt you so deeply."

"I'm sorry you were hurt, too." Tiffany rallied, pulled herself together and forced a smile. "I've also learned that all the pain and heartache I experienced with Jim was preparing me to find the truest of true loves with Blaine."

"How did you ever summon the courage to take that leap again?"

"I never needed courage to love Blaine. That's how I knew it was different from the get-go. He makes me feel safe to be myself, to sob over my dead ex-husband, to be everything and anything I want to be without the fear of losing him simply for being myself."

"What a lovely way to describe true love." It sounded, she thought, an awful lot like what she'd found with Duke.

"It's also a lovely way to live. I can't tell you what to do about this dilemma, but I can assure you that you and Jax will be just fine no matter what you decide. You're a strong, capable woman building your own business and a whole new life for yourself and your son. If you never saw a dime from him, you'd be fine. I know it."

"That means a lot to me coming from a badass boss bitch like you."

Tiffany laughed. "That might be the best compliment I've ever received, especially since I hardly feel like that on the inside lately."

"You're a survivor, and you'll survive this, too."

"Thanks for the vote of confidence."

"Thanks for the advice. It helped a lot."

"Any time."

"Now, about work…"

Tiffany laughed as she opened QuickBooks to get started on their list of tasks for the day.

CHAPTER 33

*W*ith McKenzie working late, Duke decided to go into town to see his friends for the first time in weeks. When he walked into the Beachcomber bar, a cheer went up from all the regulars, who greeted him like returning royalty.

"Look what the cat dragged in." Jace Carson poured a beer for Duke from the tap. "Where you been, old man?"

Amused by the reception, he took the beer from Jace. "I've been around."

"He's in *love*," Sierra said as she made kissy faces.

"Are you having a stroke or something?" he asked her while everyone else laughed.

"Am I wrong?"

"Nope."

"I'm *so* happy for you, Duke," Cindy Lawry said. "I met McKenzie when she came into the salon to meet with Chloe about the books. She's lovely."

"She sure is."

Jace reached across the bar for Cindy's hand. "Ain't nothing quite like true love," he said as he kissed the back of her hand.

Cindy's smile stretched from ear to ear as she gazed at Jace. "That's the truth."

"So where is she?" Sierra asked. "Did she already dump you?"

"Haha, no, she didn't dump me. She's working, if you must know. I decided to take advantage of the opportunity to come visit you losers. What's been going on here?"

"The doc has managed to knock me up again." Chelsea McCarthy grinned at her husband, Dr. Kevin McCarthy, as Summer slept in her arms.

"The doc has still got it," Kevin said.

"Spare us the gory details," Sierra replied.

"Nothing gory about it," Chelsea said with a wink for Sierra.

"Congratulations, guys," Duke said. "Happy for you."

"Thanks, we're happy for us, too," Kevin said with a warm smile for his wife. "Never thought I'd be starting a new family at my ripe old age, but it's the best thing ever."

"All this true-love bullshit is nauseating," Niall Fitzgerald said when he came to the bar for a refill of Guinness.

"What's with you?" Duke asked the Irishman, who was usually the epitome of happy-go-lucky optimism.

"Nothing is with me. Absolutely nothing."

"Uh-oh," Duke said, glancing at Sierra, who always had the lowdown on whatever was going on with one of their friends.

"Not happening with John."

"Oh no. I thought it was."

"So did I," Niall said. "I thought wrong, apparently."

"I tried to talk to him," John's sister Cindy said. "I got nowhere. I can't figure out what's going on with him since he came back from Providence."

"If you figure it out, let me know," Niall said as he took his refilled glass back to the small stage where he performed most nights.

"Poor guy," Duke said. "I liked them together."

"We all did," Cindy said. "I wish I knew what was going on with Johnny."

"How's your other brother doing?" Duke asked. "The one who was hurt in the storm."

"Jeff has been moved to rehab and is making steady progress. They're hoping to be able to come home in a couple more weeks."

"That's great news."

"It's a huge relief that he's doing so well. Jace and I are going to visit him and Kelsey this weekend."

"Tell him we're all rooting for him," Duke said.

"I sure will."

Ace, Tim and Buster from the studio came rolling in, looking as if the Beachcomber wasn't their first stop on their night out. They stopped short when they saw Duke sitting at the bar.

"*Whoa,*" Ace said. "He's finally come up for air."

Everyone in the bar lost it laughing.

"Haha," Duke said with a grin. "Where've you boys come from?"

"The Scupper. It's two-for-one shot night over there. We couldn't pass up a bargain."

That accounted for their glassy eyes, Duke thought, as he gestured to Jace to put a round for everyone on him. These were his people, the ones who'd been there for him through thick and thin and everything in between. Jace was a relatively new friend, but he'd quickly become one of Duke's favorite people. Especially after he heard more about Jace's life and how he'd ended up in prison for a very bad decision and had lost his wife and kids in the process.

"How're the boys?" Duke asked when Jace put a refill on the bar for him.

"They're doing great. Growing like weeds and full of beans as always."

His friend glowed when he spoke of his beloved sons, Jackson and Kyle, who were being raised by Seamus and Carolina O'Grady after Jace's ex-wife, Lisa, had died of lung cancer. Lisa's death had been a massive blow to everyone who'd loved her, including Duke.

"I'm so glad you get to see a lot of them."

"Me, too. I'm very thankful for the way it all worked out. Seamus and Carolina are family."

As someone who'd never had a family of his own, Duke was endlessly fascinated with the concept of "found family," or the family one created for oneself. He'd been enormously blessed in that regard, thanks mostly to the people in this room and a few others, such as Rosemary.

After sipping his second beer for more than an hour, he settled up with Jace to head home to the two people who were quickly becoming his new family.

"See you again in six months," Sierra said with a cheeky grin.

"Won't be that long."

"Bring McKenzie in sometime," Chelsea said. "We'd love to meet her."

"Will do. Y'all be good."

"Don't do anything we wouldn't do," Ace called after him as the other guys laughed like the fools they were.

"I'll do my best."

In the parking lot, he took the time to don the helmet McKenzie insisted he wear before firing up the bike for the ride home. Soon, it would be too cold for the bike, but he was enjoying it while he could. He'd also enjoyed the night out with his friends and wanted to bring McKenzie in to meet them. It'd be no big deal to bring Jax with them. Nothing was a big deal on Gansett, which was another reason he loved it so much.

He pulled into the yard and cut the engine as soon as he could so he wouldn't wake the little guy. Seeing the light on in his house filled him with a deep sense of homecoming. The house he'd loved so much for so long had truly become a home when they'd all but moved in with him over the last few weeks.

Jax now slept in an actual crib McKenzie had shipped from the mainland, along with a shocking amount of other "necessary" equipment for a tiny human. Duke's living room was littered with toys, his bathroom counter was covered with girly stuff, and his heart... His heart was full to overflowing as he stashed the bike in the garage and walked swiftly toward the house, where his love waited for him.

It had taken a few weeks with McKenzie to know for certain that he'd never been in love, truly in love, with Lynn.

This... This was love. The heart-pounding, lightheaded feeling of pure joy he experienced every time he laid eyes on her, like it was the first time all over again.

"Hey," she said with a smile as she looked up from her laptop.

"Hey yourself. Why you still working?"

"Too much to do, not enough time to do it."

He'd loved seeing her in hot demand among all the island businesses. He didn't love paying estimated quarterlies, but he did what he was told by his business manager. She'd taken a huge load off his shoulders, and he'd heard others say the same thing. "She's worth every dime," Sierra had said bluntly a few weeks ago.

Duke leaned over to kiss her. "All work and no play makes McKenzie tired and cranky."

She laughed. "Guilty as charged."

"Missed you. Long one hundred and twenty minutes away from you."

Smiling, she said, "Missed you, too. How was the visit with your friends?"

"I took a lot of ribbing, thanks to you."

Her brows came together adorably. "Because of *me*?"

"Uh-huh. I used to be a regular over there, and now I've got much better things to do with my evenings."

"Oh, I see."

"They want you to come in."

"Let's do that sometime. I'd love to get to know them." She glanced up at him, and he saw torment in her expression that immediately put him on alert to trouble. "Can we talk?"

Oh God. No, no, no. Nothing good ever came from those words. For a second, he was struck so dumb with fear that she wanted to tell him they were over that he couldn't breathe.

"It's not about us."

It took a full ten seconds for him to start breathing again.

"Duke! Come on, you know it's not about us."

"I, uh…"

She stood and wrapped her arms around him. "I'm sorry. I didn't mean to scare you."

"You didn't. Not much, anyway."

"Yes, I did, and I hate that I did. You have *nothing* to worry about where I'm concerned. Please tell me you know that."

"I do." He kissed her and leaned his forehead on hers. "It's just that you've become so damned essential to me that I could barely stand to spend one evening away from you and Jax."

"We missed you terribly. Jax didn't want to go to sleep without Doo Doo."

"Best nickname ever," he said with a chuckle.

"What I wanted to tell you is that we heard from Eric about a financial settlement."

Duke went completely still when he heard that son of a bitch's name.

McKenzie took his hand and towed him along with her to the sofa, where they settled next to each other with her legs over his lap and their hands still intertwined.

He never got over how soft her skin was or how much he craved everything about her when they were apart.

"What'd he say?"

"He offered a one-time payment of one hundred thousand, provided I sign away the right to more down the road."

"Fuck him and his money. We don't need anything from him."

"That's very sweet of you to say."

For once, he didn't react to her use of that dreaded word. He was too busy being enraged over the gall of that guy to care about being called sweet.

"But I want to do what's best for Jax."

"You do what's best for him every second of every day. He has everything he'll ever want or need, thanks to you."

"Which is very nice of you to say, but how do I let Eric off the hook, as if he bears no responsibility whatsoever for Jax?"

"You don't need him. You have me, and I have you, and Jax has us both, and we'll make sure he's the happiest kid who ever lived."

"Duke…"

"Don't tell me I'm sweet or else…"

She smiled. "Or else what?"

"I'll think of some way to punish you."

"I love when you punish me." The only way he did that was by withholding orgasms until she was begging him for relief.

"I don't want his money. I want him out of your lives forever."

"That money would come in handy if Jax wants to go to college."

"We'll pay for his college."

"Duke…"

"McKenzie…"

"I don't expect you to pay for my son's college."

"Why not? I thought I was going to help you raise him. Why can't I help to educate him, too?"

"You're serious about this."

"I'm as serious about you and Jax as I've ever been about anything in my whole damned life."

She placed her free hand over her heart. "What did I ever do to get so lucky to find you?"

"I'm the lucky one, babe."

"We both are, and we're smart enough to know it."

"That's right, and we don't need that deadbeat or his money."

"I agree, and I appreciate what you're saying. It's just that after what he did to me, the way he lied to me and deceived me and tried to make me think he couldn't have fathered Jax… I want him to pay for that. I want him to have to step up for our son, even if it's only this one time."

Duke listened to her and thought about what she'd said.

"Can you understand that at all?" she asked.

"I can, and I suppose you could invest that hundred grand and let it pay for college for all our kids."

Her brows lifted. "*All* our kids?"

"Yeah, we're gonna have a bunch of them."

"Is that right?"

"Uh-huh. My future wife is young and has lots of time left to have babies."

The minute he said the words *future wife*, her whole body went rigid, and not in a good way.

"Did I go too far?"

"One step too far. I meant it when I said I don't want to get married."

"Even to me?"

"You're the only one who could make me consider it."

"But?"

"I want us to be together every day because we want to be. Not because we're legally bound to each other."

"Can't we do both?"

"It's just so freaking awful for everyone involved if it doesn't work out."

"This is gonna work out, sweetheart."

"Everyone thinks that when they're newly in love and planning a future. But then life happens, and things go sideways. The tearing apart is brutal."

"When life happens, and things go sideways, I'll be right there with you through it all. I'll go sideways, hell, I'll go upside down if I have to, if that's what it takes. But one thing I'll never do is leave you to figure it out on your own. We'd be in this together every step of the way, because we want to be, not because the law says we gotta."

He tipped up her chin to receive his kiss. "I've waited my whole life for you and Jax. Every minute of every day and every month and every year was leading me to you and him and this family. I want us to stand up in front of our people and take vows and make a life together with Jax and that bunch of other kids we're going to have. And I want us to be ridiculously happy for the rest of our lives."

"Are you, like... um... proposing to me?"

"What if I am?"

"I, uh... Well... Wow." She huffed out a laugh. "I've never been proposed to before."

With her in his arms, he stood and returned her to the sofa. Then he knelt on one knee and reached for her hand, kissing the back of it. "McKenzie Martin, love of my life, owner of my heart and soul, would you please do me the massive—and probably undeserved honor—of being my wife, my soul mate, my life partner, my everything? If you say yes, in exchange I'll give you and Jax everything I have, everything I'll ever have and do everything in my power to make you happier than you ever thought you could be. I'll do that every day for the rest of my life, which will no doubt end long before yours does because I'm so much older than you, and then you can live in sin with some other rando, but you *cannot* be as happy with him as you were with me. That's where I draw the line."

She was laughing and crying all at once. "You're out of your mind planning my widowhood while you're asking me to marry you."

"I like to see to all the contingencies, especially since you'd be taking on a senior citizen compared to you." He bent his head over her hand, peppering the inside of her wrist with soft kisses. "I heard you when you said you don't want to get married, and I completely understand why after everything you've seen and been through with your parents and that jackass Eric and others. But here's the thing…" He looked up at her now with tears in his own eyes. "I want us to be a family. I want you and Jax to be the first real family that's truly mine. I want us all to be Sullivans, if that's okay with you. I have the best friends in the whole world, and I love them. But they all have their own families to go home to. I want that, too. I know we could achieve that without the legal shit, but call me old-fashioned… I want the big white wedding day and the vows and the party and the happily ever after. And just for the record, I never pictured that for myself until I pictured it with you."

She stared at him for a long time, long enough that a million thoughts passed through his mind—not all of them good ones. What would he ever do if she said no to him? Would he be satisfied to live with her and their kids without the vows? If that's what she really wanted, he'd do it for her. He'd do anything for her.

"First of all, it is not an undeserved honor."

He had to think about that for a second before he tied those words back to what he'd said earlier. "I'm batting way out of my league here, babe. Just want you to know I get that."

"Stop talking, Duke."

He swallowed a laugh and forced his expression to be serious. "Yes, ma'am." God, he loved when she was bossy with him.

"You deserve my love and Jax's more than anyone ever has. From the minute you showed up at Tiffany's with as many of our things as you could find in our destroyed home, you've been showing me who you are and what you're about. So I don't ever want to hear again that you don't deserve me or that I'm way out of your league. Is that understood?"

"I'll keep the thought to myself going forward."

"You do that."

"What's the second of all?"

"I meant it when I said I never wanted to get married."

He felt like a balloon that'd been stuck with a pin as he deflated.

"However... I understand you wanting a family that's all yours, and it seems I want to give you that more than I want to avoid being married."

Just that quickly, he was back in the game, breathless as he waited to hear what else she might say.

"It gives me tremendous comfort to know how much my grandmother loved you. There could be no greater endorsement for me than that, but over these last few weeks, I've also witnessed how much everyone else on this island loves you. I can't say your name without someone telling me what a great guy you are or how you helped them out with this or that or how you showed up for them time and again. And during that same time, you've shown up for me time and again, giving me a place to live and basically turning your truck over to me and helping with Jax and bringing me coffee in bed every morning and trying—not so patiently—to teach me to cross-stitch and sticking with me even though I totally suck at it."

A grunt of laughter burst out of him. "You're coming along very nicely."

"No, I'm not, but you don't give up on me."

"I never will."

"And I know that, so..."

Duke held his breath as his whole life came down to whatever she said next.

She looked him dead in the eyes. "Yes, I'll marry you, Duke."

The burst of pure joy was unlike anything he'd ever felt. It filled his heart to overflowing as he drew her into the sweetest kiss of his life.

"One other thing..."

"What's that?"

"When Kendall tells Jackass you're taking the settlement, have her ask him to sign away his paternal rights to Jax so I can adopt him. If that's okay with you."

McKenzie blinked back tears. "Of course it is."

"I'll get you a ring. Any ring you want."

"I don't care about that."

"I care about it, and it's gonna happen."

"If you say so."

"I say so. I love you, McKenzie. I love you so damned much."

"I love you just as much."

"Thank you for having the courage to take a chance on me."

"A very wise friend recently told me that when you're with the right guy, there's no courage needed."

EPILOGUE

*M*cKenzie woke the next morning wrapped up in Duke's arms, her eyes aching from the lack of sleep after a night spent celebrating their engagement.

She was engaged.

To Duke Sullivan.

Her unicorn. Her one-in-a-million. The love of her life.

McKenzie Sullivan.

She liked the way that sounded.

His hand moved from her hip to cup her breast, his thumb moving back and forth over the nipple that immediately stood at full attention.

"I had the best dream last night," he said in the gruff morning voice that sent a shiver of delight down her spine.

"Is that right?"

"Uh-huh. The gorgeous, smart, sexy, funny, bossy, delightful McKenzie Martin agreed to marry me."

"She did? I don't remember that."

In a matter of seconds, he was on top of her, looking down at her fiercely.

She laughed.

"Don't fuck with me."

"Why not?" She raised her hips to press against his erection. "It's my favorite thing to do."

"You think you're so funny."

"I am funny. You just said so—gorgeous, smart, sexy, *funny*—"

He kissed her so thoroughly that she couldn't remember what'd come after funny. Oh, right. *Bossy.* She liked that one.

"Duke?"

"What, honey?"

"I was thinking about how I'm rebuilding the cabin."

"What about it?"

"Do you know how much the insurance company gave me?"

"How much?"

"Four hundred."

"What? Wow."

"I know. They emailed me yesterday to tell me the check is in the mail. With everything else that happened yesterday, I never got a chance to tell you that."

"You can build a hell of a house for that."

"I could, or I could build a nice little cabin that we could rent out and use the rest to add on to this place to make room for all those kids you say we're going to have."

"Or we could move next door to the brand-new fancy house."

"I don't need brand new or fancy. This house already feels like home, and you love it here. Your garden is here, among other things."

"I do love this place, but the only way I'm letting you pay for the addition is if I'm allowed to make you the co-owner."

"You'd do that for me?"

"I'd do anything for you. Don't you know that by now?"

She smiled up at him. "Speaking of doing anything for each other... I was thinking about getting a tattoo. Do you know anyone who could—"

He kissed her as fiercely as he ever had. "Yeah, I know someone. What do you want to get?"

"A unicorn for my unicorn."

"MK... You stop my heart."

"I want your heart beating at all times."

"It does. It beats for you and Jax."

"So yes to my unicorn?"

"Yes," he said, kissing her. "Yes to whatever you want. But there's one other thing I need to tell you..."

"What's that?"

"Sierra told me it wasn't right that you don't know the whole story about my childhood and what it was really like."

"Is it something you feel I need to know?"

"It's the thing I try the hardest to never think about."

"Then there's no reason for you to think about it now when you're happy, unless you want to talk about it."

"Fuck no, I don't, but she said I needed to tell you. That it wouldn't be right if I didn't."

"And now you have."

"That's all I need to say?"

"Unless or until you want to say more. I'll always want to hear anything you wish to tell me, but I'd never make you talk about something that hurts you just to check a box with me. Okay?"

He nodded. "Thank you for not making me talk about it."

"A wise man once told me to focus on the positives, and the way I see it, there's a whole lot of positive to focus on around here these days."

"Sure as hell is."

And then he was inside her, loving her the way only he could as he continued to kiss her as if his very life depended upon the connection they shared.

She'd had more orgasms with him than in her entire life before him, and as he drew yet another from her, she was filled with the peace that Tiffany had described. This man, this life, this love were all she'd ever need.

"Morning," he said when they'd caught their breath.

"Morning."

"I love you."

"I love you, too."

"Are you really going to marry me?"

"I really am."

He dropped his head to her shoulder. "Thanks."

"Thanks for asking me."

"Sweetheart... You're the best thing to ever happen to me."

"Likewise."

A loud squeak came from the next bedroom.

McKenzie and Duke shared a smile before they disentangled from each other to begin the first day of the rest of their lives.

TURN the page to attend a Gansett Island wedding...

A GANSETT ISLAND WEDDING

Together with their families
Nikki Stokes and Riley McCarthy
invite you to join them as they exchange vows
on Saturday, November 30
at five o'clock in the afternoon
at the McCarthys' Wayfarer on Gansett Island
Reception to follow.

The last time it'd snowed on Gansett Island on November thirtieth was twenty-six years ago when Riley McCarthy had been four years old. The second time it snowed on Gansett Island on November thirtieth was the day he was finally going to marry Nikki Stokes.

Of course it had snowed.

Because why *wouldn't* it snow on their wedding day?

He'd woken to sixteen texts—twelve of them from Nikki asking if he could believe it was *snowing* on their wedding day.

One was from his brother, Finn: *Yo, dude. Snow? Really?*

One was from his dad, Kevin: *You just gotta laugh. It'll still be the best day ever.*

The final one was from his mother, Deb: *I read somewhere that snow*

315

on a wedding day means a lifetime of good luck. Can't wait to celebrate with you and your Nikki.

The best part of snow falling on his wedding day was that he was exempt from having to plow with his cousin Mac and the rest of their team, made up of mostly family members and close friends.

Lying in bed in the guest room at his dad and Chelsea's house, Riley could only smile, because today, he would finally marry Nik. They'd met at Eastward Look, the home her grandmother, Evelyn, had owned for decades, when he'd come to fix the roof and had fallen flat-on-his-face in love with Evelyn's gorgeous granddaughter.

And then she'd disappeared from the island for months, along with her famous identical twin sister, Jordan, who'd been going through a turbulent breakup with her ex-husband.

Nikki's departure had sent Riley into the deepest funk of his life, mostly because he'd never gotten the chance to tell her how he felt about her before she left.

He would never forget the night she'd come back to the island. He'd been at the Beachcomber with his dad, Chelsea and Finn when a news report about Jordan had come on TV, and Seamus O'Grady mentioned that her sister had been on the ferry that day.

Riley had borrowed his dad's keys for the first time in years and had driven straight to Eastward Look, startling Nikki with his unexpected arrival. They'd been together ever since, and they'd renovated Eastward Look to make it their home.

Sleeping without her by his side last night had been difficult and unsettling, but she'd insisted on staying at Eastward Look with her grandmother and Jordan, their best friend Gigi Gibson, as well as Finn's wife, Chloe, Chelsea and Summer.

One last girls' night as a single lady, she'd said.

He could've done without a last night of single life, but he'd given her what she wanted—and always would.

Finn appeared in the bedroom doorway. He and Chloe had recently returned from their wedding trip to Paris. "Saw you read my message. Dad made breakfast."

"I'll be right there."

"How you feeling?"

"I feel great. Ready to get on with it."

"Can you even believe there's actual snow when the forecast called for flurries?"

"Eh, who cares? I get to marry my Nik today."

Finn smiled. "She's the best. I'm so happy for you guys."

"You know that means everything to me." The brothers had been the best of friends their entire lives. "And likewise to you with Chloe."

"Who knew that coming out here for Laura's wedding would change our lives?"

"Right? Best thing we ever did. Tell Dad I'll be right there."

Riley showered, got dressed in jeans and a long-sleeved T-shirt, grabbed his phone and headed to the kitchen. A brief glance at the screen showed a text from his cousin Adam.

Hey, Riley—just a quick note from me, Abby and Liam (plus four new cousins coming soon) to say HAPPY WEDDING DAY! We're so sorry to miss the festivities, but we'll be there in spirit. Please give Nikki all our love and take some for yourself. We couldn't be happier for you guys and look forward to celebrating with you when we get back to the island.

Riley responded to Adam as he walked toward the kitchen and the scent of breakfast. *Thanks, man, appreciate the kind words. Hope Abby and the football team are doing okay. We'll miss you, but you're exactly where you need to be. Nik and I will be over to visit soon. Love you.*

"Are you texting your wife?" Kevin asked when Riley came into the room.

His dad was wearing Chelsea's pink, frilly KISS THE COOK apron and looked so ridiculous that Riley busted up laughing. He grabbed a photo for Chelsea before Kevin had one second to realize that the moment would be immortalized forever.

"Actually, I was responding to Adam, who texted to say they're sorry to miss the festivities."

"I talked to him yesterday. He's super bummed to miss it."

"Like I said to him, they're right where they need to be."

"Definitely."

Kevin served up eggs, potatoes, pancakes, sausage and toast.

They'd sat down to eat when Big Mac arrived with Frank, Ned and two boxes of Auntie Linda's sugar doughnuts.

"What goes on around here anyway?" Big Mac asked. "Anything special?"

"Just another day," Riley said, grinning at his beloved uncle as he and Finn reached for the doughnuts.

"Like hell it is. The last of our babies is getting married today, boys." Big Mac pretended to dab at a tear. "Hard to believe."

"Sure is," Kevin said, "but I'll remind you that Summer is not yet married, nor is her upcoming brother or sister."

"Allow me to rephrase: The last of our *original* babies is getting married."

"Better," Kevin said with a smile.

Riley knew his dad was still a bit gobsmacked to be raising a second family in his fifties, but he'd never seen Kevin happier than he was with Chelsea and Summer.

"And how is the groom feeling this fine, snowy morning?" Frank asked.

"He's feeling ready and excited," Riley said to his other uncle.

Despite Kevin's huge breakfast, he and Finn also devoured half the doughnuts.

Riley never could get enough of Auntie Linda's doughnuts.

The sound of truck doors closing outside preceded Mac and Shane's entrance, kicking off snow and generally making a huge racket before they appeared in the kitchen.

"Oh sure," Mac said. "While we're out plowing, the rest of the family is getting fat off doughnuts." He helped himself to one and then stepped aside so Shane could get his.

"We work our fingers to the bone for this family," Shane said with a mouthful of doughnut.

"Yes, we do, and no one appreciates us."

"Have you guys heard from Mac and Shane yet today?" Big Mac asked.

The rest of them lost it laughing.

Riley loved the family he'd been born into more than just about anything, but he couldn't wait to start his own family with Nikki in about five hours.

As he glanced out at the snowy landscape, a thought occurred to him. "Hey, Ned?"

"Ya?"

"You still got that sleigh you had a couple of years ago when you saved Christmas with it?"

"Sure do. Why?"

"I've got an idea."

Over at Eastward Look, Nikki was glued to the window, watching the snow come down faster by the hour. "I mean, what are the odds of snow on November thirtieth?"

"You want an actual number?" Jordan asked.

"A number would be good."

"Siri, what are the odds of snow on Gansett Island on November thirtieth?"

"Siri says she can't check the weather that far out."

"That far out? November thirtieth is today!"

"I think she means for next year."

"Well, then, what good is she?"

"Nicole, calm down about the snow and come have some of this gorgeous breakfast your sister made for you," Evelyn said. "If you don't eat, you're apt to faint during the ceremony."

"Gram is right," Jordan said. "Enough of the snow watch."

"What if Riley can't get there because of the snow?"

"Riley would crawl to the Wayfarer if that's what it took," Jordan said. "Stop inventing problems where there aren't any."

"Have you always been such a bitch?" Nikki asked her twin.

"For as long as you've known me."

"That's true."

"She's been a bitch as long as I've known her, too," Gigi said with a grin as she nursed her second cup of coffee.

"And here I was looking forward to having you home for the wedding," Jordan said to their best friend.

Gigi snorted. "I'm a bitch, too. You've known that forever."

"Enough with the bitchiness," Evelyn said as Chelsea laughed. "Honestly, you girls never change."

"Uh, yeah, we do, Gram. Nik's getting married, I'm knocked up and engaged, and Gigi's madly in love with Cooper. I'd call those some big changes."

"And yet, when the three of you are together, you're thirteen again."

"That's just how we roll," Gigi said.

"Tell us everything about how things are with Cooper," Nikki said as she buttered a piece of toast.

"Things are divine. He's... Well, he's the best."

"That makes my old heart so happy to hear," Evelyn said.

"Your heart is not old, Evelyn, so don't let us hear you say that again," Gigi said.

Evelyn smiled, fully aware of how essential she was to all three of "her girls."

Jordan reached for her phone to read a text. "Riley says to tell you to be ready at four and to not wear your dress. He has a surprise for you."

"What kind of surprise?" Nikki asked.

"The kind where he's not going to tell you until four."

"How am I supposed to wait that long?"

"We're going to have to sedate her," Jordan said to Gigi, who nodded in agreement.

Cindy Lawry arrived to help Chloe with wedding-party hair and makeup. No one wanted Chloe to overdo it and end up with sore hands later, so they'd asked Cindy to help. Chloe's rheumatoid arthritis had been flaring lately, but she'd wanted to be part of the hair-and-makeup team for her new sister-in-law. She would be doing only Nikki's hair.

Cindy was in charge of the others.

The preparations kicked into high gear, and by three thirty, everyone was just about ready.

"We should've stayed at the Wayfarer," Nikki said fretfully. "I knew I should've reserved the rooms for last night."

Riley's mom was staying there, along with a couple of his and Finn's friends from Connecticut.

Evelyn put her hands on the bride's shoulders. "You wanted to be at home with your girls last night, and it was a perfect night. Today will be a perfect day, despite the snow."

"Riley sent another text. He said to dress warmly and send your gown to the Wayfarer with us."

"What is he up to?" Nikki asked.

Jordan went to the window and let out a squeal of excitement. "Come see!"

Nikki joined her sister at the window as a horse and sleigh came down the long driveway. "Oh my God!"

"Most romantic thing ever," Jordan said, "and it couldn't have happened without the snow."

Riley stood up as the horse-drawn sleigh, driven by Ned Saunders, came to a stop in front of the house. "Nicole Stokes, will you marry me?"

Nikki was so busy staring at the man she loved that she could barely breathe.

Jordan gave her a push. "Go!"

Nikki bolted toward the door but stopped and turned back. "Don't forget—"

"I'll bring everything you need," Jordan assured her. "Don't worry about anything. Go have the best wedding day ever."

"I love you all so, so much."

"We love you, too, sweetie," Evelyn said as she wiped away tears.

Nikki pulled the hood of her warmest winter coat over her head to protect her hair as she ran out to meet Riley, who stood beside the sleigh, looking for all the world like a knight in shining armor.

She ran right into his outstretched arms.

He swept her right off her feet. "Goddamn, it's been a long sixteen hours without you."

"Too long."

He put her down and kissed her with sixteen hours' worth of pent-up desire. "Good surprise?"

"The best."

"I brought an umbrella to protect the hair."

"I couldn't care less about the hair."

"Yes, you do, so don't lie to me before you marry me." He lifted her up and into the sleigh, then got her settled under the umbrella and two heavy down blankets. "To the Wayfarer, James."

Ned grunted out a laugh and used the reins to turn the horse toward the main road.

"How cool is it that it snowed on our wedding day?"

"I'll never forget this," Nikki said. "Not for the whole rest of my life."

He kissed her. "Me either, love."

Right at five o'clock, Nikki took the arm of her beloved grandmother and went down the stairs at the Wayfarer, which had become her home away from home since she became the general manager. She'd overseen many weddings in the last year, but none as important as this one.

With music provided by Riley's cousin Evan and Laura's husband, Owen, she walked toward the man who'd renewed her faith in love after a terrible ordeal during college had nearly ruined everything.

Riley had given her so much, more than she ever dreamed possible for herself, and she had not one single doubt about the step they were about to take.

Right before they entered the room where the ceremony and reception would take place, Evelyn stopped and turned to face her. "I'm so, so, so proud of you, my darling girl. And I love you with all my heart."

"I love you, too, and this day never would've happened without your love and support."

"We're a team. Now and forever."

Nikki smiled as she nodded. "Thank you for everything."

"No need to thank me."

"I have every need to thank you." Evelyn had put her back together after a trauma that might've derailed her entire life.

"Let's go get you married, sweetheart."

Riley thought he was ready to greet his bride, but nothing could've properly prepared him for her.

His eyes filled with tears as she came toward him on Evelyn's arm. He loved her grandmother almost as much as he loved Nikki.

Finn's hand on his back helped to keep him grounded and centered for the biggest and best moment of his life.

Their cousins Mac and Shane stood next to Finn while Jordan, Chelsea and Gigi waited for Nikki. Summer was their honorary flower girl.

"Fancy meeting you here," Nikki said, smiling as she and Evelyn stopped in front of Riley.

"You take my breath away, Nik."

"Likewise, my love."

"Take good care of my girl," Evelyn said to Riley through tears.

"Always."

"Love you both. Be kind to each other and never go to bed mad."

Riley and Nikki kissed and hugged Evelyn.

Then they turned to face Riley's uncle Frank, who was presiding.

"Are we ready?" Frank asked, smiling.

Riley looked to Nikki, who nodded.

"We're so ready," Riley said.

Ahhhh, I LOVED writing Duke and McKenzie. He was so much fun to write, as was McKenzie. I loved catching up with a number of other Gansett Island friends as Duke and McKenzie's story unfolded. I had NO plans to write Jim's demise until it just sort of came to me, but I liked the way Tiffany reacted and how she and Blaine came together to support Ashleigh. The scene with Thomas and Ashleigh gave me ALL the feels! It seems like we're also inching closer to the arrival of four more McCarthy boys! But poor Abby. Nothing is ever simple for her.

Join the Renewal After Dark Reader Group at *facebook.com/groups/renewalafterdark/* and the overall Gansett Island Series Group at *facebook.com/groups/McCarthySeries*. If you're not already subscribed to my newsletter mailing list, you can join at *marieforce.com/subscribe*.

In a recent newsletter, I mentioned that I'm going to get us through the arrival of the quads and several other babies in the next Gansett Island book, and then I'm thinking about jumping the timeline forward ten years or so to when the kids will be teenagers. The thought of writing our favorite couples dealing with wild teens makes me giggle. We'll see how that transpires over the next year or two.

To everyone who has stuck with me to book TWENTY-SEVEN in the Gansett Island Series, thank you from the bottom of my heart. It's still so much FUN to write in this world, and of course, knowing you guys are eagerly awaiting the new book makes it even better. Much more to come from Gansett! Thanks for taking this journey with me!

Thank you to the team that supports me every day: Julie Cupp, Lisa Cafferty, Jean Mello, Nikki Haley, Ashley Lopez, and lately my lovely daughter, Emily Force, has been on Team Jack. Special thanks to Lisa, our resident CPA, this time around for helping me to come up with McKenzie's new career path on Gansett and checking my bookkeeping terminology. As my late mom was an outstanding bookkeeper, I had to get that right, even if I have the same reaction to the word *QuickBooks* as Duke and Sierra do! I did not get my mother's mathematical wiring. LOL

As always, thank you to Dr. Sarah Hewitt, family nurse practitioner, for letting me run high-risk pregnancy scenarios by her. Any mistakes in the final version are mine. Between the two of us, we'll be delivering quads before much longer.

Thank you to my editors, Linda Ingmanson and Joyce Lamb, and my A-team beta readers, Anne Woodall, Kara Conrad and Tracey Suppo. Also a big thanks to the Gansett Island betas: Jennifer, Doreen, Andi, Amy, Katy, Michelle, Judy, Amy and Jaime.

Finally, you may have heard that I have an all-new exciting single title romantic suspense coming September 24, called IN THE AIR TONIGHT. I'm so excited about this book! Turn the page to read the blurb and first chapter. At the end, we've included preorder info. I can't believe a summer girl like me is saying I can't wait until September!

xoxo

Marie

IN THE AIR TONIGHT

MARIE FORCE

I was there. I saw what you did.

Blaise

I wasn't supposed to be there that night, but my friend Sienna talked me into going to the party in Land's End so she could spy on her boyfriend. While hiding out in the woods, we witnessed an unspeakable crime. And we did everything wrong afterward.

Connections run deep in our small town.

I was pressured into keeping my mouth shut, even though every part of me objected. I assumed I'd always do the right thing in any situation. I was wrong about that and a lot of other things.

I was wrecked by what I saw and how the victim was treated by kids I'd known all my life. I've been sick over it ever since, even as I moved on, far away from the town where I was raised.

Fourteen years later, I learn that the guy who committed that unspeakable crime is running for Congress, and something in me *snaps*.

I can't bear the weight of that knowledge for another second.

Finally, I report what I saw, and all hell breaks loose for me and others who were at that long-ago party. Some of them will do whatever it takes to keep the truth from coming to light…even if they have to kill me.

In the midst of an epic battle, a new love gives me the strength to stay strong, to fight for my life and to right a terrible wrong.

Content warning: A sexual assault storyline may be upsetting to some readers.

Chapter 1

Blaise
NOW

I'm late getting home from work and in a foul mood after another long day with my jerk of a boss, Wendall, barking orders at me that couldn't be seen to in a month, let alone a single day. But that's what he expects—everything *right now*. Six months ago, I stopped taking his calls after hours because I don't get paid to tend to him for more than eight hours a day. That's all he gets from me now.

He didn't like that.

Ask me if I care. We've reached the point where he needs me far more than I need him, and he knows it.

My friends in the city were green with envy when I landed a job as the personal assistant to the hottest star on Broadway. They don't know he's a nightmare. No one knows that but me and the people he stars with in *Gray Matter*, the top-grossing show on the Great White

Way this year. As the show becomes more successful, he's an even bigger dick to everyone around him.

I'm giving him six more months and then moving on. Life's too short to work for someone I can't stand.

I've barely walked into my apartment when my phone rings with a call from my mother. I hesitate to take it because I'm in such a shitty mood, but she worries when I don't answer. I press the big green button.

"Hey, Mom." After kicking off my sneakers, I drop my bag on the sofa. It's got my laptop and the heels I wear at the theater where I spend my days.

"I'm so glad you answered, sweetheart. I tried you yesterday but got your voicemail."

I've told her—many times—I never check my voicemail and she should text me if she wants to chat, but she's never gotten the hang of texting. My siblings and I have tried to teach her. She says she has a mental block. I say she couldn't be bothered. "What's going on?"

"Teagan is pregnant again."

I'm shocked. My sister has four children under the age of seven. "Wow. Four wasn't enough?"

"I guess not. She's so happy. I could hear it in her voice when she called to share the news. Doug has a big new job that allows her stay home with the kids. She's thrilled to be a full-time mom now."

"I'm glad for her. That's a lot to juggle with a job."

"It was too much, and the daycare bills were sucking up most of her salary anyway."

"I'll text her to say congrats."

"I know she'd love to hear from you."

I hear the sadness in my mother's voice. How could I not? It's been there since the day I left home and never looked back. My family has asked over the years why I never come home, even for holidays I used to enjoy. I haven't been able to provide an answer that satisfies them. This is what works for me. Staying away from there, from the memories, has made it possible for me to have a life of purpose without guilt swallowing me whole.

Since I left for college nearly thirteen years ago, I've been home once—when my father died suddenly.

I've always been certain that if I go back there for any length of time, my carefully constructed house of cards will come crashing down.

My mother chats on about people I barely remember, kids I grew up with who are now parents many times over, her friends' grandchildren and other gossip from home.

"Was Ryder Elliott your year or Arlo's?"

The bottom drops out of my world at the mention of that name.

Ryder Elliott.

"Blaise? Hello? Are you there?"

I swallow hard. "I'm here. What did you say?"

"Was Ryder your year? Or Arlo's?"

All the spit in my mouth is gone, and I'm right back in the woods on the night that changed everything. The scent of woodsmoke is forever tied to that night as is the Steve Miller song "Jet Airliner."

"I, uh, my year," I somehow manage to say.

"He's running for Congress. Can you believe that kids you went to school with are now doing things like that?"

A roar overtakes me, so loud it drowns out every thought in my head. "No."

"What? Did you say something, honey?"

I'm screaming to myself. *No, no, no, no.* He's running for Congress? Oh no. No, he is not. That cannot happen. Something about those words, *he's running for Congress,* tips me over an edge I've hovered on for fourteen long years. I can't stay there another second.

I remember every detail of that night as if it happened five minutes ago. It's as vivid to me now as it was then, unlike other things that've faded into the ether.

"Mom?"

"You're scaring me, Blaise. What's wrong?"

"I'm coming home."

⁓

Blaise
THEN

MY MOM MADE MEATLOAF, one of the five meals we'd all eat. Tired of fighting dinner battles with four picky kids, she rotates from one meal to the other, but meatloaf is usually my favorite. I can barely swallow a bite because I'm so nervous. While my parents, sisters and brother keep up a steady stream of chatter, I try not to puke from nerves.

I'm a month shy of my seventeenth birthday and about to do something I've never done before on the first night of summer vacation—directly disobey my parents. Sure, I've told a white lie here and there, had a few beers and even smoked pot a couple of times. But I haven't taken the car somewhere they've specifically told me not to go.

My phone buzzes with a text from Sienna Lawton, my best friend. *Still good to go?*

We're not supposed to text at the table, so I keep the phone in my lap when I reply with Ya.

I'm going to be sick.

"What's wrong, Blaise?" Mom asks. "Why aren't you eating? It's your favorite."

"I had a big lunch on the way home from the beach. Can I wrap it up for later?"

"Sure, honey. That's fine."

"It's delicious, Mom. Thank you for dinner."

She smiles at me. "You're welcome."

I'm a good kid. I work hard at school, get excellent grades and generally do what I'm told, unlike my sister Teagan, who's three years older than me and gives them nothing but trouble. I fly under the radar and like it there. I'd never want the kind of attention Teagan gets from them, which includes a lot of yelling, door slamming and overall contention.

My brother, Arlo, a year older than me, is my hero. He manages to smoothly do whatever the hell he wants and get away with it. My parents think he's the perfect son. However, I know where most of his skeletons are buried. I'll take that info to my grave. He and I look out for each other. It's not something we ever talk about, but we've got each other's backs.

My little sister, Juniper—known as June or Junie—chats nonstop, which usually annoys me. Tonight, I'm thankful for the distraction she provides.

I'm taking the car to a party across the river in Land's End, where I'm most definitely not allowed to go. My parents say the long, dark winding roads leading to Land's End are an accident waiting for a teenager to happen. Plus, it's well known in our town of Hope that some of the kids from Land's End, who are bussed to our high school because they don't have one of their own, are partiers.

My parents would lose their shit if they knew my plans for the evening.

They don't track my phone because I've given them no reason to, whereas they pay extra for new technology that lets them track Teagan's every move. She calls me the Golden Child. It's not a compliment coming from the Merrick family's chief agitator. Just because I'm not constantly getting in trouble doesn't mean I don't know how to have fun. Granted, I'm not one of the super popular girls like Teagan was in high school, but I can live with that. I have several good friends, even if none of us are considered the "cool" kids.

Sienna sort of straddles both worlds thanks to her boyfriend, Camden Elliott. He and his older brother Ryder, who are both in our class thanks to Ryder being held back a year before kindergarten, are the most popular boys in our school. They're co-captains of the football team, as well as baseball (Camden) and track (Ryder) stars.

They're also Arlo's closest friends. You'd think that having a best friend and brother attached to the school's most popular kids would elevate me, too. You'd be wrong about that.

Sienna and Cam have been a couple for as long as I can recall. I barely remember her without him. However, things have been weird between them lately, which is why we're risking everything to go to spy on a party we weren't invited to. Cam pretended like he didn't know about the party, which made her suspicious and paranoid.

When she couldn't get her family's car for the night, her paranoia became my problem.

Upstairs, I change into denim cutoff shorts and a halter top. In the long shot possibility that we're able to talk our way into the party, I put on makeup, focusing on the blue eyes that people say are my best feature. I run a brush through the reddish-brown hair I straightened earlier. I want to change my hair color, but my mom won't let me. Try having reddish hair when your name is Blaise. I've had every nick-name from Fire Ant to Fireball. I especially hate that the boys call me Ablaze. Worst nickname ever.

As a finishing touch, I spray on some of the fancy perfume my grandmother gave me for Christmas. I'd never heard of the scent, but Gran said it's best not to smell like anyone else.

I'm ready to go, but still feel like I'm going to be sick. I knock on Teagan's door. She's only home because she's grounded—again.

"What?" She's twenty and finished her second year at community college in May, getting grades that barely kept her off academic probation. She has to do another semester to get an associate degree. Last week, she was caught at a bar in Newport, even though she's underage. My parents went ballistic and demanded she turn over her fake ID. Knowing her, she has two others hidden in her room.

"Do you have any Tums?"

She hurls the bottle at me, barely missing my head. I catch the bottle, shake out two of them and put the bottle on a desk piled high with clothes and other crap. It's never seen a school book in all the years since Mom bought desks for us at Pottery Barn Kids.

"Thanks."

She grunts something in reply but doesn't look up from the phone she earned back after the latest parental altercation by doing chores around the house.

In a way, I'm kind of thankful for her. She keeps the attention off me.

In the hallway, I run into Arlo. His light brown hair is wet from the shower, and his blue eyes give me a quick once over. "What's with you?"

"Nothing. Why?"

"You're dressed up." He leans in for a whiff. "Wearing perfume and makeup. Where're you going?"

"Nowhere." If anyone can see right through my lies, it's him, which can be comforting and annoying—at the same time.

"I'd better not see you anywhere near Land's End tonight, you got me?"

"Why would I go there?"

He gives me a withering look that big brothers have been giving their younger sisters since the beginning of time. "Stay. Away."

"I have better things to do than go to your stupid party."

"Don't tell Mom and Dad anything about it, or I'll murder you."

I roll my eyes, to say 'as if I'd start talking now'. Why would I tell them that Houston Rafferty's parents are away, and he's hosting a rager with booze? His party has been the talk of our town and LE for days. I'm surprised my parents haven't picked up the scent by now.

I land downstairs feeling moderately better after taking the Tums.

My dad is doing the dishes. She cooks. He cleans up. They get along great and only butt heads over Teagan. He's tough on her. Mom's a softie, and that infuriates my dad, who, as he says, is trying to keep her out of jail. Mom says he exaggerates, but I tend to agree with him. He's probably the only thing keeping her out of serious trouble.

Dad glances at me and smiles. "You ready to go?" His gaze takes in my outfit. He hates the crop tops that're all the rage with girls my age, but thankfully, he doesn't make an issue out of it.

I swallow the lump in my throat. "Yep."

"And you guys are going to the movies and maybe downtown, right?"

"Yes." I feel sick lying to him.

"Home by midnight?"

"I'll try. If I'm running late, I'll text you."

He hands over the keys to his Toyota SUV and kisses my cheek.

"Thank you for being so considerate. It's very much appreciated."

I come this close to spilling my guts and telling him the truth. But he'll never let me take the car to Land's End, and Sienna is counting on me.

How many times will I wish I'd told him the truth about my plans for that night?

Every day for the rest of my life.

Get *In the Air Tonight* in stores and online at your favorite paperback retailer on Sept. 24, 2024.

ALSO BY MARIE FORCE

Contemporary Romances Available from Marie Force

The Gansett Island Series

Book 1: Maid for Love (*Mac & Maddie*)

Book 2: Fool for Love (*Joe & Janey*)

Book 3: Ready for Love (*Luke & Sydney*)

Book 4: Falling for Love (*Grant & Stephanie*)

Book 5: Hoping for Love (*Evan & Grace*)

Book 6: Season for Love (*Owen & Laura*)

Book 7: Longing for Love (*Blaine & Tiffany*)

Book 8: Waiting for Love (*Adam & Abby*)

Book 9: Time for Love (*David & Daisy*)

Book 10: Meant for Love (*Jenny & Alex*)

Book 10.5: Chance for Love, *A Gansett Island Novella* (*Jared & Lizzie*)

Book 11: Gansett After Dark (*Owen & Laura*)

Book 12: Kisses After Dark (*Shane & Katie*)

Book 13: Love After Dark (*Paul & Hope*)

Book 14: Celebration After Dark (*Big Mac & Linda*)

Book 15: Desire After Dark (*Slim & Erin*)

Book 16: Light After Dark (*Mallory & Quinn*)

Book 17: Victoria & Shannon (Episode 1)

Book 18: Kevin & Chelsea (Episode 2)

A Gansett Island Christmas Novella (*Appears in Mine After Dark*)

Book 19: Mine After Dark (*Riley & Nikki*)

Book 20: Yours After Dark (*Finn & Chloe*)

Book 21: Trouble After Dark (*Deacon & Julia*)

Book 22: Rescue After Dark (*Mason & Jordan*)

Book 23: Blackout After Dark (*Full Cast*)

Book 24: Temptation After Dark (*Gigi & Cooper*)

Book 25: Resilience After Dark (*Jace & Cindy*)

Book 26: Hurricane After Dark (*Full Cast*)

Book 27: Renewal After Dark (*Duke & McKenzie*)

Downeast

Dan & Kara: A Downeast Prequel

The Wild Widows Series—a Fatal Series Spin-Off

Book 1: Someone Like You

Book 2: Someone to Hold

Book 3: Someone to Love

Book 4: Someone to Watch Over Me (Coming 2024)

The Green Mountain Series*

Book 1: All You Need Is Love (*Will & Cameron*)

Book 2: I Want to Hold Your Hand (*Nolan & Hannah*)

Book 3: I Saw Her Standing There (*Colton & Lucy*)

Book 4: And I Love Her (*Hunter & Megan*)

Novella: You'll Be Mine (*Will & Cam's Wedding*)

Book 5: It's Only Love (*Gavin & Ella*)

Book 6: Ain't She Sweet (*Tyler & Charlotte*)

The Butler, Vermont Series*

(Continuation of Green Mountain)

Book 1: Every Little Thing (*Grayson & Emma*)

Book 2: Can't Buy Me Love (*Mary & Patrick*)

Book 3: Here Comes the Sun (*Wade & Mia*)

Book 4: Till There Was You (*Lucas & Dani*)

Book 5: All My Loving (*Landon & Amanda*)

Book 6: Let It Be (*Lincoln & Molly*)

Book 7: Come Together (*Noah & Brianna*)

Book 8: Here, There & Everywhere (*Izzy & Cabot*)

Book 9: The Long and Winding Road (*Max & Lexi*)

The Miami Nights Series*

Book 1: How Much I Feel (*Carmen & Jason*)

Book 2: How Much I Care (*Maria & Austin*)

Book 3: How Much I Love (*Dee's story*)

Nochebuena, A Miami Nights Novella

Book 4: How Much I Want (*Nico & Sofia*)

Book 5: How Much I Need (*Milo and Gianna*)

The Quantum Series*

Book 1: Virtuous (*Flynn & Natalie*)

Book 2: Valorous (*Flynn & Natalie*)

Book 3: Victorious (*Flynn & Natalie*)

Book 4: Rapturous (*Addie & Hayden*)

Book 5: Ravenous (*Jasper & Ellie*)

Book 6: Delirious (*Kristian & Aileen*)

Book 7: Outrageous (*Emmett & Leah*)

Book 8: Famous (*Marlowe & Sebastian*)

The Treading Water Series*

Book 1: Treading Water

Book 2: Marking Time

Book 3: Starting Over

Book 4: Coming Home

Book 5: Finding Forever

Single Titles

In the Air Tonight (September 2024)

Five Years Gone

One Year Home

Sex Machine

Sex God

Georgia on My Mind

True North

The Fall

The Wreck

Love at First Flight

Everyone Loves a Hero

Line of Scrimmage

Romantic Suspense Novels Available from Marie Force

The Fatal Series

One Night With You, *A Fatal Series Prequel Novella*

Book 1: Fatal Affair

Book 2: Fatal Justice

Book 3: Fatal Consequences

Book 3.5: Fatal Destiny, *the Wedding Novella*

Book 4: Fatal Flaw

Book 5: Fatal Deception

Book 6: Fatal Mistake

Book 7: Fatal Jeopardy

Book 8: Fatal Scandal

Book 9: Fatal Frenzy

Book 10: Fatal Identity

Book 11: Fatal Threat

Book 12: Fatal Chaos

Book 13: Fatal Invasion

Book 14: Fatal Reckoning

Book 15: Fatal Accusation

Book 16: Fatal Fraud

Sam and Nick's story continues...

Book 1: State of Affairs

Book 2: State of Grace

Book 3: State of the Union

Book 4: State of Shock

Book 5: State of Denial

Book 6: State of Bliss

Book 7: State of Suspense

Historical Romance Available from Marie Force

The Gilded Series*

Book 1: Duchess by Deception

Book 2: Deceived by Desire

*Completed Series

ABOUT THE AUTHOR

Marie Force is the #1 *Wall Street Journal* best-selling author of more than 100 contemporary romance, romantic suspense and erotic romance novels. Her series include Fatal, First Family, Gansett Island, Butler Vermont, Quantum, Treading Water, Miami Nights and Wild Widows.

Her books have sold more than 13 million copies worldwide, have been translated into more than a dozen languages and have appeared on the *New York Times* bestseller list more than 30 times. She is also a *USA Today* bestseller, as well as a Spiegel bestseller in Germany.

Her goals in life are simple—to spend as much time as she can with her "kids" who are now adults, to keep writing books for as long as she possibly can and to never be on a flight that makes the news.

Join Marie's mailing list on her website at *marieforce.com* for news about new books and upcoming appearances in your area. Follow her on Facebook, at *www.Facebook.com/MarieForceAuthor*, Instagram *@marieforceauthor* and TikTok *@marieforceauthor*. Contact Marie at *marie@marieforce.com*.

Made in the USA
Monee, IL
14 August 2024

63850733R00190